Jodi Taylor is the author of the bestselling Chronicles of St Mary's series, the story of a bunch of disaster-prone historians who investigate major historical events in contemporary time. Do NOT call it time travel!

Born in Bristol and educated in Gloucester (facts both cities vigorously deny), she spent many years with her head somewhere else, much to the dismay of family, teachers and employers, before finally deciding to put all that daydreaming to good use and pick up a pen. She still has no idea what she wants to do when she grows up.

JODI TAYLOR

HOPE FOR THE BEST

HEADLINE

First published in Great Britain in 2019 by
HEADLINE PUBLISHING GROUP

1

Cataloguing in Publication Data is available from the British Library

ISBN 978 1 4722 6425 1

Typeset in Times New Roman by CC Book Production
Printed and bound in Great Britain by Clays Ltd, Elcograf S.p.A.

MIX
Paper from
responsible sources
FSC® C104740

HEADLINE PUBLISHING GROUP
An Hachette UK Company
Carmelite House
50 Victoria Embankment
London EC4Y 0DZ

www.headline.co.uk
www.hachette.co.uk

DRAMATIS THINGUMMY

My resolution to write books with fewer characters has been even more unsuccessful than my resolution to give up chocolate. Please don't judge me.

ST MARY'S PERSONNEL

Dr Bairstow	Director of St Mary's. One step ahead of everyone. As usual.
Dr Peterson	Deputy Director. Stubbornly refusing to act in his own best interests. Nothing new there.
Mrs Partridge	PA to Dr Bairstow. Kleio, daughter of Zeus, and Muse of History.

HISTORY DEPARTMENT

Mr Clerk	Historian.
Miss Prentiss	Historian.
Miss Sykes	Historian.
Mr Bashford	Historian and chicken lover.
Miss North	Historian. About to do her duty.
Angus	Non-egg-producing historian.

R&D

Miss Lingoss	Multi-hued weirdo. Now wearing a beanie.

MEDICAL SECTION

Dr Stone	Medical doctor. Devious, cocoa-drinking optimist.
Nurse Hunter	Still not giving anything away.

SECURITY SECTION

Mr Markham	Head of Security. Personal status still shrouded in mystery.
Mr Evans	Security guard. Not Welsh and suffering because of it.

TECHNICAL SECTION

Chief Tech. Officer Farrell	Husband, hero and bringing his own doughnuts.
Mr Dieter	Another chief technician. Rumour says if you put one in a warm, dark place and cover it in shit then you'll have another by the morning.
Mr Lindstrom	Ordinary technician. If there is such a thing.

TIME POLICE

Commander Hay	Commander of the Time Police. Doing what she thinks is right.
Captain Farenden	Her adjutant.
Captain Ellis	Matthew's long-suffering mentor. Possibly not quite as indifferent to Max as he thinks. We'll see.
Max	Former Head of the History Department. Now a lowly officer in the Time Police and making friends wherever she goes. Not so much changing History as *re-routing* it.
Map Master	Not having a good day map-wise.
Mr Grint	Grint the Grunt. Let's face it – he and Max are never going to get on.
Mr Nash	Re-routing History partner in crime.
Mr Oliver	As above.
Mr Bevan	As above.
Master Sergeant Romano	Zapped and zipped. And in her own detention centre, too. She's not going to be happy.
Greta Van Owen	Former historian. Is she leaning back towards St Mary's?
Medical doctor	Another cheerful, chatty officer brimming with social skills and joie de vivre.

Various others too numerous to mention.

OTHERS

Mrs De Winter	Former schoolteacher. Sibylline Oracle.
David Sands	Former historian. Shacked up with Rosie Lee and therefore entitled to some sort of award.
Gareth Roberts	Former historian. Beard owner.
Rosie Lee	PA to Head of History Dept. According to her job description.
Benjamin	Her son.
Ian Guthrie	Former Head of Security. Has something planned but you won't learn about it in this book.

UNPLEASANT PEOPLE

Malcolm Halcombe	Former representative from Thirsk University. About to make the biggest mistake of his life.
Major Sullivan	Halcombe's right-hand minion. If he wasn't claustrophobic before, then he is now.
His men	

SEX-CLUB OWNER AND STAFF

Atticus Wolfe	Immoral sex-club owner, trafficker, vicious and untrustworthy. Not your standard Jane Austen character.

| Demiyan Khalife | His PA. Even more vicious and untrust-worthy. Fortunately. |

Waiters, bouncers et al.

THE VILLAIN

| Clive Ronan | Heading for trouble. |

HISTORICAL PERSONAGES

| Mary Tudor | More sympathetic than might be thought. |

Her household

Various Londoners

Three men and their rabbit

Priests and priestesses of Amun-Ra

Citizens of Kush

WITH A FULL SUPPORTING CAST OF:

Bees, horses, doughnuts – ta-dah! dinosaurs, dodos, camels, a cobra, donkeys, a very pretty ram, and an enormous prehistoric snake poised to make the evolutionary leap but who now probably won't bother.

| Matthew Farrell | Insufficient data to comment. |

AUTHOR'S NOTE

There are many versions of the events that took place during the week 3–10 July 1553. And some discrepancies over the exact dates as well. This isn't a huge problem if you're studying events from the safe distance of nearly five hundred years in the future but presents certain difficulties when trying to put together an almost hour-by-hour account of the events happening at the time. I've tried to steer a middle course through all these different versions.

My usual plea – historians, please do not spit on me in the streets – is more appropriate than ever.

I was worried about what Matthew would make of his parents' disabilities, because – let's face it – neither Leon nor I were in good condition at the moment. Leon was still recovering from being blown up in Hawking Hangar and I'd been shot and then fallen off the roof – hey, shit happens – and I was so busy worrying about us that I never even considered that Matthew himself might be walking wounded as well.

Leon was getting around well and only sometimes needed his stick, but I was still in my wheelchair, looking pale and interesting. Or, if you listened to Markham, pathetic and feeble.

St Mary's, obviously, thought Leon and I were hilarious. There may be organisations where personal tragedies are treated with sympathy and support but, trust me, St Mary's isn't any of them. There were all sorts of jokes flying around which I'm not going to repeat because they were cruel and insensitive. Although the ones about Leon were quite funny.

Anyway, it was the day of Matthew's long-awaited visit. Leon and I assembled ourselves on the pan outside Hawking, awaiting his arrival. The Time Police were punctual. They always are. It's one of their many irritating features, along with no sense of humour and shooting you dead if you look at them wrong. Their pod materialised – not one of their detention pods, I was pleased to note – and Matthew, accompanied by Captain Ellis, stepped out.

I felt Leon stiffen beside me. I didn't need to stiffen. With both ankles encased in flexi-boots and my arm in a sling and flexi-glove, I was there already and, now, here was Matthew making a major contribution to the Farrell family's current lack of working limbs. His left arm was swathed in a bright blue flexi-glove that stretched nearly to his shoulder, and a large piece of sticking plaster adorned his forehead. It had an inaccurately depicted dinosaur on it.

I glared at Captain Ellis, who spread his hands defensively. 'Not my fault.'

'What happened?'

'He fell out of a tree.'

'Why?'

'Lost his grip.'

'I mean – why was he in a tree?'

'His dirigible got stuck.'

Leon said with interest, 'Still not solved the steering problem, then?'

In addition to having a poor grasp of priorities, men are very easily distracted. Especially techies.

Matthew silently shook his head. He doesn't talk much.

Leon frowned. 'Have you tried . . . ?' And the three of them embarked on some long, incomprehensible discussion of interest only to those with a Y chromosome or no social life.

I could see a change in Matthew since his last visit. He'd filled out and he seemed more confident. He still wasn't chatty – his early years as a climbing boy in the slums of London had left their mark upon him – but his silences were no longer hostile. Dr Stone had warned me that, while bright enough, he would probably

2

never develop as a normal child. 'There's nothing wrong with him, Max – he's just a product of his early upbringing. Be prepared for the unexpected.'

'Must talk to Auntie Lingoss,' said Matthew, spotting her over by the hangar and setting off across the grass towards her, without even the slightest interest in why his mother was currently occupying the St Mary's wheelchair.

'Wait until he starts harvesting you for parts,' said Leon, grimly. Noticing my expression, he added hastily, 'Wheelchair parts, I mean.'

Captain Ellis was grinning. I enquired coldly why he was still here.

'Glad to see you too, Max.'

I scowled at him but refrained from the traditional criticism of the Time Police's failure to capture the renegade Clive Ronan, because the truth was that he'd been living on our roof for quite some considerable time and we hadn't noticed. Although, to be fair, neither had the Time Police, but it was embarrassing, just the same.

We had, however, managed to get his accomplice's body out of the tree. The operation had been quite complex, involving a cherry-picker; Angus the chicken in an observer's capacity; less than helpful suggestions from Professor Rapson, hanging precariously out of his window for a good view; an inordinate amount of rope; the entire Security Section; Miss Lee, who had taken advantage of my absence to be a nosey-parker; and finally, when the situation had become desperate, Mr Strong and his chainsaw. Down came the tree, Dottle and all. I was sorry I'd missed it, but I was in Sick Bay at the time, having my bones glued back together.

It's a bit of a bugger, but the truth is that, at my age, the bones don't knit quite as quickly as they used to and I was having trouble knitting. Or so Dr Stone said. I told him I personally blamed my lack of knitting on the poor standards of medical care currently prevailing at St Mary's, and that turned out to be a bit of a mistake because the next moment he was standing over me with a syringe the size of a Saturn V rocket.

I sat up in a hurry. 'What the hell's that?'

'Nothing for you to worry your little historian head about. Good heavens, what has Mr Bashford done now?'

I twisted my head to look and the bastard got me.

'Ow,' I said indignantly, rubbing my arm.

'There,' he said happily. 'That should do it.'

'What do you mean – *should*?'

He stared dubiously at the syringe. 'Well, I have to admit I'm not completely confident because I've only ever used this stuff once before and that was on a ginger tomcat.'

'What? Did it survive?'

'Sadly, no.'

'*What?*'

'Relax. It was run over by a bus.'

I sagged back on to the pillows with some relief.

'Yes,' he continued. 'It had some sort of fit about ten seconds after the injection and ran out into the road. Don't worry, we won't let that happen to you.'

'It's a little late now, surely.'

'We thought we'd tie you to the bed and hope that will increase your chances of survival. Hold still now.'

'Bugger off.'

He grinned. 'Bet you're feeling better now.'

I hauled the bedclothes up to my chin. 'Much. I can hear my

bones knitting faster than a bunch of tricoteuses at the foot of the guillotine.'

I know it sounds as if I'd done nothing but lie around and not be tied to my bed, but I hadn't been wasting my time. While various flexi-boots and gloves did their work, soothing swollen flesh, healing broken bones and torn ligaments, and rendering me not only pain free but quite euphoric on occasions, I'd used the time to do some thinking. Quite a lot of thinking. And a lot of planning, too. I suspect Nurse Hunter was quite surprised at my docility. She was always bursting in and staring at me suspiciously, looking for signs of misbehaviour. I would stare back, looking for signs of marriage and/or motherhood. We – Peterson and I – had failed to elicit information of any kind from Markham. I don't know why we thought we'd succeed where teachers, police, magistrates, the army and Dr Bairstow had failed. And if I wasn't being either the starer or the staree then I was being surrounded by visitors.

Peterson came every day. Wearing his blues again, because he was in charge of the History Department until I was back on my feet. He seemed his usual self, but he wasn't. He was all over the place. Dottle's death and its implications had affected all of us and Peterson most of all.

I knew Lingoss had stayed with him throughout Dottle's arrest and all the subsequent drama. She brought him to visit me in Sick Bay. I think it was when they were getting Dottle out of the tree and they wanted him out of the way. Sick Bay's on the other side of the building. I wasn't feeling that brilliant myself at the time, but Peterson had a strange, lost look and I feared for him.

Lingoss and I exchanged glances. 'I'll get some tea,' she said. 'Are you allowed to drink anything, Max?'

'No one's told me not to,' I said, 'so yes.'

She disappeared.

Peterson stood by my bed. There was a chair, but I don't think he could remember what it was for.

He said hoarsely, 'Max, I . . . told her things. I did this.' He gestured at my battered state. 'This is my fault. This is all my fault.'

If she hadn't already been very, very dead I'd have climbed out of bed, broken bones and all, and slaughtered her on the spot.

He shook his head. 'How could I get things so wrong?'

'We all did, Tim. You can't take all the credit. Come and sit down, you daft bugger. Before you fall down.'

He dropped heavily into the chair and gestured at my flexi-boots. 'This is my fault.'

'No, it's not. It's mine. I should have realised sooner.'

He shook his head. 'You had your hands full last year, Max.'

'We all did.'

He said quietly, 'It was a shit year all round.'

'It'll get better, Tim. Remember – this too will pass.'

Lingoss reappeared with tea. I watched them both as she carefully handed him his and, somewhere, a neurone lifted its battered head and began to fire.

'I've put a little something extra in it,' she said.

That roused him. She did work in R&D after all.

He regarded the cup with suspicion. 'What? What have you put in it?'

'Oh, just a little something the professor and I knocked up in the lab.'

He made a huge effort at normality. 'Don't drink it, Max. You could grow another head.'

'Well, Markham's been having it on his cornflakes for years,' she said, 'and it hasn't done him any harm.'

'That's a matter of opinion.'

I sipped my tea. Of course, she hadn't put anything *dreadful* in it. That was Hunter's job – but Lingoss was doing exactly the right thing. Taking his mind off things. A bit like stubbing your toe when you've just broken your arm. I looked at the two of them. Yeeeees . . . I'd had a bit of a brilliant idea and I needed to talk to Markham.

Peterson took a cautious sip. 'Tastes like whisky.'

She beamed. 'Good. Keep thinking that.'

Markham, now firmly in charge of the Security Section, had been another visitor, and determined, single-handedly, to eat all my grapes.

Bashford, Angus and Sykes, that eternal and bizarre love triangle, visited most evenings. And Atherton. Even North turned up once or twice, presumably to check whether I was dead yet and was it too early to apply for my job?

Professor Rapson and Dr Dowson visited each afternoon – apparently for the specific purpose of ignoring me and having a massive argument about something or other over my helpless and shattered self.

Even Ian Guthrie had hobbled in. He was doing well – better than me anyway, he would say smugly. He'd only stay for half an hour – because he didn't do chatty – and then return whence he came, saying he didn't want to set his recovery back by associating with the History Department. Or damage his public image by associating with the History Department. Or . . .

'Yes,' said the History Department. 'And your point?'

Leon came every day. He would limp in. Really, said Markham, you had to go a long way these days to find a working set of legs at St Mary's. We didn't talk a lot, but then again, we didn't need to. We would hold each other's hands and then he would smile and kiss me and go away again.

So, as you can see, I'd had to do most of my thinking at night because there was a lot going on during the day.

Anyway, Matthew's long-awaited visit was here and everyone was determined to make the most of it.

He spent the first day racing around saying hello to everyone. Mr Strong reintroduced him to the horses. They all seemed pleased to see each other. The Security Section included him in their football team after first promising to moderate both their language and the violence. Mrs Mack made him a constant supply of jam tarts and sausage rolls. R&D had a whole raft of stuff for him to be involved in. Leon and I took him into Rushford to see the new *Star Wars* and he enjoyed it so much we had to take him back the next night. Peterson came too, saying he'd always wanted to see it and was too embarrassed to go on his own so I had to invite Lingoss as well. Leon raised an eyebrow, but as I pointed out with perfect logic, she had been present when he invited Peterson and it would have been rude not to have included her. He made the traditional noise techies make when we break a cup-holder, so I maintained the tradition and ignored it.

The two of them, Leon and Matthew, spent hours pouring over Matthew's carefully drawn diagrams of his dirigible and discussing the steering issue. And me? I just hung around, helping and healing as best I could.

And then, one rainy day, I was sitting at our table, painting. What with one thing and another over the past months, I hadn't had the opportunity to do very much, so I was taking advantage of my enforced inactivity. Currently, I was working on a pastel sketch of a row of sunflowers – all brilliant golds and yellows against a blue background. Matthew, as I thought, was at the other end of the room. I had no idea what he was doing, but he was doing it quietly, which was good enough for me.

I suddenly became aware he was standing at my elbow. I also became aware that despite being at the other end of the room, he'd managed to get an inordinate amount of pastel dust all over himself.

I told him he had a rare gift. He said nothing, staring at my sunflowers. Which, I have to say, were pretty good. And certainly very colourful.

I dusted off my hands. 'What do you think?'

He nodded.

To get him to talk, I said, 'Which bit do you like best?'

'All of it.'

I began to pack my stuff away.

'How does it work?'

'How does what work?'

He picked up a stick of colour. 'This.'

Never before had he shown the slightest interest in things that didn't plug in somewhere.

'Well,' I said casually, pulling out a piece of card, 'you can swirl the colour about – like this . . .' I swirled the yellows and oranges I'd used for the petals. 'Or you can use the edges and make lines or dots – like this . . .' I drew a series of lines and dots.

He frowned. 'How do you know which colours to use?'

'I can use any colours I like. It's my picture.' There was a pause and then I said, 'Fancy a go?'

9

He nodded, so I passed him over the piece of card. 'Here you are. See how you get on.'

I handed him pastels, pencils and markers. He was busy for the next ten minutes, covering the card – and himself – with a rainbow of colours. At the end of it he asked for a clean piece of paper.

'What colour?'

He thought. 'Black.'

I passed it over and left him to get on with it while I went off to wash my hands. When I came out of the bathroom he was still busy. He'd moved on to markers and rulers. There was a lot of heavy breathing and whispering to himself.

I made us both a cup of tea and put out a plate of biscuits. He ignored both.

I was conscious of a growing excitement. He'd never shown the slightest interest in anything artistic and, as I'd said to Leon, he obviously had his father's genes. Leon had rolled his eyes and said he gave thanks daily he didn't have his mother's. It looked as if both of us had been wrong.

At the end of an energetic and very messy twenty minutes, he'd finished. I was itching to see what he'd produced but first things first.

'Bathroom,' I said. 'And don't touch anything on the way in.'

I hosed him down, dried him off and chivvied him back into our living room.

'Let's have a look then.'

He held it up.

I didn't know what to say. Yes, he'd smudged a lot of it because he'd never done anything like this before but, even so, it was remarkable.

I was looking at clouds of silver and grey which appeared to swirl and shift before my eyes. Playing hide and seek among these swirls were clusters of small blue dots which surrounded larger more defined red spots – think Jupiter – and the whole thing was surrounded by a filigree of glowing lines, connecting the red points with ruler straight lines It was at one and the same time, familiar and alien. And it seemed to move on the paper. I kept having to blink and focus.

I knew better than to ask what it was. I knew what it was. He'd drawn the Time Map. Or a part of it, anyway.

'Wow – that's good. Tell me about it.'

'It's Troy.'

I sighed inwardly. Yes, he would choose to paint that, wouldn't he? There were no warriors or ramparts or ships or horses or anything even remotely recognisable. He'd painted the Time Map's representation of Troy.

I had a sudden thought. 'Is this how you see things?'

He shrugged. 'Sometimes.'

I had an idea he'd just said something important, although what I had no idea, and there was no time to talk about it because, at that moment, Leon came in, smiled at his family and then looked around him. Yes, I'll admit, we'd had a craft afternoon and the room wasn't quite as pigment-free as we might have liked.

'Matthew, Auntie Lingoss is looking for you.'

The magic words. There was a small whirlwind, the door slammed behind him and he was gone.

I sighed and enquired exactly what was going on in R&D with which his parents could not compete.

'The professor is in the throes of inventing some sort of acoustic device he says will be able to lift heavy objects and defy gravity. Speaking as someone whose job involves daily lifting of heavy objects, I'm all for it.'

'Great,' I said, gloomily, 'we'll never get him out of there now.'

'Well, I've tried explaining they don't blow things up every day of the week but the evidence is against me.'

'Never mind,' I said, beginning to put my stuff away. 'Don't you think he looks tons better these days? Putting on weight and no more fleas or lice.'

'That's probably because they've all migrated to Markham.'

Our Mr Markham is generally reckoned to be a five-star hotel for wildlife.

Leon frowned at the door. 'Speaking of no more lice, Max, your son needs a haircut. You'd better have a word.'

I looked up from packing my gear away. 'Me? Why me?'

'You're his mother.'

'And you're his father. Surely this is part of the father/son talk.'

'Nope. I only agreed to do the *when a daddy technician loves a mummy historian* bit.'

'What?'

'You know. The bit about special cuddling.'

'What?'

'You agreed.'

'When?' A thought occurred. 'Was I drunk?'

'Oh God, yes. You'd have agreed to anything.'

I moved subtly into fighting stance. 'And apparently I did.'

He grinned and glanced at his watch. 'Oh, is that the time? Must crack on. Pods don't repair themselves, you know.'

'Not yet,' I said, 'but come the glorious day . . .'

He just laughed and disappeared.

I had a bit of a think about the haircut thing. We all have long hair here – even the blokes have a kind of historian shag. I once told

Markham he looked like a tousled Shih Tzu and he sulked for days. We all have various ways of keeping it under control – except for Miss Lingoss who embraces the whole *my hair expresses who I am* thing with enthusiasm.

I met her on the way to my office. Today's hair was black and dramatic.

I stared thoughtfully.

'Max? Are you all right? Are you in pain?'

'Actually, far from it. Do you do it yourself?'

'Do I do what myself?'

'Your hair.'

'Yep. Always have.'

'Do you cut it yourself as well?'

'Of course. I had to in college – no money. I used to do my friends' as well.'

'Did they pay you?'

'In drink, mostly.'

'Before or after?'

She grinned. 'Both. And sometimes during.'

'Would you do Matthew's?'

'If he'll let me.'

I said thoughtfully, 'Leave that to me.'

We were returning to our room after lunch. Matthew waited patiently as I inched my way along at glacial speed, prior to him shooting off to R&D for a fun-filled and, above all, very messy afternoon. There would never be a better opportunity.

I moved to attack position. 'Congrats on winding up the Time Police, by the way.'

He looked up at me, eyebrows raised.

13

'The hair. You're really getting Captain Ellis into a lot of trouble. Well done. Are you working to bring them down from the inside?'

He said nothing, waiting for me to finish negotiating a corner and then said, 'Don't want it cut.'

'Oh no. Absolutely not. Although be warned – Dr Bairstow will be telling you to put it up or in a plait like the rest of us girls.'

'Uncle Peterson has lots of hair. And Uncle Bashford.'

'Seriously? You're modelling your look on those two? One of them is in love with a gender-neutral chicken.'

He snorted.

'Do you want me to tell Dr Bairstow you refuse? Quote your human rights or something?'

He shook his head.

'Well, it's the same rules for you as for the rest of us, then. Up or off.' And I carried on to our room. He followed me in, all ready for a major sulk. I could practically hear his brain working.

I seated myself on the sofa and rummaged through the pile of files on the coffee table, eventually pulling out one of Lingoss's. 'Can you take this back to R&D when you go, please,' and waited for him to make the connection.

He stared at it for a while and then said suddenly, 'Auntie Lingoss could do it.'

'Do what?' I said absently, already opening a book that was, apparently, utterly engrossing.

'Cut it.'

'Cut what?' I said, vaguely.

'My hair,' he said impatiently. 'It would be good.'

I didn't even bother looking up. 'You're *not* having a Mohican.'

'Aww. Could I . . . ?'

'You're *not* dyeing it blue.'

14

'Why not?'

'Because I say so.'

'You never let me have any fun.'

'That's very true. Well spotted.'

'Why won't you let me have any fun?'

'I'm your mother. I'm not allowed to. It's in the job description. And you have to do as you're told.'

'No, I don't. I'm your son. It's in the . . .' he fumbled for the words, '. . . job depiction.'

Well, isn't he a quick learner? I made it easy for him.

'You will not, under any circumstances, ask Miss Lingoss to cut your hair. I shall telephone her as soon as I've finished reading this chapter to make sure she understands.'

He glared at me. 'You're horrible.'

I beamed. 'Thank you.'

'Wait till I'm eighteen.'

'When you're eighteen you can have an orange and yellow flat top if you want. Until then you do as you're told.'

'I'll be eighteen soon . . .'

'Really? You know how old you are now?'

He threw me a crafty glance. 'No. But neither do you. No one knows how old I am.'

I played dirty. 'Well, by my reckoning you're only about two years old so you've got quite a way to go until you're eighteen. You could still be doing as I tell you when you're thirty.'

'No, I won't,' he shouted.

'So, when will you be eighteen?'

'Today,' he shouted and stamped out, slamming the door behind him in the traditional teenage manner.

I opened my com. 'Miss Lingoss?'

'What ho, Max.'

'He's on his way. Not a lot off, since he's a haircut virgin and we don't want him catching cold. Just tidy him up a bit.'

'You want me to take off just enough to piss off Captain Ellis.'

'That's the ticket.'

'Max, you're evil.'

'I'm a mother. It's enough to bring out the worst in anyone.'

The seven days of his visit went by all too quickly. Matthew seemed to have enjoyed himself but he obviously had no problems returning to Time Police HQ. I told myself it was good that he was so happy there. And safe. Safe was important. While Ronan was at large we couldn't risk having him here.

Ignoring the Farrell family habit of not talking about the important stuff, I casually asked him if he'd enjoyed his visit.

He nodded.

'And you'd like to come again? Soon?'

He nodded again.

It was on the tip of my tongue to say something about the picture he'd drawn, but I didn't. Yes, he wasn't the chattiest kid in the world, but even so . . . No. Safer for everyone to say nothing.

So, I said nothing.

2

A few days after he'd gone, I had my old casts off and my walking casts on and could say goodbye to the wheelchair. It took a while to get used to walking again, but I was soon inching my way around the building with all the speed and stylish panache of continental drift.

Leon took the opportunity to recycle all the jokes I'd made about him over the last months, although, as I pointed out, they weren't funny the second time around.

I spent a lot of time in our room, working on my private project. Data stacks and files covered every horizontal surface until, one day, I reached the point where I couldn't go any further. I'd been putting it off for days but the time had come. I needed to have a chat with Mrs Partridge.

I hobbled around the gallery. I knew there was no point in complaining because I was lucky to be mobile at all, but I've always moved quickly and it irked me no end not to be trotting around the building at my usual speed. The only good thing about the whole situation was that I was still considerably underweight – sorry, I just want to savour those unfamiliar words again, considerably underweight – after my spell in the 14th century, and at least being light made movement much less tiring.

Regaining weight isn't easy. You're not allowed to pile it on any old how, you know. For some reason that completely escapes me, you can't just scarf your way indiscriminately through plates of sausages and chocolate until you hit your target. You have to eat sensibly. I'd pointed out to Dr Stone that the medical profession was always coming up with new reasons for people not to scarf down chocolate and sausages and he'd said there was something in the Hypocritical Oath compelling doctors to make their patients' lives as difficult as possible. Apparently, they get Brownie points. Even after weeks of eating sensibly, my BMI still wasn't acceptable and there had been a small confusion because I had thought BMI was a car and Hunter had offered to draw me a picture.

Anyway, trudging – or rather, hobbling – back to the point, my lighter frame was a Good Thing, apparently, so I was taking advantage of this and wobbling my way to Mrs Partridge's office.

She regarded me without joy, but she always did so I didn't take a lot of notice.

'I'm afraid Dr Bairstow isn't here at the moment, Dr Maxwell. He's attending a meeting at Thirsk and not expected back until late tonight.'

'Well, actually, it was you I wanted to see, Mrs Partridge.'

She shut down her screen and pushed her keyboard away. 'How can I help you?'

Now that the moment had come, I wasn't sure I could find the words, so I got up and flicked on the red light outside her office and then sat back down again.

I thought she would tut with annoyance – she usually does whenever I'm around, but not this time. She sat, her hands in her lap, quietly waiting for me to find the words.

I felt slightly awkward. 'We've never spoken of this.'

'Is there any need to speak of it now, I wonder?'

'Yes, I think the time has come.'

There wasn't a flicker of emotion from her. On the other hand, no hostile stare, either. I swallowed. 'Mrs Partridge, you once gave me a second chance. A chance of a new life and I was grateful enough to take it and ask no questions.'

She said nothing. We'd never spoken of this in any way, of when I'd been dying and she'd swept me off to another world. One minute I was staring at the sword in my chest and feeling my life ebb away, and the next I was face down on someone's carpet in a world where Leon was alive – which was good – and the Time Police existed – which was less good. I'd fulfilled Mrs Partridge's purpose – not that I'd had much choice – and my reward had been this other life at this other St Mary's with this other Leon. I'd tried to thank her once or twice but she'd swept my words away and we'd never mentioned it again. Until now.

I continued. 'Today, I have questions. Important questions.'

I paused in case she wanted to say she had no idea what I was talking about and I was to go away immediately but she remained silent.

I struggled on. 'The world in which I find myself today is very similar to the world I left. There have been some differences, but many things that happened there have happened here as well.'

I stopped and looked at her, searching her face for some clue. I don't know why I bothered. Her face registered nothing but polite interest. I gripped my hands together more tightly and continued.

'For example, in the other world, Peterson sustained a serious wound to his arm at Agincourt. Here, it was at Rouen. Different circumstances, but it was the same wound. Same arm, even. David Sands was in a wheelchair there – here, he's lost a foot. Izzie Barclay was shot in that world,' (by me, actually, but no need to

19

go into that now) 'and then again in this one.' This time by Greta Van Owen in revenge for the death of Schiller.

Again, I waited in case she wanted to tell me to stop wasting her time, but she just stared at me impassively. I took a deep breath because this was the crux of the matter. I'd shouted at the Time Police and demanded to know why, when all the odds were with them, they couldn't catch Clive Ronan? Why did he always manage to get away? Why did he always manage to escape? I'd been quite rude. I was surprised they hadn't shot me. And then, in the exact moment when Dottle and I fell off the roof, when you'd think I would have had other things on my mind, I'd realised *why* we couldn't catch Clive Ronan. Well, I thought I had and now I was here for confirmation and she wasn't making things easy for me.

I continued. I didn't say, 'in my world,' because that implied I hadn't accepted this one and, since in the other one I'd been dying at Agincourt and Leon was already dead, I felt it implied a certain amount of ingratitude. *This* was my world now.

I came straight to the point. 'In the other world, Clive Ronan died in the Cretaceous period.'

Still she said nothing. I had no clue what she was thinking but at least she was listening. I glanced at her locked door and lowered my voice even further. 'I think the reason we can't catch Clive Ronan here is because he's not meant to die here. He's supposed to die in the Cretaceous.'

She regarded me steadily. 'Are you saying that if you can arrange a similar set of circumstances then events might follow a similar path to a similar result?'

'Yes. I think if I could somehow lure him to the Cretaceous then I will be able to . . .'

'No,' she said, so sharply that I was alarmed. 'You must not make the mistake of thinking that because the circumstances are the same, the result will be the same.'

'But things that happened there could happen here?'

'*Could* . . . yes. *Will?* Not necessarily.'

We looked at each other for a long time. She wasn't helping – but she wasn't chucking me out, either. I was at a loss as to what to say next. The silence lengthened. What did she want from me? Much more, obviously, otherwise I'd be on the other side of the door by now, but what?

I think, in the end, she took pity on me. 'Why are you here, Dr Maxwell?'

I said very quietly, 'I'm working on an idea, which I'd like to run past Dr Bairstow. I've spent a lot of time on it, but I've reached the point where I'm doubting myself and, without more information, I don't know if I should pursue it any further.'

I inched forwards on my chair. 'Mrs Partridge, might it not be quicker and easier all round if you could say, here and now, whether I would be wasting Dr Bairstow's time by troubling him with this idea?'

I sat back. I couldn't do any more. If I was wrong then all she had to do was tell me so. But if I was right? I felt a thrill of excitement. Because I was right. I knew I was right.

We stared at each other over her desk for what, to me, felt like aeons and then she pulled her keyboard forwards. 'I can pencil you in for 10:30 tomorrow morning, if that is convenient.'

'It's perfect, Mrs Partridge. Thank you.'

I was prompt. In our job you have to be. Mrs Partridge waved me through. Dr Bairstow was waiting for me.

My presentation took a long time. There were several strands to it. I worked through each one individually and then wove them all together into chronological order.

He said almost nothing all the way through, just stared at his hands, but that's what he does when he's listening, so I gritted my teeth, ignored his lack of reaction, and soldiered on to the very end. I'm accustomed to his long silences, but this one went on and on. It was a struggle not to burst into speech, to explain, to elucidate, but he doesn't like that, so I shut up and stared over his shoulder out of the window.

Eventually, he said, 'Shall we have some tea?'

Which meant he wanted me to go through it all again but that was a good sign.

Mrs Partridge brought in the tea. I thanked her – and not just for the tea. We set things up on his briefing table and went through everything. Point by point. Line by line. Lunchtime came and went. I missed it but I was too strung up to eat anyway. He picked away at everything. Not in a critical way but making sure he knew exactly what each aspect of my plan entailed. And, I suspected, making sure I did, too. Because this one was a doozy.

'You are aware, Max, there are large areas that cannot be planned in advance. Almost more than I am comfortable with.'

'Can't be helped, sir. All I can do is respond to circumstances at the time and improvise.'

'Offhand, I cannot remember any occasion where creative thinking has been a problem for you.'

'Thank you, sir.'

'Let us hope this is not that occasion.'

I shut up.

Midway through the afternoon, Mrs Partridge brought in fresh tea and sandwiches and instructed us both to eat something. I chomped my way through a chicken-salad sandwich – protein, vegetables and carbohydrates – and watched while he twirled the data stacks, referring from one to the other and frowning.

I helped myself to another sandwich and poured us both a second cup.

He sat back, stirring his tea. 'Have you discussed this with Leon?'

'No, sir.'

'Will you?'

'When you give me permission to, sir. After Dottle, I . . . I am conscious of a certain reluctance to discuss anything with anyone.'

He regarded me gravely. 'Talk to Leon about it. He will be able to provide a useful perspective.' He sipped his tea. 'You and Leon – how are you these days?'

He wasn't talking about just our physical state.

'It's like being in a kind of limbo, sir.' I put down my tea. 'Every now and then I try to work out how we ever got to this point. Years ago, we'd just catch a glimpse of Ronan here or there – we would foil one of his dastardly schemes or dodge his attempts to throw a spanner in our works and then go on our merry way. But now, everything has escalated and he permeates our entire lives. He affects everything we do. Not only can we not catch him, but the Time Police can't either. We're hobbled, sir, both in our private and our working lives and until we hunt him down we're . . . stuck.'

'I agree,' he said. 'Which is why I'm inclined to give my permission for this somewhat bizarre and very unorthodox idea of yours.'

I knew better than to get up and cheer.

He tapped the box of files and data cubes. 'This is . . . massive.'

And he wasn't referring to the size of the box and the quantity of material inside.

'Yes, sir.'

'And involves others.'

'Many others, sir.'

'Who will not always be aware they're being involved.'

'There are key figures whom I think we should inform, sir. For our own safety. And theirs. But otherwise I do recommend we tell as few people as possible.'

'Agreed,' he said, staring into space.

Suddenly he turned around and seemed to see me for the first time. 'Max, I've kept you too long. You look tired.'

I knew better than to deny it. 'Well, I am, sir, but it's a good tired.'

'Mm,' he said. 'I'm going to let you go now. Leave all of this here, if you please, I want to familiarise myself with the details. I shall meet you again in . . . a few days.'

I hadn't expected him to leap from his seat shouting, 'Brilliant, Dr Maxwell, get on with it!' but to make me wait . . .

He knew what I was thinking. 'There are people I must consult.'

Dottle's betrayal was still very fresh in my mind. I said doubt-fully, 'Of course, sir.'

'I know what you are thinking, Max, but you may rest easy. In fact, I order you to do so. When we meet again I want you fresh, rested, on top of your game, and able to answer every point I put to you.'

I stood up. 'Yes, sir.'

He paused. 'You have thought this through, haven't you?'

'Yes, sir.'

'You know the personal sacrifices it will entail?'

'I suspect there will be more than I'm aware of, sir, but the ones I am aware of I've thought about.'

He seemed to find this piece of gobbledygook satisfactory. 'By the way, Max, I have been visiting the Chancellor at Thirsk.'

'Yes, sir. Mrs Partridge said.'

'They wanted to discuss a replacement for Dottle.'

I stared at him, swallowed down my frequently voiced opinion of the University of Thirsk and their representatives, and said, as mildly as I could, 'Sir, they cannot be serious. The two we've had so far – Halcombe and Dottle – were complete disasters. For Thirsk as well as for us. I confess I've rather been hoping they'd take the hint and let the whole idea slide quietly into oblivion. And I have to ask – given the life expectancy and career damage – why would anyone there even *consider* working here?'

'That was, more or less, my own argument.'

I tapped the box. 'Sir, if they're serious, then I do feel we need to implement this as soon as possible. Before some other daft bugger turns up and starts to cause chaos.'

'Indeed. Take the few days, Max. You're going to need them. I'll send for you.'

I said again, 'Yes, sir,' and headed to the door.

3

The following Monday I went back to work properly.

Peterson had done a good job – there was hardly anything in my in-tray. I expressed my thanks and he said no problem, the job was hardly onerous, and whatever did I find to do all day long? I told him to sod off and off he sodded.

Barely had I warmed my seat when Lingoss stuck her head around the door. 'Max? Have you got a minute?'

'Yes, of course. Come in.'

She closed the door behind her. 'Can I have a quick word?'

We both paused, waiting for Rosie Lee to leave.

Nothing happened.

We folded our arms and stared until even she couldn't fail to get the message.

'I might as well finish early then.'

It was ten past two.

'You might as well,' I said. 'It's not as if you're doing anything here.'

She slammed the door on the way out.

I asked Lingoss if she wanted some tea.

She shook her head. Today's hair was silver tipped with purple. Very striking.

'So – what can I do for you?'

'Well, the thing is, Max, I wanted to ask you something.'

I had a sudden nasty moment of déjà vu. We'd had a similar conversation when she wanted to leave the History Department's training programme and join R&D and I'd lost an historian. Was she about to give in her notice? I'd do anything to keep her here, not least because, if she left, the job of babysitting Professor Rapson through his working day might fall to me. No other bugger would do it.

'What did you want to ask?'

She shifted in her chair. 'The thing is, Max, last year when, you know, when . . .' she tailed away. I wondered what on earth could cause the blunt and forthright Lingoss such embarrassment and waited patiently while she gathered her forces for another go.

'Last year, Max, after Hawking blew up and we thought they were dead – Guthrie, Chief Farrell and Markham, I mean – and you were so . . . and then you and Peterson . . . well, you know. Everyone was so pleased. Everyone thought it was such a good thing. For both of you. And then Chief Farrell came back. Which was so brilliant. But Peterson was . . . well . . . and then there was all that business with Dottle . . . and now she's dead. And then there was the steam-pump jump with Dr Peterson – as you know . . . and . . . um . . . I wondered . . . Well . . . do you think there's any hope for me?'

Strangely, I knew exactly what she was on about. I always tried to avoid thinking of that night. Peterson with his smart jacket – the only one he had, actually – standing in front of me with his neatly combed hair, pleased at the possibility that Leon might still be alive, no matter that he would be alone again.

I'd despatched Lingoss to keep an eye on him because I'd been genuinely torn. Yes, I had to go and rescue Leon, but that really wasn't a night when Peterson should have been left on his own. And then, Dottle had died . . . He was doing his best to carry on normally, but sometimes he struggled, so I'd sent him out with Lingoss on a very minor assignment and Markham had ever so slightly overstepped the brief and pushed her into the moat so she could be rescued by Peterson. Sometimes, I wonder whether having the Security Section on your side is a Good Thing or not.

But whatever he'd done, it had worked. I knew they'd been spending time together. Nothing major and all perfectly innocuous, but it was a start.

She looked at me directly. 'May I be blunt?'

I don't know why she asked – I'd never known her be anything else.

I nodded. 'Of course.'

'I don't know if you know, but on our last assignment – you know, the steam-pump jump . . .'

'The one where you fell in the moat?'

'And Dr Peterson saved me. Yes, that one.'

That wasn't quite how I'd heard it but never mind.

'Well,' she continued. 'The thing is, Max, that . . . well . . .' She took a deep breath. 'I don't mean to pry and I'm not going to ask, but . . . well . . . I don't want to be the consolation prize.'

I must have looked blank.

'I mean I don't want to be the one Peterson settles for because he can't get you.'

Ah. In all my careful plans, that was the one thing I hadn't considered. That she was holding back because she thought . . . well, never mind.

I took a long time to consider my response, eventually saying, 'I

28

remember him when he was with Helen. When she was still alive. These days, on the surface, he looks fine – but he's not. Inside, he's dying. If you can make him happy again then I swear I will move heaven and earth to help you.'

I picked up a pen and moved it three inches to the right. 'But if you're not serious about this, or if you hurt him, or if you mess him around, then I will gut you like a fish and tie your innards in a bow around your neck. Just so we're both clear on that.'

'I'm clear.'

'So – do I need to start practising my knots?'

'Not on my account. Do I have . . . ?' She stopped.

'You don't need my permission.'

'No, but I need your goodwill. He listens to you, Max. He relies on you. He's closer to you than to anyone. You could scupper my chances with a word. If you wanted to.'

'I could, but I won't. Not if you make him happy.'

'Well, I don't know about that, but I'm going to give it a bloody good try.'

'Has he said anything about her – you know – Dottle?'

'No. Not a thing. I knew she wasn't right for him even before . . . you know. I mean, she was so *wet*. Or so we thought. And given his reputation for being attracted to difficult women . . . I couldn't think what he saw in her. Honestly, I don't know how I kept my mouth shut.'

'Well,' I said mildly, 'she did turn out to be *quite* difficult.'

'And now she's dead,' she said briskly. 'Problem solved.'

'Not for Peterson.'

'Leave that to me,' she said, and left the room.

After she'd gone, I sat quietly for a while. Then I sat up straight and wiped my eyes and blew my nose. Then I thought I'd better get on with my day. Then Mrs Partridge called me up and said Dr Bairstow wanted to see me. It would seem my few days were up and he'd finished his deliberations.

I was with him for four hours. I can't divulge what was said but, as our discussion progressed, it became very apparent he hadn't wasted his time. More from things he didn't say than things he did, I began to suspect mine was only one part of a larger scheme. I had a sudden picture of him sitting, motionless, at the centre of an enormous and elaborate web whose strands reached out in directions and distances known only to him. I didn't ask because he wouldn't have told me and I had enough on as it was.

As I left, Peterson and Leon filed in. Leon had the pod files under one arm, and as I stepped aside to let them in, Markham came in as well with his scratchpad ready.

They closed the door behind them and I went off for a well-earned mug of tea and a bit of a think.

Dr Bairstow made the announcement a couple of days later, during one of his fortunately infrequent all-staff meetings.

The first item on the agenda was the ethnicity forms and our failure to realise the importance of.

Every couple of years, Thirsk bombard us with a mountain of forms variously requesting details of age/ethnicity/religion and so on. Dr Bairstow calls an all-staff briefing and silently hands out the forms. Most people regard them as an exercise in creative writing and, two days later, equally silently, he collects them back up again and bundles them off to Thirsk. I've no idea how they're received there, but I do know that one year, Bashford stated his colour was green and he'd been born on

Olympus Mons, lower left-hand quadrant adjacent to the lava tube on the right.

I should say now that, as far as I know, Olympus Mons remained his official place of birth for quite some time until a little while ago when he applied for a passport and the authorities swooped for their revenge. He was released from custody after less than a day, though not because he'd cooperated in any way – indeed, the silly sod hadn't helped his cause at all, insisting on speaking to everyone in what he called Martian but was actually Latin. A fact discovered only when an ancient academic accidentally wandered past. He was lost and looking for the bar. Recognising the lingo, he enthusiastically joined in. Personally, I'd have arrested the pair of them but they were released without charge.

Bashford was returned to us with a written warning on his record, an inconvenience soon forgotten in the joy of being reunited with a jubilant Angus. And Miss Sykes, of course.

After the ethnicity forms there was the usual stuff.

Dr Bairstow cleared his throat. 'Subsequent to last week's fire drill, may I congratulate those who, on hearing the alarm, had the intelligence to vacate the premises. I would, however, like to invite some of you to reconsider your assembly point. I cannot feel that your habit of congregating in the area adjacent to the oil tanks "because it's out of the rain, sir," enhances anyone's chances of survival during a major conflagration, although it is, of course, entirely your choice and, as always, I hesitate to interfere.'

He paused so we could appreciate his non-interference and then continued with the big finish.

'With effect from the day after tomorrow, Dr Maxwell is to be seconded to the Time Police. To assist them in their hunt for Clive Ronan. I am sure we all wish her well.'

An astonished murmur ran around the room. I folded my arms and stared at my feet, refusing to catch anyone's eye. The briefing concluded and we dispersed.

Back in my office, Rosie Lee was furious. 'Who will make my tea?'

I shook my head. 'No idea. I suspect you'll be dead of tea deprivation ten minutes after I've left. Don't forget to leave your desk tidy for your successor.'

The entire History Department crashed *en masse* through the door and talked at me for nearly thirty minutes. I smiled and, other than confirming Peterson as my legitimate heir, said as little as possible. North glared at me. She'd been after my job since the day she walked through the door. Sykes was nearly in tears and, apparently, even Angus would miss me.

I chivvied them all out and went off to find Leon who was waiting for me in Hawking. We walked around the lake because, since my discovery that our room had been bugged, we'd taken to talking about important stuff outside. In vain did Markham protest he'd swept our room three times and it was cleaner than clean – we just felt safer that way. And Dr Bairstow had decreed that, until this matter was settled one way or another, there were to be no written or electronic communications. Everything was to be face to face and in real time.

Leon and I talked together for two circuits of the lake. Or about forty-five minutes. Neither of us was very happy, but what can you do?

I spent the rest of the day closing things down in my office and packing. I wanted to take all my treasured possessions with me – my Trojan Horse, my red snake and so on – but apparently, people join the Time Police with nothing but the clothes they stand up in and a toothbrush. All right, slight exaggeration but not much.

'It's like the French Foreign Legion,' I said.

Leon stared at me. 'What?'

'You know – people have a crisis and join the Legion to forget.'

'The Time Police are nothing like the French Foreign Legion,' he said. 'And since when have *you* ever had to go abroad to forget something? I've been waiting for your signed copy of the pod schedule for a week now.'

'Talk to Peterson about it,' I said, waving my hand vaguely. 'He's got the History Department now.'

'Poor sod.'

In the end I had to narrow my packing down to what I could stuff into my sports bag. Which wasn't much. And like me, the bag had seen better days.

I asked Leon whether he thought I should close down my bank account.

He took me gently by the wrist and once again we were outside.

'Max, you're making it sound as if you're not planning to come back.'

'Well, obviously I am, but you know what we say – hope for the best and plan for the worst.'

'No, you say that. I say . . .' he stopped and looked away.

I put my arms around him. 'You don't have to say anything, Leon. I know what you say. But we'll get him. Between us, we'll get him. And then I'll be back. And I'll be bringing Matthew with me. Everything's going to be absolutely fine.'

The Time Police sent a pod for me. Markham said it was because they didn't trust me to get there on my own, but I suspected they had stringent security at TPHQ and any pod attempting an un-authorised landing would probably be vaporised on the spot. Together with its occupants.

Leon walked me down to Hawking. We didn't say anything. It had all been said the night before. Dr Bairstow, Peterson and Markham stood at the far end. The gantry was empty. Only Dieter and Mr Lindstrom were around, standing outside Number Five and ticking things off a checklist. Our footsteps echoed loudly in the concrete cavern.

Dr Bairstow turned. 'Ready, Max?'

I nodded.

He said quietly, 'I will clear the way for you, Max. I promise.'

I nodded again, not trusting to my voice.

'Good luck.'

It was only as I shook hands with him that the full impact of what I was doing hit me. That was the moment when I wondered what the hell I thought I was playing at. A dark, unknowable future gaped at my feet and I stood on the brink. I closed my eyes for a moment, fighting off combined vertigo and panic. Everything swayed around me and I think that, at that moment, if anyone, anyone at all, had said, 'I really don't think this is a very good idea, Max,' then I would have agreed with them and suggested we all go back to the main building for breakfast.

They didn't, however, so I didn't either, and the feeling passed.

Leon heaved one of the sliding doors open. It screeched in its metal runners. We stepped outside. It was a cold, raw day. A thick early morning mist hung heavy in the air.

They were already waiting for me. This was it. Half of me thought – so soon? And the other half was glad there would be no hanging around.

I walked with Leon to the Time Police pod. The ramp came down as we approached and an officer stepped out. I'd hoped for Matthew Ellis – a familiar face to make this a little easier, but I didn't know this one. Silently, he took my bag from me and, displaying an enormous amount of tact for the Time Police, disappeared inside, leaving me alone with Leon.

Leon took my ice-cold hand and held it between his own. Despite the dawn chill, his hands were very warm. My heart was thumping away but I'd come too far to back down now. Besides, I'd never live it down.

'Well,' I said, lightly. 'This is it.'

'Yes. Gainful employment at last. Who'd have thought?' His grip tightened. 'Max . . .'

'I will,' I said. 'I'll take care, I promise you.'

'I was going to ask you if you'd got everything but, yes, the taking care thing is good as well.'

'You too, Leon. I don't want to do the whole heroic return thing to find St Mary's in flames.'

'I think you'll find St Mary's is only ever in flames when you're around.'

'Hurtful but true.'

'Look after yourself.'

I really didn't want to do this. How do I get myself into these situations?

'And you, Leon. I'll see you soon.'

'You'd better. Give my love to Matthew.'

I nodded. Someone coughed nearby and I looked round. The officer was back and holding my bag. Silently he unzipped it and displayed the contents. There were one or two personal items but I suspected it was the enormous plastic bag containing my own bodyweight in tea bags that was causing the problem. Tea was taxed out of existence in their time. Everyone glared at me. I think they suspected me of attempting to undermine the Time Police Culture of Evil by using tea bags as bribes, currency, rewards and so on. And for hot beverages, of course.

It would appear my bag hadn't made it through customs.

'You won't need any of this,' he said and held it out to Leon, who took it with a look that indicated he'd always known I'd be in trouble but hadn't realised it would be quite this soon.

And then, suddenly, the moment arrived.

I took a breath. 'I'd better be off.'

He kissed my hand and then my cheek. 'Good luck, Max.'

I nodded, suddenly unable to speak.

He stepped back and I entered their pod. The ramp came up behind me.

I turned my back on St Mary's and faced my future.

A quiet voice said, 'Commence jump procedures.'

'Commencing now.'

The world flickered – and that was it.

I couldn't help feeling smug. Typical Time Police – all mouth and no trousers. St Mary's does it much better.

The landing at TPHQ was much more impressive. We landed so smoothly and gently that at first, I didn't realise we'd arrived at all. It was only when they started shutting things down and the officer said, 'This way, please,' that I realised we were actually here. All right, the Time Police do that better, but I rather missed Peterson and his bouncing-bomb landings.

I shouldered my bag and followed the officer down the ramp. We don't have ramps on our pods – not only does it reveal too much of the interior but it makes it difficult to fight off curious dinosaurs, mammoths, pitchfork-wielding villagers and so on.

I paused at the bottom and looked around. I was in the bowels of TPHQ, buried beneath the iconic Battersea Power Station. Given the size of the space in which I stood, I might even be under the River Thames itself. Probably best not to think about that.

Captain Farenden, Commander Hay's adjutant, was waiting for me.

'Max, welcome to Time Police HQ. Nice to see you again.'

'Thank you,' I said.

An awkward silence fell.

'Big pods,' I said, gesturing around. 'With ramps.'

'We usually need to get as many feet on the ground as quickly as we can, to say nothing of plant and materiel. This is the best way of dispersing our forces.'

'Oh, right. You feel that a helicopter hovering over 15th-century Florence isn't going to attract any attention at all?'

He grinned. 'Where do you think Leonardo got the idea from?'

This equivalent of Hawking Hangar was massive. I don't want to worry anyone, but if anything ever goes wrong, then half London will disappear in a flash and a bang and a gigantic puff of smoke. Along with most of the southern counties. If you want to be a safe distance away when the inevitable happens, may I suggest Reykjavik?

I'd been here before, of course. On several occasions and for various reasons. Sometimes conscious – sometimes not. This was the first chance I'd had to get a really good look around.

On the far wall, two swing doors led to their really excellent medical facilities. Another door in another wall opened into their stores and repair areas. The technicians – no, sorry, the Time Police call them mechs – had an office at the far end. Unlike St Mary's, everything was bright and gleaming and modern. And functioning properly. I doubt they even knew duct tape existed.

I don't know what material they'd used in the construction, but this was no echoing concrete cavern. Voices were subdued and easily absorbed by very effective soundproofing. There wasn't even a tinny little radio belting out popular tunes of the day. Music was probably a little too frivolous for the Time Police.

I thought I might be taken to see Commander Hay immediately, but apparently there was a great deal to do first. I suspected the delay was also to reinforce my new position as lowest of the low.

To begin with, I had to have a medical to prove I was fit for purpose. I think we all felt a bit dubious about that, but I scraped through somehow. I'd brought a message from Dr Stone saying this was as good as I was ever likely to get and welcome to his world.

They had several doctors at TPHQ – apparently their casualty rate was even higher than ours – and I had the unnervingly silent one who'd treated Leon. We gazed at each other and then he sighed heavily, bleeped some sort of electronic device and I was officially A3.

I protested. Back at St Mary's, I was A1. He shook his head and said I was with the Time Police now and they had higher standards. I enquired when we were likely to see any evidence of that.

'Underweight and puny,' he said, typing something into his machine.

'I'm so sorry I don't fit into the narrow band of weight the medical profession has deemed acceptable for women *today*. Should we wait a week or so for that to change?'

'I don't think you realise *the medical profession* – as you so disparagingly refer to it – has only your wellbeing at heart.'

'Well, I don't think anyone realises that, do they?'

His finger hovered menacingly over A4 so I took the hint and left.

Only one step from physical decrepitude I might be – according to their medical team, anyway – but apparently, I did have some sort of status because I wasn't shoved into a dormitory with the other lower life forms but found myself in the same guest suite in which Matthew and I had stayed before. I tried to feel this was because they valued me as an asset, rather than regarding me as some troublemaker from St Mary's who had to be kept separate to avoid contaminating the others.

It was quite nice, actually – even though it didn't have Leon in it. I found myself facing the future with a small sitting room enjoying an amazing view over the river, two tiny bedrooms, a kettle and a jar of coffee.

Someone tapped at the door. I went to open it, remembered I didn't have to and called, 'Come in.'

The door opened automatically. It was Matthew.

'Hello,' I said, really pleased to see him. 'How are you?'

He nodded to indicate he was fine.

'Oi!' said someone behind him and gave him a poke. 'Speak.'

'Very well, thank you,' he said, politely.

'That's better,' said Captain Ellis. 'Max, welcome to TPHQ.'

'Thank you. It's very nice to be here.'

There was a short pause during which I remembered you're not supposed to tell fibs in front of children.

'Well,' he said. 'As you can see, your uniform is on your bed. Your list of duties is on your desk downstairs. Here's a map of the building showing the few areas you have access to and the many more that you don't.' He handed me a sheet of paper. 'Plus, the usual *Things You Should Know* folder, as well.' He handed me a folder. 'We'll leave you to unpack and then come and collect you.'

'Done that,' I said.

He looked around at the small featureless room entirely bereft of any personal possessions. 'Oh. OK.'

'If you can give me a minute to get changed I'll be with you.'

'Before you go, there's something we need to discuss.'

My first thought was *only one thing*? but I nodded. 'What's the problem?'

'No problem at all, but we need to discuss where this young man is going to sleep in future. Would you like him to join you here – that's why we gave you this suite – or . . . ?'

40

Or remain in the dormitory with his friends was what neither of them were saying.

My first impulse had been to say, 'Here, of course,' but I swallowed that down. 'Well, sleeping here is a nice thought, but I'm probably going to be coming and going at all hours of the day and night. It's up to you, though, Matthew. What would you like to do?' He would want to stay with his friends. Of course, he would. I made it easy for him. 'Would you prefer to stay where you are for the time being?'

He nodded.

'Speak,' said Ellis sternly.

'Yes, please.'

I swallowed down my disappointment. I had hoped . . . well, never mind. 'All right then.' I was struck with an idea. 'Tell you what, this Friday, if you're not doing anything, come round and we'll watch a holo. I'll get a pizza, you bring your favourite movie and we'll have an evening together. What do you think?' I looked at Ellis. 'Not a school night, so no problem.'

'Well,' he said, reluctantly, 'there's usually a nine o'clock curfew.'

We both watched Matthew work out that his mother probably didn't do nine o'clock curfews. 'Yes, I'd like that.' He looked at me severely. 'No anchovies.'

'In that case,' I said, 'no *Transformers*.'

'*Attack of the Killer Zombie Robots*?'

'Sounds good. See you Friday, if not before.'

He nodded and looked at Ellis who said, 'Off you go, then.'

He disappeared.

Ellis looked at me. 'Nicely played, Max.'

'Yep, here less than an hour and undermining all your good work already. Um . . . can I ask you something?'

41

He looked wary. I didn't blame him. 'What do you want me to do?'

'It's something I don't want you to do.' I stopped, a little unsure.

'Yes?'

'I think Leon . . . I mean . . . well . . . Not sure how to say this . . . And don't think I'm – we're – not grateful for what you're doing with Matthew, but I know Leon is looking forward . . . Well . . . could you *not* teach Matthew to shave?'

There was a moment's silence and then he said, 'Well, I don't think that's likely to be an issue for a while yet, but yes, I do understand what you're saying. Inasmuch as anyone can ever understand St Mary's.'

He did understand. I felt rather mean. 'I don't want you to think we're not aware of . . .'

'It's not a problem,' he said. 'I volunteered and I don't regret it. Now, we need to get a move on.'

'OK. Give me two minutes.'

Nothing had changed since my last visit. We walked down long, anonymous beige corridors, each one labelled with its floor number and tower name – North, South, East or West. Doors opened off either side. Other than their numbers, there was nothing to identify any individual rooms or their function. None of them were labelled. Every corridor was almost identical to the others. It was very easy to get lost. Intentionally so, I guessed.

We headed first for Commander Hay's office – the big one at the front, overlooking the river. The one with the wonderful view out over the Thames crowded with river traffic and with airships chugging slowly overhead.

I strode along beside Ellis in my stiff, unfamiliar uniform. Black

T-shirt – long-sleeved in my case because I feel the cold. Almost everyone else wore them short so everyone could admire their bulging muscles. Even the girls. Not having any muscles – or indeed bulges of any kind – I kept my sleeves down. I also wore the black combat trousers and what I persisted in referring to as Batman's utility belt. There were pouches and loops for all sorts of equipment. Not having any equipment to speak of, mine jangled emptily.

'You'll soon acquire all sorts of bits and pieces to hang off them,' said Ellis, 'and then they're bloody heavy, let me tell you.'

All officers were permitted to go armed and I rather hoped I'd get one of their big sonic guns. Not because I intended to shoot anyone but because I thought it would make me look like one of those movie heroines, heaving around some massive piece of weaponry while inexplicably – but they all do it for some reason – stripping down to my vest. Sadly, no one else shared my vision and I remained weaponless. The uniform was comfortable and practical, though, and in no way resembled the skintight bodysuits all professional women seem to feel obliged to wear in today's movies and holos.

I wore my own boots. They weren't Time Police regulation issue but they'd seen some action over the years and looked much tougher than I did. There was even a possibility they might still have some Time Police DNA on their toecaps. They were boots that would be respected in a place like this and I reckoned I could bask in their reflected glory.

We clumped along what seemed like miles of their featureless beige maze. For an organisation inhabiting one of the most iconic buildings in the world, their interior designer had seriously missed the mark.

I asked him if they'd done the décor themselves.

'What décor?' he said, looking around.

'Well, I think that answers my question.'

Commander Hay was waiting for us in her office.

I'd encountered her before on several occasions. We'd both been at the treaty-signing after the Battle of St Mary's. She was a very different person from Colonel Albay, former head of the Time Police. I hadn't liked him at all, not least because he'd tried to strangle me. That sort of thing can put you off a person.

Commander Hay was, on the face of it, a much more benign person than Albay. Until you remembered that there weren't that many women in the Time Police so for her to rise to this position was an enormous achievement. And she'd fought in the Time Wars – that period of anarchy when the secret of time travel was out there for everyone to grab. The story was that that was when she'd incurred the injury to her face. There'd been an emergency extraction and the door had blown off the pod. Everyone had died except Marietta Hay but, when they were eventually able to get to her, one side of her face was older than the other. As always, I wondered what she thought when she looked in the mirror every morning.

She'd been appointed because she was the more acceptable face (no pun intended) of the Time Police. The bad old days of Colonel Albay were gone. Under her leadership, the Time Police were working hard at being nice people. A bit of a struggle for some of them but I was sure they'd get the hang of it. One day.

As part of her *We in the Time Police are lovely people, really* scheme, they'd opened up the ground floor to the public. A beautifully designed atrium was the focus of the public side of the organisation. There were indoor trees and gardens and a splashing fountain. There was a lot of smart glass and shafts of sunlight made exciting patterns on the floor.

Crocodiles of chattering children could frequently be seen wandering around the place with their lunchboxes and worksheets. There were lectures and holos open to all. Discreet offices staffed by specially selected officers – those with if not friendly then at least less-scarred-than-usual countenances – who encouraged people to report any suspicions they might have about something sinister being built in their neighbours' garage. Friendly, cheerful, smiling Time Police officers stood in full view, all ready to direct arrivals or answer questions and not shoot anyone. Not in front of the children, at least.

We were shown in by Captain Farenden. Despite his having the bad taste to work for a bunch of psychotic thugs with a thing for black clothing, I quite liked him. He was a former helicopter pilot and another who had been injured in the Time Wars. His helicopter had been shot down and only his first-rate piloting had avoided a heavily populated area and major loss of life. He smiled at me as he ushered us into Commander Hay's office and took his place at a side table, his scratchpad glowing expectantly.

Commander Hay stood up as I entered, which I thought was pretty good of her, considering I was now just an anonymous oik in her organisation. Her face, however, even allowing for its natural lack of expression, was not that friendly.

'Dr Maxwell, good morning.'

'Good morning, ma'am.'

'Welcome to the Time Police.'

'Thank you, ma'am.'

She seated herself and clasped her hands on her desk. I was not asked to sit.

'Before we go any further, I want to be absolutely clear that *you* are absolutely clear about your duties and responsibilities during your secondment to us.'

You can never go wrong with yes, ma'am. 'Yes, ma'am.'

'You will forgive me if I say that, given your past behaviour, I find that hard to believe. Gentlemen, if you could give me a moment alone with Maxwell, please.'

As they were leaving the room, she said sternly, 'Please understand that while you may use the public areas, the atrium and some of our facilities, there are many other areas you may not access. For instance . . .'

The door closed quietly behind them and we were alone.

'Sit down, Max. Everything all right so far?'

'Yes, thank you, Commander. My accommodation is very comfortable, I've unpacked, I've seen Matthew and now I'm ready to get to work.'

'Not everyone is happy with your presence here.'

'I'll just have to live with that, ma'am.'

'How soon before you're in trouble, do you think?'

'Hard to say, ma'am.'

'Try.'

'I shall endeavour to live up to expectations, ma'am.'

She paused a moment and then said, 'There is another dimension to our problem of which you might not be aware. At least, I hope you are unaware.'

I waited.

She shifted in her seat. 'There are certain factions here within the Time Police who are unhappy with the direction in which I am taking them.'

I nodded, remembering the gardens outside. The beautifully

landscaped atrium. The lines of excited children all clamouring to join up. The guided tours. The smiling face of the Time Police.

She sighed. 'The Time Wars are finished. Over and done with. Mostly.' Unconsciously she touched her face. I wondered if she had been young and half her face had aged more quickly as a result of her accident, or had she been middle-aged already and half her face had become younger. If the former, what would happen when the other half of her face caught up?

I made myself concentrate. She was still talking. 'Or we thought they were over and done with. Colonel Albay . . . ?' She cocked an eyebrow at me and I nodded.

Don't get me wrong. They were the right people for the right job at the right time. Unlicensed time travel was at epidemic levels and doing nobody any good at all and the Time Police got out there and quite literally saved the world. The trouble was, they hadn't known when to stop. These days, it was very apparent to everyone that their *shoot first, destroy everything in sight and sell the survivors into slavery* approach might possibly need some slight modification.

Poles apart ideologically, St Mary's and the Time Police had always been on some sort of collision course and there had been a massive firefight which we won and they lost, and Colonel Albay celebrated by trying to strangle me in a particularly unpleasant manner – a fact I tried hard not to hold against them and usually succeeded.

After the famous Battle of St Mary's, we'd thrashed out an agreement, which all parties had signed – and, give them their due, they'd pretty much stuck to it. There was no doubt, however, that many of them hankered back to the good old days.

She continued. 'Colonel Albay might be dead but his spirit

lingers on. We are, at the moment, a divided force. They call themselves the Albayans. There aren't that many of them, but they are vociferous, pugnacious, and well-connected. And they're just waiting for an opportunity. They disapprove of my approach. They certainly disapprove of me.'

I nodded. The small number of women in the Time Police suggested they were not an enlightened organisation. On the other hand, you could argue that most women had more sense. And I'd signed up. Make of that what you will.

I cast my mind back. 'But it's working, isn't it? You'd never have caught that idiot who jumped back to 1536 if his girlfriend hadn't grassed him up. Crisis averted. Obviously, it pays to be approachable.'

'At the moment, I have the upper hand. My people hold most of the key positions. There is no doubt, though, that our failure to capture Clive Ronan is seriously weakening me.'

'Well,' I said cheerfully, 'we'd better get him, then.'

She smiled. Only half her face moved. 'I'll let you get started. Please be clear – there will be no preferential treatment. To single you out in any way would look suspicious. You are, on the face of it, simply an ex-member of St Mary's, here to provide historical background and perspective to our jumps. I shall protect you as much as I am able but you will need to make your own way here, Max.'

'I understand completely, ma'am. And I do think a certain amount of friction between us will make my inevitable treachery so much more believable.'

'Good luck, Max. You're going to need it.'

'Thank you, Commander.'

* * *

I was allocated a study carrel in one of the libraries, all done out in grey, sound-deadening material. It was quite large, actually, almost a small room. I had three shelved walls, a desk, a moderately comfortable chair, and two screens, both voice-activated – one to access the internet and one for the intranet. There was a firewall the size of China between them. On my desk sat a much better scratchpad than I was used to back at St Mary's, four or five blank notepads, a mug of pens and pencils, and a list of passwords to the sites I was able to access. Each of the screens read *Welcome, Dr Maxwell*, which I thought was a nice touch. Sadly, there was no kettle – only a drinks dispenser at the far end of the long room. Still, exercise is supposed to be a Good Thing.

A blue folder revealed a list of forthcoming Time Police projects. Three were asterisked, denoting they were for my attention. Officially, I was here to provide detailed historical background to their missions. I don't know how Commander Hay had persuaded her people these would form an important part of future assignments, but she had and it was up to me now.

The first was to industrial Liverpool, 1826. The purpose of the assignment had been redacted, but I'd expected that. The Time Police are not St Mary's. They don't give a rat's arse about History. It's the timeline and the maintenance thereof that floats their particular boat. Someone, somewhere, was doing something naughty in Liverpool, 1826. Their job was to sort it out and mine to assist them in doing so.

After a few false starts, I got the hang of things and started to pull up the information available. My programme said the briefing was for 11:00 tomorrow. Whether I would present my own findings or pass them on to someone else was unclear. In fact, it wasn't even clear whether I'd be allowed to attend the briefing at all. I really was at the bottom of the pile again.

I sighed, opened a notebook, selected a pen, and got stuck in.

I did attend the briefing. And I did the presentation as well. It didn't go too badly. For one thing, I remembered my audience and briefed accordingly. I kept it short and simple. A bit like me, really. I didn't bang on about not interfering with History because I could go on about that all day and they still wouldn't understand me.

I stood in front of a room filled with about thirty officers. I gave them the background. I told them what they could expect to see, what they should look out for, areas where they might expect to encounter problems, and so on. I even gave them a quick outline of subsequent events, just to put things into context. I'd given myself ten minutes to get all this across, reckoning this was about the limit of their attention span. Any longer and they might start throwing things. Or shoot me.

It went well. They listened. One or two actually took notes on their scratchpads. I think there was a general air of things having gone better than anyone – including me – had thought they would. I didn't stay for the rest of the briefing, slipping out of the door before we all suffered the embarrassment of me being asked to leave.

I went straight back to the library, did my best to enjoy the cup of lukewarm brown water that could have been either coffee or gravy because they're very similar, and reckoned things weren't going too badly.

Obviously, not everything went that well. They were the Time Police and I was St Mary's. There was always going to be friction, which I intended to exploit to the best of my ability, and it wasn't very long before the first opportunity arose. They'd scheduled me for weekly sessions of self-defence and there was trouble right from the word go.

'Right,' said Ellis. 'Pair off. One of you to disarm the other. *Disarm* only. I don't want any casualties due to over-enthusiasm. Pretend your opponent is a little old lady.'

'No problem there,' said my partner, a thickset yob named Grint, sneering unpleasantly at me. So, bearing in mind Ian Guthrie's advice – always get your licks in first – I hooked my leg behind his and helped him to the ground. It was only an unfortunate coincidence that he banged his face on my knee on the way down.

There seemed to be an enormous amount of shouting and one second later I was surrounded and two seconds later we were all in Commander Hay's office. I don't remember my feet touching the floor at all.

I think 'irked' is the best word to describe her expression. 'I understand there has been an incident.'

Everyone else was silent so it was obviously up to me. 'I was disarming my opponent. As instructed.'

Ellis said in exasperation, 'With your knee?'

'The situation appeared to warrant the element of surprise. I didn't realise I was being too rough for him.'

He was even more angry. 'You broke his nose because you didn't adhere to the approved protocols.'

'Why would I? The unexpected is always good.'

'They are designed to keep you safe.'

'I can do that for myself. As this morning proved.'

'You were lucky.'

'No – I was underestimated. By everyone.'

51

'You're part of a team. Your team is there to protect you.'

'Seriously? Do I look like I need protecting?'

'I am responsible for you and I'm following my orders. You should try it some time.'

'Your man was about to shove a gun in my face. What was I supposed to do – scream and collapse on the floor?'

'In moments of crisis – yes. It takes you out of the game and we can get on with things without injuring you. Although why that's such a priority is a mystery.'

'Everything's a mystery to the Time Police.'

As one they took a step towards me, fists raised.

I screamed and collapsed on the floor.

I lay there, inhaling carpet and praying someone had a sense of humour. This used to happen to me a lot during my training at St Mary's. They pit one short historian against three security guards and then get upset because she doesn't play fair.

A pair of boots appeared right in front of my face and Captain Ellis said, 'You see – you can do it if you try.'

'Get her up,' said Commander Hay and I was hauled to my feet.

'In the phrase popularised by idiots down the ages, I think lessons have been learned today.' She paused. 'By everyone.'

I smiled brightly because I've been told that's very irritating.

She sighed. 'I am about to return to my desk and open a file. When I look up none of you will still be here.'

She did and we weren't.

Yes, there were a few bumps along the way, but from my point of view, everything was going quite well. This was a strange new world and I was eager to investigate. Unfortunately, that wasn't so easy. They had a library. Actually, they had three, scattered around the building, but for me, certain books were banned. And I certainly wasn't allowed just to browse. Books were selected for me. Almost all non-fiction was banned and if I did get what I wanted, most of it was so redacted as to be almost useless.

I picked up various bits and pieces along the way, of course. They worked me hard but I kept my eyes open because, as I said, as an historian it was my duty. They did let me outside – which surprised me because I thought they'd be completely up their own arses about the future contaminating the past and so on. I did have to sign an enormous number of documents promising never to divulge anything about the future. I probably shouldn't say this, so look away now if you don't like spoilers, but if anyone wants to put their money into zeppelins, canals, dirigibles, energy-generating walkways, green roofs, intelligent glass and especially **[Information Redacted]** then now's the time. You didn't hear any of that from me.

Some things had barely changed at all. Doors and windows were still in the same place – although they were now voice controlled. As were the light panels in the walls and ceilings. Clothes were made mainly of a cotton mix and rarely required washing. Which was good. And, for me, there were still the same anti-period injections but without the side effects – which was even better.

I have to say the weather was dreadful. They'd had a bash at climate control, apparently, but it was as hit and miss as normal weather so hardly worth bothering with. In fact, I thought they'd just made things worse. Until they told me how unstable things had been until recently, and then I had to concede they hadn't done a bad job at all.

Interestingly, there were now three official worldwide languages – English, Spanish and Mandarin – and because people lived all over the place these days, each news bulletin was in all three languages. So that everyone could check they were all getting the same news, Ellis told me later.

As always, the main concerns were with the US. America had found yet another way to be at war with itself and was now split along roughly east-west lines with California as a separate country. No one would answer any of my questions about it so I can't tell you any more. Sorry.

Marriage was finished. A couple of years ago I'd have led the cheers, but now I wasn't so sure. These days people signed a contract for either seven or ten years – there were tax breaks for those undertaking the ten-year sentence – at the end of which term the contract could either be terminated or extended. I was intrigued enough to do some digging around on the internet. I was looking for statistics on which gender terminated most, but either the figures weren't available to anyone or just not available to me. I'd learned not to probe too deeply into matters not strictly related to the Time Police because if I did, sooner or later, someone would appear in the doorway of my carrel and frown at me.

Sex was no longer for the purposes of reproduction and most women were artificially inseminated with the sperm of their choice at the time of their choice.

'So,' I said to Matthew Ellis. 'Sex is for pleasure only.'

'Depends how you do it,' he grinned and would say no more despite my gentle probing.

Doctors were scarce and worked only in hospitals. Most people had home-scanners that diagnosed and prescribed. If you opened your eyes and found a real doctor bending over you then you were in serious trouble. Nothing new there then.

World population had peaked and was now declining slightly, but not by enough and not quickly enough. The deserts were being greened, which was interesting, and attempts were being made to farm the oceans. With mixed success.

Taxation was sky-high, with most resources being poured into slowing climate change. The Gulf Stream was all over the place and the temperature in London was now slightly cooler than before. Winters in north-west Europe were colder and wetter and snow was so frequent that even England had stopped grinding to a halt every time a teaspoonful of the stuff drifted across a motorway.

Around the world, some cities were moving underground. Canada was almost completely subterranean. I asked if I could visit and was told no.

Most interesting of all – if you were politically inclined – there were a handful of major international corporations now more powerful than most governments. I gathered this was causing a certain amount of friction.

So, we hadn't managed to blow ourselves to bits, or completely exhaust the world's resources, but it certainly wasn't the Utopian paradise so beloved of all science-fiction writers and – and this, for me, was the real tragedy – still no flying cars.

Matthew and I established a nice little routine. I often saw him during the day even if it was only to wave. He would visit on Friday evenings and we'd do a holo and pizza together. Sometimes, afterwards, he would stay to talk about his schoolwork, or to show me something he'd made. One night, when it was much later than either of us realised, he stayed in the other bedroom. And the next Friday as well. Then he moved one or two things in and, after a while, staying with me on Friday nights became an accepted thing. Captain Ellis congratulated me on my strategy.

But I was lonely. Very, very lonely.

I missed Leon a lot. Much more than I thought I would. We'd been apart for long periods before, but I was usually too busy trying to survive to have time for moping and feeling sorry for myself. Here, I had plenty of time on my hands and thoughts of Leon filled most of it. And not just Leon. I missed Peterson and I worried about him. And Markham. Even Rosie Lee. The people here were perfectly pleasant and we were all making heroic efforts to get along together – we could have done a holo for the UN had they still been in existence – but they weren't St Mary's. Evenings were the worst, with no Leon to curl up with. I even missed all the football I'd had to watch because he'd fallen asleep on the remote and I didn't want to disturb him.

I threw myself into my work and my briefings went well. My room was bland but comfortable. The food wasn't bad. The facilities offered inside the building were excellent. Sadly, they weren't a light-hearted bunch. Well, they were the Time Police, so frivolity had no place in their lives. As I said, some of them were quite pleasant, but bloody hell, it was dull.

I had no means of communication with Leon but I had to do something so I wrote him letters in my head, telling him how Matthew and I were getting on. He was working hard at his reading and writing. Matthew, I mean. He still attended a normal school in the mornings and got his Time Police education in the afternoons. They were treating him well and he seemed happy. His old, suspicious, glowering look had all but disappeared.

All in all, I had no complaints. I kept my head down and my mouth shut and people actually listened to my briefings. I think they were surprised I wasn't preaching at them, but if they were able to rampage through History and get away with it, then who was I to interfere? I just stood up, gave them the facts and sat back down again. On a good day, one or two people might come to see me afterwards to seek clarification on one point or another.

So, there I was – working for the Time Police, and mainly doing a good job. There was the odd incident – there probably always would be; Captain Ellis usually smoothed everything over afterwards but I knew that, in one or two areas, there was bad feeling. No one ever sat with me to eat and my evenings were pretty solitary.

But – things were going fairly well. Right up until the moment when they weren't. The moment when the manure heap well and truly impacted the ventilation system and nearly derailed all my careful plans. And – before anyone says anything – it wasn't my fault. It was Matthew's.

I'd expressed a curiosity and Captain Ellis had invited me to the Map Room. Officially, it was on the list of places where they would shoot me if they found me unescorted, but I was interested and he offered, so off we toddled.

We fought our way through Commander Hay's public attempts to convince people the Time Police were members of the human race, across the echoing atrium with its exciting visuals, professional landscaping and teeth-gritting Time Police tour guides and back into the private areas.

The room housing the Time Map was just around the corner, through a discreet key-coded door, along another anonymous corridor and through another, heavy door which required not only Captain Ellis's card, but his thumbprint as well.

Being the Time Police, of course, the equivalent of the St Mary's version of the Time Map wasn't anything like good enough for them. I think they thought ours was a bit girlie. Theirs did not sit within the confines of a data stack. Theirs was a giant holo, about three storeys high. I suppose that, in an almost exclusively male organisation, size is important, but even I had to admit it was spectacular. I made a note to keep Miss Lingoss away because if she ever clapped eyes on this then I'd lose her forever. I know the Time Police are a bunch of idiots, but this was one thing they really had got right. And yes, it did make our Map look more girlie than a pink handbag in Girlie Land.

Unlike the St Mary's version, which is vaguely hourglass-shaped, theirs was a huge sphere, incorporating two axes – one horizontal and the other vertical. The horizontal axis denoted space and the vertical showed time. Where the two intersected was the ever-changing here and now. Everything above now was in the future and everything below denoted the past. I tilted my head back, trying to take it all in at once.

I had no idea how many streamers they'd needed to keep this going. Hundreds possibly thousands – of pinpoints of light glittered like stars from the ceiling, the walls, even the floor, all converging on this enormous, impressive Time Map.

'You'll get a better view from the observation ring,' said Ellis. 'This way.'

He steered me along a curved corridor and out on to the observation ring. As I stepped into the silver light, I could hear a low, droning hum as the Map slowly rotated.

The ring was situated about halfway up the Map, thus giving an excellent view both up, down and all the way around. A giant silver filigree of light stretched way up above my head and down to the floor beneath. Thousands and thousands of tiny, glowing silver points were all connected in a vast network of fine, shimmering lines. Scattered throughout, tiny blue, green and purple dots of light denoted various jumps. Almost every jump that had ever taken place, as Matthew Ellis proudly informed me, although I doubted it. Yes, they'd tracked down Matthew when he'd been taken, but they'd failed to capture Clive Ronan . . . or Adrian and Mikey . . .

Superimposed over the jumps, glowing red dots indicated major historical events.

'Points of reference,' he said. 'They're only there to enable us to navigate our way around the Map. They're just history. It's Time that's important.'

I nodded politely because what else can you do in the face of such folly?

Each dot was joined to the others around it because, as anyone from the History Department will tell you, nothing exists in isolation. Everything is connected to everything else. If you interrogated our St Mary's Map and pulled up our Troy jump – although I'd rather you didn't because it's still a bit contentious, even today – not only would you find details of the establishing Pathfinder jumps, but all the known circumstances leading to that particular event. Trade wars, border disputes, kidnappings, murder – all the rich pageant of human History. And the consequences, too. The subsequent fall of Troy. The increased importance of Mycenaean culture, the murder of Agamemnon and Clytemnestra – been there, seen it, got the T-shirt – and so on. Which reminded me that one day I really was going to have to go back and observe Odysseus's adventures as he hacked his way around the Aegean and Ionian Seas trying to get home, because who wouldn't want to check out a Cyclops?

Anyway, back to their Time Map. Which, admittedly, was magnificent. As was the structure in which it was housed. Three floors high – and beyond, possibly. I tilted my head back but still couldn't see the very top, lost in darkness. A bit of a metaphor for the future if you think about it.

The room was curved, to follow the shape of the Map. People hunched over consoles built on gantries at all levels around the walls, constantly updating and amending, because, as we all know, time waits for no man. And the Time Police don't hang about, either.

Captain Ellis stood back to let me take it all in. And it took some taking in, I can tell you. I stood watching the constant interchange, trying to trace the almost imperceptible but never-ending passage of time. To watch a point emerge over there, or a line extend itself by the tiniest fraction just here. The whole thing was quite mesmerising. I have no idea for how long I stood, face lifted, watching time – sorry, Time – unfold in front of me.

I was so absorbed in the Map, working my way from point to point around the ring, that I didn't notice the other people in the Map Room until Ellis nudged me. I looked away, blinked to refocus my eyes and saw the top of Matthew's head, down on the ground floor below us.

I assumed it was one of his tutorials because he was clutching his scratchpad and listening with the sort of rapt attention I, as his mother, could only dream of inspiring.

The Map Master herself was demonstrating something and, as I watched, one of the frighteningly young people at the consoles leaned aside for Matthew to have a better look at his screen.

'Want to go down and say hello?' said Ellis.

I nodded and we slipped away from the viewing area, down a discreet spiral staircase and back into the Map Room itself. The Map reared above us, humming more loudly at ground level. From down here looking up, it was colossal.

Unfortunately, being so close meant I could hear the ongoing dialogue between Matthew and the Map Master.

'My mum said you would be able to tell me because the Time Police know everything.'

I don't think she was quite sure how to take that.

'Yes,' he continued, his piping voice clearly audible to everyone in the Map Room, if not the entire bloody building. 'She says the

Time Police think they know everything, but actually they couldn't find their own arse with both hands.'

Oh great – months of taciturn silence and now he decides to get chatty.

'And a torch.'

To her enormous credit, because she didn't know I was standing behind her, she made a real effort. 'I think . . .'

'And a map.'

'Perhaps we could . . .'

'And a team of Sherpas.'

'Yes. Enough.'

There was a short silence. I could feel Ellis shaking with laughter beside me.

The Map Master took a deep breath and soldiered on. 'Obviously, the Time Map can only show what we put in and . . .'

'Yes,' he said. I could see the shifting colours flickering across his upturned face. One minute his face was brilliantly lit – the next moment in deep shadow. 'But you've put some of it in wrong.'

'Indeed,' she said, a trifle frostily, I thought. 'Well, I expect we can discuss that later. What I wanted to talk about today – and I know this is difficult for you to understand – but if you try to imagine space-time as being like a rubber sheet . . .'

He interrupted. '. . . Distorted by the presence of heavy objects.'

'Exactly. Well, much the same thing can happen to Time . . .'

He started to walk towards the Map. 'Where Time is distorted?'

'Yes, and . . .'

'What sort of heavy objects?'

'Well, usually it's human intervention or . . .'

'What happens when it stretches? Does it snap? What makes it snap? What happens when it snaps?'

She looked down at him. 'You do remind me of your mother.'

He looked up at her, puzzled. 'Whose mother should I remind you of?'

I swear I don't know if he does these things by accident or not.

'Well, anyway,' she said, soldiering on again. Perhaps she had children of her own. 'This is our Time Map and . . .'

'It's different from the one at St Mary's.'

'Yes. That's because we're not so much interested in history as Time itself. We really don't care if Odysseus look twenty years to get home or the Vikings landed in Nova Scotia in . . .'

'Mum says History's important.'

'Well, I daresay she does, but . . .'

'Because when History goes wrong everything goes wrong.'

'Yes, I'm sure, but . . .'

He frowned and pointed. 'Like that bit there.'

'Anyway, today we . . . What?'

He pointed. 'That bit's wrong.'

She smiled. 'I don't think so.'

He put down his scratchpad. 'Yes, it is. Can't you see? You have the funny criss-cross lines but they criss-cross in the wrong place. Look.' He pointed again. 'They should be . . . there . . . which makes that line wrong . . . which makes that bit wrong . . . which makes . . .' He pulled on the gauntlets she'd left lying on a console and moved his hands.

'Stop,' she said sharply. 'Don't touch the Map.' But it was too late. He stood, a little dark figure in front of the massive luminous Map and waved his arm. A section disengaged. He waved his arms to enlarge it and made a series of wide scything actions. Various lines either disappeared or rearranged themselves. The disengaged segment took on a different shape.

Around the Map Room, lights began to flash on various consoles. Someone got to his feet, calling a warning. The humming noise increased in volume and pitch. He didn't let that stop him, raising his voice to be heard. 'Look. Now you can see that this area here is wonky. The History has gone all funny. My mum says you must never discount History.'

The Map Master wasn't listening. She was standing helplessly, watching quite a large section of her precious Map disintegrate before her very eyes.

Everyone was standing helplessly watching quite a large section of the Map disintegrate before their very eyes.

The disturbance began to spread outwards – like an ink blob on blotting paper. More lines buckled or twisted and what had been a complicated and intricate dance became chaos. Lines broke away and waved aimlessly, lacking a destination before slowly fading away completely. A darkness began to spread. Somewhere, a harsh alarm sounded. And then another.

The Map Master wheeled around and strode from console to console, barking out a series of orders. People hunched over their screens, their hands a blur as they sought to keep up. To compensate. The heart of darkness spread further. More alarms sounded. The humming increased. People were running hither and thither, shouting instructions to each other.

'Freeze it. Freeze it,' she shouted and I understood. Unable to keep pace with the changes, she'd ordered the Map frozen until they could understand the extent of the problem and work out how to fix it.

In the meantime . . . I began to work my way towards Matthew, getting there just as the Map Master, glitter-eyed with rage, rounded on him.

To be fair to her, she was presiding over a catastrophe but I don't really think she would have hit him. However, I wasn't taking any chances. I slipped between her and him, saying quietly, 'Yes? Can I help you?'

She was beside herself with fury. 'Did you see what he did?' She wheeled on Matthew. 'You're banned. Forever. Get out of my sight. Now. Don't ever let me catch you in here again.'

I could feel him shaking. He doesn't deal well with anger and he'd been in here often enough to know what he'd done.

Other officers congregated around us, shouting and gesturing. We were surrounded by a ring of hostility. I felt him press close to me and it suddenly occurred to me that no matter how well he was treated, the black and violent days of his early life would never really leave him.

I dropped my hand lightly on his shoulder and said, 'I think I'll take him away now. You can thank him later.'

She stopped in mid-sentence. '*Thank* him?'

'Yes. I'll admit his method was a little crude, but you know as well as I do that his social skills need work. But what a good job he noticed your mis . . . that mistake. From where I was standing, it looked quite bad. Obviously, I'm no expert, but it looks to me as if that whole section is about to implode. And you hadn't noticed. Well done, Matthew, but we really should let them get on with their repairs. You can finish your lesson another day. Map Master. Captain Ellis. Good afternoon.'

I nodded at the pair of them and got him out of the room before anyone could pull themselves together enough to stop us. I don't know which of us was shaking most. This whole mother business isn't easy, you know.

I took him back to my room. If anyone wanted him – and they

very probably would because he'd just committed a major sin – they would have to come through me first.

Channelling Dr Stone, I made him a cup of cocoa and we sat down. He huddled at one end of the sofa. Until I saw it reappear, I hadn't realised how much he'd lost his old, suspicious, watchful, careful expression, from when there was no kindness in his world and no one was to be trusted. Not even for a second. Adults were people who exploded into violence at a second's notice. In that moment, I kicked everything into touch. My plan, the Time Police, Clive Ronan, everything. It could all disappear up its own rear end as far as I was concerned. If things got nasty for him here I'd take him back to St Mary's, and Leon and I would rethink everything.

. I looked down at him. At the hollows in his temples where the blue veins showed through his skin. At his thin, bony hands. My heart ached for him. He was so vulnerable. He probably always would be.

He finished his cocoa but it hadn't done him as much good as I had hoped. He hadn't said a word the whole time, just huddling into the corner of the sofa and trying to make himself as small as possible.

I had a brilliant idea, leaned over, and pulled one of his jigsaws from the drawer. Once, when everyone thought Leon was dead, we'd sat every night, not saying very much but doing something simple together. I wanted to give him something safe and familiar to do. To give him a chance to get himself back together again.

The picture showed the Tower of London and part of Tower Bridge, both of which were just downriver from us. Or possibly upriver. I was never really sure.

I refilled his mug, he shook the pieces out of the box and we sat quietly, as we used to do, looking for the corners and the sky.

Neither of us spoke, but slowly, the colour returned to his cheeks. He stopped turning pieces over at random and began to concentrate.

Until someone knocked at the door.

He jumped a mile and turned anxious eyes to me.

I winked and said, 'Seriously? How long have you known me?' and the door opened to reveal Captain Ellis.

'Hey, Max,' he said lightly. 'Matthew here?'

I nodded.

There was a pause. 'May I come in?'

'Well, that rather depends.'

He held up his hands. One of which contained a pizza box. 'I bear a gift.'

'Pizza? On a school night?'

'I think Commander Hay is rather worried there might be no more school days.'

'I haven't yet taken that off the table.'

'Perhaps I could come in and talk for a moment?'

'Again, that rather depends.'

'I haven't come to cause trouble, Max, so climb down off your high horse and give your kid a lesson in how to handle conflict gracefully.'

'Hey, I'm not an ear-boxing Map Master.'

'And neither is she. It wouldn't have come to that. But he broke the rules.'

'And highlighted a problem you had no idea existed.'

'That's what I've come to talk about. With pizza.'

He flourished the box again.

'If you shout at him, I will kill you where you stand.'

'Duly noted.'

I sighed. 'Come in.'

I stood well back, arms folded, radiating protective maternal hostility, but I have to say he handled Matthew beautifully. He sat beside him at the table, unhurriedly turning over various pieces of the puzzle, not saying anything. The minutes ticked by. He gave no sign of being hurried, or hostile, or critical. All I could hear was the occasional murmur of, 'I think that might be a bit of tree.' Or, 'There's a piece of the bridge that goes with that bit.' Gradually, the emotional temperature began to drop.

I opened the pizza, and because I'm a godless heathen, Matthew's the son of a godless heathen, and Ellis is in the Time Police, we didn't bother with plates; we rolled it up and scarfed it straight from the box. It tastes better that way. When we'd nearly finished, I made Ellis some brown water, and Matthew had a glass of milk.

It was Matthew himself who brought the subject up. 'Are they very cross?'

'They were,' said Ellis, using his thumbnail to scrape cheese off the inside of the box, 'but now they think you've done a Good Thing.' He grinned. 'It's safe to go back.'

Matthew shook his head. He still looked pale.

'I'll go with you if you like,' I said. 'And then you can show her where her Map was wrong and I can show her what will happen if she ever frightens you like that again.'

'Yes,' said Ellis, thoughtfully. 'I'm pretty sure everyone was hoping that we'd call all that water under the bridge and just move on. Better for everyone.'

He winked at Matthew. 'Adults don't like to be reminded they've made a mistake. On the other hand, young Matthew, you know the rules. You don't touch the Map.'

He nodded. 'But it was wrong.'

'True, but next time, just point, there's a good lad. Saves a lot of emotional wear and tear on your mentor.'

'So,' I said, joining them at the table and casually turning over a few more pieces of puzzle, keeping things low-key, 'what was the outcome?'

'The outcome is that we have a problem. No, nothing you did,' he added hastily, as Matthew got wild-eyed again. 'The problem is with the 16th century.'

'What?' I said jokingly. 'All of it?'

'Yes,' he said seriously. 'Most of it. And it's spreading. Very slowly, but it's serious.'

I shot Matthew a glance. He was to all intents and purposes engrossed in his puzzle but I could practically feel the breeze from his anxiously flapping ears. 'So, what's this problem then?'

Ellis drained his mug and set it down. 'Well, I need to put this in terms St Mary's can understand ... It's a bit like a bluebell wood, isn't it?'

I blinked. 'Is it?'

'Yes. Actually, that's rather good, because it's *exactly* like a bluebell wood.'

'What is?'

'Time.'

I resisted the temptation to roll my eyes. We'd been ticking along nicely and now here he was banging on about Time. You'd think Time would be the same as History, wouldn't you? I think I'd mentioned this once and the shocked silence had warned me never to make that comparison again.

I said, carefully, 'Time is a bluebell wood?'

'Well, no, obviously not, but yes. You understand I'm keeping it simple for you.'

Now I did roll my eyes. 'Go on then. Explain to me how Time is like a bluebell wood.'

'OK – stop me when I get too technical. Think of the 16th century as a bluebell wood. Very pretty. Very popular. Very interesting. There's a lot going on and everyone wants to visit.'

He paused, presumably to give me time to catch up.

'Anyway – as we know – a lot happened in the 16th century. And not just in England, but in Scotland, France, Europe, and America as well. Things were happening everywhere. New countries. New religions. Larger than life personalities all over the place. When time travel was available to the public, the 16th century was where everyone wanted to be. What everyone wanted to see.'

I nodded. He was right. The entire 16th century was an international dance of diplomacy, religion and death. The century when everything changed.

He'd stopped again. I wasn't sure if he'd finished or was waiting for me to catch up, so I nodded encouragingly. It wasn't so very different from dealing with Matthew. The younger Matthew, I mean.

'Right,' I said. '16th century. Bluebell wood. Got it. What's the problem?'

'Well, imagine you're strolling through the 16th century . . .'

'The bluebell wood . . .'

'Exactly. You're strolling through the bluebell wood, enjoying the birdsong, the sunshine, the lovely colours . . .'

I said impatiently, 'It's the 16th century – you mean the religious intolerance, the torture, the paranoia, the violence . . .'

'If you like, yes. But now, you look behind you and there's another group of people following on. And another, bigger group behind them. And another even bigger group behind them. And so on. And slowly, the nice little path that you've been following

70

gets wider and deeper and more and more churned up as more and more people use it. So, what happens?'

I opened my mouth but I wasn't quick enough. He was well into his stride now.

'People step off the path – that's what happens. They make a new one. One that avoids the muddy bits. And then *that* one becomes the path. But, of course, in only a very short time, that one becomes unusable as well, so people make yet another path. Or they just wander off into the wood on their own, trampling the bluebells, damaging the trees, frightening the birds and, before you know what's happened, the entire bluebell wood has been destroyed. Everything has disappeared into the mud and all that's left are a few dying flowers.'

'So,' I said slowly. 'You're saying the 16th century has been trampled into the mud.'

'Pretty much, yes.'

'Collapsed under the weight of sightseers.'

'Exactly. I don't know if you've heard the expression, "The act of observing changes that which is being observed."'

'Once or twice,' I said. 'It's a favourite of Dr Bairstow's.'

'And he's perfectly correct.'

'He always is,' I said, gloomily. 'So . . . how do you fix it?'

He added another piece of bridge, not looking at me. 'Well, I suppose you could say – we put down decking.'

I began to wonder if the Time Police weren't more similar to St Mary's than anyone had suspected. 'Decking?'

'Yes, decking.'

'The Decking of Time.'

'Exactly, Max. Well done. I never thought you'd grasp things so quickly. We make another path with decking and then the bluebells can begin to grow again.'

71

I thought about this for a while and then said meaningfully, 'But they're not the same bluebells.'

He sighed. 'Yes, for your own peace of mind, you might not want to dwell too long on that.'

'Why?'

'Look, you're not going to be happy, so let's just give the next bit a miss, shall we?'

'Let's not.'

'OK. We . . . rebuild . . . the bluebell wood.'

I shot to my feet. Bits of jigsaw went everywhere. 'You what? And don't wrap it up in pretty stories about bluebell woods and birdsong. *You change History?*'

'We rebuild Time.'

'You can't *do* that.'

'We've already done it.'

'What? When?'

'Well, not lots of times, but once or twice.'

'I don't believe you.'

'Well, that kind of makes my point, Max. You never noticed. No one ever notices. No one ever knows anything about it.'

'That doesn't make it right.'

'Look, I accept that we have different values and different goals. We leave you to do your job . . .'

'No, you bloody don't. You're always crashing through our door trying to shoot us.'

'. . . and you should leave us to do ours. Can I invite you to contemplate the meaning of the words *Time Police,* Max? *Time. Police.* It's what we do.'

I knew I was never going to win this argument but that didn't mean I wasn't going to go down fighting. I waved my arms around

– the sign of a perturbed historian. 'How the hell are you ever allowed to get away with this?'

'Strangely, that's a question we often ask ourselves about St Mary's.'

I waved that aside. 'So how exactly do you set about rebuilding this bluebell wood?'

'Well, we need to go off and have a bit of a chat about what to do next. No,' he said quickly, noticing Matthew's alarm. 'Not you. You can stay and finish your puzzle.'

'But Mum's going.'

'Yes, but I have to take your mother, because if I don't, she'll eat her way through the walls to find out what's happening.'

Well, that was rude.

I said to Matthew, 'Will you be all right on your own? Because I don't have to go.'

He nodded.

'Sure? I don't mind staying.'

He shook his head.

Damn. I wasn't too sure I wanted to listen to a group of Time Police criticising Matthew and plotting to overthrow History.

Actually, I should probably say now – most of what was to come was my idea.

Sorry about that.

The Map Room was a place of some disorder.

The Map stood silent, dark and unmoving. Frozen in a moment of chaos. The irregular dark patch reminded me of a black hole, devouring everything around it. Not a bad analogy, actually. We had a black hole in Time. In contrast to the frozen Map, crowds of technicians and specialists were racing around, peering at screens, shouting at each other, scanning printouts and generally behaving like headless chickens. There was an air of barely contained panic. I felt quite at home.

The Map Master saw me first.

'You!'

She began to elbow her way through the throng to get to me.

I gave her my best *Come on, then. Come and have a go if you think you're hard enough* look. The one used in academic circles everywhere when a cherished theory is called into question.

'Before you start,' I said, pre-empting trouble in the traditional manner, 'he didn't cause the damage. He discovered it. Without him, you'd be sitting here playing Battleships and wondering what to have for tea as the entire 16th century disintegrated around you while you weren't looking. So yes, I will pass on your grateful thanks while warning him, in future, for his own protection, to let all other anomalies go unreported.'

I turned to go. The trick to all conflict resolution is always to have the last word. Indeed, not to let the other party have any words at all if you can manage it. Alas for me, she was made of stern stuff.

'He touched the Map.'

'He did,' I agreed, 'and Captain Ellis has already instructed him never to do that again. I'll admit I find your enthusiasm for maintaining an inaccurate map to be a little confusing, but if that's the way you like things in the Time Police, then who am I to criticise. I'm only a guest here.'

She took another step towards me. 'That's easily remedied.'

I, too, stepped forwards and we stood, chest to chest, invading each other's space as hard as we could. 'As you wish. My compliments to Commander Hay and please advise her that Matthew and I will be gone within the hour.'

Yes, I was pushing it a bit, here. If they let me go, then my lovely plan for capturing Clive Ronan would crash to the ground in flames. I think if it had been just me then they'd have let me go quite happily, but my threat to take Matthew with me made them pause.

Captain Ellis saved the day. As the two of us stood glaring at each other, he cleared his throat. With the result that now the both of us were glaring at *him*.

'Max, Commander Hay would like to see us in her office. Immediately, please.'

It was a face-saving solution. We held our hard-woman stares until the very last moment – like two tomcats fighting over possession of a dodgy kipper – and then allowed ourselves to precede him through the door.

* * *

I hadn't been in her office since the bijou problemette with Grint's nose. She looked up as we entered and said, without any preamble, 'We have a problem.'

Ellis nodded. 'Yes, ma'am, we were there.'

'I don't mean the damage to the Map.' She looked at me. 'Which we will be discussing later. I'm alluding to the current instability in the 16th century.' She sighed and continued in a slightly softer tone. 'Max, I have bad news. The Map is not particularly reliable at the moment but our people have cobbled information together as best they can. It's all looking bad, but the worst part is that such information as is available leads us to believe that, while none of our own people are in harm's way, members of St Mary's are – so to speak – in the eye of the storm.'

I bristled immediately. 'They can't possibly be held responsible,' I said with more loyalty than accuracy.

'We're not holding them responsible. Our concern is that if anything happens to the fabric of time while they are still there – and we very much think it's happening now . . .' She paused. 'Max, there's no good way to put this. If this particular reality rolls up and disappears – as it could do at any moment – then it will take everyone and everything with it. Including everyone from St Mary's who happens to be in that particular time.'

I remembered those silver lines, waving aimlessly and then slowly fading away.

She continued. 'Based on what we can deduce, we think they're in 1588. Max, why would they be there? What would they be doing?'

I cast my mind back to the assignment list pinned to my office wall. 1588 – the Spanish Armada. 'Can you be more precise, ma'am? Do you have a location?'

'We have a date of 19th August. London.'

That was worrying. Very worrying. Elizabeth was addressing her troops at Tilbury on that day. They should be there. What would they be doing in London?

'Elizabeth is making her famous speech at Tilbury,' I said. 'You know the one. Heart and stomach of a king and a King of England, too. Are you sure they aren't there?'

She said crisply, 'Positive. But for whatever purpose they are in London, they need to be extracted. And as quickly as possible.'

The Map Master nodded. 'My team are already on it, ma'am, but the Map only reflects what is happening. The problem needs to be addressed at source.'

'Indeed,' she said. 'Captain Ellis will lead a rescue team and assess the situation. You, Dr Maxwell, will provide the expertise and liaise with the St Mary's team. They will probably listen to you more readily than they would to us.'

A good decision. Without someone to mediate, there would almost certainly be some sort of massive punch-up and someone would be shot.

It was as if she read my mind. 'You will all work together. Those are my instructions and they would be Dr Bairstow's if he was here. Are there any questions?'

We shook our heads.

'Then go and get them out.'

It was only when I was on the other side of her door that I remembered Matthew. Was he ready to be left alone? In the end, it wasn't something I had to worry about. When I got back to our suite, an old friend was waiting for me.

'Max!'

'Greta. Is that you?'

Greta Van Owen was ex-St Mary's. She'd left in a hurry after shooting and killing Isabella Barclay. Dr Bairstow would have sheltered her, I was certain, but she'd elected to leave and the Time Police had yielded to a compassionate impulse and taken her in.

I was delighted to see her again. 'Good to see you. How are you?'

'Absolutely fine, thank you.' She laughed. 'God, it feels good to say that again.'

'Why haven't I seen you here before?'

'Sick Leave, plus Annual Leave, plus a spell of light duties in Admin. I was only signed back on again this morning and the first thing I get is this young man.'

'Bad luck,' I said.

She turned to Matthew. 'How's your dad?'

Van Owen had been with Leon and Guthrie when Ronan blew them back more than eight hundred years and two thousand miles.

He nodded.

I said, 'Speak,' and he said, 'OK, I think.'

'You can tell me all about it while your mum's away. Don't worry, Max. I'll keep an eye on him for you.'

'Thanks. You might want to keep him away from the Map Room for a bit.'

'Yeah, I heard about that. Not a problem.'

As I shot out of the door I heard her say, 'So how's everyone back at St Mary's then?' as the door closed behind me.

The Time Police don't normally bother with costumes. They wrap themselves in sinister black cloaks which they consider constitute a sufficient disguise. One day I'm really going to have to tell them.

Today, however, whether in deference to me or circumstances in general, they wore variations of brown leather doublets, knee trousers and boots, and someone had set aside a linen chemise and a mud-coloured kirtle for me that looked vaguely of the right period. I kept my boots on and no one objected. I wondered how long it would be before I succumbed to bad Time Police habits. While they'd provided the obligatory sinister black cloak for me, there was nothing for my head.

I blame the influence of TV and historical holos. These days no one is interested in historical accuracy when it comes to costumes. For one thing, in any of Calvin Cutter's abominations, no one's clothes stay on long enough for anyone to notice. And – and this really upsets Mrs Enderby – his characters never have anything on their heads. I wouldn't be in the slightest bit surprised to hear the Time Police gleaned their historical knowledge from Calvin Cutter's heirs and successors.

I sighed loudly and one of them – Nash, I think – demanded to know why it was important.

'Because I don't want to be solicited as a prostitute, accused of witchcraft, or mistaken for a young girl.'

Complete silence implied one of these was very unlikely.

I stood my ground, radiating deep historian disapproval.

Eventually, one of them rolled his eyes and disappeared, returning moments later with what looked like a tea towel. Everyone watched as I draped it over my head, tied two corners at the back of my neck and then tucked the rest under. A couple of hairpins held it in place. When I checked in the mirror I had TPHQ over one eyebrow but I could live with that.

Everyone was armed except me. Not even a stun gun. I protested, but Captain Ellis informed me I'd never be out of his sight the whole time so why would I need a weapon? In the interests of inter-unit cooperation, I kept my mouth shut.

We stood silently in the lift. No one spoke. I never thought I'd say this, but I rather missed Sykes and North bickering in the background.

We were decanted into the basement. The lights were full on today, and now I got to see how big the space really was.

In Hawking, the pods stand against the walls in two neat rows, with our big pod, the recently rechristened Tea Bag 2, at the back. Formerly known as TB2, it had been rebuilt after Ronan's effort to blow us all up and someone, looking around at the mountain of tea-making equipment and mugs left inside it by the overworked and exhausted Technical Section as they struggled to get it built, fitted out, aligned and working in record time, had christened it Tea Bag 2.

The Time Police had four times as many pods, which stood in clusters, ordered by use. Over there, near to the doors leading to the Medical Centre, were their four hospital pods, big and white and with every international medical symbol painted on the walls. Alongside those were two enormous pods – almost portable aircraft hangars – and I couldn't for the life of me think why they would need anything that huge.

'Troop movements,' said Ellis curtly, catching me looking. 'For when we need a show of force. And for any equipment and materiel we might need, of course.'

'Ah,' I said, thinking of Captain Farenden's helicopter over Florence.

'And over there,' he said, pointing, 'our detention pods.'

'Ah,' I said. I'd seen those before.

'And over there the clean-up pods.'

The clean-up pods were just small boxes. No attempt had been made to camouflage them. I suppose if you've reached the stage where the clean-up crews are on site, then everything's gone properly tits-up and any disguise is a waste of time. Clean-up crews are bad news. They do what they say on the tin. I had a nasty feeling about this.

I turned to Ellis. 'Is that a clean-up crew coming with us?'

'Only because we don't know what we're going to find, do we? So yes, a squad will accompany us in case we need them.' This was Time Police speak for doing whatever necessary to neutralise whatever threat was presenting itself at the time.

A clean-up crew consists of four members. The Time Police tend to travel in fours with a team leader. They stood waiting for us. Armoured and visored. They were wearing those helmets with the antennae. They'd made no attempt at all at 16th-century dress. Of course, the 16th century might not be around long enough to protest.

Our pod was just an ordinary, bog-standard Time Police pod which was a bit of a relief. Ellis's crew consisted of him, me and four others. Grint, the one whose nose had collided with my knee, Nash, Oliver and Bevan. And the clean-up crew, of course.

We all filed on board and the door closed behind us. Things were a little snug and some of them were closer than I was completely happy with.

I was still fiddling with my headscarf when I heard Ellis say, 'Commence jump procedures.'

'Jump procedures commenced.'

And off we went. Just like that.

St Mary's still does it better.

London 1588 was a disaster zone. Some dreadful cataclysm had occurred. Or was occurring. Or was about to occur. We had to verify the coordinates twice because none of us could quite believe what we were seeing.

Time Police pods have four screens, one on each wall, so there was no crowding around the console, which, and I speak from experience, can be irritating. Each of the four screens showed a different view and every single one of those views was very, very bad. We were looking at the end of the world. I moved from screen to screen, staring open-mouthed, and I wasn't the only one.

Supposedly, we were in Southwark, on the south bank, within sight of London Bridge. I'd been here so many times in the past that the view was quite familiar. Over there should be The Globe. Except it wasn't. Over there should be London Bridge. Except it wasn't the London Bridge I knew. Nothing was as I'd known it.

First things first. Careful to keep any hint of criticism from my voice, I said, 'Why are we here?'

'Because this is where your team is,' said Ellis, absently, watching the screens.

I opened my mouth to say, 'Are you sure?' and then closed it again. Of course they were sure. They were the Time Police. The explanation of why St Mary's wasn't at Tilbury was something I looked forward to hearing. Although, when I thought about it, given what was going on outside, where else would they be?

Ellis turned to me. 'Max, can you tell us what's happening here?'

'I don't know,' I said, still unable to take my eyes from the screens. 'I honestly have no idea. Something's gone horribly wrong somewhere.'

Something had indeed gone horribly, horribly wrong. London appeared to be in the midst of some sort of massive catastrophe. What that catastrophe had been or was about to be, I had no idea, but every street, every lane, every alleyway was clogged with people, all of them screaming and fighting with each other. Some were even trying to scramble over roofs, so desperate were they to escape . . . something.

Grint had turned the volume down and we were watching screaming hysteria happen in silence. Mouths opened and closed, red in dirty faces. People were knocked down and then others fell over them, slowly crushing the life out of those at the bottom. I caught glimpses of desperate faces and even more desperate arms held out for help. I saw a man's face, blue and congested, and then another pile of people was added to the heap and he was gone. Others were silently crushed under trundling wagon wheels.

We tend to associate silence with calm or stillness or peace, but this was the very opposite. This was pandemonium, turmoil, madness, even. Someone, Grint, I think, reached out to adjust the sound.

'Don't,' said Ellis quickly. 'It won't help.'

And all the time, smoke from fires on both sides of the river drifted across the streets. Orange flames danced in the distance.

This was no ordered evacuation with people being directed to the quickest way out of the city. No one was in charge. It would seem that law and order had completely broken down. Shops and

83

stalls had been broken into and their contents strewn everywhere. It was, I think, a measure of people's desperation to get out that no one stopped to pick anything up. Bolts of once-beautiful cloth lay trampled in the filth. Crates and barrels lay shattered, their contents spilled across the road, and no one even noticed.

From what we could see, the people on the north bank were struggling to get across the bridge to our side of the river and the people on our side were trying to fight their way north. No one was directing the traffic or attempting to clear a way. Where were the soldiers? What was happening? Yes, all right, the Armada was on its way but there was no record of this level of terror. These people were blind with fear. The carnage was horrible.

Worst of all, the River Thames – London's main thoroughfare – was jam-packed with boats and small craft. Barges, wherries, small rowing boats, the larger and more ornate ferries belonging to the well-off – all were crammed together in a frantic, heaving tangle from bank to bank and as far upriver as the eye could see. There was no order and certainly nothing was moving. Just hundreds of boats all jostling against each other as they tried to escape. Watermen were waving their arms and roaring silent curses at each other as they tried to force their way through. Oars that weren't irrevocably entangled were wielded with vicious precision but to no avail. Boatmen swore and their passengers screamed. Even as I watched, a young noble in an obviously privately owned wherry wobbled to his feet and attempted to make his way to the bank, stepping from boat to boat. I think he successfully negotiated two boats, leaving them precariously rocking in his wake, before an infuriated boatman fetched him a blow that knocked him clean into the water. Boats closed in over his head and I never saw him again. No one made the slightest attempt to save him.

To go downriver was impossible because London Bridge had been blockaded. I could see massive chains stretched between the starlings, and each narrow area of water between the arches was filled with small boats. And each of those small boats was packed high with barrels.

'Gunpowder,' said Ellis in disbelief. 'They're going to blow the bridge. Why would they do that? What could be so bad they're going to destroy the only bridge in London?' He turned to me. 'Max, help us out here?'

I tried to stay calm because panic wouldn't help. There was enough of that going on outside. 'I'm sorry – I don't know. Yes, there was alarm over the Armada . . .'

'Wasn't Drake so cool about it he finished his game of bowls first?'

'Well, that's the story, but it's possible the tides weren't right for the fleet to sail at that moment. They were all dependent on the tides and weather in those days, so, unable to sail, he finished his game and scored a point for style. But this . . .' I gestured at the chaos. 'This is almost a rout. It's as if the enemy is already at the gates. According to records, Elizabeth should be at Tilbury, addressing the troops. And Clerk, Bashford and North should be there, and probably Evans, too, and yet you say they're here?'

'Grint, can we get a fix on any of the St Mary's crew?'

He shot his eyes to me in an *is this something we want her to know?* look and then, at a nod from Ellis, consulted some sort of proximity detector.

'Yes and no. Their readings are flickering. They're here. Which is why we're here. We've homed in on their tags, but where they are in all this . . . Let's face it, they could be twenty feet away and we'd never know.' He shook his head.

'They'll have a handle on what's going on here,' I said, with more confidence than I actually felt. 'We should go and find them and get them out.'

'In this?' The pilot gestured at his screen again.

'You're right,' I said, rather pissed off with this *let's all stay safely in the pod* attitude. I could have done with a bit of that when they were chasing me and Leon up and down the timeline. We were falling over the buggers everywhere we went.

I picked up my cloak. I don't know why. It was August out there. 'You're right. I'll go and find them and you all stay in here where it's safe.'

'No one is to hit her,' said Ellis, without looking up from the console. 'That's my job.'

Obviously, they all came with me. Except for Grint who remained with the pod. Even the clean-up crew came along. And very glad I was to have them because it was murder out there.

The pod door opened to a cacophony of noise. You couldn't hear yourself think, let alone speak. The streets were packed solid with people all trying to go in different directions and all screaming at the tops of their voices. An unending clamour of bells was sounding as every church in the city raised the alarm, while over them all, almost opposite us on the other bank, the single Great Bell of Bowe Church rang the death knell of England itself.

I couldn't understand what was going on. It was as if someone had shoved a stick in an ants' nest. There was no order. No authority. People weren't fleeing in one direction away from a peril behind them. They were just milling around all over the place, leaderless and terrified. The whole city appeared to be one massive logjam of panicked people going nowhere. The injured and dying were left to lie where they fell. A distressing number of them were children or old people. I suspected either they hadn't been able to keep up or they'd just been abandoned to their fate. People ran straight over the top of them. I don't think they even noticed they were doing it.

Watching the scenes from inside the pod had been bad enough but it was a hundred times worse to be part of it. The noise was horrendous. Thousands of people were all screaming at everyone else to get out of their way. The few horses we could see were foam-flecked and terrified, lashing out at anyone who came close. Fights were breaking out everywhere. The smell of burning was overwhelming. Smoke caught at the back of my throat and made my eyes stream.

I'd never seen anything like it. Not even at Pompeii. People were killing each other in their desperation to get away. But from what were they trying to escape? From which direction was the danger coming and which was the way to safety? And where, in all this, was St Mary's?

We flattened ourselves against the side of the pod while we got our bearings. London Bridge was to our right. A church was at our backs. On the opposite bank stood the Fishmongers' Hall, surrounded by wooden quays and warehouses. Bowe Church rose majestically from the smoke. Further to our left across the river stood Old St Paul's.

As far as I could see in each direction, the river was bordered by wooden and stone-gabled buildings and warehouses. Each had a set of steps leading down to the river and were chaotic with people at the top trying to get down to the shoreline while those at the bottom attempted to force their way up.

Nash consulted his hand-held reader and shouted, 'They're . . . over there. I think. West. About a hundred yards. I think.'

I tried to stay calm. Not easy in all this turmoil when we had to scream at each other to make ourselves heard. 'Can't you tell?'

'Not in all this, no.'

We battled our way through the crowds. It wasn't a case of struggling against the flow. There was no flow. We were buffeted on all sides, pushed this way and that. An angry man shouted in my face, his spittle flying in all directions. Bevan took hold of my left arm and someone else my right, otherwise I'd have been swept away. Sometimes we allowed ourselves to be carried along because it was easier than fighting the crowd, but mostly, with the clean-up crew at the front, we fought our way westwards.

Nash was counting down. He put his head close to Ellis and shouted, 'Only twenty yards to go, sir, but we've drifted too far to the left. Next opportunity we get, we should head back towards the river.'

Ellis nodded and we took a moment to catch our breath.

We shouldn't have stopped. A hysterical woman grabbed my arm. The strength of her nearly pulled me over. She screamed something – I think she was looking for her child. I felt a huge stab of sympathy. I tried to disentangle myself as gently as I could. I didn't want one of the clean-up crew pulling her off and throwing her into the crowd.

We did our best, battling our way along. The ground underfoot was bumpy and uneven. Once, I think something tried to grab my ankle. I tried hard not to think about what I could be standing on. And tried even harder not to trip over any of it.

I could hear the beeping from the tag reader, increasing in frequency and rising in tone. They couldn't be that far off, although how would we find them in all this . . . They could be ten feet away and we'd never know in this solid wall of people.

Ellis made a sign and we halted, hot and panting, in the shadow of a low-hanging roof. 'Nash, Oliver, get yourselves up there and tell me what you see.'

They clambered up and stood rather precariously on the loose thatch.

'Can you see anything?'

Oliver shook his head. 'Wall-to-wall people. This is useless.' He put a hand on his belt. 'Sir?'

He looked down at Ellis who nodded reluctantly. 'Very well, but not here. Let's get down to the river. Best place. Visible from both banks and the river itself.'

We struggled to the bank. It was August and the stench from the river easily overcame the smell of smoke and sweaty, frightened people. The tide was coming in, washing over the wet mud glistening in the hot afternoon sunshine. The shoreline was littered with discarded possessions, broken boats, dead animals, shattered planks of wood, tangled nets and the occasional body.

'Ready, sir.'

'Do it.'

They fired a fizzer. They fired a bloody fizzer. I could see their thinking – the people here obviously aren't terrified enough so let's give them a hanging red ball in the sky, shall we? It stabbed silently upwards into the sky, leaving a brilliant white trail some twenty feet high. I thought it looked like the finger of God and I wasn't the only one. The panic around us shifted up a gear.

I rounded on Ellis, furious. 'What the hell are you doing? You fired a fizzer? Here? Now?'

'It's a flare,' he said calmly. 'And fairly discreet. As opposed to the St Mary's version which sends a brilliant red ball screaming into the sky, where it hangs around for ages frightening the living daylights out of contemporaries. Of course, we can always just find somewhere to sit down and wait for your lot to turn up of their own accord. Except we don't have the time because we need to get them out of here as soon as possible. Time is not stable here, Max, so shut up and let us get on with our job.'

Well, that told me. I shut up and let them get on with their job.

The first thing that happened was that the crowd, catching sight of this dire portent in the sky, collectively screamed and stampeded. We were swept along, desperately trying to hang on to each other and keep our feet. We were pushed around a corner and the second thing that happened was that I collided with something bony and hard which turned out to be Bashford. Of course, it would be him, wouldn't it?

'Mr Bashford?'

If I was surprised, you should have seen him. He stared as if he couldn't believe his eyes. '*Max?* What the hell?'

I seized his arm in case he was swept away. 'Where are the others? We've been looking for you.'

'Here. Somewhere.' He raised his voice in a bellow and waved a stick on which he'd tied a piece of material. He does sometimes have moments of near intelligence. There was an answering shout and the next moment Evans appeared, with North in the crook of one arm. She, too, was carrying a stick. There was blood on it. I guessed she'd been laying about her again. Damn – I'd missed it. Clerk panted along behind, bringing up the rear.

'Max? How did you know?'

I gestured around. 'What the bloody hell's going on here? There's all sorts of alarm bells going off everywhere at TPHQ. Have you managed to break the 16th century?'

He wiped sweat off his grimy face. 'It's the Spanish.'

90

'The Armada? Here already?'

'The word is out. They're sailing up the Thames . . .'

'Why?'

Someone cannoned into him and nearly knocked him sideways. I don't think he even noticed. I'd never seen him so rattled. 'It's all gone to shit, Max.' He was shouting at me. Sweat had run clean channels down his dirty face. One of the Time Police offered him a drink and he took it thankfully. 'We've lost, Max. Drake and Effingham have been defeated. The English fleet is scattered. Or sunk. Gone, anyway. But that's not all of it. The Scots have poured across the border. Berwick is burned to the ground. Completely destroyed. Durham and York have been occupied. The word is they're marching south on London.'

I was bewildered. 'The Scots? What have the Scots got to do with this?'

'Not just the Scots. It's the Auld Alliance again, Max. The French have landed at Dover and they're marching towards the capital. London will be caught between the two and the Spanish are sailing up the river.'

Now I could understand the sheer panic around me, but not how this had happened. None of this was supposed to happen. I said, more to the uncaring universe than anyone in particular, 'How could this happen? What is going on here?'

Bashford took two or three deep breaths and tried to speak calmly. 'Three armies are converging on London. They're killing and burning everything in their path. The whole country is ablaze. We're in the middle of a massacre. People are desperate to get out but there's no way for them to go. A secondary Spanish force is making its way up the Severn Estuary for the sole purpose of torching the Forest of Dean.'

'What?' said someone. 'Why?'

'The forest provides the timber for English ships. One of King Philip's stated aims was its complete destruction. The end of the Navy. And that's only the beginning, Max. They're going to carve up the country between them. This is the end of England as we've known it.'

'So, the queen's not at Tilbury?'

'The queen's not anywhere, Max. She's long gone. Fled to Holland two or three days ago.'

I shook my head. 'No. I don't believe that. Elizabeth would never flee.'

He sighed and looked at me. I felt the fingertips of fear run down my spine.

Perhaps because he was speaking quietly, his voice cut through the turmoil around us. 'That's what I'm trying to tell you, Max. Elizabeth isn't the queen.'

I couldn't take it in for a moment, repeating stupidly, 'Elizabeth isn't the queen?'

He shook his head.

I had to have this spelled out for me, saying stupidly, 'So Mary Tudor is still queen? Elizabeth never ascended the throne?'

He shook his head again.

I raised my arms in frustration and fear. 'So, who? For God's sake, what is happening here?'

'I'm trying to tell you, Max. Elizabeth was never queen. Neither was Mary.'

I gaped like an idiot. Captain Ellis, the Time Police, I forgot them all. 'Well, who's queen then? There's no one left.'

'Yes, there is. There's one left. The one and only Queen of England.' He took a breath. 'Jane Grey.'

I clutched his arm. 'What?'

'I know how it sounds and I didn't believe it myself, but it's true, Max. Somehow – don't ask me how – the Nine-Day Queen has ruled England for thirty-five years.'

I know we historians are carefully trained – or so we tell people. And so are the Time Police – apparently. But this caught us all unprepared. We all stood and stared at him like a bunch of trainees confronted with an unexpected question during Friday afternoon exams. None of this should be happening. History was way off course and careering in the wrong direction. I saw again the Time Map's broken silver lines, blindly feeling their way towards the wrong destinations.

I took a deep breath to enquire further, but Ellis cut in.

'We can't stay here. It's not safe. Where's your pod?'

Clerk gestured. 'Behind St Mary Overie. About two hundred yards over there.'

We all surveyed the mêlée around us.

'Right,' said Ellis. 'Our pod is closer. Everyone back to my place.'

'Good idea,' said Bashford, wiping sweat off his face. 'I'm gagging for a cup of tea.'

This didn't seem the moment to tell them.

They stuck me and North in the middle. I could have told them they'd do better to put her at the front and just follow meekly on behind, but it was their assignment so we did things their way. The clean-up crew took up their positions at the front – like black-cloaked icebreakers, the rest of us clustered behind them – and we fought our way back to Ellis's pod, down alleyways, along blocked streets, occasionally even dropping down to river level to avoid the worst bits.

We weren't that far away – I thought I could catch a glimpse of the pod between groups of fleeing people – and I was looking forward to getting out of this crush and being able to take a moment to think things over properly – when London Bridge exploded. I'd completely forgotten about it and, judging by the expressions on their faces, so had Ellis and his crew.

We were trying to get off the foreshore, fighting our way up a flight of slippery wooden steps, and therefore had a first-class view I could well have done without. I don't know whether they'd lit long fuses – probably – or floated a fireship – unlikely given the river congestion – but I saw a white flash that hurt my eyes, followed by a series of short, sharp cracks that ran from one starling to another and hurt my ears, followed by a massive boom that made the ground shake beneath my feet and, finally, a long, loud rumble that seemed to go on forever. The shockwave flung me backwards off the steps and into the mud and North landed on top of me. Everyone else flung themselves to the ground anyway.

Almost in slow motion, the bridge blew apart. A lot of it went up. Some of the structures on it were seven storeys high and solidly built and they disintegrated like children's building bricks. There was no warning. They hadn't bothered to clear the bridge, although in all fairness, it was hard to see how they could have. I saw scores of people flung, cartwheeling, high into the air, black silhouettes against the bright blue sky.

Great lumps of masonry cracked and tumbled on to the boats

beneath. There was no escape for anyone on the river. Giant waves capsized those boats not crushed beneath the bridge itself.

And then, because what goes up must come down, massive pieces of stone plummeted downwards, wiping out the few boats that had somehow managed to stay afloat. Great plumes of dust swirled through the air, but through them I could see the river and both banks were a scene of devastation.

Stone and rubble dropped around us. I curled into a ball and trusted to the god of historians.

The rumble went on and on and what remained of the bridge cracked apart, broke up and toppled slowly into the water. Whether they'd intended it or not, the river now was not only uncrossable but completely impassable, too. It would be years, if ever, before anyone could get a boat upriver again. Dirty water swirled around me. Someone caught my wrist, otherwise I'd have been washed away. Already, the water was beginning to rise behind the newly formed dam. As if London didn't have enough to contend with, there was about to be massive flooding, too.

Those buildings on both banks not already destroyed by fire had been flattened by the blast. The church was on fire. Shattered buildings and burning thatch had been blown everywhere. People lay like broken dolls, either stunned or dead. I kicked a burning plank off my legs and tried to sit up. I didn't seem to have incurred any great injuries but it looked as if a small cottage had fallen on Bashford, and Clerk's legs were protruding from beneath a pile of smoking thatch. I could only hope the rest of him was still attached.

I thought at first that the screaming had stopped. That this catastrophe was just one too many and people had no more capacity for terror. Then I realised the blast had made me deaf. I waggled my jaw about to try and clear my ears.

The smell was stomach-churning. Sulphur is not a good smell, but the smell of roast meat is much, much worse. Especially when you realise who the meat had been. I climbed on to my knees and heaved, bringing up the pizza that seemed rather a long time ago now. Fortunately for me, most of it missed Miss North. She would never have forgiven me.

The state of the citizens was pitiful. Where there had been shouting, screaming chaos, there was now just stunned silence. I hadn't gone deaf after all. People hunched, white-faced, staring at the place where their bridge had been, struggling to take it all in. One by one, slowly, they tried to get to their feet. I could hear the occasional whimper.

Someone heaved me to my feet. The river was beginning to surge around us. I could hear the gurgle of rising water. We needed to get out of here. Ellis was checking over his team. Clerk, emerged from the thatch, was checking over his. I was checked by both of them, as befitted my anomalous position. A foot in both camps, so to speak.

We gathered around Ellis. 'Back to our pod,' he ordered. 'Clerk – Maxwell, keep an eye on your people.'

The rest of our journey back to the pod was by no means so arduous. Most people were sitting or lying motionless, huddled together in shock. One or two wandered, dazed and lost – the rest had sought shelter. Doors were being bolted, windows made fast. I think Londoners were realising there was no escape now and their safest bet was to lock themselves away and hope for the best.

The pod was almost buried and we had to kick aside a great deal of charred debris before we could get in. Fortunately, pods are very robust.

We crowded inside and sat, squashed together, on the floor.

Time Police pods are not over-endowed with facilities, although there was a kettle in this one. Clerk peered dubiously at his paper cup of brown water, politely said thank you, and then carefully set it on the floor beside him. 'Nice headdress, Max. I see you're wearing the Time Police brand.'

There was a pause. Clerk played with his cup of alleged coffee, turning it round and round on the floor beside him.

'Well, go on,' I said. 'Report.'

He nodded to North. 'If you would, please, Miss North.'

Good choice. A complete lack of empathy with the human race and an inbred conviction of superiority dating back to the Conquest means that North briefs better than anyone.

She cleared her throat of London dust and began. 'We landed in Tilbury. The whole place was on fire. The few ships that were still there were burning or deliberately scuppered. Like you, we couldn't believe what we were seeing. We couldn't get anyone to talk to us or tell us what was happening and when we tried to question some men outside a tavern, some soldiers turned up and things got rather ugly. There were accusations of enemy agents and spies, so we decided we'd be in a better position to find out what was going on in London itself.'

'And no one thought to return to St Mary's to report these anomalies and get permission to investigate further?' asked Ellis.

St Mary's stared at him in complete incomprehension.

'Who calculated the new coordinates?' I interrupted.

'I did,' said North, 'with Mr Clerk. Mr Bashford checked them.'

'Well done.'

She inclined her head, accepting the praise with practised ease and continued. 'We arrived this morning and found the situation to be not quite as bad as it is now. Clerk and Bashford went to

The Tabard to see what information they could gather. Mr Evans and I walked the streets, talking to anyone we could persuade to stop and give us the time. There were all sorts of rumours flying around. The fleet had been sunk. The queen had fled. The French had landed. The Scots were burning the north. And so on.'

She paused. 'Like you, I assumed that when they said queen, they meant Elizabeth. No one had mentioned any names – it was always *the queen had done this* or *the queen hadn't done that* – and we were quite a long way into the conversation before someone actually said Jane. We were talking to some old drunk at the time and as soon as he said Jane, I requested Mr Evans escort our friend to a more discreet location where we could question him more thoroughly.'

Ellis was regarding her with admiration. I made a note to tell him that if he made me a decent offer he could have her.

'No point in messing about,' said Evans modestly. 'I picked him up by the scruff of his grubby neck, took him round the back of a church and threatened to thump seven shades of shit out of him if he didn't tell us what we wanted to know.'

'And did he?'

'Mr Evans was very persuasive,' said North calmly. 'And there was a rain butt nearby. I think it was probably the first time most of him had seen water for years.'

'It was a long business,' said Evans. 'We had to keep giving him time to recover. And he threw up twice, but we got there in the end.'

'For God's sake,' I said. 'Don't tell me you've just invented waterboarding?'

'It was Miss North's idea,' he said quickly.

It probably was, too.

'Anyway, to cut a long story short, as far as we could ascertain,

Mary and Elizabeth didn't live long enough to ascend the throne. When Edward died, Jane became queen. And is still on the throne. Or would be if she hadn't fled to Holland.'

'Hmm,' I said. 'I don't think either Elizabeth or Mary would have run away.'

'I am inclined to agree.'

'Wait,' said Ellis. 'You're telling me that Edward died and they couldn't dredge up a male heir from anywhere? What about Scotland? Didn't they have a couple of spares knocking around up there?'

'That was the whole problem,' said North, turning to him. 'There were seven legitimate heirs to the throne after Edward's death and every single one of them was female.'

'You're kidding.'

I shook my head. 'Don't ever let anyone tell you the Tudors weren't all about women. Even setting aside all Henry's queens and their impact on History, his older sister, Margaret, had a grand-daughter – Mary Stuart, Queen of Scots – and no one wanted her. His youngest sister, Mary, had two daughters, one of whom was Frances Brandon, who herself had three daughters, Jane, Catherine and Mary Grey. Henry himself had only two surviving children – Mary and Elizabeth. Mary was a staunch Catholic and not even to be considered and I suspect Elizabeth was showing signs of being a proper little madam even then.'

North nodded. 'The Lord Protector, Northumberland, deter-mined to manipulate the succession to his advantage, allied with the Brandons and they selected the supposedly docile, impeccably Protestant and, above all, easily controlled Jane Grey. Which, it would seem, has turned out to be biggest mistake of their lives, although to be fair, she was very much an unknown quantity at the time. Anyway, Edward was dying. Northumberland saw his opportunity and married Jane to his son Guildford.'

A number of Time Police shifted impatiently. It had been a long time since they'd been allowed to shoot anyone and were probably going through withdrawal symptoms. I asked Ellis if we should throw them a banana, but only because I knew their weapons were safely out of reach by the door.

'Anyway,' said Clerk, picking up his drink, sipping it and putting it down rather quickly, 'there she is – little Jane Grey, outwardly living the life of a high-born Protestant maiden with royal connections. Well educated, very intelligent, rigorous in her duty to her family and to God, and, although no one knew it at the time, a bit of a monster.'

North frowned at him and continued. 'We know she was initially reluctant to marry Guildford but, with hindsight, that might have been because secretly she had her own ideas. As did her father-in-law, Northumberland, who concealed Edward's rapidly failing health while he laid his plans and got his people into position.'

Clerk took up the tale. 'The first thing he does is send for Mary and Elizabeth. They must be brought under his control and neutralised. Both of them set off – that we do know, but this is where it all goes to shit, Max. At some point, Mary is poisoned *en route*. Probably by another of Northumberland's sons – Robert Dudley.'

'The one who goes on to become Elizabeth's boyfriend?'

'That's the one. Except that now he doesn't because Elizabeth never reached London either. Mary's death left her dangerously exposed as the last remaining direct descendent of Henry. She was ambushed outside the city and never seen again. It's thought she was executed there and then – at the roadside – but no one really knows. Or if they do they're not saying.'

She paused and glugged some water. 'So that's both Henry's legitimate heirs dead. Edward died on 6th July, although the news was withheld until Jane was proclaimed queen on the tenth and Northumberland rubs his hands together in triumph.'

I nodded, fascinated by this alternative timeline. 'And then?'

'And then it all goes wrong for him. Having been crowned queen, Jane breaks free of his influence. She refuses to make her husband king. Worse than that – he dies under mysterious circumstances.'

I was trying to keep up. 'Guildford? Guildford dies? How? Don't tell me she killed her own husband?'

I don't know why I was surprised. After all, Mary Stuart murdered her husband and Fat Harry changed his wives more frequently than his underwear.

Clerk emphasised the point. 'Well, she was a Tudor, after all. Religiously fervent. Pragmatic. Determined. And utterly ruthless. As she showed with Guildford's death. Northumberland, by now probably in fear for his own life and feeling his power draining away by the minute, is summoned to her presence and arrested.'

I could picture him sweating in his fine robes in the hot summer sunshine, as he suddenly realised he'd created the instrument of his own death. A monster who had turned on him.

'And now the religious factor kicks in. England wasn't yet wholly Protestant but it was on the brink. At that point the country could have gone either way and with Jane on the throne it went Protestant. Big time. They talk of rivers of blood, Max, and Jane has waded through oceans of it. As of this moment, she has burned, beheaded, hanged, tortured and mutilated more people than all her Tudor predecessors combined, earning herself the soubriquet "Bloody Jane". It's a real reign of terror. There

102

are widespread arrests and people mysteriously disappear all the time. And don't confuse her with Fat Harry, roaring his way down the corridors of power, loud, fat and imposing. Jane is small, slight, softly spoken and utterly deadly. Everyone is terrified of her. She's escaped so many attempted assassinations that the Pope has publicly proclaimed her to be in league with the Devil and has offered a free pass to heaven for anyone who can get rid of her.'

'What's happened to her parents?' I asked, curious.

'Father under house arrest. Mother just . . . disappeared.'

I nodded. 'I've often wondered why Frances Brandon wasn't proclaimed queen. As Jane's mother, her claim was even greater than Jane's.'

North shrugged. 'I suspect one reason was that Frances was married and therefore legally submissive to her husband. North-umberland had better control over Jane. Or thought he did. My suspicion is . . .'

'What?' said Ellis.

'Jane had her killed.'

I nodded. Half an hour ago I'd have scoffed at the idea. Now . . . now I was more than prepared to believe six impossible things before breakfast.

'And what does the rest of Europe have to say to all this?'

'Well, the Emperor Charles V was furious over the murder of Mary. She was his cousin, of course. He invaded twice. 1554 and 1555. The Pope sanctioned Jane's murder by making it widely known that political assassination of the enemies of Christ would incur God's pleasure. And Philip of Spain, of course, had two problems. Not only was he very keen to prevent any sort of alliance between the Protestant Netherlands and England, but there was always his long-standing fear of France. Spain was always wary of any agreement between France and England which would tip the balance of power in Europe.

'Jane herself doesn't help, making enemies wherever she goes, especially in Scotland. Apparently, she took to calling herself the rightful queen of Scotland as well, declaring the Catholic Mary Stuart a false pretender.'

'Yes – what of Mary Stuart?'

'Publicly beheaded at Fotheringhay and people didn't like it. Really, it's not surprising everything blew up in Jane's face – the only wonder is that it took so long.'

There was a long silence.

'Well?' said Ellis to me.

'I don't know what to say. This is . . . unbelievable. How could any of this possibly have happened?'

He shrugged. 'Someone somewhere has changed something. It's as I said, Max, the 16th century was very popular. Wherever you looked there were people trampling the bluebells. It would prob- ably have been something tiny and inadvertent and no one noticed.'

I sat back, thinking. Whoever had done it was almost certainly dead anyway. History would have dealt with them, but whatever they had done had given birth to this . . . this spur . . . this false timeline . . . this bubble. Call it what you will.

I turned to Ellis. 'So, is the temporal instability the cause of this . . . this rogue History, or is the rogue History the cause of the temporal instability?'

'A very good question.'

We waited.

He spread his hands. 'I'm sorry, we'll probably never know and at the moment it's not important. Our main problem is how to put it right. And the first thing we must do is get St Mary's out of here.'

I looked up at the screens. The scenes were sickening. London burned before my eyes. The only people remaining now were those too old, sick or injured to drag themselves out of the way of the armies who would crush them in a three-pronged approach.

England was a battleground. Protestantism would die under the twin hammers of Spain and France. The Inquisition would come to England. I wasn't sure about the Stuarts – given their inclination towards Catholicism they might remain as puppet monarchs, but the Hanoverians would never happen. No Industrial Revolution. England would become a theocracy. The ramifications spread far and wide. There might be no America. The French and Spanish would split the continent between them – the French would take the northern territories and the Spanish would hoover up the rest.

How? How could this have happened? What tiny event sparked this massive catastrophe? We'd never know. History was well and truly off the rails and we had to do something about it. And quickly.

I gestured around. 'For how long will this timeline be stable?'

'You mean in this particular bubble? No idea. Could be ten minutes. Could be a hundred years.'

'How can we fix it?'

'Well, I rather think this might be a St Mary's area of expertise, Max. Somehow, we have to find the tipping point. That moment when some little detail changed and re-routed the 16th century.'

'And having found it – use it to put things right.'

'Exactly.'

'OK,' I said. 'Can you give us thirty minutes?'

'To . . . ?'

'To have a bit of a think.'

'Fancy another coffee?'

'What a good idea,' I said brightly.

10

There was silence in the pod. Even the Time Police sat staring at the floor, apparently lost in thought. Except for the pilot, Grint, who fiddled with the controls on his console, awaiting instructions and apparently completely uncaring. I think he was slightly taken aback by our collaborative approach. Time Police operations do tend to be more *These are my instructions. Go away and carry them out or die.*

'OK,' I said slowly, 'this tipping point . . . and feel free to stop me at any time.'

They nodded.

'It's Mary. It all goes wrong because Mary never gets to London because she's poisoned on the way.'

North nodded. 'I think that could be correct.' I ignored the slight note of surprise in her voice. She probably didn't know she was doing it. I was just grateful Sykes wasn't here because the two of them would be locked in some kind of death-struggle by now.

She continued. 'Northumberland's invitation is a trap. Both Mary and Elizabeth set out. Mary doesn't make it – poisoned on the way. And with Mary dead there's no need to keep Elizabeth alive so she's executed. We think.'

Clerk frowned. 'Instead of Jane. It's Jane who should have been executed – not Elizabeth.'

'Wait,' said Ellis. 'Why was Jane originally executed?'

'Because,' I said slowly. 'Because of Thomas Wyatt's Rebellion. Early in Mary's reign, there was a plot to replace her with Elizabeth – the Protestant princess. Elizabeth somehow managed to convince Mary of her innocence, but Jane was considered too dangerous to live and she was executed. Here – in this . . . this . . .'

'Bubble,' said Ellis, helpfully.

'. . . in this bubble . . . *Mary* died, which meant Elizabeth had to die, too, and Jane lived to become queen.'

I began to speak more quickly as my idea took hold. 'So, all we have to do is keep Mary away from London. Because if she lives, then so will Elizabeth. Mary will be crowned, which means Wyatt's Rebellion *will* take place and Jane will die. As she should do.'

'So,' said Ellis, 'what you're saying is that if Mary lives, then Elizabeth lives also. And if they both live, then Jane doesn't and we're back on track.'

'Could be,' said Clerk, thinking.

'That seems very . . . simple.'

'Mm . . .' I said, thinking.

'I think . . .' said Bashford and stopped.

I looked at him. 'Go on.'

'Well . . .' He stopped again and looked at the Time Police, uncertain what to say.

I turned to Ellis. 'What Mr Bashford is saying is that we need two teams. One in 1553 to safeguard Mary and ensure her succession, and the other in 1554 to make sure the rebellion happens and that Jane safely dies.'

'Before she starts displaying her monster qualities, yes?'

Clerk stood up. 'We'd better get cracking, hadn't we? Coming, Max?'

Ellis shook his head. 'I can't allow that.'

St Mary's stiffened.

'No – and before you all look at me like that – firstly, Max is a member of the Time Police now and answers to me. I will decide her role in all this. Secondly, you're all going home. You shouldn't be here at all. The 16th century is extremely unstable at the moment. Our purpose here is to get you out safely and then *we* will assess the situation to decide what action *we* should take. *You* won't be involved in any of this because *you're* going home. Now.'

Clerk looked at me.

'That's all true,' I said. 'You should get back to St Mary's and leave the Time Police – us – to deal with things here.'

He looked them up and down. 'And they know what they're doing?'

'Of course not,' I said, 'but half the time neither do we.'

'Max . . .'

'No,' I said. 'My word on this is final. I mean Captain Ellis's word on this is final. Back to St Mary's.'

'OK,' he said casually, heading towards the door.

'And Officers Bevan and Nash will escort you,' said Ellis, equally casually. 'Just to make sure you get back to your pod safely.'

This time the silence was pregnant. For some reason, everyone looked at me.

I nodded at Ellis and said to Clerk, 'What he said.'

'Max, they're not – with respect, Captain Ellis – they're not historians.'

'No,' I said, 'but I am. Leave this to me. And the Time Police, of course.'

Clerk was still reluctant. 'If you're sure, Max.'

'I am. You're going to have to trust us on this one. And Dr Bairstow needs to know what's happening here.'

'He's got a lot on at the moment,' said Bashford, quietly. 'This won't help.'

I turned to him. 'Such as?'

'Oh . . . um . . . well, they don't really tell us anything, do they?'

'Well, they do,' said North, 'but you're usually too busy making love to your chicken to take it in.'

Time Police heads swung towards Bashford. 'Angus is very intelligent,' he said indignantly.

'More intelligent than you, certainly.'

'She can count.'

'*Much* more intelligent than you.'

'You should go now,' said Ellis quickly, as Bashford began to bristle. 'Nash, Bevan . . .'

'No, wait,' I said quickly. 'I've been thinking. Yes, I accept your point about getting them out of the way – this is an unstable environment – but before you dismiss the idea completely, you might want to consider the advantages of having a couple of historians along. Yes,' I said, as Time Police heads all turned to look at me. 'I'm sure you're all excellent at what you do, but the point I'm making is that you don't do *this*. History, I mean. But we do. It doesn't make sense to have expertise and not use it. If you amalgamate Mr Clerk's team, together with your excellent clean-up squad here . . .' I gestured and they blinked, '. . . you'd actually have expertise *and* muscle. Vital ingredients for any successful rebellion. Which means that our team,' I gestured at Ellis and the others, 'are free to concentrate on Mary.

'And,' I continued, before Ellis could open his mouth to say no, 'I think you should also consider the possibility you may have to split your team even further. Mary writes to the Privy Council declaring herself Edward's heir and claiming the throne. That letter *must* reach London. Robert Dudley is out there somewhere so you might want to consider detailing a few people to ensure that it does actually arrive.'

St Mary's, experts at cutting the ground from underneath an opponent in an argument, and well aware of the pitfalls of over-egging the pudding, sat back quietly to let the implications sink in.

'Our mission was to pull St Mary's out.' There was just the very slightest trace of doubt in Ellis's voice. And he'd used the past tense.

I pursued the advantage. 'And you will still be able to do so once they've assisted your people to a successful conclusion. I'm not criticising anyone, but how many of your people could recognise Edward Courtney or James Croft or Peter Carew, or understand the implications of their actions? Or are even able to communicate effectively with them? Captain Ellis, I formally recommend the inclusion of one, some, or all of this St Mary's team. It's ridiculous to have expertise and not avail ourselves of it.'

'And,' said Clerk politely, 'another point, which I'm sure has only not occurred to you because you haven't had time to think about it yet, is that you don't have enough pods. If this lot . . .' he nodded at the clean-up squad, '. . . heads off to 1554, then that leaves you lot . . .' he nodded at Ellis and his entourage, '. . . pod-less. At the mercy of whatever happens. You can't tell me that's good practice.'

Everyone from St Mary's had the sense to keep quiet and look as if good practice was something that happened to them every day.

'I can return to TPHQ for reinforcements.'

I shook my head. 'You said it yourself, this is an unstable environment. Every time someone jumps in or out it will become that little bit more unstable. And Time is not on your side on this one. In fact, I think we should get a move on.'

I shut up and left him to think about it. Clerk and the others knew when to remain silent as well. We all sat and watched him think it through. Even the clean-up crew said nothing, although to be fair, I wasn't sure they'd all mastered speech.

'If,' said Ellis, 'we didn't have to factor in a dodgy timeline then I might be tempted, but . . .'

'What will happen if the bubble bursts?' asked Clerk. 'Or if the timeline rolls up? Or any other colourful Time Police metaphor for catastrophe?'

'I really don't know,' said Ellis.

Something in his voice made me pause. 'This sort of thing has happened before, hasn't it?'

He paused and then said reluctantly, 'We think so, yes.'

'Don't you know?'

'Well, that's kind of the point I'm trying to make, Max. We don't know. We rebuild what we can and assume everything goes back to the way it should be.'

'Or the way we think it should be,' said Grint helpfully.

'Or the way it should be but wasn't,' said Bevan.

'But now is,' said Nash.

I looked at them grimly. 'Just a tiny hint-ette, guys – never bullshit a bullshitter.'

'No, listen,' said Clerk, leaning forwards. 'We can handle the rebellion. We're St Mary's. We'd be good at that.'

I nodded. 'From experience, I can confirm they'd be very good at that.'

'And,' said Bashford, 'you'll be allocating tasks according to abilities. We take a team back to 1554 and identify the potential causers of trouble. We whisper in a few ears and let events take their course.'

'Everyone plays to their strengths,' said North. 'A logical course of action.'

'I don't think any of you realise,' said Ellis, in exasperation, 'that a successful conclusion puts us in even more danger than before. As soon as everything is back on track this timeline *will* disappear. And possibly us with it. Which is *our* risk – but not yours.'

'We can take steps to minimise that risk,' I said. 'It shouldn't be a problem.'

Ellis was silent for a moment and then said, 'All right, consider this. There are two main areas on which to concentrate, which means splitting our forces because we can't go back and get more people. In fact, it would be dangerous to do so. Reluctantly, I agree. We should split into two teams.'

'OK,' I said. 'One team to cover Mary in 1553 and the other . . .'

He sighed. 'The other needs to jump on ahead to 1554 and do what they can to foment a rebellion. I'm aware of St Mary's natural talents in this direction, Max, and I'm prepared to include your people. You, though, I think I'd rather have with Mary.'

I nodded. That made sense. When dealing with a woman, other women are always useful. I could just imagine Grint, for example, strolling into Mary's bedroom somewhere and saying, 'Hey, listen up, doll . . .'

'Max, you and I will lead the team to intercept Mary. With your permission, we'll be in the St Mary's pod. The others,' he nodded at Clerk and the clean-up team, 'will handle the rebellion from this pod.'

I nodded. All that made good sense.

He turned to the clean-up squad. 'As soon as you're done, you jump to The Tabard. You know it?'

'I do,' said Clerk. 'Been there – drunk the beer.'

'Good. Bevan and Nash – you'll follow the letter. As soon as it's safely delivered, you get yourselves to The Tabard also. Rendezvous with the clean-up squad and jump back to HQ.'

'What about you?' asked Bevan.

'Max and I will make our own way back in the St Mary's pod.' He turned to Clerk and said, with all the politeness of one who would go ahead and take it anyway, 'With your permission.'

Clerk nodded.

'No one hangs around. As soon as your part is completed, you return to TPHQ.'

'What – not even time for a beer?' said Bashford.

'Actually . . . no,' said North, thoughtfully.

I thought she'd been a bit quiet.

She'd found a scratchpad from somewhere and was frowning deeply. 'I think we might have a problem.'

'Which is?'

'Time.'

'You mean . . .' I gestured around us and assumed a portentous tone. *'Time . . .'*

She ignored this frivolity. 'No, I mean time as in we might not have enough of it.'

'Explain,' said Ellis, curtly.

'Well, I don't think the rebellion will be a great problem. We know that it did happen. We just need to ensure that it does happen. But the Mary part of the assignment might be a little trickier. Forgive me, this isn't one of my areas of expertise, but Mary rides from Hunsdon?'

114

I nodded. 'Yes, she has no idea of the extent of Edward's illness so she's in no rush.'

'And her first stop is Hoddesdon?'

'As far as we know, yes.'

'Where she's warned?'

'There are differing accounts but, yes, she could be.'

'Hoddesdon's not that far from Hunsdon. Which is good and bad. It means you'll only have a short walk that day. But – the minute that letter sets off then we're on the clock. Because, as the crow flies, Hoddesdon's only about twenty miles from London. It's a longer route by road, but I would imagine they'll cut across country. I estimate, with a fast horse, the letter should take between two and four hours to get to London. Perhaps slightly longer if they're unfamiliar with the route, but say only three hours to be on the safe side.'

'Yes? And?'

'You'll be leaving the pod behind you at Hunsdon. You travel six or seven miles to Hoddesdon, do the business . . .'

'Oh,' I said. 'Shit.'

'Yes – you'll have only three hours to get back to the pod. Possibly less. And that's barring accidents, getting lost, or falling over. And you'll be tired because you've already done the seven miles there.'

There was silence in the pod.

'If we assume – and I think we should – that putting events back on track will mean the end of this particular . . .'

'Bubble,' said Ellis.

'. . . bubble, then you could find yourself seven miles from your pod, in a strange environment, possibly in the dark, and with only three hours to get out. That's a very narrow margin.'

'We'll come for you,' said Clerk.

'No,' I said. 'You won't. And that's an order.' I turned to Ellis. 'What will happen if we don't make it back to the pod in time?'

He shrugged. 'I don't know. Let's hope for the best but plan for the worst. Let's say we have three hours from Mary despatching the letter . . . The letter goes one way – Mary goes another. And at great speed, probably. She won't want to hang around.' He stopped, worried.

'She'll head for her estates in Norfolk,' I said. 'We can do it. They . . .' I nodded at the clean-up crew and Clerk's team, '. . . rendezvous at The Tabard and jump. We tidy things up with Mary, race back to the pod and jump. Jobs done and done.'

'Why not just take the pod to Hoddesdon and wait for her there?' asked Bashford.

'Because we need to keep an eye on her,' I said. 'We don't know at what point Northumberland plans to have her poisoned. Don't forget Robert Dudley's out there somewhere, waiting for her. We can't afford to let her out of our sight.'

'Three hours,' said Ellis, doubtfully. 'Shit.'

'Possibly less,' said North, just to cheer him up, 'if they have good horses.'

'It will surely take some time for events to play out,' I said, from a position of massive ignorance but with even more massive optimism. 'As long as everyone takes their pods and jumps as soon as their task is completed, we'll be fine.'

That last sentence had the hollow ring of bravado. All our lives we've been taught not to interfere with History. Grant died at Peterloo because he tried to save a woman and child. Randall was knifed in Rouen when he tried to put Joan of Arc out of her misery.

He died in the pod in a pool of his own blood. Hoyle was trampled to death in his desperate and doomed attempt to kill Henry Tudor at Bosworth Field. You can't change History. History doesn't like it. There are always consequences.

On the other hand, History had already been changed. Among all the traffic in and out of the 16th century, someone, somewhere, had done something. It could have been a tiny thing. We'd never know and the person responsible was surely dead. It might not have been maliciously done. It was probably an unknowing accident, but the implications were spreading outwards like ripples on a still surface.

I was still having difficulties with Ellis's Decking of Time explanation, but I'd seen the Time Map disintegrate in front of my eyes. I'd seen the darkness spread. I'd watched new paths form, new points emerge. I'd watched History change.

It wasn't yet too late, according to Ellis. We'd located the tipping point. Well, *a* tipping point, anyway. A little – a very little – cautious intervention and the day would be saved. History could be back on track.

I'd done something similar once before when Mary Stuart – that headstrong little minx – wasn't behaving according to the History books. Clive Ronan had been behind that particular episode. We'd put things right. Well, I had, and I'm still not proud of what I did but, on that occasion, History had worked with me. I'd been conscious of having my way smoothed. Luck had been with me all the way. Opportunities had offered themselves and I'd availed myself of them. This could be a similar situation. I hoped. Because if it wasn't ... If it wasn't, then any attempt to interfere could bring disaster crashing down upon us. And it wasn't as if there wouldn't be plenty of opportunities for disaster out there. But we didn't have a lot of choice.

We didn't have a lot of time, either. If this was one of those bubble universes and it was too fragile to live long then it could burst at any moment. With us inside it.

11

The clean-up crew stood quietly by the door. None of them were saying anything but they always had the air of people who didn't say much. They weren't thugs, but I wouldn't want to cross any of them. I certainly didn't want to speculate about some of the things they might have done in the course of their duties.

We'd given them a quick ten-minute briefing on Wyatt's Rebellion. They listened with flattering attention. I was feeling quite pleased with myself until I realised they were regarding this as a military operation, rather than an historical assignment, but perhaps they were right to do so. Whatever floated their boat, anyway. I contented myself with warning them, sternly, not to kill anyone. All they had to do was keep an unobtrusive eye on things and let Clerk and his team do the rest. Actually, since this was the 16th century and plots and rebellions abounded, they probably wouldn't have to do much at all, because the most important part of the job was to ensure the plot was discovered at the appropriate moment. There was no time for any more. They'd have to pick up the rest on the job.

The plan was thus:

Team One – the unlikely combination of St Mary's and the clean-up team, with Grint in command, would jump to 1554 and . . . yes, facilitate is a good word . . . and facilitate Wyatt's Rebellion.

They should be safe enough. By that, I mean the rebellion actually occurred so they should be safe from History. Whether the 16th century and its inhabitants would be safe from them was another kettle of fish. Looking at them, my money was on the clean-up crew. I've just realised I never knew their names.

We – Ellis, Nash, Bevan and I – would jump to July 1553 and attempt to dissuade Mary from obeying the summons to London. It shouldn't be too difficult. In the original timeline, she was actually warned not to go. All we had to do was ensure we were the people warning her.

In the original timeline, having been advised she was walking into a trap, Mary writes a letter to the Privy Council, claiming the throne under the terms of her father's will, so our task would be twofold. Firstly, to prevent Mary travelling to London and, secondly, to make sure her letter arrived safely. Because Robert Dudley was out there somewhere, under orders to intercept her, and given that in this timeline Mary was poisoned, we could all guess at his instructions.

'How will you safeguard the letter?' I asked Nash.

'We'll follow at a distance,' he said. 'Close enough to intervene should anyone have any ideas about intercepting it.'

'But how will you manage? You'll need horses, surely. Where will you get horses from?'

They looked at me pityingly and I resolved to shut up and stop embarrassing myself.

'Right,' said Ellis. 'Good luck, everyone. Don't forget – no hanging around. Job done and go. No arguments.'

They nodded.

By now, the streets of London were worryingly deserted. No attempt was being made to defend the capital. Far, far in the distance, the horizon glowed red and orange. I could hear a muted roar. Like the crowd at a far-off football match. We needed to get out of here.

Number Five was exactly where Clerk had said it would be. I called for the door and the next moment we were inside. I closed my eyes and inhaled. It was wonderful to be back. Trust me, cabbage never smelled so good.

I opened my eyes to see my colleagues looking around. Bevan sniffed disparagingly. I caught them all exchanging glances. Presumably no one ever vomits or bleeds in a Time Police pod because they all smell faintly of pine air freshener.

'Right,' said Ellis. 'First things first, Max.' He unzipped his pack and pulled out a small box. 'With your permission . . .'

He plonked the box on the wall.

I peered suspiciously. They were the Time Police after all. 'And that is . . .'

'Standard issue. For when we have to travel some distance from the pod. Homing beacon. You don't have them?'

We don't normally travel that far from the pod but to say so would make us sound a bit girlie, so I said airily, 'We normally manage to find our own way home without artificial aids.'

A statement received with complete disbelief by everyone – even the person who uttered it.

There's a pod etiquette, observed even by the Time Police, so I was the one who did the coordinates. And I was the one to lay them in, as well.

'Biometrics,' I said to Ellis. 'So stop sulking.'

'Great. So, if anything goes wrong and you're dead then we're stuck here.'

'Pretty much, yes. You'd better let me have the return coordinates as well, please?'

He looked at me and frowned.

'It's the way we work,' I said. 'It saves time.'

He frowned some more.

'You're St Mary's now,' I said. 'We often have to leave in a hurry. Trust me.'

He sighed and I laid them in. 'Ready when you are.'

'Let's do it.'

I smiled to myself and said fondly, 'Computer, initiate jump.'

'Jump initiated.'

And the world went the most wonderful shade of white.

If I'd done it right – and I had – this was 6th July 1553. Either today or tomorrow, Mary Tudor would set out from her house at Hunsdon in response to her summons to London. Terrified of missing her, we were there just after dawn.

Hunsdon had been a favourite with all the Tudors. Unexpectedly large and imposing, it even had a moat. I remembered it had been extended by Henry VIII. All his children had spent time here. It was at Hunsdon that Mary had taught Elizabeth to play cards. The building itself was beautiful. Built of redbrick, it glowed happily in the summer sunshine.

We'd landed in a small copse about a few hundred yards away. At first glance, things did not look promising. The house was very much bigger and grander than I had expected. There was no way we were going to be able to blag our way inside. On the other hand, the wall wasn't high and the unguarded gates stood open. That didn't mean there were no guards around, though. Not in these unsettled times.

122

We carefully circumnavigated the building and grounds, finally settling on a site opposite the gates a little distance away. Gently rising ground gave us a reasonable view of the house.

We'd each brought a small pack containing water and those really rather grim, hard, brown survival biscuits. The ones guaranteed to keep you on your feet for twenty-four hours, taste like ceiling tiles and give you three months' constipation. And then we settled down to wait. A lot of my job is waiting. Or running, of course.

The good news was that she was definitely leaving today. Even just after dawn, the place was in turmoil. We couldn't see much through the gates, but we caught glimpses of male servants running hither and thither, chivvied from A to B and back again by scolding women wearing wide dresses. Their clothing – male and female – was dark and sombre with white frills at the neck. A mountain of trunks and boxes were already stacked on the grass.

'Good job it's not raining,' said Ellis.

We watched as the alp of baggage grew ever higher.

'Is she taking everything she owns?' asked Nash in amazement.

'It's very possible,' I said. 'Wealthy people often took their furniture with them – including their beds. I don't think that's happening here, but she'll probably be accompanied by a sizeable entourage – she is the daughter of a king, after all – and they'll all bring a ton of kit as well. It'll all be loaded on to pack horses and mules and into carts and carriages. The best thing is that they'll only be able to travel at a snail's pace and we'll have no difficulty keeping up.'

'Are we actually joining them?'

I nodded.

'Won't they notice?'

'I doubt it. We won't be the only ones. Travel is still quite hazardous. People band together for safety. There'll be Mary and all her entourage – including her guards – and others will join on at the rear. No one will notice us,' I added hopefully. 'With luck, the newcomers will think we're part of the baggage train and Mary's men will think we're just hangers-on. Just look stupid and unthreatening. Yes, that's very good.'

Sometimes I just can't help myself. On this occasion, however, they restrained themselves. They still looked doubtful, though, and I considered telling them about my intervention with Mary, Queen of Scots, and how well that went. But, for a variety of reasons, not least that you never voluntarily tell the Time Police anything, I decided not to worry them with it.

The morning wore on. I'd been right – carts and mules were being loaded up. There was a great deal of shouting and even more female twittering. Apparently, everything had to be just so.

'Bloody women,' muttered Nash. 'They've made them repack that bloody mule three times now and they're still not satisfied.'

Progress had been made, however. A ragged line of carts, mules and packhorses was formed and, with a great deal of shouting and waving, slowly and ponderously the front of the line began to move away.

'They're off,' said Nash, levering himself up from his stomach. We were watching the goings-on from underneath a straggly hawthorn hedge. 'Shouldn't we get a move on?'

'Relax,' said Ellis. 'It's Mary we're following, not her baggage. She'll have breakfast and set off later and catch them up. But it's time for you two to earn your pay.'

Nash and Bevan inched their way backwards, got to their feet and disappeared.

'Where are they going?' I said in some alarm.

Ellis grinned. 'They're going to nip back to the stables and help themselves to anything with four legs that hasn't already been commandeered.'

'Won't someone notice?'

'Of course they will, but they'll just think someone's forgotten something, or they need spare horses or something. They'll probably even help saddle them up.'

'Oh,' I said, admiring. 'Neat.'

'Naturally.'

And actually, that's exactly what happened. They reappeared a while later leading two sturdy brown horses, bridled but not saddled. Obviously, tack was more difficult to steal.

Ellis and I backed up and edged our way around the hedge. We found ourselves a neat spot from where we could see everything and settled down to wait. Behind us, I could hear the Time Police bonding with their horses.

The sun rose higher in the sky and the day promised to be hot. A small crowd began to gather at the gates. To catch a glimpse of Lady Mary, we assumed. Whatever the reason, we welcomed their appearance.

'We can get lost in the crowd,' said Ellis.

And then, finally, around mid-morning, the front doors were thrown open and a small woman appeared, escorted by a man I assumed to be the chamberlain or steward of the house. No prep meant I didn't know his name. His wife stood slightly behind him and, behind her, some five or six other women.

The small woman – who must be Mary, given the deference being shown her – paused, drawing on a pair of gloves. She said something over her shoulder and as she did so, the horses were brought round.

I knelt up to see better.

Ellis pulled me down. 'Stay down.'

'I can't. It's my job. I'm the historian. I study historical events. You're the Time Police. Go and count your crayons.'

Someone behind me wondered aloud why they let me live.

'I've no idea,' said Ellis. 'Perhaps she'll come in handy one day.'

'And if not?' Was it my imagination or was there a hopeful note there?

'*Then* you can kill her.'

That seemed to mollify them but I'd lost interest, staring instead at Mary Tudor. Given her enormous father, she was so small and slight. Her waist was tiny. She wore a brown dress pulled back over a lighter underskirt. Her headdress was small and close-fitting. Probably so as not to be blown away as she rode. All her clothes looked plain and practical.

She was surrounded by what seemed like hundreds of women. I know she always had a large household, even when suffering under Henry's displeasure, but trust me, there were a lot of women here. I wracked my brains for names. Frideswide Knight. Several Franceses – Aylmer and Jerningham. A Mabel Browne. Another Jerningham – Anne? I wished I was better prepared. Normally I'd try and befriend one of them and attempt access to Mary that way but that might not be possible here. I'd interrogated the Time Police computers but although they were spot on with dates, they carried little personal information about actual people. And none at all about ladies-in-waiting.

There are various versions of events which I suppose isn't that important if you're studying them from a position four or five hundred years in the future, but a bit of a bugger if you're actually on site waiting for everyone to get a move on and wondering what will happen next.

Some say Mary was warned while actually on the road. Some say a message was sent from London. Others that she was warned by Lady Burgh at Euston Hall. Or that Lady Burgh simply confirmed what Mary already knew. So many versions of events. Well, the beauty of this situation was that we could make our own.

Ellis grinned at me. 'All set, Max?'

I nodded.

The crowd around the gates sent up a cheer and here she came, mounted on a rather nice-looking bay. Her household and escort cantered along behind her.

She slowed for the crowd, smiling and waving. The crowd waved back. She seemed very popular locally.

We slipped out from under the trees and fell in about a hundred yards behind. Within sight but not close enough to be threatening. Especially not to an armed party.

The day was lovely with a light breeze and birdsong. I could hear the gentle clump of hoofbeats behind us and an occasional snort I assumed was from one of the horses. Everything was very peaceful. It's easy to forget how quiet the world used to be.

They rode for about two hours and at a very gentle pace. We'd worried she might race off after her baggage, but perhaps she was enjoying the day. We had no trouble keeping up. Ellis and I went first, followed by Bevan and Nash leading the horses. They'd thrown their cloaks over them in case anyone recognised them.

Ahead, two soldiers went first, heading the procession. Mary followed on next, with one of her ladies at her side. I've no idea which one. They were all dressed more or less identically. Her other

127

ladies followed on behind. Behind them were various members of her household together with their assistants and staff. More soldiers brought up the rear.

Every now and then the Tudor equivalent of Markham would peel off and trot down the line, looking for trouble and generally keeping an eye on things. Occasionally a couple would canter on ahead to check out the road. I don't know if anyone was expecting trouble – they were alert, but not nervous. They had no idea Robert Dudley was somewhere in the vicinity. They didn't even know that Edward was very seriously ill, if not already dead. There was no indication that anyone was aware Mary was going to her death.

It wasn't an unpleasant walk. We stayed far enough back to avoid the dust. Though there was a lot of it. No wonder Mary had chosen to travel separately from her baggage train. Noon passed. The afternoon was hot but with just enough breeze to keep us comfortable. No one stopped to eat so we didn't either – just a glug of water every now and then.

We saw the manor house at Hoddesdon long before we reached it. Well, we saw its tall chimneys peeking above the surrounding elm trees. And then the mellow red roof. We rounded a bend and there it was. Another lovely redbrick building drowsing in the mid-afternoon sunshine. Everything was hot and still and peaceful. A whole world away from the murderous paranoia of Tudor court life.

The garden was walled but the gates were open. The baggage train must have arrived because a small welcoming party had gathered. We watched them greet the royal party with great deference. The horses were led away and Mary's party was escorted slowly towards the house. We strolled casually past the gate and then Ellis and I snuck back for a closer look, hiding in the long grass opposite.

The house had small windows – it would be gloomy inside. Especially if the rooms were panelled with the usual dark oak. I had a bit of a think. It was a lovely day. And she hadn't come that far. She might want to rest but I was betting she would want solitude even more.

I could imagine the turmoil inside. The flurry of feminine activity. Hot and agitated women flitting from room to room, skirts swirling around them, scolding even more hot and agitated servants for delivering the wrong chests and trunks to the wrong rooms. Everyone would be stressed and losing their tempers. Her hosts would be flustered and anxious. The traditional flurry of an arriving guest. A *royal* arriving guest.

Mary might well want to take herself away from all that. To find somewhere to gather her thoughts. Possibly even to pray. There was a small, private garden, enclosed by high walls. She would be safe enough there. Surely, she would seek a little privacy. If not, I'd have to think of something else.

I sat back on my heels and looked around. In the distance, behind another stand of trees, I could see more thatched roofs. Might this be the farmhouse attached to the manor house? A deeply rutted track led from the road, down past the house and towards the farm. I might be able to access the garden from the rear. I could leave Captain Ellis and his men here at the front in case anything happened.

The most difficult part was getting him to stay behind.

'Listen,' I said, for what seemed like the umpteenth time. 'You'd never get anywhere with Mary. I probably won't but you *definitely* won't, so you need to stay here and keep an eye on things. And you two . . .' I looked at the other two officers, 'need to be ready to go at a moment's notice. It's very possible she'll write to the

Privy Council without any prompting from us. Dudley and his men could be anywhere around here and that letter must get through.'

Ellis didn't like it. None of them liked it but, as I pointed out because I can be very irritating, that didn't mean it wasn't the right thing to do.

I scrambled to my feet and tried to tidy myself up a bit. I shook out my skirts and brushed off the worst of the Thames mud, re-tied my tea towel and was ready to go.

'I'll give you an hour,' said Ellis, stubbornly.

'Better make it two.'

He sighed in resignation. 'Until dark then.'

'Keep an eye on things here and make sure Nash and Bevan are ready to go after that letter. Don't wait for me and lose your opportunity.'

He nodded and I set off down the cart track. The ruts were very deep and hard. There hadn't been any rain for quite a while. I had to watch where I put my feet. Turning an ankle now would not be a good idea.

Insects buzzed around me – there seemed to be a lot of bees about, and there were a lot of flowers as well, growing wild in the long grass. I assumed there must be hives nearby. A tall brick wall ran parallel to the track. I was hoping this might be the garden wall and on the other side Mary Tudor might – just might – be taking a peaceful stroll while her harassed and probably grateful hosts got everything sorted in her absence.

A thick hedge ran down the other side of the track which could be useful if I had to hide. The grass was at knee height so I was guessing that apart from farm traffic, no one ever used this path. I hoped.

I rounded a bend and the track opened up into an equally rutted farmyard. They must be up to their knees in mud in the winter. Dilapidated buildings lay haphazardly around. I was surprised at their smallness but, of course, there was no large agricultural machinery to house in this time. Apart from a barn, most of the wooden sheds were little higher than a man.

A part-stone, part-timber building stood slightly apart and I guessed that must be the farmhouse, but architecturally it was only a tiny step up from the outhouses.

Best of all, though, everything was deserted on this hot afternoon. Not a soul in sight anywhere. No smoke drifted from the chimneys. There wasn't even a barking dog to give warning. I wondered if they were all in the fields. Or had they bunked off to catch a glimpse of Lady Mary? Not important right now. Because best of all, there was a gate in the wall. A back gate into the property.

I scooted over and tried the handle. This could be easier than I thought. History was with me.

No, it wasn't. The bloody thing was locked. Bloody bollocking hell.

I sighed. I'm St Mary's. This sort of thing isn't supposed to dismay me. I stepped back and looked up at the wall. It was in goodish repair. A few bricks looked a bit dodgy and a lot of the mortar was loose. But it was covered in ivy. I seized a thick stem.

In books people are always scrambling up ivy-covered walls. They do it all the time. You try it. In real life, the ivy comes away from the wall and you land on your arse. I was really glad there weren't any Time Police around. Pick yourself up, Maxwell, and try again.

This time I ignored the ivy and concentrated on the bricks. None were actually missing, but one or two were loose. I chipped away

131

with a small rock as tiny pieces of mortar pinged painfully at my hands and face and then had another go.

It wasn't graceful. It certainly wasn't elegant. And I had to tuck my dress into my anomalous knickers. I couldn't help thinking this was probably not the best way to approach a Tudor princess but I scrambled up somehow, skinning fingers and knees, until I could peer cautiously over the top of the wall.

I'd misjudged. This wasn't a pleasure garden. I was looking into an orchard. Trees stood in neat rows. I could see apples, pears and plums and, in a corner, a giant mulberry tree that was preparing to shed its dark fruit everywhere.

Half a dozen wooden beehives stood in another corner. So I'd been right about that. One or two bees buzzed around my head. I refrained from flapping my arms and politely requested them to leave me alone because I've heard that bees respond positively to that sort of thing. Don't ask me where I get all this information from when I don't even know who the current prime minister is but, in my defence, the thing about bees is important and the thing about the prime minister definitely isn't.

Over on the opposite wall another gate might give me access to the private gardens and, with luck, my strolling princess.

Getting down the wall was a piece of piss because gravity took over and I landed in a bit of a heap at the bottom. I picked myself up, pulled my dress out of my knickers, dusted myself down, and looked around. Apart from some very sleepy bees, the orchard was deserted.

I was just about to set off for the door in the other wall when it opened of its own accord. I only just had time to duck down behind the hives. The bees didn't seem to mind. Politeness pays.

History hadn't abandoned me after all, for which I was very

grateful, because it was Mary Tudor walking into the orchard. And she closed the gate behind her which I took to be a signal she was alone and wanted to remain that way.

Once, when I'd done something like this before, there was a moment when everything fell into place. When – and forgive the fanciful exaggeration – History was working with me instead of against me. Doors opened that shouldn't have. Opportunities arose out of nowhere. I even managed to escape more or less unscathed. This might be another of those times. When, suddenly, everything comes together with no striving, no effort, no grief, and you just know – this is it. Everything falls into place and you can fly.

I didn't make the mistake of rushing over to speak to her. No matter how pushed we were for time, running up to an apparently unescorted, apparently unarmed Tudor princess would never be a good move. Alone she might appear to be, but there were bound to be attendants nearby. I had to make sure she didn't call them.

I retreated quietly back behind the hives. An old wooden box sat half hidden in the long grass. I used it to sit on while I considered my strategy.

And then I had another thought, stood up and opened the box. Yes! Among all the other rubbish I found a wide-brimmed hat and a veil. They'd been in the box a long time and were dirty, torn and probably forgotten, but just what I wanted.

I put on the hat and draped the veil over the top. As bee protection, the veil had more holes in it than a political party's election manifesto, but as camouflage it was perfect.

Mary had seated herself on an old bench at the other end of the orchard. I rather thought she might be praying.

I became amazingly busy doing nothing. Anyone who, at half past three on a Friday afternoon, has decided they really can't be arsed to do any more work will be familiar with my actions.

There were all sorts of old tat tucked behind the hives. I had the wooden box, a dilapidated old wicker basket, some sort of broken rake, and some old terracotta pots. I began by picking everything up and diligently moving it from one side of the hives to the other.

Then I picked up half of them and moved them back again. Never once did I look at her directly.

Ambitiously, I fiddled with the nearest hive but the humming increased alarmingly so I packed that in pretty sharply.

Finally, after about ten minutes of useless activity, when I judged she might be used to my presence, I picked up the wicker basket and began to move around the trees, picking up the small windfalls. God knows what I thought I was going to do with them. Feed them to the bees, probably. I think bees like apples. Everyone likes apples.

I lifted the veil up over my hat so she could see my face and slowly and aimlessly worked my way towards the still figure sitting on the bench.

I was surprised at how pretty she was. Much prettier than the Antonis Mor portrait. Never mind burning Protestants – she'd have been better off burning the artist. Perhaps being queen would age her. Or being married would age her. It had certainly aged me.

Her hair had faded to an indeterminate light colour but still had streaks of red in it. She was very pale – naturally so, I thought, with long dark eyes. She had a small mouth with deep creases at the corners. As if she was continually pressing her lips together. Keeping secrets. Holding her tongue. Unusually for this age, her complexion was clear and she had small, plump, pretty hands. Antonis Mor really hadn't done her any favours at all.

She hadn't even changed her dress. I could clearly see roadside dust clinging to the folds of brown velvet. Now, however, she wore a large pectoral cross, simply made. She'd come to pray. Which could present a problem. Not because I'm a godless heathen, but

135

because she wouldn't take kindly to being disturbed. But I had to take a chance. Time was short and I was certain she wouldn't be allowed to remain alone for long. And, as I continually tried not to remind myself, this universe could roll up and disappear at any moment.

I was putting it off. I'd forgotten how heart-stoppingly terrifying this sort of thing is. I swallowed, heaved my basket on my arm and approached her from an angle. She could see me coming. I was quiet but not stealthy.

Unsure whether to bow or kneel, I did neither. I sat, unthreateningly, under a tree, about ten feet away from her. She was between me and the gate. I took another quick look around but we were alone.

I didn't know how to address her, either. Edward was dead or nearly so. She might already be queen but if I said, 'Your Grace,' she might well suspect entrapment. I couldn't remember whether, at this point in her complicated life, she was Princess Mary or only the Lady Mary so I compromised, saying softly, and in Latin, 'Madam, heed my words.' And waited. If she screamed or raised the alarm then I'd be off and over the wall and into the woods. On the other hand, I was willing to bet she had a dagger among all that brown velvet. She might well do for me herself. She was a Tudor after all. Something Northumberland – who had casually dismissed her as a weak old woman – was about to find out, I hoped.

Because this was Mary Tudor, born into and brought up in the most dangerous court in the world; she was far too wily to commit herself in any way. She remained perfectly still. I suspected that was so she could claim afterwards she hadn't heard me. Or had been asleep.

I started to take the tiny apples out of the basket and lay them in a neat row on the grass. 'Madam, you must heed my words. Do not travel to London.'

Again, I waited and again she said and did nothing.

'Madam, Northumberland has despatched his son to intercept you. You will never arrive in London.'

I started on a new row of apples. 'Beware of poison.'

'Guildford?' Her voice was just a whisper on the wind.

'Robert, madam. You must avoid him.' And remembered, too late, that dreadful things happened to men who used the word 'must' to her sister, Elizabeth. I had to walk a fine line between not sending her screaming for help or getting a knife in the ribs. Not for the first time – or even the thirty-first time – I thought about an office job.

The afternoon continued hot and silent. There was no breeze in this still place. The only sound was the faint humming of the bees. Another minute slipped by. I tried not to stir impatiently.

She was still cautious. 'My brother the king? How does my brother?'

I looked up at the afternoon sun. Edward might be dead by now. I didn't know. She didn't know. No one knew. Northumberland was suppressing the news while he moved his people into position.

I took a chance. 'Madam, His Grace is with a merciful God.'

Her face didn't change but I saw her knuckles whiten. 'The king has summoned me.'

'Madam, the king is dead.'

'But we have heard nothing. There has been no message. The bells do not toll.' A gentle wind stirred the leaves. 'I must go to London.'

'Madam, you will never reach London alive.'

'The king has summoned me.'

137

'The king is dead.'

She said nothing. To discuss the death or possible death of a monarch was treason. I expected her to say nothing but she clutched her cross and closed her eyes. I didn't know whether she was praying for her brother or for herself. I waited, forcing myself not to speak. Surely, we wouldn't have much longer in this quiet place. Her household would be coming for her soon but I had to be sure she understood.

I started another row of apples.

'Madam, you are the rightful Queen of England. The message I have for you is that you should write to the Privy Council with all speed.'

'From whom does this message come.'

'From your many friends, madam. Those who have not forgotten whose daughter you are. Your throne is slipping from your grasp.' I swallowed. 'You must assert your right. You are in the gravest danger.'

She was silent for a long while. I could feel the sweat running down my back and prickling under my hair. One by one, I began to put the apples back in the basket. She was deeply suspicious. She didn't believe me and why should she? Some oddly dressed woman who had appeared from nowhere and started messing around with apples? I wouldn't have believed me.

I made one last effort. 'Madam, you will hear this news again. Robert Reyns awaits you at Euston Hall. Lady Burgh also will tell you. I speak truly and from the heart. God has put me in your path today. Heed my words.'

I stood up to go.

'Wait. What of Elizabeth?'

Now that was interesting. Rivalry for the crown had not yet

sundered these two sisters. There was genuine concern in her voice. They had been good friends once.

'Madam, her life hangs with yours. If you die then so will she. They will be too afraid to keep her alive. If you live then so will she. They will be too afraid to kill her. You hold both your lives in your hand. Avoid London if you would live. Now I must go.'

I left the basket and the apples by the tree and backed away to the far end of the orchard. To the corner where I'd come in.

There was ivy on this side, too. Pulling off the hat and veil and chucking it behind the hives, I scrambled up, finding holes in the brickwork to put my feet. Another load of ivy came away as I did so, but there was nothing I could do about that. I pulled myself up and sat astride the wall for a dangerous moment, looking back.

She was on her knees, clasping her cross in both hands, praying. What she was praying for I had no idea. Was she seeking guidance? Giving thanks? Praying for her dead brother? Not a clue. A bit of an enigma, our Mary Tudor. A shame. I would have liked to have known her better.

I more or less fell off the wall again, landing with a bump on the farmyard side. Fortunately, there was still no one there and the farmyard dreamed softly in the heat haze. I took a hasty look around and then trotted off back up the cart track.

I was hot and bothered when I arrived back. Ellis and the others were resting under a tree. The two TWOC'd horses grazed peacefully nearby.

'Don't get up,' I said, dropping to the ground beside them.

They passed me some Tudor water which I would probably regret later on. I drank deeply, mopped the sweat off my face and adjusted my tea towel.

'Well?' said Ellis. 'What happened? Did you see her?'

'I did,' and gave them the details. I nodded towards Bevan and Nash. 'If she believes me she'll write to the Privy Council. You'll need to be ready to move at a moment's notice.'

'*If* she writes the letter,' said Ellis.

'If she writes the letter,' I agreed.

The minutes ticked by.

An hour passed.

Nothing happened. No one galloped out through the gates with an important letter for the Privy Council. I tried not to panic but, deep down, I was convinced I'd failed.

'Not necessarily,' said Ellis, trying to reassure me. 'It's still only late afternoon. It's midsummer – the days are long. There's plenty of time for her to despatch a messenger.'

I shook my head despondently. Even allowing for her prayers, she'd had plenty of time to return to the house, gather her thoughts, compose her letter, seal it, summon a messenger and send it off. More than enough time. She hadn't believed me. We were going to have to think of something else.

I said to Ellis, 'Do we have a plan B?'

He shook his head.

That was a bit of a bugger. And we couldn't come back. There are no do-overs in History. If we screwed this then everything was screwed. And – more to the point – how much longer could we remain here? And Clerk and the clean-up team? What was happening to Wyatt's Rebellion? If we failed then so would they. They could hardly instigate a rebellion against a Catholic monarch who'd never made it to the throne. And if they failed then we failed because Jane Grey wouldn't be executed. The whole thing just went around and around in my head until I was dizzy. Either

140

way, we didn't have much more time. What was happening to the fabric of the 16th century? If it all suddenly disappeared, would we ever know anything about it? Would we miraculously appear somewhere else? Probably not. When this particular bubble burst, we'd go with it.

I took off my tea towel to let my hot head get some air before my brain exploded.

Nash sat up suddenly. 'There.'

Something was happening. They were opening the gates. Two riders flew out between them before they were even half open, wheeled sharply and disappeared down the road in a cloud of dust.

'You're up,' said Ellis to his men, but they were already swinging themselves on to their horses.

'Nothing must happen to that letter,' I said, still in the throes of near terminal anxiety.

'It won't,' said Bevan. 'Get out of the way, Max.'

I leaped aside and they cantered away after the riders. We watched them out of sight.

And then – amazingly – out of the blue – another thunder of hooves behind us. I spun around. My first thought was that Dudley's men were here already, pursuing the letter.

I was wrong.

It was a good job Ellis was there because I was too busy gawping like an idiot to get out of the way. He yanked me to the side of the road. I caught a confused glimpse of six big brown horses and their riders. The first two were well-dressed and heavily armed. They wore swords. The one nearest to me had a pistol in his belt and a dagger in his boot.

The last two were ordinary soldiers. The muscle.

The two in the middle were women. Mary Tudor, hooded and

cloaked, thundered past me, her face white and set. Her cloak billowed behind her. She wore a long knife at her belt. Beside her, a younger woman was similarly armed.

This was no gentle ride across country. They were really moving. They looked neither to right or left. If we hadn't moved they would have ridden over the top of us. Mary Tudor was heading to her estates in Norfolk. To raise her standard and claim her throne. Seconds later, they were out of sight. The sound of hoofbeats lingered only a moment longer.

'Well,' said Ellis, 'it's out of our hands now, Max. And we can't afford to hang around. We need to be getting back to the pod. Come on. It's only seven miles.'

'I've already done it once,' I said grumpily. 'To say nothing of falling off that bloody wall. Twice.'

There's no doubt that when you're working for History, History works for you. So far – flawless. However, now we'd done our bit, we were no longer important, so half an hour later the rain came down. We did our best, keeping under the trees at the edge of the road, but it was the wrong sort of rain and we were soaked in minutes. And it got dark quite quickly as well. Ellis had a torch and a compass and swore he knew how to use them both and when we got a little nearer – he said – we should be able to pick up the signal from the homing beacon.

The rain really slowed us down. There was mud everywhere. There seemed to be two types of road in Tudor England. The hardened, rutty, dusty sort that turned your ankle and broke your axles, and the wet, sticky, muddy sort that sucked at your shoes and soaked your hem. Each is as uncomfortable to walk on as the other.

And you get so tired. Well, I did. My stupid wet skirt kept wrapping itself around my legs, considerably hampering my progress. In the end, I just hitched it up and struggled on as best I could. Our progress was slow and we dared not deviate from the road. Not by very much anyway. We did have to detour sometimes to avoid the worst of the bogs, puddles and swamps.

Despite the pace, I was shivering all the time and it seemed a very, very long way back to the pod.

'That's because it is a very, very long way back to the pod,' said Ellis.

There was no time to eat. I couldn't remember when I'd last had food. Although I had seen a pizza go by twice. Drinking as we ran was not successful. I suggested a pit stop every thirty minutes or so, but Ellis pushed us on. He didn't say anything, but I know he was concerned about how much time we might or might not have left. We'd done our part. Mary was warned. Her letter was on its way to London, safeguarded every inch of the way by Nash and Bevan, who would then go on to the rendezvous with the others at The Tabard.

Clerk and his team were in 1554, facilitating Wyatt's Rebellion. As soon as the conspirators were discovered, they and the clean-up team would jump to the rendezvous point, meet with Nash and Bevan, and get the hell out of the 16th century.

And everyone's instructions were very, very clear. At the first sign of this timeline dissolving there was to be no lingering. Whether the job was completed or not there were to be no heroics. Everyone was to return to TPHQ and safety. Regardless.

And if we weren't back at Number Five we'd dissolve, too. So, we ran.

We ran and ran. The road was a quagmire but we squelched and splattered along as quickly as we could.

And then, on one of our detours around a boggy bit, I fell over a rabbit. Hey – these things happen. It was dark. It was wet. I wasn't looking where I was going. It had been a long day. Let's see anyone else do better. It's typical, isn't it? We'd done the job and now the god of historians had abandoned us. Sometimes I think these deities need a good talking-to.

Actually, it wasn't the rabbit itself I fell over, but the snare stretched between two pegs, so – you know – quite forgivable under the circumstances.

If this was one of Calvin Cutter's masterpieces then I – as the heroine, obviously – would have broken my ankle and have to be carried along by the hero who would randomly have to tear off his shirt. As it was, I cursed horribly, scrambled to my feet, aimed a kick at one of the pegs and missed. Ellis stood solidly nearby and showed no signs of removing any sort of garment.

'You should look where you're going,' he said, mildly enough, and I was all set to incinerate him on the spot but at that moment something rustled in the undergrowth. Someone was out there. This was Tudor England. No one went out in the rain and murk unless they were up to no good. Just like us.

I think the same thought went through both our heads – Robert Dudley and his men were out here somewhere.

A chilling thought. We hadn't reckoned on Dudley being so close. I knew he'd brought a couple of hundred men into Norfolk. In the original timeline he'd missed Mary and spent his time capturing towns, including King's Lynn where he'd proclaimed Jane queen. But this wasn't the original timeline. This was unexpected and alarming. That he or his men could be so close . . .

'Follow my lead,' said Ellis and before I had time to say or do anything, he pushed me to the ground.

I managed to get as far as, 'What the hell?' when he began to fumble underneath my skirt.

Fortunately – for both of us, because he had only micro-seconds to live – the undergrowth rustled again and suddenly there were three men standing around us, together with either two very short men with cold, wet noses or a couple of dogs. They had a lantern with them and there was no chance of escape.

We blinked in the sudden light and did our best to look like two people so carried away by passion they hadn't noticed the pouring rain. Not that easy.

I was unsure whether they were Dudley's men, engaging in a little light poaching to supplement their rations – in which case we were in trouble – or actual poachers, come to check on their traps – in which case we were in trouble – or gamekeepers who thought they'd caught a couple of poachers – in which case we were in trouble. Whichever it was, there seemed to be a common theme and it would be sensible not to hang around.

Ellis rolled off me and we both stood up. Ignoring the men around us, I rounded on him and shouted in English.

'What the hell was that all about? Are you some sort of pervert?'

He yelled back. 'Well, you don't think that was a particularly pleasant experience for me, do you? There are any number of women whose skirts I would like to investigate more closely but, trust me, you're not any of them. Besides, Leon would rip out my spleen.'

'Never mind Leon ripping out your bloody spleen – I'll do it myself. Just stand still a moment.'

I could see the men watching us. The lantern cast dramatically long shadows in the half-light. The dogs were completely uninterested, all their attention on the dead rabbit. The men were grinning. Good.

Ellis hadn't finished. 'And quite honestly, Max – and I say this as a concerned friend – you've really let yourself go a little, haven't you? I mean, I know a lot of women regard having a baby as an excuse not to . . .'

I uttered a scream of rage. 'Who are you kidding, buster? If I'd known that one day you were going to be firkling around my

146

nether regions, I'd have had six kids at least – and possibly major psychiatric counselling as well. Left.'

I swung my left hand, going for an open palm slap. Partly because the sound effects would be good and it would do him less damage, but mainly because I always forget to untuck my thumb when I punch.

The slap echoed around the trees. I swear one or two men winced. Even the dogs looked up.

He rode the blow as best he could – although I suspected we were going to be discussing this for at least the next two miles or so – and staggered backwards, not coincidentally kicking the lantern over as he went.

Sudden blackness fell.

He seized my wrist. At least, I assumed it was Ellis – although at that moment it's fair to say I would have gone off with anyone – and we raced off into the gloom under the trees.

There was an instant's surprised shouting behind us but we were a considerable distance away by that time. And they were in darkness. They'd have to find the lantern, check it wasn't broken and whether there was still any oil in it, find their tinder boxes and get it lit again. By the time they'd done that we'd be in the next county.

It was the dogs I was worried about, but they'd been ratty, terrier types, more suited for plunging down rabbit holes than pursuing people and ripping their throats out. Had they been mastiffs or hounds I'd have been seriously concerned.

We flew through the trees with Ellis flicking his torch every few seconds, to avoid bumpy ground and low-hanging branches. I was just feeling we could reasonably slow down and catch our breath a little when suddenly there wasn't anything under my feet.

I toppled sideways. Ellis fell on top of me and we rolled for what seemed like a considerable length of time. Where had the trees gone? We were in a wood and just one to halt our progress would have been useful.

We landed in a tangle. I couldn't move. My skirts had wrapped themselves around me and I had a Time Police officer on top of me. I was soaked, muddy and lost. 'Get off me, you great lump.'

'Hey, I just saved us both.'

'Really – that's the Time Police idea of a successful getaway? Bouncing off the trees and falling off a cliff? To say nothing of assaulting a female colleague. I'm reporting you for harassment in the workplace.'

'You don't think I enjoyed it, do you? Trust me, I am washing this hand as soon as I possibly can. Decontaminating, even.'

'Oh, don't be such a baby. And while we're on the subject, try that again and you could lose the entire arm.'

'I don't doubt it for a moment. For how much longer are we going to lie in the rain yelling at each other?'

'Until you tell me where we are.'

'How should I know? Thanks to your left hook I have major concussion.'

'From that teeny tiny slappette? I had no idea the Time Police were so fragile.'

'Do you think they were Dudley's men?'

'Could be. Although I didn't see a badge, did you?'

'No, too dark. We need to get a move on.'

He hauled me to my feet. We plunged into the gloom again and ran straight into three horses tied to a tree. And I do mean straight into them. Markham himself couldn't have done a better job.

They snorted and plunged a little, but none of them tried to eat us. It seemed unlikely that poachers would have horses, so it seemed reasonable to assume they had been Dudley's men. It also seemed reasonable to assume the god of historians hadn't completely abandoned us, after all. If I hadn't fallen over the rabbit then we'd never have found the horses. I felt a little guilty.

'Quick,' said Ellis, flashing his torch.

I scrabbled at a wet knot. Voices sounded in the distance and I thought I saw a light flashing among the trees.

I pulled the tether free. The horses were haltered but not hobbled. Note to self: write thank-you note to god of historians.

I seized a handful of wet mane and heaved myself aboard. 'Which way?'

He consulted something. 'South-east-ish.'

'You go first. I'll follow.'

It was raining. It was dark. And the horses didn't want to move. A stubborn yellow horse flickered across my memories. Anything was better than being on foot, though.

We pushed on through the woods. At this rate, now that we had horses, we would reach the pod with plenty of time to spare.

No problem at all.

14

We reached the road again and Ellis flashed his torch. 'I have good news and I have bad news.'

'Give me the good.'

'We're back on the road again.'

'And no sign of our pursuers?'

'No,' he said. 'They'll be legging it back to their camp as fast as they can go.'

'With their rabbit.'

'With their trampled rabbit, yeah.'

'To find their horses gone.'

'Yeah,' he said with satisfaction. 'We've really ruined someone's day, haven't we?'

'And the bad?'

He flashed his torch up and down the road. 'I'm so turned around I don't know where we are.'

'Wait,' I said, with the practised non-panic of the frequently lost. 'Let's start using our brains.' I paused for any comment he might feel behoved to utter but he said nothing. The horses stood quietly, heads hung low. The rain pattered down around us. 'I know time is short but there's no sense in us careering off in the wrong direction and ending up even further away from the pod. We need to think. A socking great baggage train passed this way recently. It must have left some trace.'

'It's pouring down,' he said. 'Everything will have been washed away. Or turned to mud.'

'Yes, but you saw the size of the ruts in the road. I bet a lot of people will have done what we did and walked on the verges. We look for hoofprints, footprints, whatever, and take it from there.'

We poked about for ages. The trouble was that, prior to the rain, the ground had been so hard and dry there were no footprints of any kind. In any direction. I stayed back and held the horses well out of the way while Ellis ranged up and down, looking for some signs a number of people had passed this way and, most importantly of all, in which bloody direction they'd been travelling. I couldn't believe he didn't have some sort of direction-finding device.

'I can't believe you don't have some sort of magic box. You are the Time Police, after all.'

'I do have a magic box. It bounces signals off the ionosphere. In layman's terms, the beacon broadcasts on high frequency.'

'Well, that's good.'

'Not really. It has a very limited lifespan and therefore won't kick in until it's remotely activated by our signal.'

'Well, that's bad.'

'Believe it or not, Max, we don't want to go polluting the timeline with unnecessary tech so everything has built-in obsolescence in case we have to leave it behind for some reason.'

'How limited is the life expectancy?'

'About two days.'

Something bleeped.

'There you go,' I said, preparing to mount. 'Problem solved.'

'Not quite.'

I had a sudden and very nasty feeling.

'That wasn't the beacon, Max. That was our timer. Our three hours is up.'

Bloody hell – that was quick. But at least now we had nothing to lose. I was about to say, 'Look, just choose a direction and we'll go with that. At least we'll have a fifty per cent chance of being right,' when he said, 'Aha.'

'What? Aha what?'

'Broken twigs – and yes . . . something here.' He straightened up and said with conviction, 'This way.'

I swung myself aboard my horse and as I did so the bleeper bleeped again. Because that's what they do and it's bloody irritating.

Now we knew the way we could go faster. And we did. We still had a couple of miles to cover and heavy clouds were obscuring the moon, which slowed us even further, but he set a good pace and I followed on behind. We seemed to be cantering through the darkness for considerably more than two miles. Surely we should have picked up the beacon by now. I called to him. 'How much further?'

He pulled up and I moved alongside him. He wasn't looking at me and I realised what he'd done.

I said, 'That thing about knowing which way to go – you made it up, didn't you?'

He nodded, still not looking at me. 'Yeah. I couldn't see much in the dark so I took a chance. Looks like I was wrong.' He couldn't look at me. 'Sorry, Max.'

I put my hand on his forearm. 'No, you did the right thing. I would have done the same.'

'Which direction would you have chosen?'

'Same as you,' I said, because there was no point in saying anything else.

'Max, I've dragged us two miles in the wrong direction.'

'Not your fault. It's this stupid mist. Everything looks different.'

Something beeped again.

'That bloody thing's getting on my nerves. We know our time's up. Can't you switch it off?'

'I . . . did,' he said slowly.

We sat like a pair of idiots until realisation kicked in. It was the homer. I turned to him, a sudden hope in my heart. There might be a chance for us after all. He was staring at some sort of readout.

'Bloody hell, Matthew. How much further?'

'I'm not sure . . . the signal's not brilliant.'

'Curse this lack of Tudor orbiting communication satellites.'

'Indeed,' he said absently. 'Whatever were they thinking? A little less religion and a little more technical progress would have done everyone some good. But I think . . . under a mile, Max. Maybe a little less. We're nearly there. We've nearly made it.'

I said hoarsely, 'Matthew . . .'

He was busy fastening his pouch again. 'Mm?'

'Matthew . . .'

'What?'

I had to swallow hard. 'Behind us.'

He turned around, stared for a moment and then said softly, 'Shit.'

We both stared. I'd thought it was just white mist. Just ordinary white mist. The sort you get in a woodland area after heavy rainfall. And then the sun comes out and there's a lot of steaming and smelly, wet earth and then it all burns away in the sunshine and everything is fine again.

Not this time. This was the wrong sort of mist. And now that there was no sound of hoofbeats, now that we were alone in the silence, I could hear a faint buzzing. No, not a buzzing – more a sort of hum. The sort of noise you hear sometimes if you stand near a mega pylon.

I became aware the rain had stopped as well and a rather nasty silence had fallen. I could hear no birdsong, no woodland noises, not even the plopping sound of moisture falling from leaf to leaf. I felt the hair on the back of my head lift.

The horses didn't like it either. Tired they might be but they knew that mist did not bode well. Ellis's horse snorted and plunged. Mine was trying to walk backwards.

'Easy,' I said. 'Everything's fine,' but horses are considerably more intelligent than people and they knew very well everything was not fine. Ellis's horse reared again.

'Get down, Max,' he said. 'They're not happy and it's not far now. We can't risk either of us being injured.'

He was right. I scrambled down and no sooner had I done so than my horse ripped the reins from my fingers and they both thundered off into the woods. Away from the mist. And much good it would do them.

We stood and stared at the billowing misty silence. And beyond that – nothingness. There just simply wasn't anything there. Not blackness or whiteness or fog or anything. Just a deep, endless nothingness. An absence of anything. I'd once experienced something very similar and it hadn't been pleasant then. It was even less so now.

I felt my stomach turn over. Ellis was gripping my arm. Hard. I hadn't really given much thought as to how it would happen. My mind had been completely taken up with thoughts of Mary Tudor

154

and her letter. I know we'd blithely talked about the universe rolling up – as if it was an old carpet no one wanted any longer – and disappearing. We'd talked about bubble universes which presumably would just pop out of existence, but it dawned on me now, with a rather sick feeling to my stomach, that I hadn't really thought *how* it would happen.

The mist was creeping closer. It wasn't fast but it was inexorable. No power on earth could stop it. No barrier could even slow it down. It simply enveloped everything in its path. Slow, silent and unstoppable. I couldn't drag my eyes away. There was something hypnotic about it. My legs felt heavy and useless. I think that, left to myself, I'd have just stood and watched it bear down on me.

'Come on,' said Ellis, and his voice had that dead quality you get in an acoustic room. 'We have to move.'

We did move. We were faster than the mist but we couldn't go on forever. We were already tired. We'd been blown up in London. We'd walked seven miles. We'd interfered with History. And then we'd part-walked and part-ridden most of those same seven miles back again. And some of us weren't as young as we used to be.

Ellis led the way. I fixed my eyes on his back and ran, slipping, sliding, occasionally tripping over some hidden obstacle but never stopping. My lungs began to burn. My heart was pounding fit to burst and that wasn't because of the exertion. I didn't dare look behind me.

For God's sake – how much further?

I glanced from side to side as I ran. White mist was everywhere around us but whether this was post-rain mist or end-of-the-world mist I couldn't tell and I certainly wasn't going to take the time to investigate.

Ahead of me, I could hear Ellis's proximity meter blipping away.

'Half a mile,' he shouted over his shoulder. 'Probably less,' and, indeed, I thought I could see the chimneys of Hunsdon, dark against the mist.

That was a nasty moment. We had assumed the mist was behind us but suppose it was all around us instead. Suppose everything centred on us. Suppose – my heart and legs both failed me here – suppose the pod had already gone. Swallowed up into nothingness. Suppose there was nothing to do but wait at the centre of an ever-contracting world. Accept our fate. We'd saved the timeline – I hoped – and our reward was annihilation.

I spared a thought for Clerk and the others. Had they made it out? Or were they also trapped in another contracting bubble awaiting their own fate?

Ellis slowed and stopped. I just avoided running into him. He was looking back over my shoulder so I did the same.

Shit. It was going to be bloody close. Too bloody close. We weren't going to make it.

I honestly thought we'd get away in time. We always did. We're St Mary's. Well, one of us was. I think I even thought a grateful History would smooth our way a little and I'd been wrong about everything.

No, I hadn't. History hadn't abandoned us. History had caused me to trip over the rabbit. And yes, History had put those men in our path, but more importantly, had put their horses in our path. Literally. My forehead still throbbed from the impact. The horses had bought us the extra minutes we needed and we'd been given those extra minutes for a reason, I was convinced of it.

The bleeper was bleeping like a mad thing so we knew we weren't far away.

The humming noise had increased. I could hear it over my own

156

heavy breathing. White tendrils of mist curled silently among the trees.

'There,' I said suddenly, pointing.

We ran. I could see the mist creeping along the ground everywhere. What would happen when it touched me? Would I lose my feet? Would I have to drag myself to the pod on bleeding stumps? Where do I get these thoughts from?

I had only enough breath to pant, 'Door,' and we crashed into the pod, which was a festival of flashing red lights. The computer was shouting, 'Warning. Warning. Warning.' Presumably in case we'd failed to notice anything amiss.

I shouted, 'Shut up. Shut up.'

'Yes,' said Ellis, panting. 'Shouting at a machine. Always a sign of advanced intelligence.'

I got the door closed and hit the mute control.

In the silence I could hear a faint buzzing. I stared wildly round. Was it in here with us? Where was it?

'It's in there,' said Ellis, pressing his ear against the door to our tiny toilet.

'Keep that door shut.'

'Don't worry.'

As if that would make any difference.

Was it my imagination or was the door beginning to waver? I remembered Commander Hay's face. No time to stop and think. I thanked my forethought in having the return coordinates laid in ready.

'Computer – emergency extraction.'

The world went black.

We landed with a crash that threw us both to the floor. I decided that with the sort of day I was having, it was probably wisest to stay put. We both did.

Ellis groaned. 'I have to say, Max – and no offence – but the Time Police do it better.'

I wiped blood off my nose. He might have a point but I was so happy to be in one piece I couldn't be bothered to argue.

I heaved myself to my feet and inspected our impressive array of flashing red lights. There was some damage to a few minor systems but the structure appeared to be intact so I reckoned I could ignore most of it.

I reached down and offered Ellis a hand up. 'All right?'

He was carrying out a limb check. 'Everything seems to be here but I am *not* having a good day.'

'This is a St Mary's pod,' I said. 'Therefore, St Mary's terms and conditions apply.'

'What?'

'Are you still alive?'

He patted himself. 'Yes.'

'Then according to St Mary's, it's a good day.'

'St Mary's can piss off,' he said, rubbing his elbow.

Bloody ingratitude.

We decontaminated, I got the door open and we exited the pod. Very carefully. I'm sure they were expecting us and therefore we wouldn't die in a hail of fire as we emerged but nevertheless . . .

We were back at TPHQ and the first thing I saw was the clean-up squad waiting for us. Why were they back already? I blinked. Why were they here and not instigating riot and rebellion across the land? Bollocks. Typical Time Police. Obviously if you want a good riot you stick with St Mary's.

'What happened?' I said in alarm. 'What went wrong?'

They ignored me, addressing their remarks to the important member of the team. Everything had gone well, they said to Ellis. No need to panic, they said to me. Queen Mary was safely on the throne. The main conspirators had been identified, had their ears whispered in, been threatened, been bribed, been intimidated, whatever it took. It hadn't been that difficult, they said.

'Did everyone get back safely?' asked Ellis.

A mech nodded. 'You're the last. And just in time by the looks of it.'

I turned to look at the pod.

Oh shit.

The back right-hand corner seemed to have borne the brunt. The outer casing there was black and bubbled. As if it had been burned. Or incinerated. Or melted. I reached out and touched it. Hard and cold. I had no idea what Leon was going to say but the structure itself appeared intact so, with luck, he'd only complain for a week or so.

Ellis was still looking down at himself.

'Ah,' said a mech, wandering past. 'Wet, muddy and bloody. You've been out with St Mary's, haven't you?'

I turned. 'Speaking of which . . . ?'

'Safely returned. They decontaminated, had a quick check-up and a hot meal and then we dropped them off at St Mary's. Maxwell, you're to meet them there when you've finished here. Oh, and Commander Hay wants to see you and your reports as soon as possible.'

Everyone was really interested in the mist and the disappearing world.

There was a polite interest in my stellar work with Mary Tudor but it was the vanishing universe everyone wanted to hear about. I was writing reports about it for two days.

The original timeline was reasserting itself, Ellis assured me. Apparently, this wasn't the first time something like this had happened, but hadn't everything gone well and thanks for the help, Max. Couldn't have done it without you.

I still couldn't quite believe what I'd done. And God knows what Dr Bairstow was going to say.

I wanted to get back to St Mary's as quickly as possible. Firstly, to catch up with Clerk and the others and, secondly, to report to Dr Bairstow, because I wasn't too sure how he was going to react to our efforts to restore the timeline. And to see Leon, of course. And to have a decent cup of tea. Several decent cups of tea. And to see what the History Department had been up to in my absence. And to see if Lingoss and Peterson were inching their way towards an understanding. And to see how Hunter was. And to check up on the loonies in R&D. And a million other things as well.

The Time Police, though, had other ideas. Bloody Time Police and their bureaucracy. On the upside, their decontamination procedures were so good that, despite all that Tudor water, I didn't have to spend any time in their medical centre.

'This isn't St Mary's,' said Ellis. 'We move straight on to the next assignment. We don't spend all our time lolling around and eating grapes.'

I saw Commander Hay alone, so it was safe to talk.

'Mr Clerk and his team were returned to St Mary's nearly three days ago now, Max. There were no casualties. They were dropped off at the usual place. I understand Mr Clerk was somewhat apprehensive of Dr Bairstow's reaction and felt matters would proceed more smoothly if . . .'

'If the Time Police weren't actually on the premises.'

She smiled. 'Something like that. I understand you have been able to offer some useful insights into unstable bubble universes.'

'That's kind of you to say so, ma'am. Although I should point out I was nearly blind with terror at the end.'

'You are comparatively uninjured, however.'

I agreed that I was comparatively uninjured. 'Will this have affected our plans at all, Commander?'

'I don't think so. It's been a slight – a very slight – delay. Nothing more.' She paused. 'I think Matthew's role in all this is quite interesting, don't you?'

I tried to downplay Matthew's quite interesting role in all this. 'Mm? No, not really, ma'am.'

I could see she wanted to talk about Matthew and I didn't, so I distracted her by requesting permission to jump back to St Mary's to return Number Five to its rightful owners, check on Clerk and his team's story, and to report to Dr Bairstow in case they had any more 16th-century assignments planned. I told her it seemed sensible for St Mary's to avoid that period until things had settled down a little.

She blinked – possibly at my use of the word 'sensible' – and hesitated, but it was a perfectly reasonable request. And I'd laboured day and night for them for weeks with no time off. And it was reasonable to want to see my husband again. She had no reason to say no and she didn't. I was granted three days' leave. I thanked her politely and went off to make preparations.

Given the state of Number Five, I was expecting all sorts of grief from the Technical Section, who tend to take this sort of thing personally. I don't know why – the outer casing is only cosmetic – a bit of duct tape and some string and it would be fine. It would be interesting to see whether Leon's pleasure at seeing me was greater or lesser than his dismay at the damage to one of his beloved pods. Anyway, I was braced for criticism and condemnation when I opened the door – and there was no one there.

There was nothing anywhere. I don't mean the rather nasty Nothing of the 16th century, but the nothing of no Leon, no techies, no pods, no nothing. Just a vast, empty, echoing hangar with a couple of broken packing cases in one corner and a flatbed with a stack of empty archive boxes in another. Leon's office was empty. As was IT. And not just empty of people. Empty of everything. Just four walls, a ceiling and a floor. I could see marks on the wall where various bits of equipment had once been. Even the traditional calendar of cute kittens doing various cute things was gone.

All of Hawking was empty, which was puzzling because even if everyone was out on a Big Job, there would be some techies here. And Polly Perkins' IT staff should be either staring at incomprehensible screens or shouting at people for getting toast crumbs lodged in their keyboards.

The blast doors were up so they hadn't all blown themselves

out of existence and there were no scorch marks on the walls so there hadn't been a fire. This was weird.

I left the hangar and set off down the Long Corridor for the Great Hall.

The silence should have warned me, but I was passing the time rehearsing my arguments and explanations to Dr Bairstow, intending to finish with a triumphant, 'So you see, sir, hardly anything for you to worry about after all.'

The Hall was empty. Gone were the tables piled high with files. And the scribble-covered whiteboards. There were no scrappy bits of paper pinned to the walls with people's passwords scrawled on them. No historians arguing, or waving their arms around, or building data stacks, or scarfing biscuits and tea on an industrial scale. The silence was deafening.

The dining room was empty. No one was troughing through their second plate of shepherds' pie.

Wardrobe was empty. No chatter. No half-completed costumes hanging around the room. No whirr of sewing machines.

I stood in the empty Hall, looking about me, confused and bewildered.

St Mary's had gone.

I couldn't take it in. I'd been at St Mary's for almost all of my working life. It's my home. No matter how badly things have gone – and sometimes it's been quite spectacular – St Mary's had always been there waiting for me.

For some reason – and don't ask me why – I was reminded of Bashford telling me that after uni he'd been quite reluctant to leave the parental nest.

'I was on to a good thing, Max. Board and lodging at a very affordable rate. My laundry done every Wednesday. As far as I was concerned, I was there forever. My parents dropped tons of hints and I ignored them all. Then one day I came back from holiday. I'd been to Marbella. This was in the days when you could, of course. I staggered in through the front door, heavily tanned and even more heavily hungover, clutching my duty frees and my straw donkey, and my dad said, "Don't bother unpacking, son. We've sold the house. Me and your mum have bought a bungalow in Skegness."'

I'd laughed when he told me the story, but now I knew exactly how he'd felt.

In the interests of giving everyone the complete picture, I've spent some time describing all the many things that weren't there. Time to move on to what actually was there.

There were six very large men pointing very large weapons at me.

They certainly weren't Time Police. Having spent some time with them, I reckoned I could pick one out from ten miles away. In the dark. With my eyes shut. I didn't know who this lot were, but they weren't Time Police.

I said, 'Good morning,' quite politely, because Markham always insists on standards being maintained.

No one returned my cheery greeting.

'Well,' I said, backing away. 'I'm obviously in the wrong place. Sorry to have troubled you. I'll be off now.'

There were two more behind me. Bollocks.

I turned back again.

'Put your hands on your head.'

'No.'

'I won't tell you again.'

'Good. I'm glad you've grasped my intransigence so quickly.'

I looked around, trying to think. My first thought was that these were Ronan's men, but my second thought told me they probably weren't. They wore official badges and insignia and looked quite a considerable step up from the sort of people he usually had working for him.

They were military. Shit – this wasn't good.

I tumbled to the truth at the same time as he appeared at the top of the stairs.

Malcolm Bloody Halcombe.

Bloody, bloody bollocking hell. Out of the frying pan, into the fire.

16

Time for a quick word of explanation, I think.

Mr Halcombe – or the idiot Halcombe as he was usually known – had been Thirsk's representative at St Mary's. St Mary's had had a spot of trouble with which I was not unconnected and, in retaliation, Thirsk had foisted him on us in what he, Halcombe, fondly imagined was a supervisory category. We'd packed him off to a leprosy clinic – you honestly don't want to get on the wrong side of us – and then Dr Bairstow had very publicly sacked him and we'd thought we'd seen the last of him.

Well, I thought we'd seen the last of him, although I suspected Dr Bairstow had had other thoughts. Now – now that it was too late – I remembered he'd once warned me about his possible successor. Had he been sacked? Was Halcombe now in charge? And then I remembered that Hawking was empty and that St Mary's was deserted. If he was in charge, he was presiding over nothing.

On the other hand, he did appear to have brought his own army. Had St Mary's all been arrested and bundled off to some maximum-security unit somewhere?

'Oh,' I said, because I can't help myself. 'You're back. How nice. And you've brought some of your little friends with you.'

He regarded me without any particular joy. 'Mrs Farrell.'

166

I sighed and surpassed him in joylessness. 'Malcolm Halcombe.'

I don't know why I bothered. There was a huge hole where his sense of humour should be.

He waited for me to ask what was going on and I refused to give him the satisfaction. 'Bit foggy today, don't you think?'

He said heavily, 'Where are they?'

Well, wasn't that interesting? Wherever St Mary's was, he hadn't had anything to do with their disappearance. I emphasised my own ignorance. 'Who?'

That wasn't a good move. I got a gun in my face. 'Answer the question.'

I fell back on the old favourite. 'I take my instructions from Dr Bairstow.'

'He's not here.'

No, he wasn't. None of them were. But at least they weren't all dead in the basement. Halcombe didn't know where they were either, but I had the advantage over him because I could hazard a very good guess.

We have a remote site. Its location in time and space is a closely guarded secret. Leon and Dr Bairstow set it up years ago. It's a refuge. A safe haven. A place for our pods and archives. The pods for obvious reasons, because you don't want any of those falling into the hands of the wrong people, and the archives because they are a record of events as they actually happened. Before History could be rewritten by the winners. Or by those idiots who want to portray events in a more ... contemporary ... light. Or by religions trying to airbrush some of their less compassionate actions. Or leaders whose stupendous military triumph turns out to be not so stupendous after all. Or a politician who says or does something stupid.

167

You'd be amazed at the number of people who want to rewrite History. Sometimes their reasons for doing so are quite benevolent. Or so they tell themselves. Sometimes they mean well. But you can't do it. It doesn't matter why you want to do it – you can't. You shouldn't. Because once you start messing about with it, the actual truth becomes distorted, then blurred and then finally lost altogether, which is why our job is to record and document major historical events in contemporary time and file the results in our archive. Dr Bairstow once said our archive was our heart and he was correct. So, he and Leon had established the remote site. A place of refuge for St Mary's while they avoid whoever thinks tampering with History is a good idea. A place to wait until everyone comes to their senses.

I was pretty certain that was where they were now. And it was no use asking me where and when the remote site was because I didn't know. Dr Bairstow obviously knew, and so did Leon. Major Guthrie would have known, so Markham would now know. And that was probably it. I wasn't even sure whether Peterson as Deputy Director would know. He wasn't here, so he probably did.

'Actually,' said Halcombe, bringing me back to the present crisis. He was standing in Dr Bairstow's old place on the half-landing – obviously he'd been picking up tips from the master himself – 'I'm very glad to see you. I have some questions for you.'

I shrugged. 'Ask away. I don't work here any longer so I've no idea what's been happening recently. Can't help you, I'm afraid.'

'I'm quite sure you can't; only an idiot would entrust you with important information. But I do think you might be instrumental in helping me get the answers I require.'

I gave him my best *I doubt that* look, but inside I was suddenly very, very afraid.

And for good reason. They were marching Tim Peterson down the stairs. Closely followed by North, Clerk and Bashford. But no Evans. Where was Evans?

Halcombe must have read my thoughts. 'I'm afraid Mr Evans isn't very well at the moment. He's having a – what shall I call it? – a lie down.'

I knew exactly what he meant. Evans was stocky and pugnacious and the nearest thing we had to a tank. I could only imagine what it had taken to put him down. And the others weren't in much better condition.

They all looked exhausted. Peterson in particular looked as if he hadn't slept for days. As he stood alongside Halcombe under the roof lantern, I could make out faint bruising high on one cheekbone and around one eye.

He grinned at me and it was a very creditable effort.

'What ho, Max.'

I laughed and that was a very creditable effort as well. 'Don't let Markham hear you say that.'

'What are you doing here?'

'Oh, I just popped in as I was passing. You?'

'Keeping an eye on things. As you do.'

I turned to the others. 'Mr Clerk, I believe congratulations are in order. Good work with Wyatt's Rebellion.'

'And you too, Max. You found her then? What was she like?'

'More amenable and less religious than I expected.'

'Ah, well. Give her time.'

'Indeed.'

Halcombe interrupted our pleasantries to repeat himself. 'I'm very pleased to see you this morning, Mrs Farrell,' and we all blinked at the unlikeliness of that statement. 'I believe you may be instrumental in getting me what I want.'

'Which is?'

'I'm not sure I'm quite ready to divulge my objective just yet.'

I rolled my eyes. Something I would never have dared to do with Dr Bairstow. 'Another example of muddled thinking, Halcombe. If you don't tell me what you want, then you can hardly complain if I am unable to assist, can you?'

'Actually, I had intended your role to have more of a passive nature. Until Dr Peterson tells me what I want to know, of course.'

Shit. I didn't like the sound of that. Obviously, he wanted to know where St Mary's was. I wondered if he was aware of the existence of our remote site. Something inside me said yes, he was. Not that it would do him any good. He could ask me until the cows came home but I couldn't tell him what I didn't know. The information was above my pay grade, so to speak.

He descended the stairs slowly so I'd have time to experience the fear and apprehension he thought he engendered, whereas the reality was that, despite my predicament, I was hard put not to laugh. Until I looked past him to Peterson, who suddenly had that blank, expressionless look that indicated he was very worried indeed – and if Tim was worried, then so was I.

Halcombe stood in front of me. Two soldiers took up positions on either side. I'm not sure what they thought I was going to do.

'So, Mrs Farrell, St Mary's seems to have disappeared.'

I looked around. 'Have they?'

'A great shame. I had an important assignment for them.'

'They don't take their instructions from you, Halcombe.'

'They will now that I have you.'

'They take their instructions from Dr Bairstow. We all do.'

'Not any more, you don't. I am now in command at St Mary's.'

I stared around at the empty building. 'How's that working out for you?'

A soldier stepped up. He wore the rank of major. He raised his gun. Halcombe put his hand on his arm. 'Not just at the moment, Major. Let's give her a chance, shall we?'

I shrugged. 'You can call yourself Titania, Queen of the Fairies, for all I care. It looks as if there is no St Mary's here to command. It's all gone. Nothing left.'

'I think we both know that's not true any longer, don't we?'

I went suddenly cold, because he was talking about Number Five, squatting, battered, on its plinth in Hawking. Suddenly, thanks to me, Halcombe had acquired a pod. And now I would have to be very, very careful.

I shook my head. 'No. Sorry. Not with you.'

'Oh, I think you are.'

'No, I'm not. Really.'

'Allow me to enlighten you.'

'No, it's OK. I don't want to put you to any trouble. I'll just take myself off.'

I'd made a huge mistake coming back to St Mary's. I couldn't be in a worse place at a worse time. I had to get the pod out of here as quickly as possible. I didn't dare look at Peterson and the others. As calmly as I could I said, 'I told you, Halcombe, I don't work for you. I'm under no obligation to you. I don't actually work for St Mary's any longer, as everyone here can attest. I don't know what you want but I'm unable to give it to you.'

I turned to go. I'd actually taken two or three steps when he said, 'But now, thanks to you, we have a pod.'

Shit. Shit, shit, shit. Bloody, bloody bollocking hell. I said calmly, 'I'm sorry – were you talking to me?'

'You came here in a pod, I believe, thus providing the final ingredient. I had historians but no pod but now, thanks to you, I have both. You just couldn't stay away, could you? I knew if I waited long enough you would turn up. And here you are. I have historians, I have a pod. And now I have you.'

He paused so I could fully appreciate the trouble we were in. And we were. I didn't dare look at Peterson. I stared down at the floor, keeping my face as expressionless as I could, and tried to think.

Yes, I'd been stupid to come back here. But, to be fair, I hadn't known that at the time. Dr Bairstow had obviously gone to a great deal of effort to clear St Mary's out of harm's way and I'd gone and landed them straight back in it again. It was small consolation that Halcombe would have had Number Five anyway if Clerk and the others had returned to St Mary's in the normal manner. He'd still have been waiting for them. That must be why Peterson was still here – to give them the coordinates for the remote site so they could all jump there together. So, Peterson did know the location. But Halcombe had turned up before Clerk and the others. The Time Police had dropped them off and jumped away because they never hang around and Clerk's team had walked straight into trouble. And now I was here. With a pod. Bringing even more trouble. I was suddenly very, very afraid for Peterson.

I started walking towards the doors. I couldn't think of anything else to do.

'Turn around, Mrs Farrell.'

Reluctantly I turned. Peterson and North each had a gun to their heads. Clerk and Bashford had been pushed against a wall.

'Well, Mrs Farrell?'

'Well, what, Halcombe?'

'Which of your friends would you like me to begin with?'

There was a cold lump in my stomach. The only thing I could do for them was to convince Halcombe they were unimportant. That whatever he threatened them with meant nothing to me. Somehow, I managed to shrug. 'I don't care. Whichever you like. As long as it's not me.'

I started walking again. It was a long way to the door. I was never going to make it.

I heard a shout behind me and the sounds of a scuffle. When I turned back, Peterson was struggling with three of the guards. Two of them pinned his arms – the other reversed his gun and struck him in the face. They let him fall to the ground.

'As you can see, I mean business,' said Halcombe, calmly. 'One down. Who will be next, I wonder?'

I considered. What would happen if I forced him to kill us all? He'd have no hostages left, but then he'd just ship the pod off to somewhere. They'd strip it down and reverse-engineer it. I'd no idea how easy that would be or how long it would take but that wasn't the point. We'd all still be dead.

I had to start using my brain. The first priority was to get the pod away from Halcombe. The second priority was to rescue the hostages. The third priority was to get these bastards out of St Mary's.

'What exactly do you want, Halcombe?'

'I want you to open the pod for me.'

'And then?'

'Lay in some coordinates.'

'What coordinates?'

'That's not necessary for you to know.'

173

'Don't be so bloody silly. Of course I need to know. No historian in their right mind would programme in unverified coordinates. The wrong sequence at the wrong time and the whole pod could be blown to kingdom come.'

It couldn't, actually. Programme in the wrong sequence at the wrong time and the computer would just sigh heavily and request assistance from the nearest technician. But it was enough to make him hesitate.

I folded my arms.

On the floor, Peterson stirred. North pulled herself free of her captors and went to kneel at his side.

Halcombe appeared to come to some sort of decision and took out his wallet. For one mad moment I thought he was going to give me some money. Alas. He rifled through the contents and finally pulled out a piece of paper folded very small which he passed to me.

Curious, I took it from him and unfolded it. I recognised the arrangement immediately. Temporal and spatial coordinates.

I frowned. There was nothing there I recognised. The configuration was completely unknown to me. 'What's this?'

'Your next assignment.'

'What assignment?'

'The one I am instructing you to carry out.'

'Or?'

'Or the condition of some of your colleagues will take a sudden turn for the worse.'

Pillock. 'What are these coordinates?'

'Your destination.'

Dear God, it was like getting blood from a stone. At that moment

I was granted an insight of how truly irritating I can be. Keep plugging away, Maxwell.

'What destination?'

He hesitated but only because he was spinning out the moment. He really, really wanted to tell me. I could see it in his face. I began to have a very bad feeling about this.

I said again, 'What destination, Halcombe?'

Now he was openly smiling. 'Jerusalem. 33AD.'

17

Believe it or not, we do have rules at St Mary's. And yes, I've broken a few of them in my time. For instance, only a few days ago I'd re-routed History. But there's one thing we won't do. As Dr Bairstow puts it, 'We're not in the business of propping up faltering belief systems. Or any belief systems.'

Most of us at St Mary's are godless heathens. Given some of the things we've seen, it's hard to believe in any sort of benign intelligence presiding over human affairs. Especially when you see what's been done in the name of some of those benign intelligences. Most of us have chosen to place our fate in the hands of the universe – or the Technical Section, to give it its mortal manifestation – rather than any specific deity. In a crisis, I myself tend to call on the notoriously unreliable god of historians, and then sort everything out for myself because it's easier and quicker that way.

Of course, occasionally, some idiot will say, 'Oh, why don't you go back to Bethlehem or witness the Sermon on the Mount? Imagine,' they say with enthusiasm, 'if you could prove the Crucifixion actually happened. Wouldn't that be amazing?'

Well, no, is the simple answer to that one.

If you stop and think about things – which would do the most damage? Proving the Crucifixion did happen? Or that it didn't?

And it's not just Christianity. We're equal-opportunity spoil-sports. We have specially designated Sites of Special Significance. They're marked on our version of the Time Map – Triple-Ss. In red, just to make the point. We're not allowed to visit any of them.

Not Mecca. Nor Bethlehem. Nor Medina, nor Benares, nor Bodh Gaya. We don't go anywhere near any of them. And Jerusalem is very dodgy. There isn't much of its History that hasn't got a thumping great red Triple-S stamped across it. By forbidding access to these sites, we protected ourselves from those who wanted information too perilous to know. Religion is dangerous enough. Imagine if you could definitively prove the existence of *a* God – but it wasn't *your* God. We'd all be dead by next Tuesday.

'It's forbidden,' was always our excuse and our answer: 'We can't go there.' Until now, it would seem.

I myself always think God's a bit like the Loch Ness monster. An exciting and mysterious concept which would be too wonderful for words if it were true and too disappointing for words if not. Far better not to know, but to believe. To have faith. After all, isn't having faith what religion is supposed to be all about?

From the look on Halcombe's face, however – no. To him, religion was about something much more important. I suspected money. Or power. Or both. I shrugged my shoulders. I'm a godless heathen. What would I know?

I handed back the piece of paper. 'The date of the Crucifixion is unverified. Jumping to these coordinates would be a waste of time.'

He handed it back to me. 'Current research has narrowed it down to two dates. This one is the most likely.'

I handed it back. 'Too much uncertainty.'

'Not at all. Recent geological studies have managed to pinpoint the date of the earthquake that occurred at the time. There is a very good chance these coordinates will put you right at the centre of events.'

I shook my head. 'I can't do this. I won't do this. The implications are massive.'

'Yes, you will. You will do exactly as you're instructed, Mrs Farrell. Rather a novel experience for you, I think. You will do as I say in this matter. *I* command St Mary's now and, from this moment, this unit will begin to earn its keep.'

I was desperate to learn more about this so I said contemptuously, 'Rubbish,' and turned away.

'No, Mrs Farrell. Not rubbish. Simply good business. After the successful completion of this jump – something that I think will really put us on the map – this unit will undertake a series of sponsored jumps and investigate events on our sponsors' behalf.'

I felt my blood run cold. No wonder Dr Bairstow had cleared St Mary's out of the way. This was his worst nightmare. St Mary's had always made it perfectly clear there were certain things it would never do. Suppress its findings. Amend its records to reflect political bias or current politically correct thinking. Plunder the past for valuable artefacts. Interfere in History at the behest of vested interests.

I worked very hard at keeping my voice calm. 'You mean people will pay you to jump to the historical event of their choice in order for you to "verify" exactly what they tell you to verify. They'll be buying both you and the results. And from there, of course, it's only one step to "arranging" events so the outcome is agreeable to your sponsor. You *idiot*, Halcombe. Who do you think these sponsors will be? Once word gets out that . . . time travel . . . is possible, for how long do you think you'll be allowed to keep it? No,' I said thoughtfully. 'You're just the front man. They've shoved you here

178

with instructions to make this jump because no one knows what will happen if you do but, believe me, if you survive, they'll never let you keep St Mary's. You're just their fall guy.'

As soon as I said the words 'fall guy', I had a sudden memory of a dying Lawrence Hoyle and his 'shadowy figures'. The shadowy figures who had planted him at St Mary's. They'd promised him the opportunity to alter History. To ensure Henry Tudor lost at Bosworth Field. That had been an obsession of his. He'd been manipulated and it had cost him his life. And very nearly mine and Markham's as well. Were these same shadowy figures responsible for Halcombe and this current idiocy?

My priorities had re-written themselves. This had to be stopped. And by me because I couldn't ask anyone else to do it. I had to shut this down right now. At whatever cost. Shame about my plan to take down Clive Ronan, but someone else could pick it up. Someone would get him in the end but that was all in the future. This threat was real and immediate. Always deal with the now first.

I had a plan and it was simple. Well, I hadn't had time to think of anything complicated. I'd do it. Whatever it was they wanted me to do – I'd do it. I'd get the pod out of here, away from them, and then ... Well, it wouldn't be making the return trip. Yes, I'd lay in the coordinates and we'd jump back to wherever he wanted me to be and then one of two things would happen. If the Time Police had fixed the Time Map then our hugely illegal jump would light the place up like Guy Fawkes Night at St Mary's. And if they hadn't – and I had a horrible feeling they wouldn't have because the damage had looked pretty substantial to me – then, once we'd landed, I'd simply shut down the pod and there we'd stay. I wouldn't switch on the screen. I wouldn't even open the door. We'd last a couple of hours – until the air ran out. We'd all die there – including, regrettably, that promising historian Maxwell – but most importantly, the pod would never come back. It would be out of Halcombe's reach forever. It would be out of everyone's reach until the Time Police tracked it down. But, with luck, I'd have sent a clear message. That there are some jumps you never come back from.

One day, St Mary's would reassert itself and the pod would be brought back. Too late for me, of course – too late for any of its occupants – but that was just my tough luck. My duty was clear. Get the pod away from Halcombe. Nothing was more important. And I had to make sure I was the one who did it. I couldn't – wouldn't – ask anyone else to do this.

I also had to be careful not to give in too easily.

'I'm not doing this, Halcombe. You're insane. Are you trying to start a global war?'

'I'm trying to start a global peace. Imagine if we could do away with the uncertainty. Imagine if we could actually *show* people the Crucifixion taking place. The benefits would be . . .'

I cut across him. 'And suppose we come back and say it didn't. That everything people think they know happened never actually did. That it's all one big fairy story. What would be the effects then?'

'Well, obviously, we wouldn't tell people *that.*'

And that, folks, is the difference between time travel and investigating major historical events in contemporary time.

I shook my head. 'I don't care. I still won't do it. None of us will.'

'I had anticipated such an attitude. So really, it's just a case of deciding who to use to make my point.' He began to pace, thoroughly enjoying his big moment. 'Let us all think carefully.

180

Who here has the least value? Who has annoyed me the most?' He turned to face me. 'Who is in need of a much-deserved lesson?'

'No idea,' I said.

'Oh, I think you do.'

'Well, yes, I do, but I thought it would be rude to point out it's you. Not in front of your men. Although it would be good to stop you talking before everyone dies of boredom.'

'I don't think you'll find the next hour boring at all, Mrs Farrell.'

'I wouldn't be too sure of that. I have a really short attention span.'

'Oh, I think this will focus even your wandering mind.' He thrust his face into mine. 'You fell off the roof, didn't you? I'm sure you remember that?'

My mouth went horribly dry. Yes, I did. I remembered it very clearly and I was in absolutely no hurry to repeat the experience.

'I have no doubt, Mrs Farrell, that your ego would allow you happily to sacrifice everyone here but I see no reason why anyone should suffer because of you, so I will issue this instruction – just once. You will take a team consisting of Major Sullivan and two of his men and jump to these coordinates. You are at perfect liberty to refuse and I must confess I rather hope you will.'

He turned slowly. The little man still enjoying his big moment. 'Major, escort Mrs Farrell to the roof. Offer her one last opportunity to save herself, her friends, her unit and so on. If she won't see reason then push her off. Then pick her up, drag her back up the stairs and push her off again.'

He smiled. 'Remember how much it hurt the first time? Now imagine how much it will hurt the second time. And then the third. And we'll keep at it, Mrs Farrell, until either you do as I say, or you're dead, or you're just a blob of jelly on the ground, in which case we'll simply leave you there and start on the next person. Someone will give in. They always do. And if they don't, well, we'll simply make arrangements to transport the pod back to our own facility, leaving you here to finally perform one useful function in your pointless life and be something's lunch. Shall we begin?'

Now was the perfect time to allow myself to be persuaded. I let panic into my voice. Which, trust me, wasn't that difficult.

'You can't do this. It's madness. For God's sake, stop and think about what you're doing.'

Major Sullivan made a gesture. Two soldiers grabbed my arms. There were shouts of protest from everyone. Especially me. They started to drag me up the stairs.

I swallowed and shouted, 'All right. All right. I'll do it.'

He smirked. 'I thought you would. Not so brave now, are you, Mrs Farrell?'

Peterson, who, I think, knew very well what I had planned, croaked, 'Max,' in a shocked voice.

I wheeled on him. 'What choice do I have?' And we both knew what I meant.

'Very wise, Mrs Farrell.'

I stared down at the floor presenting, or so I hoped, the picture of a defeated historian. After long moments, I became aware of the silence. Looking up, my heart sank. I hadn't won yet.

He was still smirking. 'I am aware you think I'm stupid, Mrs Farrell. This *everyone but me is an idiot* attitude of yours is really quite offensive, you know.'

A cold hand of panic clutched at me. Had he guessed my intentions?

He was continuing. 'Major, I think you'd be wise to take a hostage with you. To ensure Mrs Farrell's continued good behaviour.

Time travel is a hazardous business and it's very easy for something to go wrong. I'm certain the presence of . . . let's see . . . Miss North . . . will ensure a problem-free jump. Miss North, if you would step forwards, please.'

No. No, no, no. It was all very well for me – Peterson says I've had a death wish for years – and it was my plan and my decision and my responsibility and my everything else, but I couldn't do this to North. I couldn't take her on board knowing that in an hour or so she'd be expiring on the floor, gasping for breath, possibly pleading with me to open the door . . . to let them out, for God's sake . . . I couldn't do it.

I looked up and she was looking at me. She knew. She wasn't stupid. She knew what I was going to do. What I had to do. She knew.

I found I couldn't speak. I couldn't say a word. My mind played snapshots of Miss North. I remembered how good she was at briefings. Her perpetual arguments with Sykes. I remembered her beating the living daylights out of Herodotus with a wooden tray.

I swallowed and said quietly, 'Celia . . .'

'I know,' she said. 'But you must do your duty, Max. We all must.'

Typical North. She always did her duty and she expected others to do likewise. I think it was her family motto. In Latin, of course.

I looked at Tim, still sprawled on the floor. His face was covered in blood. He was looking at me. He knew what I was up to as well. I hoped to God it wasn't that obvious to everyone else. I couldn't even say goodbye to him, my dearest friend. I couldn't give any clue at all that we wouldn't be back in a couple of hours.

I said, 'That man needs medical attention.'

183

'And he will get it,' said Halcombe. 'As soon as I get what I want.'

I made one last effort. 'The pod will be crowded with five people. I'm not sure we'll even be able to get Miss North in. It's not the Tardis, you know.'

He brushed that nonsense aside and I dared not protest any longer in case I aroused his suspicions. 'I'm sure you'll manage it, Mrs Farrell. Shall we go?'

So we went.

18

Never had the Long Corridor seemed so short. I listened to our footsteps echoing around the empty St Mary's, walking as slowly as I could because I had some vague thought that the longer I could spin this out then the more chance there would be of either a benevolent universe intervening or the god of historians putting in a solid ten minutes' work and getting me out of this.

Actually, I have to say, as I approached Number Five, the damage to the pod looked slightly worse than it had back at TPHQ. As if I didn't have enough on my mind without worrying about structural integrity as well.

I walked around the pod, surveying the melted corner from every angle.

'Goodness gracious,' said Miss North, throwing me a lifeline. 'You cut things a little fine there, Max. Is it safe?'

'Probably not.' I turned to Halcombe. 'You realise this pod could disintegrate in mid-jump.'

He appeared unconcerned. 'I'm told they're very robust.'

'Says the man remaining safely behind.'

I ran my hands over the rock-hard bubbles. 'Everyone needs to be very aware there will be no bathroom facilities on this jump. I hope you all went before you set out.'

Silence.

'Well,' I said, planting the seed. 'If we don't come back then you'll know the reason why.' I turned to Sullivan. 'Don't worry – they say you never know anything about it.'

Not a flicker of expression from any of them. Bollocks.

Halcombe smiled and patted the pod in a proprietary manner I didn't much care for. I bet the pod wasn't that impressed, either.

'I think this is going to turn out to be an extremely profitable enterprise for everyone, don't you? Open the door, please, Mrs Farrell.'

There was no escape. The moment had come. I said, 'Door.'

The door opened.

'Really?' said Halcombe. 'Is that all it takes?'

'Yes, but it has to be said by someone really, really special.'

'For the time being,' he said smugly.

The one thing I really regretted – apart from my long, lingering death, of course – was that I wouldn't be here when the pod failed to return. I wouldn't be around to see that smug look wiped off his stupid face, as days, weeks, months, possibly even years passed with no sign either of the pod or its occupants and it slowly dawned on him he'd let the opportunity of a lifetime slip through his non-leprous fingers.

Ah well – in every life, a little rain must fall and it was my duty to provide the thunderstorm. *Après moi, le déluge*, so to speak. I could speak to Dr Bairstow about making that our motto. And then I remembered – no, I couldn't.

Entering the pod, it occurred to me I might have been a little over-optimistic about our chances of survival. We might not live long enough to die slowly of suffocation. Even setting aside the less than pristine condition of Number Five, no one had ever done this before and there was every possibility that the penalty for jumping to a Triple-S site was instant annihilation. That the pod would explode immediately on landing.

Someone poked me in the back. I hadn't realised I was still standing in the doorway.

'Right,' I said. 'I get the big chair. Pilot's privilege. Miss North will assist me. The rest of you fit yourselves in where you can and if you can't all get in then that's your problem. We jump the minute I've done the preliminaries and laid in the coordinates whether you're ready or not so everyone shut up and let me concentrate.'

'I shall want to oversee you laying in the coordinates,' said Sullivan, pushing North aside. 'If you have any thoughts of taking us somewhere that isn't 1st-century Jerusalem, forget them now. I've been briefed and I know exactly what to look for so don't mess me about. Unless, of course, you want to see your colleague's brains splashed up the walls.'

North gave him a look that would have curdled milk. I was full of admiration. I was probably taking her to her death and she was as steady as a rock. The least I could do was the same.

'I said to shut up. Historian working.'

Sullivan seated himself alongside me. They nudged North into a corner where she waited, her face expressionless. I didn't dare look at her. I didn't trust myself not to say, 'Look, this isn't going to work. Let's have a rethink, shall we,' because actually, in the scheme of things – in *this* scheme of things – North and I weren't important. We're St Mary's and we're all of us very aware of the importance of ensuring neither our pods nor our archive fall into the wrong hands.

My own hands shook as I began to fire up the pod. I could only hope Sullivan and his cohorts would put it down to nerves.

He sat beside me, watching my every move. I worked my way

through all the pre-flight checks. Typically, all the lights were green. I watched hopefully in case any ill-effects from our recent 16th-century jump were about to manifest themselves, but nothing. Curse these robust and well-maintained pods. There was no reason not to proceed. I propped the piece of paper up on the console in front of me and began to lay in the coordinates. Normally, not even the most irresponsible historian would lay in unverified coordinates, but since there was a very real possibility none of us would survive this jump, it hardly seemed important. I think I might have harboured a faint hope that the computer wouldn't accept them but no such luck. The console stayed green across the board.

He checked the readouts against my piece of paper, nodded and leaned back. 'Do it.'

Normally, I would have warned people to brace themselves, especially since we were jumping into the unknown, but maybe, during possible post-jump bouncing, an opportunity would present itself. And as an old hand, North was braced anyway.

I wiggled my bum in the seat, took a breath, and said, 'Computer, initiate jump.'

'Jump initiated.'

No miracle intervened and, sadly, the world went white.

19

We landed with a minor bump that would have been one of Peterson's finest efforts. My passengers staggered but kept their feet although that didn't prevent a great deal of bad language and complaint.

I was about to tell them they were lucky I wasn't Peterson when every alarm in the pod went off. I'd been expecting something of the sort and so had North, but Sullivan and his team, already apprehensive over their first jump and in unknown and unfamiliar territory, nearly shot through the roof.

Every light flashed red. Every alarm sounded. Worse was to come.

My relationship with our computer has always been moderately amicable. There's always the very slight suggestion of eye-rolling as it responds to any requests for info and a kind of *I can't believe you didn't know that* tone to its pleasant, female, albeit slightly bossy voice, that sometimes sounds uncannily like Mrs Partridge, but the whole transaction is usually carried out in an atmosphere of calm goodwill. Suddenly, however, everything was different. A male voice, rough and angry, filled the pod.

'Warning. Extreme hazard. This jump is not within permitted parameters. Site of Special Significance infringement. Implement immediate evacuation. This pod will terminate in four minutes fifty-nine seconds.'

189

'Well,' I said to North. 'Looking on the bright side, at least we're not going to suffocate to death.'

She nodded. 'I always think it's important to accentuate the positive, don't you?'

Already on edge, Sullivan was even more rattled. 'What the hell is that?'

'I tried to tell you,' I said. 'You've jumped to a Triple-S site.'

'What does that mean?'

These days I make an effort to moderate my language – you know, mothering responsibilities and all that – but frankly, at that moment, I couldn't be bothered. Some of you might want to look away.

'It means we're fucked, you monumental pillock. This pod will terminate in . . .' I peered at the console, '. . . four minutes forty-nine seconds.'

'Switch it off,' he shouted.

'Well, if you say so, but it won't help.'

'I mean – shut it down.'

'No can do.' I made myself comfortable. 'Sorry.'

'Open the fucking door. Let us out.'

And here we go. 'Nope.'

'This pod is about to blow. Let us out.'

'Nope.'

He thrust his gun painfully into my ribs. 'Get us out of here.'

'Nope.'

'Four minutes thirty seconds.'

He leaned over my shoulder and stabbed buttons at random. Nothing happened. Of course, it didn't. What did he expect?

'I'm ordering you. Open that door.'

'No.'

190

He thumped a clenched fist on the console, roaring, 'Open the fucking door.'

'No.'

I think that was the moment he began to realise this was a situation over which he had no control.

I swivelled the seat around. 'Celia, I'm so sorry.'

She even managed a smile. 'Not your fault, Max. You have to do your duty.'

'Yes, but I hadn't planned on doing it all over you.'

Sullivan swung around to face her. 'What do you mean? What are you talking about? Tell me. Tell me now.'

'I'd be happy to,' I said. 'If I could get a word in edgeways.'

He took a couple of deep breaths, regaining control. 'What's happening?'

'Nothing. Nothing's happening. Nothing's going to happen. We're here. That's it.'

His two men with him were looking around. They were worried but not panicking. Not yet. That would come.

Sullivan continued. 'What do you mean – that's it?'

I spread my hands. 'That's it. We're here. I've done my bit. My assignment is completed.'

'What assignment?'

'To remove this pod from Halcombe's reach. To remove enough of his team to weaken his position at St Mary's. To demonstrate very clearly, and without ambiguity of any kind, exactly what happens to those stupid enough to try this sort of thing. And, of course, to ensure we all die here and the pod is destroyed and can never be used again.'

Sweat gleamed along his top lip. 'I don't believe you.'

'Four minutes remaining.'

I shrugged. 'What you do or do not believe isn't important. All *you* need to understand is that you'll never leave this place. Ever. We're all going to die.'

He was shouting now. 'Discontinue the countdown.'

'Of course,' I said, pleasantly, and turned to the console. 'Computer – discontinue countdown.'

'Three minutes fifty seconds.'

'Oh dear, that doesn't seem to have worked, does it? What would you like me to do now?'

His brain was still working. 'Can you freeze it?'

'I don't know,' I said, honestly. 'I've never actually done this before.'

'Do it.'

'Computer – freeze countdown.'

'Three minutes forty-five seconds.'

He was still banging around the console. 'Isn't there any way to stop it?'

'I don't know. Jumping away might do it. Not that that will do you any good because I still won't open the door. So even if we get out of this – which we probably won't – in about two hours' time – probably much less because you've overloaded the pod – you'll be on the floor, purple-faced, desperately trying to suck in air that isn't here. I can tell you now it's not going to be pleasant.'

I turned to his men because I'm a troublemaker and can't help myself. 'Of course, he could always increase the amount of air available by shooting you two.'

I could see by their faces exactly the same thought had occurred to them.

He thrust his gun in my face again. 'I could shoot you.'

'If you want. Although you will be shooting fifty per cent of the people here who can actually save this pod so I doubt you'll do it. You'll never give up the hope you can persuade me to change my mind, so I'll be the last to die.'

He pointed his gun to North. 'True, but I could shoot her. To save on oxygen and change your mind. So, open the door or I'll do it.'

North smiled faintly. She was very white but holding up well. Not so Sullivan and his team. He was red-faced and getting sweatier. To be fair, I could feel sweat running down my back, too. It wasn't my imagination. Inside the pod, things were getting very warm.

'Three minutes fifteen seconds remaining.'

'Stop it,' shouted one of his men. I looked at him properly for the first time. He was only a young man. 'Stop it,' he shouted again, spittle flying. There was a note of hysteria in his voice. 'Make it stop. Shut it down.'

I shook my head. 'Sorry, I can't do that. I tried to warn you. Well, I tried to warn your boss, but you know what he's like. He obviously considers you expendable.'

He stared at the console. The computer was barking out its Triple-S warning again. He had to raise his voice to make himself heard. 'I don't understand. What's happening?'

I was irritated. These were my last minutes on earth and I didn't want to spend them talking to idiots. 'It's telling you what's happening. Why don't you shut up and listen for once? You've jumped to a Site of Special Significance. It's a forbidden area. We're not allowed to be here. It's part of the safety protocols built into the pod.'

The other soldier was banging on the door with his gun butt. 'Let us out. For God's sake, let us out.'

'Tell them to stop,' I said wearily. 'No power on earth can open that door if I don't want it to open. There's nothing you can do.'

'You think?'

The blow came out of nowhere. I never even saw it coming. Straight to the kidneys. I fell against the console and from there to the floor.

He lost all control, wading in with boots and fists and most of it bloody hurt, I can tell you. The only thing saving me from a real beating was that the pod was too small for him to really get going. Plus one of his men, together with North, was shouting and trying to pull him off me. I guessed that the gist of the argument was that if he killed me then they'd never get out of here. The other soldier was curled in the corner, crying. Time travel doesn't suit everyone, you know.

Eventually, the shouting stopped. I think his man had prevailed. I climbed back into the seat, bent double with pain. The sound of his panting filled the pod.

He made an exasperated sound, shrugged off his man, wiped the sweat off his face and stared at his feet. I'd like to think he was engaging in a little rational thought but I wasn't optimistic.

I was panting, too. There was blood on the console. Leon would do his nut about that.

There must be some damage to my ribs. I was struggling to get my breath. I tried to breathe slowly and smoothly, trying not to jerk my ribs too much, and then I realised that it wasn't just me. Everyone was panting for breath. This wasn't the smallest pod but there were still five of us in it. And they'd used up a great deal of oxygen by panicking, threshing around, shouting, hitting me . . . If there's a shortage then the accepted practice is to sit quietly and keep as still as possible. We hadn't really been doing that, had we?

There was a big splat of nose blood on the console. I used my finger to draw a tiny heart with an L in the centre.

The man who had restrained Sullivan made a huge effort and said quietly, 'Isn't there anything we can do?'

I shook my head. 'Nothing.'

Sullivan intervened. 'What do you mean – nothing? You can return to base. Return to base immediately. That's an order.'

In an instant he had North pinned against the wall, a gun at her head.

I shrugged. 'Fire that in here and this pod never goes anywhere again. You're really not bright, are you?'

Suddenly he was ice-cold and dangerous. 'Brighter than you,' he said quietly. 'This fires bolts, not bullets. Something along the lines of a humane killer. I'd like to think she'll never know anything about it but I suspect she will.'

And still, in the background, the computer was counting away to itself. The two soldiers were shouting themselves hoarse. My whole body throbbed. The temperature was soaring. My back was soaked in sweat. The emotional temperature was even higher.

'Open the door,' he shouted. 'Now. Let us out or she dies.'

It was never going to happen. This was Jerusalem. The thought of them running around out there . . . They had weapons. They weren't prepped. With or without a crucifixion, Roman-occupied Jerusalem was a powder keg.

North turned her head until she was looking directly at him. The bolt was an inch away from her right eye. He smiled at her. I swear he was enjoying himself. 'You are going to die.'

She shook her head. 'You really don't understand St Mary's at all, do you?'

I was sitting quietly, but inside I was frantic, desperately formulating and discarding stupid, crazy, ridiculous plans to get us out of this. I couldn't think of anything. Obviously, the Time Police hadn't fixed the Time Map because otherwise they'd have been here faster than . . . I couldn't think of anything at that moment. I was so angry with them. Yes, they'd only been a faint hope, but I was still pretty miffed they were letting me down. Typical Time Police. Whenever I'm up to something dodgy they're about three seconds behind me and here I was, doing something very dodgy indeed but in a heroic manner, and where were they?

I tried not to remember it was my own son who'd broken the Time Map.

Celia North was very white but very calm. Because, for her, it had always been all about duty. The overriding principle of her life. And of her family, back through the ages. Yes, we'd joked about them crushing the peasants and so on but doing one's duty had been bred into her bones.

And so should I. I had to do *my* duty. I had to take the straight path. No hedging or dodging or evading the hard decisions. I had to do my duty. She was doing hers. I must do mine. It was the least I could do for her.

Sullivan was screaming. 'I'll do it. I swear I'll do it.'

'Two minutes remaining.'

I looked at her and she looked at me. I could vaguely hear the background noises of the pod. Men were shouting at me but Celia and I were the only people here. The only people who mattered, anyway. She nodded. I nodded. And the deal was done.

Sullivan was shouting now. 'I'll do it, you know. I will do it.'

We both ignored him.

She smiled slightly. 'You have to do your duty, Max. For both of us.'

I would have stood but I knew my legs wouldn't hold me. 'Miss North, St Mary's thanks you for your exemplary service.'

Her voice wasn't quite steady. 'An honour and a privilege, Max.'

It was like a scene from hell. The heat. The flashing red lights. The screaming. The inexorable voice . . . counting down to oblivion. There were bloody handprints on the door where they were trying to force it open. I was killing people . . .

Someone thumped on the door. From the outside.

'One minute thirty seconds.'

I sighed. It's typical, isn't it? You decide you're going to die. Bravely, obviously. You forgive all your enemies – or not, in my case – you turn your thoughts towards higher things, you make your peace, and then some bugger bangs on the door. It's just not good enough.

I ignored it. Things in here were complicated enough. There was no way I was opening that door. I could just see Sullivan and his men erupting out of the pod, shit-scared and desperate and causing all sorts of grief. If you think St Mary's can be a bit volatile, you should try 1st-century Jerusalem on what might, just possibly, be Crucifixion day.

Actually, don't think I hadn't considered it. Not opening the door, obviously, but definitely activating the screen. Who wouldn't want to see events unfold. I'm St Mary's. We always want to see . . .

But – no. Whatever was happening on the other side of that door must go on unhindered by St Mary's. Events – whatever they were – were all progressing as they should do. All thanks to me. I did think it was rather a shame the Christians were never going to give me the credit I deserved. I should be up there with the greats. St Max. There should be statues. They could name a chocolate after me. I realised I was rambling. My thoughts were scrambling themselves. But the thing about the chocolate was good. I could see it now.

'I'll have a big bar of Max, please.'

'Certainly, madam, plain Max, milk Max or white Max? Caramel Max is on special offer this week.'

I rather liked the sound of that. Caramel Max . . .

Sullivan was banging on the door. 'Help. Help. Open the door. We're trapped in here. Get us out.'

Bloke was an idiot. Well, he worked for Halcombe so that was a given. You see, this is what happens when you bring amateurs on a jump. I wondered if I could be bothered to tell him he was wasting his time.

Nah . . . I went back to Caramel Max. Looking good . . .

Whoever it was knocked again. And not just any old knock. The old shave-and-a-haircut knock.

Well, that was odd. From everything I'd seen of contemporary pictures, the men of those times had never met a barber in their life. Big biblical beards burgeoned boldly. Hey, that was quite good. Who said I was passing out through lack of oxygen?

They knocked again. Shave and a haircut. OK.

Someone grabbed me and shouted, 'Open the fucking door, you stupid . . .'

Well, that was a very rude word.

We were all panting now. The sweat was pouring off me. Or it might have been blood. That's St Mary's for you. Blood, sweat and tea. Hey, that was good as well. I was on fire today.

The young lad in the corner lifted his head. His face was mottled with tears. For some reason – lack of oxygen, whatever – the years rolled back and I saw Matthew Ellis, a young lad abandoned by his colleagues at Pompeii. I saw him trapped under the wreckage as pumice rained down upon both of us. I saw him struggling to keep his face clear of the suffocating ash. I saw him look up at me.

Oh, for God's sake. I'm such a sucker for young men.

I flipped on the screen. I couldn't see much. Either it was dark or there was a massive storm going on. And, of course, we were scheduled an earthquake later on, as well. But, storm or not, there they stood. Four Time Police officers. The one looking up at the camera was Matthew Ellis.

I wondered idly what he was doing here.

Someone shook me violently and all the aches and pains that had begun to subside fired themselves up again and I became Mrs Throbby. And my chest was beginning to hurt with the strain of breathing.

I said to no one in particular, 'I've had better days, you know.'

The lad was still looking at me. 'Please.'

I turned to Sullivan. 'See – that's all you had to say,' and opened the door.

Warm, dusty air flooded into the pod, heavy with spices and animal dung.

I could hear their blasters whining. 'Max – what the hell?'

'One minute remaining.'

'Tell you later,' I said, scrabbling at the controls. 'Need to leave. Now.'

'Where to?'

'Anytime but this.'

'Move on ten years.'

I nodded. 'Copy that.'

I slammed the door closed, moved the coordinates on ten years and trusted to luck he'd taken himself out of range.

'Computer –'

'Fifty seconds.'

'Initiate jump.'

'Jump initiated.'

The world went white.

And with a whole forty-five seconds to spare.

Piece of piss.

200

We landed like a feather. It was really a shame Peterson wasn't there to see it. Given my stress levels, it was a bloody miracle. There was a nasty moment or two while the computer weighed up our new coordinates and decided they were acceptable. 'Countdown cancelled.'

Five people exhaled all at once.

I looked around. Crisis over. Back to business.

'Right, you lot – I suggest you lay down your weapons. You are about to be on the receiving end of the Time Police and if you think I'm a bit of a cow you just wait until you meet them. Or not, of course. I really don't care if they shoot you on sight. It's up to you.'

Reluctantly, they put down their guns. Major Sullivan was the last to do so but he really didn't have a lot of choice. We waited and eventually he broke his gun and laid it on the console. I moved it out of his reach.

'I'm opening the door to let in some air,' I said. 'I don't advise making a break for it. They'll shoot you where you stand.'

The light outside was soft and peach-coloured. The sun, out of sight, was casting long indigo shadows. It was early morning or late evening. We'd lived to see another day.

The Time Police were about four minutes behind us. I think it was a sign of Sullivan's demoralisation that no one tried to make a bid for freedom. His two men slid down the walls to sit with their hands over their faces and just enjoy being able to breathe normally again. North joined me at the console. Sullivan stood. We waited in silence. I'm not sure what words would have been appropriate anyway. Apart from, 'You're going to die, you utter bastards.' Always a useful fallback phrase.

Ellis appeared in the doorway. Two others I didn't recognise stood behind him with Mr Personality Grint behind them. Considering our ordeal, Ellis was insensitively cheerful.

'Sorry we couldn't get here sooner, Max. We've literally only just finished repairing the Time Map. The Map Master switched it back on again and not only did the whole thing light up like a Christmas tree but every alarm in the building went off as well. Obviously, we knew it would be you and here we are. Just in time to save the day. Again.'

Euphoria was kicking in. 'Rubbish,' I said. 'Miss North and I had the situation well in hand. There was no need for you to rush.'

'In fact,' said Miss North, loyally, 'we didn't need you at all.'

He took in the scene. Celia North, flushed and dishevelled. Me, definitely not looking my best, and Sullivan and his men. I could see I didn't have to explain anything at all. Which was just as well because I still wasn't sure I could put coherent words together. I rather thought someone else could do the thinking for a little while.

Without a word, Ellis gestured and his men bustled about collecting weapons. All except Sullivan's humane killer, currently lying on the console. This man would have killed North. One of my people. In my mind I saw the heavy bolt shatter her skull. And heard him speculating on whether she'd know anything about it. And how she'd stood firm.

Perhaps it was time for me to send a message of my own. I

looked at Sullivan. I looked at North. And then, slowly, I reached across and picked up his gun. It was considerably heavier than I expected. I turned it over in my hand. I looked at Sullivan.

Ellis held out his hand. 'Give it to me, Max.'

I looked at Ellis but I saw Celia North. Prepared to do her duty. Right up until the very end.

I snapped it together and slid the bolt into place. Suddenly the pod was very, very quiet.

'Don't do it, Max.'

I looked at Sullivan. I saw my own arm raise the weapon and level it with his right eye.

There was complete silence in the pod. There was complete silence in the entire world.

'Max, I'm ordering you. Don't do it.'

I could hear my own voice saying to Sullivan, 'You are going to die,' and I think he could, too, because there was the sudden acrid smell of urine.

The moment dragged on. Nothing moved. Except it wasn't Sullivan I saw, but Helen. That tiny black hole over one eyebrow. She was looking at me. A voice said, 'You mustn't do this, Max,' and whose it was I couldn't have told you.

The moment dragged on and on. I honestly don't know if I would have pulled the trigger but before I could come to any sort of decision, Ellis put a gentle hand on my arm.

'Don't do it, Max. I know you. You'll regret it forever.'

I saw poor, battered Peterson, his face covered in blood. And I remembered that I hadn't seen Evans at all. 'His hands aren't clean.'

'They aren't – but yours are.'

'He would have killed us all.'

'He would, but you have no authority over him. I do. He's contravened the Triple-S rules, Max. Leave us to take care of this. It's what we do. Put the weapon down.'

I strung it out for another four or five seconds then slowly lowered my arm. There was the sound of people not holding their breath any longer.

Sullivan did not go quietly. Well, I suppose he had nothing to lose.

'I represent the government,' he announced, struggling between two colossal and impassive Time Police officers.

Ellis was unimpressed. 'Your government signed a treaty giving the Time Police the authority to deal with all illegal time travel.'

'This is not illegal. I am operating within my legal remit.'

'I should perhaps warn you that every word you say digs you deeper into the mire. Seriously, I'd shut up if I were you.'

'You have no authority over me. I answer to His Majesty's government.'

'That's the one that signed the treaty, is it? I'd really shut up if I were you.'

'You can't arrest us for contravening rules we knew nothing about.'

'I told them,' I said swiftly. 'On several occasions. They knew the jump was illegal. They forced us to carry it out.'

'Yes,' said Ellis, turning to me. 'I can't wait to hear your brilliant idea for getting out of that particular crisis.'

'Actually,' I said, loftily, 'I had two.'

'And I can't wait to hear either of them.'

I shrugged. 'They were belters. Simple, effective and one hundred per cent successful.'

'And the first one was . . . ?'

'To let the computer do its job and blow us all to pieces.'

'Good grief, Max. And the second?'

'Not to open the door so we all suffocated,' I said.

He nodded. 'Yeah, that would have worked as well. But, fortunately for you, the Time Police have saved St Mary's – yet again.' He gestured with his head. 'Get them out of here.'

They put black hoods over their heads and led them away. Actually, the hoods came as a bit of a shock. I did wonder if they were going to take them round the back of the pod and shoot them there and then, but common sense kicked in and said it was so they wouldn't see what was going on around them. This was still 1st-century Jerusalem, after all.

Ellis remained behind. He obviously wanted to talk. I imagined it would proceed along the lines of – you left us less than an hour ago, what the hell sort of situation have you got yourself into now? – and there would be criticism and recrimination and, frankly, all I wanted was a nice cup of tea.

Ellis was speaking again. 'For crying out loud, Max, barely have we fixed the Time Map than the whole alarm system goes off again, courtesy of yet another member of the Farrell family.'

I shook my head and muttered, 'Sorry.'

'What's going on here?'

'I don't know. I don't have any answers.'

'I mean, why are you here?'

I glanced at North. 'No choice.'

'Who were those men?'

I fell back on ignorance and half-truths. 'I'm sorry, Matthew – I don't know. I don't know who they are, where they came from, or what they want – I don't know a single thing.'

'Has Dr Bairstow gone insane?'

I sighed. 'He's not there any longer. St Mary's is under new ownership and they thought they'd kick off with something spectacular.'

'You nearly died!'

I shrugged.

'What aren't you telling me?'

'Nearly everything.'

There was a long silence and then he said quietly, 'Max, I thought we had fought our way to a place where we could trust each other.'

'Hey, don't talk to me about trust. I trust you to look after my son.'

'I think,' said Miss North, with all the social grace for which St Mary's was not famous, 'I'll see if I can assist in the other pod. Statements and so on.'

We watched her disappear out of the door.

'Listen . . . Matthew . . . if it was your organisation and something had gone wrong and you didn't know what and you didn't know who was on your side, wouldn't you want to wait and gather more info before deciding who to involve and who not? I mean, I bet Commander Hay doesn't go blabbing about the Albayans to just anyone.'

'I'm sorry you think I'm just anyone.'

'I don't and you know it, so don't pull the pathetic routine with me. I'm telling you the truth. I don't know what's happening or what I should do about it, so rather than just rushing in, I'm going to do a little discreet poking around first. I thought you'd be pleased.'

'Pleased?'

I nodded towards the door. 'Will you take North back to TPHQ and keep her there for me? She'll be safe and she can handle all the legal stuff much better than I can.'

'All right.'

'And keep an eye on her, would you? She's not anywhere near as calm as she likes people to believe.'

'You're not coming back with us?'

I shook my head. 'Not just at this moment.'

He said quietly, 'Max, what's going on at St Mary's? Do I need to go and check things out?'

I looked straight at him. 'You remember, just now, you said to trust you.'

'I remember.'

'Will you trust me?'

'What should I be trusting you to do?'

'The right thing.'

I waited for him to say that the St Mary's right thing and the Time Police right thing were not always one and the same thing, but he didn't, which was just as well because at that moment, I honestly didn't know what to do for the best.

The easiest option was to take Ellis and his men back to St Mary's, point to Halcombe and instruct them to kill him. But then they'd find out something had gone very, very wrong and, from there, it was a short step to them keeping us under close observation 'as a safeguard' – I could just hear Commander Hay saying it – and we might never be rid of them.

No. My priority was to find Dr Bairstow, dump the problem squarely in his lap, and then follow his instructions.

I'd need to be careful. I wasn't going to go anywhere near Halcombe because it was much more effective to leave him to wonder. To leave him to explain the absence of both the pod and

207

his people to his superiors. To leave him to try to find an acceptable explanation. Because they would never know what had happened to us and uncertainty can be a killer. It certainly wouldn't do Halcombe any good. Extreme disfavour from his bosses – whoever they were – might be the least of his problems. I'd like to see him talk his way out of that one. But, at the same time, while keeping me and the pod away from Halcombe, I had to go back to Peterson and the others and do what I could for them and find out what had happened to St Mary's.

I smiled in what I hoped was a reassuring manner. 'I've just got a few things to sort out and then I'll be back to work.'

'Off your leave,' he said sarcastically.

'That's right. Leave me to sort this out and you won't find yourself involved in the sort of thing Commander Hay wouldn't like at all but would be unable to avoid.'

'For God's sake, Max . . .'

'I'm on leave, remember?'

'I don't think leave covers what you've got planned.'

'I don't know what I've got planned.'

'Max – you should come back with us.'

No, I shouldn't. I didn't want one of our pods anywhere near Time Police HQ. There might suddenly be all sorts of reasons why it shouldn't leave. And all sorts of reasons why I shouldn't leave either. I might be doing them a huge injustice – I probably was – in which case I'd apologise for it later.

And, for me, anyway, the top priority was always Ronan. I couldn't afford to be distracted by the Time Police. And something, somehow, told me he and Halcombe were not unconnected.

Grint tapped at the open door. 'All safely stowed, sir.'

'Thank you.'

208

He stood in front of me and I groaned inwardly. Grint the Grunt. Just what I needed right now.

'Take your top off, Max.'

I recoiled. 'Piss off, pervert.'

He flourished his med kit. 'Let's have a look at those bruises.'

Not without some difficulty, I pulled my T-shirt over my head.

Quite a lot of me had gone red and dark blue and purple. He sprayed away with something that smelled like drain cleaner. Whatever it was, it worked. The throbbing didn't go away completely but it became much more bearable.

He pressed two fingers against my ribs, moving up and down. He'd closed his eyes and, out of appreciation, I closed mine.

'No,' he said eventually. 'Nothing broken.'

'Are you sure? It certainly feels like it.'

'I could break one if you like and we can do a comparison.'

'Grint,' said Ellis warningly.

'It's no trouble, sir. Wouldn't take a moment. You'd be inundated with volunteers.'

'Piss off, Grint,' I said.

He grinned and they both departed.

I didn't go straight back to St Mary's. I'm not that stupid. I needed to rest a while. I knew from experience that tomorrow my bruises would leave me as flexible as a banker negotiating his annual bonus. I needed a refuge.

But, before that, I made myself a cup of tea, sat back, closed my eyes and wrestled with the devil.

Because, ten years back, while pretending to Sullivan that I was shutting down the pod, I'd 'accidentally' switched on one of the cameras. Of course, I had. Why wouldn't I? True, I'd had no idea of our location within the city of Jerusalem, but a quick glimpse outside might be all I needed to work out what was going on. On this day of all days, the simplest of clues could tell me what was happening. I reasoned thusly:

- Deserted streets with Roman patrols everywhere – something important was happening.
- Riots, crowds and civil disturbances – something important was happening.
- Everyone going about their business as usual – nothing important was happening.

So – when I hit 'replay' – what would I see?

My hand hovered over the controls.

And stopped.

I'd been in Jerusalem on one of the most important days in History. I'm an historian. Here, in front of me, was this once-in-a-lifetime opportunity. People would kill to be where I was now. All I had to do was instruct the computer to replay – if it would comply – and I'd *know*. I'd be the only person in the whole world who would know. The only person in the whole world who would ever know.

Still my hand hovered.

I should look. This was a true record of events. This was what St Mary's was all about: having a true record of actual events. To know what actually happened. It needn't necessarily be of the event itself. Even just the briefest glimpse of the city would enable us to extrapolate. And I had it here. Now. In front of me. I alone would know what actually happened. I could hold the fate of millions of people in my hands. I could put an end to doubt and uncertainty.

Or watch the world end in blood and fire. My choice.

I hit the appropriate key. 'Computer, overwrite, delete and destroy file.'

'File overwritten, deleted and destroyed.'

Christians – you owe me. Send chocolate.

I landed on her back lawn and it was a good job I missed her rotary drying thingy this time, because she was actually hanging out her washing.

I opened the door, leaned against the door frame and grinned at her.

If it had been anyone else I would have used the word gob-smacked. 'Max!'

I was almost too stiff to move. 'Mrs De Winter.'

'Oh, my dear, you look terrible. Come inside at once.'

I closed the door behind me and followed her into her house. She sat me at the kitchen table while she bustled about.

'Mrs De Winter, I'm sorry to impose. I'm in desperate need of shelter. And a bath and some hot food. And a cup of tea.'

'And you shall have all of that and welcome,' she said. 'On the condition that I am involved.'

'In what?'

'In whatever crazy adventure you have planned.'

'What crazy adventure?'

'Well,' she said comfortably, pouring out the tea. 'We are going to get St Mary's back, aren't we?'

Mrs De Winter is an old teacher of mine. I don't mean she's old – in fact she didn't look a day older than the day she tossed a pile of books and papers across her desk and instructed me to give her fifteen hundred words on the nature of ma'at. By Friday. Her intervention had changed my life. Those had not been good times for me but, through her, I'd escaped the manifold horrors of family life and again, through her, I'd eventually arrived at St Mary's. Oh – and she's sister to Mrs Partridge, so if anyone knew what was going on, it would be Sibyl De Winter.

I sipped my tea. 'So, if you can, please tell me what happened.'

She stirred her tea. 'Edward has been expecting this for a very long time now. Certainly long enough for him to have his plans in place. The archive was packed away, the pods all serviced and prepared, grab bags packed and so on. St Mary's isn't alone, you know. He has friends in some very high places. As does the Chancellor, of course. And then, one day, he received a telephone call.'

'Who from? I mean – from whom?' I said, reaching for a sandwich as she frowned at me.

'He didn't say. He, Dr Peterson, Chief Farrell and Mr Markham put their heads together and I think it was generally felt the time had come and they should go now before it was too late.'

'How do you mean – too late?'

'Before his leaving St Mary's was more . . . involuntary.'

I thought. 'Is this anything to do with Lawrence Hoyle's "shadowy figures"?'

'I believe the two things are not unconnected.'

'Did they get away in time?'

'He held off until the very last moment.'

'Why?'

'Because Mr Clerk's team was still out there, Max. They were away and had no idea what was happening back at St Mary's.'

And Clerk's team, having missed Elizabeth at Tilbury, had gone on to London to investigate, and then made a further jump to 1554 to instigate Wyatt's Rebellion. Even if Dr Bairstow had despatched someone to bring them home, by the time they found them it would have been too late. I remembered Ellis saying, 'And no one thought to return to St Mary's to report . . .' If they had done so, then they'd have been in time for the evacuation and a great deal of workplace stress would have been avoided.

'But Dr Bairstow could have contacted me.'

Dr Bairstow has a system for contacting the Time Police. I'll tell you but everyone has to promise not to scoff. He writes to them, giving details of the assistance required, when and where. He actually writes them a letter. Mrs Partridge posts it. It sits in a postbox in London and, apparently, some young sapling jumps back from the future, assimilates the contents and reports back. The Time Police then present themselves wherever and whenever requested and make a troubled situation even worse.

'His back was to the wall, Max. I think he felt that wasn't a good idea at this stage.'

I *knew* I'd been right not to involve the Time Police.

'And, of course, it's never a good idea to put all one's eggs in one basket. I think he rather relied on you being . . . apart . . . as it were.'

I nodded. That was very true.

'I imagine you were quite astonished to find St Mary's gone.'

I helped myself to another sandwich. 'Astonishment hardly begins to cover it. I barely had time to draw breath before Halcombe ambushed me. But never mind that. Did they evacuate? Did they all get away safely?'

'They did, but only by the skin of their teeth.'

214

I nodded. This was going to be easy. I was getting all the information I needed. She could tell me where they were; I could fire up the pod. With luck, I could be talking to Dr Bairstow in half an hour.

'So where did they go?'

'I'm sorry, Max. I can't tell you.'

I opened my mouth to argue but she forestalled me. 'I don't *know* where they've gone.'

Oh. Well, I had no reason to doubt her but that chucked the cat into the works. Or a spanner among the pigeons. One of the two. I was very tired.

I frowned. 'I find it very hard to believe Halcombe is the one in charge, don't you?'

'Oh, I agree. More tea? He's so obviously being used, isn't he? He's certainly taking instructions from someone else.'

'Someone who's not going to be very happy he let me and a pod slip through his fingers.'

'Very probably.'

I thought some more. 'It's Peterson that's been bearing the brunt of all this, isn't it? At least until Clerk's team turned up. And as time goes on, Halcombe isn't going to be a happy man at all.'

'I fear that is correct but not for a little while. You – and he – have a few days' grace before they start to worry about your non-reappearance. That was a good thought, Max. They won't hurt Peterson or any of the others during this period. But I think we should be aware, as the days pass and there's no sign of any of you, not knowing what has happened to you will render them helpless and frustrated. And we know who they'll take it out on.'

'But I have a little while.'

'Yes – you have a breathing space.'

'A very small one. And I don't think I've fooled Captain Ellis at all.'

'Yes – tell me what happened there.'

I told her what had happened after we landed in Jerusalem, ending with a slightly despairing, 'If only I hadn't come back.'

'Well, you did,' she said firmly. 'You returned to St Mary's to report to Dr Bairstow. Which, from your point of view, was absolutely the right thing to do. You weren't to know what was happening here. It all happened so quickly, Max, but no one has died and not only was a huge Triple-S violation avoided, but you've got the pod away from them. Which was the priority. If you hadn't then they would certainly have taken it and all of you away. They would have got inside sooner or later. Certainly, none of you would ever have been seen again. And if they had managed to open the pod, who knows what secrets would have been revealed. As it is, Max, none of that has happened.'

She was right – it was hard to see what else I could have done but even so . . .

'So,' she said, pushing the last sandwich towards me. 'What is your next move?'

I sighed. 'I really don't know.'

'One thing, Max – whatever you decide, you can't do it alone. You're tired and injured and there's only one of you.'

I shook my head. 'There isn't anyone else.'

She leaned forwards and topped up my tea again. 'Isn't there?'

OK, time for a little backstory. You might want to put the kettle on.

A while ago I did something very wrong. Even more wrong than usual. I put together a small team of historians – and Markham as well, because you can't keep him out of anything – and for reasons

216

which seemed very good at the time – and still do – we stole a sword from Thirsk. We drove to their Northallerton campus, lied like stink to everyone, and stole the sword. Obviously, they knew it was us because we hadn't tried to cover our tracks in any way, and Dr Bairstow was waiting for us when we got back.

Several bad things arose from this – the most serious being the imposition of Halcombe and his then-assistant, Miss Dottle – but, in support of our actions, two of my historians, David Sands and Gareth Roberts, both gave in their resignation. David Sands was now a successful writer – well, he was shacked up with Rosie Lee so if anyone deserved a little good in his life it was him – and Gareth had returned to Wales and now taught at the University of Ceredigion. I still had the occasional email from them and Rosie Lee kept me up to date as well.

The point of all this being that somewhere out there were two historians. Two people I could call upon for assistance. *If* they were in a position to render assistance. But, even if not, I should still warn them that unwelcome attention might soon be heading their way.

I stood up, not without some difficulty; I must have looked like one of those jointed rulers trying to unfold.

'Where are you going?'

'I wondered if I might use your telephone?'

'You may,' she said, 'but only after a hot bath and something more to eat.'

'But I need to contact Sands and Roberts.'

'They've been perfectly safe up until now. There is no reason they won't continue to be so for a few hours longer. You can use your time in the bath to think through the facts, marshal your arguments and come up with a plan.'

She was perfectly right. I could make a series of dramatic telephone calls and confuse everyone, or I could take a few hours and do the job properly.

'This way,' she said.

It was as I was halfway up the stairs – and making very heavy weather of them – that I had a sudden thought. 'Did Mrs Partridge go with them?'

'Of course,' she said. 'Why would she not?'

For some reason I suddenly felt much happier.

22

A hot bath, a plate of egg and chips – with second helpings – and two cups of tea later, I could have conquered the world. Albeit very, very slowly and stiffly. Grint's spray was wearing off. I reckoned it was going to be a day or so before I could limbo dance again.

I put on my jacket and walked to the front door.

'Max . . .'

'It's fine,' I said. 'I need to keep moving and it's not far. And he'll probably give me a lift back, so please don't worry.'

'I can drive you myself.'

'Exercise,' I said. 'I have to keep moving.'

She sighed. 'As you wish.'

Of course, I was regretting it before I'd gone more than twenty yards down the road. Fortunately, there wasn't far to go. David Sands and Rosie Lee live in a little house down by the river. There is a short row of modern houses built on the site of a demolished warehouse. The front gardens are so tiny that the front doors open almost on to the street.

Once before, when St Mary's was under threat, Rosie Lee had elected to leave. She'd taken a lot of stick for it which, typically, she never mentioned. This time, however, according to Mrs De Winter, she hadn't been offered the choice. Ignoring all her protestations, Dr Bairstow had made things easy by having her escorted to the gates. Exactly who had undertaken this task and the extent of their injuries remained unclear.

I paused outside and looked around but the street was empty. Of course it was. No one was following me.

I knocked and waited.

A light went on in the hall and I could see a dark figure approaching. Someone pulled the door open and there stood David Sands. Tall, handsome, and looking exactly as he had the day he'd escorted a tearful and furious Roberts out of St Mary's.

I said, 'Knock, knock.'

He smiled slowly. 'Who's there?'

'Someone who needs help.'

We looked at each other for a moment and then he stepped out and enveloped me in an enormous hug. All my bruises started up again and I couldn't give a toss. I hugged back.

He said, 'Hey,' into my hair.

I said, 'David.'

'Come in.'

The house was tiny, warm and colourful. The downstairs was open plan and I could see straight through to Rosie Lee, stirring something at the cooker.

Her son, Benjamin, was at the table, doing his homework by the looks of it. It was a peaceful domestic scene – something I'd probably never experience – and I felt a sudden surge of guilt at bringing trouble to their home. I blinked hard and swallowed down a lump because this was Rosie Lee and you should never show fear.

'Max.' And then she scowled horribly. 'What did they do?'

I remembered she had no love for the Time Police. A more than normally intelligence-impaired officer had once attempted to investigate her bosom area. A large number of people had nearly died.

She dropped the spoon and came over. I braced myself.

'Max, you look like sh— dreadful. David, don't keep her standing there. Sit down, for heaven's sake.'

I was chivvied into an armchair.

'Whatever are you doing here? We thought you were in ...' She paused. '... London.'

I glanced at Benjamin. Sands took the hint.

'OK, Benjy, forget the homework for a few minutes. Do you want to go upstairs and watch TV?'

He didn't need to be asked twice. I could hear him clattering up the stairs. Somewhere a door opened and closed.

'So,' said Sands. 'What's up, Max?' I told him.

At some point a glass of something very acceptable turned up and was refilled twice. At the end, I sat back, exhausted, and put down my empty glass.

They looked at each other. 'What do you want from us, Max?'

'I don't know. Initially I want you and Gareth back.'

'Is there any danger?' asked Rosie bluntly.

'I don't know,' I said again. 'I honestly have no idea what's going on. I'm winging it from one moment to the next. I have no idea if, as past historians, either you or Gareth are in any danger but to me it just makes good sense to have us all together in one place.'

'What about Benjy?'

'Again, I don't know, but after what happened today I'm not inclined to take any chances. David, if you want to stay with Rosie and Benjy then I'll completely understand and I'll go away at once. Or after another glass of whatever that was, because it's really good stuff. If you do want to be involved, then I would say, Rosie, that maybe you and Benjy might want to go away for a few

221

days. I'm sure you'd be quite safe here, but I'm not in the mood to take any chances.'

Sands topped up my glass again. 'Can you give us a minute, Max?'

'Of course,' I said, glugging away and they, too, disappeared upstairs.

Their house was very warm and cosy. If I closed my eyes I could easily imagine them sitting here in the evenings. Rosie, after avoiding a hard day at St Mary's and David working on his latest book. Benjamin would be doing his homework or watching the TV. It was a comforting picture and I was halfway to dropping off when Sands reappeared. He had his coat on and was carrying a sports bag with him. I could have cried. But only because I was very tired.

'What about . . . ?' I looked up at the ceiling.

'They're packing. I'm going to call them a taxi. They're going away for a couple of days. Don't know what we're going to say to his school. Take your kids out of classes during term time these days and they tend to put you against a wall and shoot you.'

'Dr Bairstow will sort it out,' I said with a confidence I wish I actually possessed. 'Do you have a number for Mr Roberts?'

He pulled out his phone and hit speed-dial. 'Gareth? . . . Yeah, fine. Listen, mate, can you get away for a couple of days? . . . No, I want you to think of it more as a walk down Memory Lane . . . Oh yeah . . . dead trouble. This is serious . . . Well, we knew it would happen one day and if you want to give it a miss I wouldn't blame you . . . Yeah, OK. See you tomorrow. I'll text you the address. Yeah. See you, mate.'

He turned to me and grinned his wicked grin. 'Done.'

We saw Rosie and Benjamin off in their taxi and then he locked

222

up and we headed back to Mrs De Winter's. It was getting dark as we drove through Rushford. Lights were on in the windows but the curtains not yet drawn. I could see bright little snapshots of people's lives.

Mrs De Winter had the door open for us. 'Come in, come in. Mr Sands, how very pleasant to see you again. Have you eaten?'

Roberts turned up the next morning. Just in time for breakfast. He'd bulked out and his voice wasn't anywhere near as squeaky as I remembered. And he'd grown a beard. At last.

'Dear God,' said Sands, leaping to his feet. 'There's something living on your face. Keep back, Mrs De Winter. I think I can save us all.'

Gareth dropped his bag on the floor and we looked at each other. 'Max.'

I was *not* going to cry. 'Gareth, it's very good to see you again.'

I had another hug. 'Missed you, Max.'

'Me too.'

Releasing me, he turned to Sands. 'Sands, you old bugger.' They looked at each other for a moment and then Roberts punched him on the arm and Sands returned the favour. British manhood at its demonstrative best.

We talked for a while. Nothing important – just catching up. Sands, as I think I've already said, was well on his way to becoming a well-known author with his bestselling novel on time travel. Which might soon be made into a film.

Mr Roberts showed us a picture of his young lady.

'She's very pretty,' said Mrs De Winter and I nodded.

'Shame there wasn't room for her guide dog in the photo,' said Sands, and I realised how much I'd missed them both.

Eventually, when there was no putting it off any longer – we got down to business.

I hadn't wasted my time in the bath. I stood on the hearthrug – a bit creaky, but functioning – outlined my plan and then sat down again so the storm of protest could go over my head.

'I'll do it,' said Sands.

'No, I will,' said Roberts. 'I'm the one with the beard.'

Now for the really difficult bit. 'It's very kind of you both to offer, but physically, I don't think either of you will be able to do it.'

'Well, I'll admit they've probably only just invented doors in Wales,' said Sands, 'so that rules out young Roberts here, but I'm perfectly familiar with their operation.'

'I'm not going through any doors.'

'Well, you'll never get through the windows because they're either locked or thirty feet in the air. And St Mary's has a pretty good security system, Max. And Hawking will be under close guard. The front doors are the only way to go.'

'St Mary's has a huge hole in its security system,' I said, recent memories coming to the fore. 'Clive Ronan lived on our roof for a time and no one even noticed.'

I'd had a bit of a think about this in the bath. Would Dottle have told Halcombe about the roof? My guess was no. Firstly, knowledge is power and you don't give either away. Secondly, she hadn't been working for Halcombe. She'd never worked for Halcombe. She'd used him. So, my guess was no. Actually, that's not accurate. My hope was no.

Sands sat up. 'Even so, you'll never actually get up there without anyone noticing.'

'I've got a pod.'

'All right, you land on the roof. How are you going to get inside? There's no access from outside.'

Oh yes, there was. Time rolled back. As clear as anything I heard Matthew's piping voice.

'You have good chimneys here.'

And he'd said it not just once, but on several occasions. Right out of the blue. 'You have good chimneys here.' And then carried on with what he was doing.

And I myself had been instrumental in burning down the medieval St Mary's which led to the remodelling of the Great Hall with – wait for it   a whopping great chimney. I even remembered thinking Matthew himself would have approved.

I braced myself. 'I'm going down the chimney.'

There was a babble of protest, which I'd anticipated, so I remained quietly sitting and let it all go over my head again.

'Look,' I said when everyone had run out of things to say. 'It's a good chimney but you're both too big and heavy. I'm not. Thanks to the 14th century there's a lot less of me than there used to be. I land on the roof, nip down the chimney, find Peterson, have a chat, and then get back out again.'

'Do you even know where Peterson is being held?'

'No. If he's in the cellars then I'm in trouble because the entrance is at the same end of the building as Hawking, where I suspect most of them will be congregated waiting for me to come back. But if, as I hope, he's in his own room, then it's just out of the fireplace, up the stairs, out of the window, across the flat roof and in through his window. Which is always open.'

'You don't know that. How do you know that?'

'Well, actually, I recently fell out of a corridor window . . .'

'As you do,' said Sands and I ignored him.

225

'. . . on to the flat roof and had to climb back in through Peterson's window,' I said airily, hoping my face wasn't as red and hot as it felt. I still can't think about that without wanting to curl up into a ball and die of embarrassment. If my plan went badly I might get my wish.

Roberts frowned. 'Max, there are massive flaws to this plan.'

'There are massive flaws to all my plans. We usually manage to work through them.'

'What about the pod? Are you going to leave it on the roof?'

'No, one of you will accompany me, lower me down the chimney and pull me back up again. If I don't make it then you'll bring the pod back here and formulate your own plans for rescuing us.'

Off they went again. 'You can't surely be planning to climb back up the chimney.'

'I don't think I have a lot of choice, do I? Although looking on the bright side, if they catch me then it won't be a problem.'

There was a short silence during which none of us said that if they caught me then my problems would only just be beginning. All our problems would only just be beginning.

Sands said heavily, 'I can't even begin to think how many things can go wrong.'

'Then don't try,' I said crisply.

'All right,' said Roberts. 'You're inside. You're alive. Then what?'

'I find Peterson. And possibly the others if they're all together, but definitely Peterson, because he's the one who knows the location of the remote site.'

Now there was a longer silence because no one would say it.

'Suppose he's already told them where it is?'

'He won't have.'

'Max,' said Sands gently. 'You don't know that.'

'Yes, I do,' I said stubbornly. 'It's Peterson. He wouldn't.'

'He may not have had any choice. If they put a gun to Bashford's head and demand the whereabouts . . .'

'He wouldn't tell them.'

'Max . . .'

'You underestimate him,' I said, trying not to get angry.

'And,' said Mrs De Winter quietly, 'remember Max wouldn't give in when they threatened Miss North. Dr Peterson would do no less. No matter at what cost to himself and others.'

'There are drugs,' said Roberts.

'And this is why I have to get in there,' I said. 'Before they start using them.'

'And out again,' murmured Roberts.

'I have to get in there, find out what I can, and then get off to Dr Bairstow as soon as possible. We have a few days at least before they expect us back from Jerusalem. People always make the mistake of thinking that if three days have elapsed there then the same amount of time will have elapsed here.'

'To return to my original question, how will you find him? There are bound to be guards.'

'I don't know how many men Halcombe has but there are three less of them now.'

'And, as you say, he might well have the bulk of them stationed in or near Hawking awaiting your return,' said Sands. 'So, the majority of his people could be at the other end of the building. Max, I think you might actually have a chance but I still think we should come with you.'

'No. If I'm caught – and I might well be – your job is to come and rescue us. You'll get us all out and we'll go into hiding until

227

this is over. If we all go together we risk being caught together. So far, Halcombe has no idea you're back in the game. Let's keep it that way.' I looked at them anxiously. 'You are back in the game, aren't you?'

'Never out of it,' said Roberts.

'She said *in* the game, not *on* it. Plonker.'

I sat back and let them get on with it because if they were bickering quietly then they weren't asking the big question. Halcombe had no pod but he still wanted the coordinates. Yes, he'd had one briefly but he'd been stupid enough to let it slip through his fingers. He'd concentrated on the short-term prize and by doing that he'd lost it. Peterson *could* give him the coordinates. Actually, he could set them to music and do a small dance – but without a pod to get there they were completely useless. None of this made any sense unless somewhere, there was someone standing behind Halcombe. Someone who did have a pod.

I know I'd said Peterson would never give away the coordinates but Sands and Roberts were quite right. He might not have any choice.

I had to get him out before it was too late.

There was a certain amount of preparation first. We don't just recklessly propel ourselves into trouble, you know. We make meticulous preparations. We try to foresee every contingency. We hope for the best but plan for the worst. And *then* we recklessly propel ourselves into trouble. Sands and Roberts disappeared into town to the outdoor sports shop, coming back with a harness and some rope. Mrs De Winter procured a pack of paper coveralls. I lay around watching my bruises change colour and kidding myself I felt better every minute.

By late afternoon we had everything we needed. I practised getting myself in and out of the harness. It wasn't difficult. Left leg, right leg, pull it up to my waist, tighten and check. I practiced with my eyes shut until I could do it in the dark – because I'd have to – and until I could do it without falling over. Which took slightly longer.

Despite my protests, both Sands and Roberts insisted on accompanying me. In vain did I say one would be sufficient and that it made sense not to put all our eggs in one basket. Neither of them was happy with my plan and actually I can't say I was looking forward to it much, either.

'What will you do if you get stuck?' asked Roberts, putting into words the one thing I was trying to avoid thinking about.

'I honestly don't know,' I said, honestly, because I didn't know.

Being 'stuck' was a very real problem for climbing boys. It's where the term 'stuck' originated. You're working your way up the chimney and somehow your bottom drops below the level of your knees and then you're stuck. You can't move either up or down. You're stuck. And if your master can't somehow manhandle you back out again then you die. And if that happened to me then the only way to get me out would be to demolish the stack. They couldn't just leave me there. After a couple of days, the smell would be awful and I'd be dribbling down the chimney.

'They'll probably just light a fire and smoke you,' said Roberts, cheerfully, and then caught Mrs De Winter's eye. 'Sorry.'

'It'll be fine,' I said. 'My son was a climbing boy. It's obviously in the blood.'

We assembled outside the pod. Mrs De Winter watched from the doorway.

I wore a paper hazmat suit, which literally covered me from head to toe, with the harness over the top. My boots were tied around my neck. It's easier to climb in socks and we didn't want sooty footprints everywhere. Sands carried the worryingly thin but apparently incredibly strong rope. I'd drawn the line at one of those orange hard hats – health and safety people look away now, please – because if I banged my head the impact would echo down the chimney, whereas banging my naked head wouldn't make half so much noise.

'All set?' I said brightly, and they nodded.

We waved to Mrs De Winter and entered the pod.

'Computer.'

It trilled helpfully. Obviously, its previous attempt to murder me was just so much water under the bridge.

'Computer, re-activate access to Sands, D and Roberts, G. Authorisation: Maxwell five zero alpha nine eight zero four bravo. Confirm.'

'Access granted Sands and Roberts. Confirmed.'

'Get your passwords banged in as soon as possible. You might have to leave in a hurry.'

They nodded and suddenly there wasn't anything left to say.

'Right,' I said, 'be clear on this. Never mind what happens to me. Your main priority is for God's sake to make sure you and the pod aren't discovered. Otherwise they'll have you back to Jerusalem before you know what's happening, and we'll all be back to square one again.'

They nodded again.

We landed without a bump. 'Speaking of which,' said Sands wickedly, 'how is Peterson these days?'

'I'll tell him you asked after him.'

He sighed. 'One last time, Max, are you sure about this?'

'Absolutely,' I said. 'Let's get this show on the road, shall we?'

We stared at the screen.

'I can't see anything anywhere,' said Roberts, moving the cameras around. 'And there's nothing on the proximity meters.'

'Doesn't mean there isn't anything there,' said Sands.

I picked up my bag. 'Let's find out, shall we?'

We switched off the lights, opened the door and slithered out into the dark. And it was dark. The chimneys were darker masses against a dark sky. I don't know where the stars had gone. They probably didn't want to be involved.

Sands nudged me and I remembered to switch on my night-vision goggles.

231

The big chimney – the one in the Great Hall – was right in the middle of the building. I remembered them starting to build it back in the happy days of 1399. Theoretically this should be a walk in the park. Or a fall down the chimney.

'Come on, Santa,' whispered Sands and lifted me up on to the stack. There was no chimney pot to remove which was a huge bonus. In fact, this chimney was lower than the other, more modern ones which tended to be taller and narrower. I'd never have stood a chance with any of those.

I peered downwards. Everything looked green and eerie. A long, rough stone shaft stretched downwards and then doglegged out of sight. I hated to admit it, but it wasn't anything like as wide as I had remembered. Bugger.

I wondered if it was too late to knock all this on the head and go down the pub instead. I have to admit – it was a close call.

I sat on the lip and Sands clipped on the allegedly strong rope, whispering, 'Ready when you are, Max. Remember – any problems, yank on the rope and we'll haul you back out again.'

I nodded, my mouth too dry to speak. How do I get myself into these situations? Because if I became stuck there was no way they could get me out and we all knew it.

I'm going to have a bit of a whinge. Skip ahead if you like.

I'm an historian. Yes, I know I'm not famous for looking ahead but, after I'd graduated, if I thought about my future at all – which I didn't really because I don't do that – I suppose I thought I'd spend most of my time in sun-dappled libraries pouring over obscure documents and making the occasional groundbreaking discovery.

Or – if I was hip and trendy – becoming a TV historian and standing dramatically on the ramparts of a fallen hill fort and making History hip and trendy for all. I never thought, for one moment, I'd end up swinging like a pendulum in a medieval chimney. Who would? I mean, I chose History because, apart from a little genteel digging in the sun, there was very little heavy lifting and it was out of the wind and rain.

I sometimes think History's having a bit of a laugh.

I made an awful noise as I scrabbled around for my first foothold. Sands and Roberts took the weight. I could only hope the chimney was as solid as it looked. I could just see myself losing my grip, slithering and crashing into the fireplace and finding myself surrounded by armed men. Or falling with sufficient speed to wedge myself in the dogleg and die there. Very slowly.

My foot found a projecting stone. I let it take my full weight, reckoning if it gave way then at least I was still in a position where Sands and Roberts could easily pull me out.

The stone held. I groped for another and found it. I took a deep breath. Here we go.

OK – tips for those climbing down chimneys. Nice rough stone is brilliant for handholds and footholds. Nasty rough stone barks your shins, knees, cheeks and elbows. Gloves might have protected my already skinned fingers but would have been too clumsy to get a grip. So, I left a fair amount of flesh and blood on the inside of that chimney.

But, it was sound. Trust Dr Bairstow to keep his property well-maintained. We only ever used this fireplace for the Yule Log, ceremonially brought in every year, and I know he had the chimney swept regularly so there would be no great dollops of soot to send crashing down into the fireplace and give the game away.

The goggles were a waste of time because I couldn't see downwards past myself. I couldn't actually see anything. And the chimney was so narrow I had to keep my arms above my head in case they became wedged at my sides. I had to work very hard at not thinking about what would happen if my arms became wedged at my sides. A dark chimney is no place to have a panic attack. I resolved never, ever, *ever* to have another brilliant idea for as long as I lived. Which might not be that long.

It struck me that if I hadn't been trapped in 1399, if I hadn't set fire to St Mary's – well, it wasn't actually all me, but the idea was mine – then they wouldn't have rebuilt the Hall to include the very chimney in which I was currently very definitely *not* having a panic attack of any kind. I was the author of my own misfortune. Or, if I wanted to put a slightly more positive spin on things, my actions now were direct descendants of my actions then. Hmm . . . not that much more positive. Just get on with it, Maxwell.

I developed a kind of rhythm, never relinquishing a handhold until I was certain the stone I was standing on was solid. Right foot. Right hand. Left foot. Left hand. And so on. The stones were irregular and painful. I was not enjoying this.

The chimney seemed endless. I had no idea how long I'd been in there. Time was happening to someone else. The only good thing was that it was so clean I wasn't swallowing down choking mouthfuls of thick black soot. I moved slowly but surely and tried really, really hard not to think about what would happen if the chimney suddenly narrowed. Or if, for some reason, they'd decided to line the lower parts with bricks and all my footholds disappeared and I had to brace myself against the sides and lower myself that way.

Occasionally I looked up, but even with the goggles I could only make out a square of slightly lighter sky and two darker green patches that might have been heads but I'm pretty sure I was kidding myself.

My fingertips were rubbed raw. And I was worrying about what

234

would happen when I reached the dogleg. Which couldn't be much longer surely because I felt as if I'd been doing this for years.

What did happen when I reached the dogleg was that my wildly waving leg found nothing, my sweaty hand slipped and I fell. I only just managed not to yell, tried to grab at something – anything – and failed miserably. I tried to brace myself against the sides – which didn't work either – and skidded down the wall, skinning my palms and banging my knees and elbows on everything, until finally I landed, with no small crash, in the fireplace.

I lay, sprawled in a heap, looking back up the chimney. If Halcombe had turned up at that moment I would happily have surrendered to him.

After a while, I got my breath back and it dawned on me no one was shouting at me. No one was poking me with their guns. OK, so far so good. I could have lain there all night, but I had work to do.

Firstly, I had to get out of this suit and get my boots on. The suit was only paper and I ripped it off, bundled it all up with the goggles, and tied it to the rope. I yanked hard a couple of times and watched it all disappear back up the chimney into the gloom.

I was down. I was in. And I was safe. And no bones broken. Frankly, if you'd asked me to put money on it I'd have laughed in your face. I like to think Matthew would have been proud.

The next step was to ensure I was alone. I crouched in the back corner of the fortunately massive fireplace, checking around. The Hall was deserted – as it should be at this time of night. Apart from the ghostly green glow over those doors designated fire exits, there were no lights. You'd be amazed the amount of detail you can make out by the glow of the words *Fire Exit* and the traditional running man. And it wasn't as if I didn't know the place like the back of my hand anyway.

I sat back on my heels and had a bit of a think. The lights were out. Did that mean there were no patrols? Or that no one was monitoring the CCTV cameras? Had they just activated the sensors and gone to bed? I could hear Markham saying, 'Sloppy, very sloppy,' and I would have to agree.

The problem for me was that while patrols could be dodged or outwitted, laser sensors were a little trickier. Especially since I didn't know where they were. However, I couldn't stay here all night. Things to do, people to see.

I started to stand up and just as I did so, all the lights snapped on. For one ghastly moment I thought I'd triggered something and the game was up. I just had time to scoot as far back into the fireplace as I could get and pull the neck of my dark T-shirt up over the lower half of my white face before two men appeared at the top of the stairs.

They descended in silence and then two more appeared from the direction of the Long Corridor. If I'd been a minute earlier they'd have caught me.

'Anything?' said one from the first lot.

'Still no sign,' was the reply.

That was good – they were still awaiting our return.

'All quiet upstairs,' said another.

Someone grunted and they all trudged across the Hall and back to the Long Corridor. Someone even turned the lights out. You see – sometimes things do go well, even for an historian. They'd told me what I needed to know. My people weren't in the basement. They might all be together – they might not. I'd head for Peterson's room first.

I was up the stairs in a flash – keeping to the edges so they wouldn't creak. I flew around the gallery, turned left at Dr Bair-

236

stow's office, and ran along the corridor where I'd once tried to spy on Leon and Peterson and fallen out of the window instead.

The end window was the one I wanted.

I was certain it wasn't alarmed. Almost certain. Almost.

I took a deep breath. There's no point in doing this sort of thing by inches. I knew from experience this window could be noisy. If I tried to ease it up it would shriek protestingly every inch of the way. I heaved it up just enough for me to wriggle through and drop heavily on to the flat roof below. All my bruises started up again but I couldn't afford to hang around so I sloped off to hide in the shadows behind an air vent. Just in case. Once again it would have been nice to lie there, just for a while, but fortune usually favours not only the brave but those who don't lie around wishing they had an office job.

I waited, listening for signs of anyone coming to investigate, but there was nothing. I suspected they'd ended their patrol in the traditional manner with a bacon buttie and a cup of tea. It seemed likely.

I scooted across the roof and counted windows. That one was Markham's so this open one must be Peterson's . . .

I clambered in as quietly as I could. I didn't want to frighten the living daylights out of him. I knew he was here because I could hear him breathing.

Skirting the bed, I tried the door to the landing outside, because it would have been a bugger if I'd done all this only to find I could have just strolled in through the door. It was locked, however, which was good, because if I was discovered, then having to unlock the door might give me that extra half second to make my escape.

Back to the bed. Now that my eyes were accustomed to the gloom I thought I could make out the heap that was Peterson.

Crossing my fingers that it was his foot, I grasped something firmly and wiggled.

There are those who wake if someone coughs in the next street. Peterson is not one of those people. A voice said, 'Wha . . . ?' and then the heavy breathing started up again.

I waggled his extremity a little harder, hissing, 'Tim.' Not easy with a word with no sibilants.

'Mm?'

'Peterson, you pillock, wake up.'

There was the sound of someone turning over. 'What?'

'It's me,' I whispered. 'Shh.'

'Max? About bloody time.'

'How long has it been?'

'Four days.' The springs squeaked as he sat up. 'They weren't too bothered to begin with. Halcombe reckoned you would stay the three days. You know, do the whole empty-sepulchre thing. Now they're just beginning to worry.'

'He does know time travel doesn't work like that, doesn't he? That three days there is not three days here?'

'Course he doesn't. Bloke's an idiot. You're back so I'm assuming it went well.'

'Everyone lived,' I whispered, glad that in the dark he wouldn't be able to see the state of me. I had an idea I was still looking battered. 'It was touch and go and then, believe it or not, the Time Police turned up and saved the day. Sullivan and his crew are out of the game. Listen, I want to put North forward for a commendation. Can you do that?'

'Of course. But tell me later.'

If there was to be a later.

I couldn't see his face – he was just a shape in the darkness.

'Max – this is the last place you should be. I don't know how you got in but you need to get out. Quickly. Halcombe is not happy and it's going to get worse.'

'I know but I need to know what's going on. I've come to get you out.'

He pushed the covers aside and swung his legs out of bed. 'Let's go into the bathroom.'

Long-standing caution kicked in. 'Are you going to pee on me?'

'You're never going to let that go, are you?'

He closed the door behind us and switched on the light. He looked awful. Exhausted, careworn, and with a bit of a crust around his nose and a fresh bruise on his cheek.

I thumped his arm. 'You daft sod. Why don't you just keep your head down and your mouth shut?'

'I know,' he said, 'but every now and then I just get this over-whelming urge to take the piss out of him. I often think I must be channelling you.' He examined his face in the mirror. 'He doesn't have much of a sense of humour.'

I sat down on the loo and he perched on the edge of the bath and we looked at each other.

'Bloody hell, Max.'

'Looks worse than it is,' I said. 'I'm actually absolutely fine.'

'Of course. Stupid of me not to have realised.'

'You don't look so good yourself. A bit like a zombie who hasn't had a decent meal recently. Should I be concerned for my safety?'

'Zombies eat brains. Whatever makes you think you'd be in any danger?'

We looked at each other some more. 'So,' he said, changing the subject. 'Clerk says you've been changing History. Should I be expecting a thunderbolt any moment now?'

I thought of Halcombe. 'It's already here, isn't it?'

He shook his head. 'We're living in exciting times again, Max. What's all this I hear about the No Longer Nine-Day Queen?'

I waved that aside. 'All sorted now. What's happened here? And should you be worrying about bed checks?'

He looked at his watch. 'Every hour. Forty-five minutes to the next one.'

'OK. Talk fast. But quietly.'

'There's a lot going on, Max. Not just Ronan. There's a new government.'

'Is there? Any better than the old one?'

'Of course not. Anyway, there's been talk for some time about getting better value for money from St Mary's . . .'

'Oh God, this is the usual political euphemism for meddling with History, isn't it?'

'I think they see it more as minor tweaking. And perhaps not even that.'

'Just the occasional tweakette.'

'We have a choice. Either agree to the occasional . . . tweak-ette . . . or cease to exist altogether. Their argument is that if they can't plunder the past or change events to their advantage, then what's the point? Dr B was ordered to comply or resign. Well, we'd had warning – everyone was on standby – bags packed – word came through – and he and St Mary's disappeared. It was touch and go. Leon got the last pod out just as the first black helicopters set down on the South Lawn.'

I looked suspiciously around his tiny bathroom – I don't know why I did that; unless they were hiding in the cistern, we were alone – and lowered my voice. 'They've gone to the remote site?'

He nodded.

'And you didn't go?'

'Someone had to stay behind to mind the shop. Clerk and the others were still out there somewhere. And what could Halcombe do? There was no one here. No records they could rifle through. And, until you came back, no pods to travel with.'

I put my head in my hands.

'Not your fault, Max.'

'I should never have come back.'

'Max, you broke one of our cardinal rules. You interfered with History. Of course, you had to come back and report to Dr Bairstow. And you weren't to know. When Clerk's team left, everything was normal.'

I shook my head. 'I dropped a pod right in his lap and North nearly died.'

'Shh. Keep your voice down. *You weren't to know*.' He made a feeble attempt at a joke. 'See – this is what happens when you obey the rules.'

'And you stayed behind because of Clerk and the others. Don't tell me you didn't volunteer. And now look at the state of you.'

He said nothing, just sat on edge of the bath and stared at his feet.

I said nothing, either. He'd stayed because he felt he had nothing to lose, that what happened to him was no longer important. I didn't know how to deal with that so I started to think properly, working things through, piece by piece.

'St Mary's won't know when it's safe to come back. Someone will have to go and get them.'

'When it's safe to do so,' he said quietly.

'That's why you're here.'

He shook his head.

'Yes, it is, Tim. You're the one who has to go and get them.'

He shook his head again.

'Yes, Tim, it must be.'

'I don't know the location.'

It didn't go in to begin with.

'What?'

'I don't know the location of the remote site.'

I stared at him.

'Why would I, Max? Suppose they gave me drugs or tortured me? I'm very brave,' he said bravely, 'but sooner or later I'd have told them. And then it would all have been over.'

Realisation dropped more heavily than me falling down a chimney. Would it? How would it all have been over? Yes, suppose for example that the remote site was in . . . say . . . Albania . . . in the 19th century. Halcombe couldn't get there. Not without a pod. Wherever and whenever they were, St Mary's was perfectly safe. No one could reach them unless . . . unless they had their own pod. Or access to their own pod. Or more than one pod. And the experience to operate it. We stared at each other. Halcombe was not the threat. He was the visible face. The real threat stood behind him in the shadows. I was more convinced than ever that somehow, Halcombe and Ronan had found each other.

Tim looked at his watch again. I didn't have much longer. I pushed aside thoughts of Halcombe and Ronan because that wasn't important at the moment. I needed to deal with the now.

And then everything fell into place as smoothly and neatly as one of Matthew's jigsaws. Peterson didn't know the location of the site. He knew the location of the location of the site. Dr Bairstow had left something behind and Tim was the guardian.

I said very quietly, 'Tim, where is the location of the coordinates for the remote site?'

He smiled at me. 'Agincourt, Max.'

24

For one moment I honestly thought I was going to have to go back to Agincourt. Except I couldn't. I'd already been there. And so had he. And Dr Bairstow knew that. Then I realised.

Brilliant. Absolutely bloody brilliant. They could have tortured or drugged him and all he would – could – ever have said was, 'Agincourt'. And who would take any notice of a drugged and semi-conscious historian muttering, 'Agincourt'?

I got up and went back out into his bedroom. As I did so, a key scraped in the lock. Shit – they were early.

For a split second I was paralysed with fright and then Peterson said, 'Quick,' and I rolled under the bed just as the door opened. The light snapped on. I peered through the dust bunnies but all I could see was a pair of boots and nothing else.

'What?' mumbled Peterson from the bathroom.

'Why are you out of bed?'

'Pee break.' He pulled the chain, switched out the light in the bathroom and closed the door behind him. I heard the creak of ancient springs as he climbed back into bed. 'Turn out the light when you go.'

The door slammed and he left the light on. That's the sort of bastard we had to put up with these days.

Neither of us moved. I could say neither of us was stupid but that sort of remark tends to provoke unwarranted mirth. And besides, the guard hadn't locked the door behind him. Minutes ticked by and then, without warning, it was flung open.

'Hello again,' said Peterson. 'Just can't stay away, can you? Perhaps I should warn you that even if I swung your way I'd never swing with you. If you catch my drift.'

The door slammed again and this time he turned the key. We gave it another couple of minutes just in case.

Eventually I rolled out from under the bed and wiped my brow. The last few days had really taken their toll on me. I'm not quite as young as I used to be. Well, none of us are, of course, but I was convinced I was ageing more rapidly than most.

'Say that again.'

'My instructions are to say "Agincourt". That's all I know.' He leaned back against the headboard and grinned at me.

I thought for a moment and then went out into his sitting room.

My books are neatly shelved. Fiction by order of enjoyment and non-fiction in chronological order. Peterson's were all over his room, piled up on every available surface. Including the floor. I told him he was a disgrace.

Disgrace or not, I was betting what I wanted was here. My room was at the top of the building and on the other side. I'd never get to it undetected. I was beginning to have a lot of faith in Dr Bairstow and his forward planning.

Hiding in plain sight is always the best way to go. The more complicated the hiding place the more easily discovered. I looked around. My by now rather battered book on Agincourt was the second one down in the pile on his coffee table.

I looked back at him. He was leaning in the doorway, watching me. So, Dr Bairstow had left a message for me and Peterson knew

245

nothing of it, only its location. Sensible. You can't tell people what you don't know.

And he hadn't.

'You need to go now, Max.'

Something in his voice made me pause. He was here alone. Bearing the brunt of everything all by himself.

'Tim, come with me. When I don't come back they'll turn on you.'

He shook his head. 'I agreed to this, Max. I'm the decoy. If they're concentrating on me then they're not chasing anyone else. Not yet, anyway. And I won't leave Clerk and the others. Evans is in a bit of a bad way. He kept telling them he wasn't Welsh and for some reason that seemed to enrage them. I'm not leaving them, Max. You wouldn't, either.'

'But . . .'

'I don't know anything. I can't tell them what I don't know. Separation of information. That's the whole point. I don't have the location of the remote site but I knew where the location of the location was. Only now I don't because you're taking the book away with you. A simple idea but it worked. The rest is up to you. You've got the pod. You know what to do.'

'I came to save you, Tim.'

'You save me every day, Max. Now go, before they find you here.'

'I don't want to leave you.'

'I'll be fine. They still think I know something. By the time they realise I don't, you'll be heading up the rescue team as it kicks its way through the front door to save us all.'

'Tim . . .'

'You have to go, Max. Please make this easy for me.'

I stared down at the floor, blinking hard.

'Don't do that,' he said, gently.

'Don't do what?'

'Cry. This is my choice. My duty. North did hers. You're doing yours. Please, Max, allow me the honour of doing mine.'

I sniffed and said again, 'I don't want to leave you.'

'Well, I don't want to leave Clerk and Bashford.'

I nodded. 'Good point.'

'You should go now. Leave that window open. It makes such a noise I'm surprised no one heard you. I'll try and find an opportunity to close it myself tomorrow.'

There was no time to examine the book so I stuffed it down the waistband of my jeans and pulled my T-shirt over it. 'I think mine is the easier job.'

'Oh, I don't know. All I have to do is sit around and look stupid.'

'Well, in that case I'll leave you to it.'

'I'm not doing it *now*.'

'Sorry. Sometimes it's hard to tell with you.'

We both stopped talking. Suddenly I was in his arms. 'For Christ's sake, take care, Max.'

'You too.' I paused. 'Tim . . .' and stopped, wondering how to put it.

He gave a shaky laugh and tried to make a joke. 'I know what you're going to say, but please don't tell me to find myself a nice girl.'

'God, no. I was going to tell you to find the worst girl ever and just let her have her wicked way with you. It would do you so much good.'

'Actually . . . could you do me a favour?'

'Anything.'

247

'If you . . . when you get to the remote site, can you . . . could you, um . . . give my regards to . . .'

'To Miss Lingoss,' I said, crisply. 'Certainly.'

'Wait. No. Hold on . . .'

'What? You don't want me to give your regards to Miss Lingoss? Have you thrown her over already? I had no idea you were so flighty. Now what am I going to say to the poor girl?'

'How did you know?'

Because Markham and I fixed it up between us and you never stood a chance was the straight answer he was never going to get so I just grinned mysteriously. Just to get on his nerves.

He helped me back over the windowsill out into the night. Which seemed extremely cold after the warmth of his room. The temperature had dropped considerably and everything was damp. I shivered and set off again.

I didn't look back.

St Mary's was silent. Utterly silent. A bit of a first, really. Under normal circumstances there's always something going on somewhere. Techies congregating in the kitchen claiming that pulling an all-nighter entitles them to their own weight in bacon butties; or something that probably should never see the light of day oozing out of R&D; or even the odd insomniac historian. But not any longer. Complete and utter silence. The sort where you could hear a mouse sneeze three floors up. Night was definitely not the time to be creeping clandestinely round a silent building occupied by unpleasant people with hostile intentions.

I sat on the floor because I still can't stand on one leg without toppling over and removed my boots.

Very slowly, very quietly, because to be discovered now, with the key to the remote site stuck down my jeans, would be the worst thing that could happen, I snuck around the gallery and down the stairs. One at a time. Stealth was more important than speed. I reckoned most of the probably by now quite nervous patrols were at the other end of the Long Corridor, or checking the grounds, or congregating in Hawking, all anxiously awaiting my return. The idiot Halcombe had a lot riding on this. Either magnificent success or total failure and, if Ronan was involved, death. There was no middle ground.

Arriving at the foot of the stairs, I stood close to the newel post and spent a long time waiting in the dark and listening. Nothing happened. I took the long way around the Hall, away from the windows, keeping close to the walls – a bit like a spider running around the skirting boards – and staying in the shadows until I was back to the fireplace again.

I stood on tiptoe, groping around for the rope. I couldn't find it to begin with. I was just about to panic that they'd pulled it up and departed without me when my fingertips brushed something that swung away from me. I caught it on the return swing and tugged three times. Someone was up there because it dropped down three feet or so.

No need to bother with the paper suit, but I needed the harness. Carefully, so it didn't chink in the dark, I held it the right way around and stepped in to the leg loops. All those hours of practice with my eyes closed had paid off because I got it right the first time. I tightened the waist strap, clipped myself on, and was ready to go.

Facing the back of the fireplace, I tugged hard again. Immediately, the slack was taken up and I was on my way.

Believe it or not, it was easier going up. Much easier. They kept the rope taut, but I came up in my own time. It was almost – not quite but almost – like going up a ladder.

I moved as quietly as I could. I really didn't want to screw things up now. I kept my head lifted and climbed slowly and methodically. Right hand. Right leg. Left hand. Left leg. And so on. Every few moments I checked the book was still safely tucked away. To lose that now . . .

It took me far less time to climb up than climb down. Or so it seemed to me. The air cooled, I felt hands scrabble at my shoulders and then someone had me under the arms. They heaved and suddenly I was clear of the chimney and sitting on the lip again.

The air smelled fresh and cold. Hands were unclipping the rope and harness.

We didn't speak. We didn't hang around, either. We ran quietly across the roof. I called for the door and the next moment we were inside.

Nobody wasted any time asking how it had gone. I touched the book one last time and subsided into a seat and said, 'Computer, initiate jump.'

And the world went white.

25

We landed in the by now familiar back garden. It was only when we touched down that I realised my body was aching with tension and tiredness. Sands and Roberts both sighed and sat back.

'I can't believe we got away with that,' said Sands.

'Me neither,' said Roberts. 'I'd forgotten you have the luck of the devil, Max.'

I began to shut things down. My hands were shaking and the tips of my fingers stung like the devil.

Sands said, 'How are they?'

'I only saw Peterson. He wouldn't come back with me.'

'How is he?'

'Not good.'

'We shouldn't leave them there much longer.'

I wriggled the book free and waved it in front of him. 'With luck, we won't have to.'

We poured over that bloody book for hours. Other than the odd tea stain there was no clue of any kind.

'I thought perhaps the page numbers would be ringed,' said Mrs De Winter in disappointment. 'To give us the coordinates, I mean.'

I shook my head.

'Perhaps the clue is in the name,' suggested Roberts. 'They're at the site where Agincourt will one day take place.'

'Maybe it's a numeric code,' said Sands, 'based on the date – 1415. You take the first letter, then the fourth, then the first again, then the fifth again and so on.'

All of that only produced gobbledygook. Sands passed it over to Roberts who looked at it in surprise. 'What am I supposed to do with this?'

'Given the lack of vowels I thought it might be in Welsh.'

'TTKNMEERPRPSUPWWSDWS is not Welsh.'

'Are you sure? It looks Welsh.'

'It looks nothing like Welsh. Please stop insulting the land of my fathers.'

'One plus four plus one plus five equals eleven,' said Mrs De Winter. 'One plus one equals two. Perhaps it's every second word.'

'The of great Court turned way this Salic lily narrow blue the journey,' read Sands. 'This is useless.'

'No,' said Roberts, in great excitement. 'I think you've got it. That last bit made sense.'

'Which bit?'

'This is useless.'

'That was me, idiot.'

'Oh.'

The world's most inept codebreakers drooped, disappointed, over their teacups.

Sands picked up the book and shook it.

'Careful,' I said, 'it's very old.'

'I just thought there might be something tucked between the pages.'

There wasn't.

I took the book back, laid it on the table and smoothed the cover. I'd had this book for years. It was special to me. Which was probably why Dr Bairstow had selected it. At St Mary's, a book on Agincourt could sit quite anonymously on anyone's shelf, concealing the devilishly clever code therein. The codemaker had had a brilliant idea. Such a shame the codebreakers weren't quite up to the job.

I stared. We weren't, were we? Between us we had a room full of talent. Just not the right talent. As Dr Bairstow would surely have known. Yes – no one had a more accurate assessment of his people's talents than Dr Bairstow. There was no code. Not inside the book, anyway.

I picked it up, took off the dust jacket and examined the hardcover. Nothing. I poked my finger down inside the spine. Nothing. I peered at the end papers. Nothing. I picked up the dust jacket and stared at the design on the front. Henry, in full armour, knelt, grasping his sword, his eyes turned heavenwards, looking as if he was having some sort of religious experience.

I read the blurb on the back but there was nothing I could see. I flattened it out, turned it over and laid it on the table.

'Wait,' said Mrs De Winter suddenly. 'Do that again.'

I turned the dust jacket over.

'No, blank side up.'

As I did so, she angled the lamp closer and there it was. Faintly in pencil, two rows of numbers. They'd been written in hard pencil and were extremely faint. You had to hold them to the light to catch the indentations in the paper. If we hadn't been looking for them in the first place then they would have been almost invisible. And, just to muddy the issue further, the numbers were Roman.

'Brilliant, Max,' said Sands. A phrase I never tire of hearing and yet, sadly, is uttered distressingly infrequently.

'Well,' said Roberts to Sands. 'That's a little disappointing. I'm not at all sure I'm happy with Dr Bairstow's opinion of our codebreaking abilities.'

'Accurate though it was.'

'Insulting is what it was.'

'But accurate,' persisted Sands.

'But insulting.'

I could see this going on for quite some time.

'Yes,' said Sands, 'because we were taking such huge strides forwards in the field of codebreaking, weren't we?'

'Well, I'm just saying. It's a bit unspectacular, don't you think? We dangled Max down a chimney for that.'

'Cherish the moment,' I said, 'because I'm never doing that again.' I stood up.

'You're going now?' said Sands.

'I think she has to,' said Mrs De Winter. 'While I am delighted to play host, I think your pod should be removed as soon as possible.'

'What do you want us to do?' said Roberts.

'Wait here,' said Mrs De Winter firmly. 'We will reconnoitre St Mary's and what's happening there.'

'Don't get too close,' I said, slightly alarmed.

'We won't. We'll establish a base in the woods above,' she said, sounding more military than could normally be expected from a former schoolteacher.

'And then when St Mary's returns, we'll be able to give them a full report.'

'Will you come back?' asked Sands to me.

I looked at the tattered book jacket in my hand and realised that once again I was jumping into the unknown.

'Yes,' I said firmly. 'Or someone will. Just have patience for a little while. And don't get yourselves caught.'

They followed me outside. Dawn was coming up on yet another day when I hadn't got a clue what I was doing. It was getting to be a habit. Me not knowing what I was doing, I mean – not dawn. Dawn tends to happen regardless.

We stopped at the pod. 'Guys,' I said. 'What can I say? Thank you.'

'You can say, "See you very soon and not only will I give you a full explanation of everything that's going on but I'll bring beer as well,"' said Sands.

I grinned. 'Look after each other.'

'We shall,' said Roberts. 'We're going back now to set up base in the woods and prepare to storm the building. There will be siege engines and trebuchets and boiling oil. It's going to be great.'

Mrs De Winter smiled. 'I'll keep an eye on them for you, Max.'

'Take care, guys. And thank you, Mrs De Winter.'

'An honour and a privilege, Max. Now – off you go.'

I took a great deal of care with the coordinates. They were very faint and I've never been that good at Roman numerals. I can never remember whether a letter modifies the symbol before or after it. I did think about running it through the computer, but if anything went wrong at any time – and it would because it always does – then there would be an electronic record of the coordinates and I didn't think that was such a good idea. So, I did my best. I laid in the coordinates and said, 'Computer, initiate jump.'

The world went white. Again.

26

I retain very little memory of the remote site. I mean, I can remember what it looked like, but mostly my memories are of a series of conversations. Some of them not important. Some of them very important.

I shut everything down very carefully and somewhat wearily stepped outside. Recent events had made me a little more cautious than usual, so I took the time to stand under a tree and have a good look around before I went careering down into possibly even more trouble.

The first thing I noticed was the crisp, sparkling air. It was amazing and I drew in great lungfuls of it that made my head spin. Wherever we were, the air was so clear I could see for miles and miles. As far away as the rolling hills in the distance and, behind them, a range of jagged snow-capped mountains. This was wonderful. My lungs weren't accustomed to air of this quality and for a moment I felt quite light-headed. Although probably quite a lot of that could be put down to the events of the last few days.

I was looking down on flat grasslands, rolling down to a wide river, sparkling in the sunshine. Behind me, deciduous woodland was touched with autumn colours. Red, gold and orange trees stood bright against a deep-blue sky hung with thin, wispy, white clouds.

Wow. I had no idea when or where I was but if ever I got the opportunity to build a log cabin somewhere – this would be the place.

And there was St Mary's – right in front of me. From up here, I had an excellent view of their campsite. The pods were arranged in groups of three – our traditional configuration – all facing inwards for defensive purposes – and with the big pod, Tea Bag 2, standing slightly off to one side. I guessed the pods were being used as accommodation only with all electronic functions shut down so as not to generate a signature. Just in case anyone was looking for them.

I could see people moving busily from one pod to another. It looked as though they'd been here for some time. Little plots of earth had been cultivated. Salad crops, I suspected, grown for fresh produce to vary their diet.

A solar-powered cooking unit stood some distance apart – in case of fire, possibly, although that seemed rather too sensible for us – and I was certain I could smell bacon.

Professor Rapson and his team were swarming around some sort of contraption linked to the river. I frowned but no doubt I'd get to hear about it sooner or later and since nothing was on fire and no one appeared to be drowning, I decided to let someone else deal with that.

They'd certainly made themselves at home. Each pod had a tarpaulin covering a pile of firewood stacked alongside and several campfires were dotted around. Some for cooking and some for hot water. Three or four lines of washing hung unmoving in the still air. It was reassuring to know that rudimentary hygiene rules were being adhered to.

Major Guthrie had to be here somewhere because two latrines had been dug with a kind of woven, waist-high fence for a bit of privacy. Only a bit though – it certainly wasn't high enough to prevent anyone from sitting in the afternoon sun with their favourite paperback and waving to their friends.

You have to hand it to St Mary's – wherever we go we make ourselves comfortable. I basked in the reflected glow of their achievements, craning my neck, looking for Leon. He'd be here somewhere and I very badly wanted to see him again.

There's a kind of literary tradition that after a prolonged absence, the hero and heroine fall romantically into each other's arms and indulge in three pages of athletic sex – gruelling for both reader and participants alike. You might want to brace yourself for disappointment. Firstly, because Leon hadn't been well for some time which meant . . . well, you know. And secondly because Markham jammed a gun in the back of my neck and tried to shoot me. Some days I don't know why I bother to get out of bed.

'Don't move,' said his voice behind me. 'Stand very still and raise your hands.'

'Make up your mind,' I said. 'Do you want me to stand very still or do you want me to raise my hands? Typical Security Section.'

'Password?'

'Horse's Arse. Actually, not so much a password – more a comment on the Security Section and its leader.'

The gun was removed. 'What ho, Max.'

I turned around. Another one with a beard. 'Tell me – did you wake up one morning and decide that facial hair was just the thing for Hunter to regard you more favourably?'

'She'll love it. She's always saying she likes a man with texture. Anyway, what are you doing here? We're all getting on very well without you, you know.'

'No, you're not. You're only one step from disaster just as you always are. This time next week you'll be reduced to eating each other and, as usual, I'll have to step in and sort everything out.'

'I look forward to hearing you say that to Dr Bairstow.' He spoke into his com. 'Stand down. It's an old friend.' He lowered his gun. 'I've got to say, Max, I've seen you look better.'

'I was just about to say the same of you.'

He holstered his gun. 'You've been back to St Mary's?'

'I have.'

'Did Clerk and the others turn up OK? We had to leave without them.'

'They did. All safe. Well, safe-ish.'

'And Peterson?'

'Stubbornly refusing to act in his own best interests.'

'So . . . normal, then.'

'Pretty much, yes.'

Gesturing down towards the camp, he said, 'Shall we go?'

'Do you still want me to put my hands up? You know – make you look good. Although with that beard it might be beyond even my massive talents.'

'Just walk or I'll shoot you and then claim I thought you were a bear.'

'You have bears?' I said as we set off down the hillside towards the camp.

'We have everything,' he said proudly. 'It's like one of those wildlife programmes. I keep expecting that bloke to pop up out of the undergrowth and start talking in a hushed whisper. Are you limping?'

'Nope.'

'Fell off the roof again, did you? I don't know why Leon lets you out on your own.'

'You haven't asked why I'm here,' I said, trying to divert him from my light bruising.

'I know why you're here,' he said smugly. He stopped and I stopped with him. 'Um . . . Max . . . do you know if there's any news of Hunter?'

I was startled. 'She's not here?' I swallowed hard and then said very carefully, 'She's not still at St Mary's, is she?'

'God, no. She's . . . elsewhere.'

'Where?'

He turned to face me and just for a moment he hadn't quite got his face under control. 'I don't know, Max. I don't know where she is and she doesn't know where I am. And Leon didn't know how you were and none of us knows about Peterson.' He pulled himself together to make a feeble joke. 'I know we're always saying St Mary's is all over the place but, these days, we really are.'

I put my hand on his arm. 'I'm here. I'm certain Hunter's safe and well. And Peterson was alive and kicking when I saw him last night.'

'Jolly good,' he said, without looking at me. 'I wasn't really worried about him. Not really. I knew he'd be fine. I was just wondering if you'd heard anything about Hunter.'

I narrowed my eyes and brought my keen intelligence into play. So, Hunter wasn't here and I bet I knew why. She *was* pregnant and she wasn't here in case she gave birth. She would be able to leave afterwards, but her child wouldn't. You're not supposed to take contemporaries out of their own time. You can – sometimes – but you wouldn't believe the grief and chaos it causes. I tucked away the information as a treat for Peterson. For when I next saw him again.

'No, I haven't,' I said. 'But absence of bad news is good news so try not to worry.'

But he would worry. He wouldn't be able to help himself. I wondered how long Dr Bairstow intended them all to remain here.

'I'm not worried,' he said, after a pause that was just a fraction of a second too long. 'Not worried at all.'

I stared at him, but you don't get anything from Markham unless he wants you to. Even so . . .

'Is this to do with that letter you received? The one after the steam-pump jump? It's not the results of some test, is it? There's nothing wrong?'

'No, no,' he said, hastily. 'Nothing like that.' And more he wouldn't say.

To change the subject, I enquired as to the purpose of all the R&D activity down by the river.

'Ah, you'll be impressed by this, Max.'

I doubted it. 'Go on.'

'He's making fuel. For the generators.'

I frowned. This sounded like a typical R&D thing – quite harmless on the surface, useful, even, but with the capacity to generate a global extinction event.

'How? Are you drilling for oil?' Before he could reply, I followed through with the question I should possibly have led with. 'From what is he making this fuel?'

'Liver.'

I might have staggered. All right, I did stagger. 'You can make fuel out of liver?'

'Professor Rapson says he can.'

'Li—? Is that even possible?'

'How should I know? Go and ask him.'

I had a nasty thought. 'For God's sake, tell me it's not human liver.'

261

'All right. It's not human liver.'

'Could you say that with more conviction?'

'No. That was my best shot.'

I shook my head. 'In that case, I'm going to leave it all in your capable hands. None of this is anything to do with me.'

'Well, apparently, if he pulls it off then we'll all be rich beyond our wildest dreams. Except you, of course. You'll still be poor.'

I found I couldn't let it go. 'Human liver?'

'If it helps, I can assure you he's not using anyone from St Mary's.'

'God, no,' I said. 'The alcohol content alone would surely render the mixture too unstable for safety.'

'You wouldn't specifically need liver for that,' he said cheerfully. 'Any body part from St Mary's would do. But Dr Bairstow says it keeps him quiet and occupied. And here he is now.'

Dr Bairstow was standing outside Number Three with Leon. I smiled for Leon alone and then greeted Dr Bairstow, who nodded.

'Dr Maxwell, welcome. Do I gather your presence here means events are on the move?'

'Faster than a cheese down Cooper's Hill, sir. And about as controlled. I've come to report.'

He motioned me into the pod. Leon followed us in and the door closed behind us. I breathed a sudden sigh of relief and let my shoulders sag. Until I was here, safe and being handed a mug of tea, I hadn't realised how wound up I'd been.

'Well, Dr Maxwell – your report, please.'

'With your permission, sir, I'll work through things chronologically and you yourself can decide their order of importance.'

I took a deep breath and gave him everything from start to finish. The Time Map, Queen Jane, Wyatt's Rebellion, Halcombe, Jerusalem, the Time Police, North still at TPHQ, Mrs De Winter, Sands and Roberts, Peterson – the lot. It took quite a long time.

He said nothing throughout until eventually my tongue cleaved to the roof of my mouth and I ground to a halt. When I'd finished, he said, 'Very well, Dr Maxwell, that seems quite satisfactory.'

I wasn't sure he'd grasped the full extent of my misdemeanours.

'Are you sure, sir? We – the Time Police and I – actively sought to influence both Mary Tudor and the leaders of the Wyatt Rebellion. You might say that without us there might not have been a rebellion.'

'I am perfectly cognisant of your rebellion-initiating talents, Dr Maxwell. Although I must say it is gratifying to see you using your powers for good, just for once.'

'But we didn't stop there, sir. We breached a Triple-S site and the Time Police turned up and now they know we're having problems.'

'An unexpected circumstance, but not, I believe, an insurmountable obstacle to our eventual success.'

'Good of you to say that, sir, but if I hadn't taken the pod back to St Mary's . . .'

'Max, you were not to know. You carried out your duties to the best of your ability. As you always do.'

Leon had chosen to focus on a different part of my tale. '*You climbed down the chimney?*'

'I *fell* down the bloody chimney,' I said bitterly. 'Climbing might be slightly exaggerating my involuntary descent.' I looked back to Dr Bairstow. 'Sir, I have some concerns for Dr Peterson's safety. And the others.'

'As do I,' he said. He turned to Leon. 'I think the time has come.'

Leon nodded. 'Then if you'll excuse me, sir, I'll go and start

263

things moving.' He paused on his way out and then said meaningfully, 'I'll see you later, Max.' He left the pod.

Dr Bairstow regarded me. 'I suppose you are aware of the most interesting part of your tale?'

'I am indeed, sir. Where did they get the Jerusalem coordinates?'

He looked at me for a long time. 'I think a better question is who gave them the coordinates?'

'Well, I think we both know the answer to that one. Mr Hoyle's shadowy figures.'

'And one shadowy figure in particular. Clive Ronan. He's been too clever for us, Max. Somehow he's ingratiated himself with the right people in London and is moving against us from behind the scenes.'

'But you have friends in high places, too, sir. You had enough warning to evacuate everyone safely.' I looked around. 'Actually, as a matter of interest, where are we?'

'We are somewhere on the left-hand side of the land mass that will one day be known as North America.'

I nearly dropped my tea. 'What?' I looked around as if expecting catastrophe to strike at any moment and lowered my voice to a whisper. 'Sir, the rules state very clearly that given North America's current state, the slightest misstep in their past could have the most unfortunate consequences for the future. Their history has been overwritten so many times it isn't stable any longer.' I drew myself up and said, in my best Dr Bairstow voice, 'Do you think this is wise, sir?'

'I am always amused when you assume you are the only one who ever breaks the rules, Dr Maxwell.'

I gave in. 'As always, sir, I am in awe of your talents.'

He waved this aside. 'You report that you have taken it upon yourself to re-recruit Dr Roberts and Mr Sands.'

'I have, but only temporarily. They may not wish to stay. Mr Sands has his writing career and Dr Roberts is Deputy Head of the History Department at the University of Ceredigion.'

'Good heavens, that sounds almost respectable.'

'Well, it is when comparing him with the bestselling writer of far-fetched and completely implausible time-travel novels, sir.'

'May I enquire as to Dr Roberts' area of expertise?'

'History of the European Union.'

He frowned. 'Well, that can't take him very long.'

'I believe he goes in for an hour every other Thursday afternoon, sir.'

He smiled and rose to his feet. 'I think we need to bring things forwards, Max. We no longer have the luxury of waiting for events to unfold around us. We need to take the initiative. Are you ready for the next phase?'

'Yes, sir. I definitely think it's time St Mary's comes out of hiding and goes on the attack.'

'Good. In the meantime, I need to call everyone together to apprise them of events. Will you join me, please?'

St Mary's sat quietly through his briefing. Then I stood up and updated them on events in the 16th century and 1st-century Jerusalem. Excited chatter broke out everywhere.

Dr Bairstow stepped forwards and held up his hand to forestall the avalanche of questions and comments.

'Traditionally, I finish each briefing by asking if there are any questions. At this moment, I understand your professional interest and I regret that, at this moment, other matters must claim our attention. Time is now pressing. All department heads to report to me immediately on conclusion of this meeting, please. Thank you, everyone. Dismissed.'

He limped away. I went in search of Leon and found Adrian and Mikey instead.

These two were not formal members of St Mary's. For a start, they were too young. They were still in their teens and both of them were whizz kids. Geniuses even. They'd built themselves an illegal time machine that closely resembled a teapot – which was probably what drew us to them in the first place. They'd turned up one afternoon to 'visit'. To witness St Mary's in contemporary time. Dr Bairstow had been greatly taken with the awe and respect with which they'd regarded him and offered them sanctuary should they ever need it. Given that they were being pursued up and down the timeline by the Time Police, who would certainly have them executed if they ever caught them, the offer had saved their lives. We'd taken them in again when Mikey was wounded, hidden them, lied like stink to the Time Police, and then, as Leon had said, 'When you bring them home and give them a name you have to keep them.' So, we had. And very useful they'd been, too. With their pod concealed somewhere so secret that Leon wouldn't tell even me about it, Adrian was assisting in the Technical Section and Mikey had found a natural home with R&D.

I was pleased to see the pair of them and I think they were pleased to see me. In fact, Mikey was grinning her head off. She was also very wet. 'Max. Good to see you.'

'Why are you so wet?'

'Fishing,' she said. 'With Adrian.'

I looked across at the even wetter and unbelievably dirty Adrian. 'Are you using him as bait?'

'Don't need to,' she said. 'We're very good. We have fresh fish most days.'

'And Angus provides the eggs,' said Sykes as she joined us.

'Really? How many?'

'Today? Or so far?'

'So far.'

'She's a bit stressed at the moment,' she said, which I suspected was Sykes-speak for none at all. Ever. Most of us were quite convinced Angus had never really got the hang of being a chicken.

'Has anyone seen Leon?'

'Over by Tea Bag 2.'

I set off again and was accosted by Lingoss. Today's hair was . . . a beanie.

I blinked. 'What are you wearing?'

She fell in beside me. 'It's an old favourite.'

'Yes, but why?'

'My hair's growing out. I look like a section of particularly chaotic geological strata. You know – different-coloured layers.'

'Well, never mind, we'll all soon be back at St Mary's and you can celebrate with the complete rainbow.'

She slowed. 'Actually, I'm not so sure.'

'About . . . ?'

'Well, you know – my hair. I'm beginning to wonder if, somehow, it's not a bit . . . over-exuberant.'

I blinked. 'What's brought this on?'

'Well, you know – some people might not like it.'

'As far as I know, Dr Bairstow has no problems. He's never said anything to me.'

'No, not Dr Bairstow.'

I was cunning. 'I can't think of anyone else who would object. Did you have anyone specific in mind?'

'No,' she said, much too casually. 'No one in particular. But I wondered if . . . you know . . . someone quite senior might find it . . . well . . . not suitable.'

I'd been away too long. I'd lost the ability to understand my own department. 'Sorry – not with you.'

'You know – they might be too polite to say so.'

'I'm assuming this is not someone at St Mary's.'

'Well, yes, actually.'

'Too polite?'

She stared at the ground.

I was firm. My own personal life is frequently in turmoil but I'm really good at organising everyone else's. 'Do *you* like your hair?'

'Yes, of course.'

268

'Then there's no more to be said. Changing your hair because you think someone else might not like it isn't something you should do and, if that someone doesn't like it, then it's their hard luck, although if it's the person I think it is, then he's fine with it, so why are you worrying?'

We both took a moment to disentangle that sentence.

'Well, you know – he's Deputy Director.'

'His hair looks like a haystack on a windy day and no one ever says anything to him.'

'Yes, but it's . . .' She tailed away.

'Well, you can't do anything at the moment,' I said, 'and I wouldn't rush into anything when you get back either.'

'OK,' she said dubiously. '*If* we ever get back.'

'You will,' I said, with a confidence born of expectation rather than experience. 'I'm working on it now. Have you seen Leon?'

'With Mr Dieter, I think.'

I could see them on the other side of the camp. They were a little apart from everyone else. Their heads were close together and it looked serious. I set off again.

Sadly, I was so busy concentrating on Leon that I failed to dodge Dr Stone.

'There you are,' he said, beaming at me in a manner he probably thought made him appear benign and reassuring.

'What do you want?' I said, keeping a safe distance between us because I've been caught like this once or twice before.

'I thought I'd just give you a quick check-up.'

'Have you nothing better to do? Professor Rapson's out there somewhere distilling probably-not-human livers. Markham's almost certainly providing a welcome for every bug and parasite known to man – together with a few that aren't – and you're bothering with me? How is this good use of your time?'

'I know,' he said, motioning me towards a pod. 'Sometimes my devotion to duty astounds even me. Shall we see what you've managed to pick up since I saw you last?'

It didn't go well. Not from my point of view anyway.

'Well,' he said, as I shrugged my jacket back on again. 'Good job I checked. You have a ganglion.'

'Yes, I know.'

'How do you know?'

'I Googled it.'

'Well,' he said, huffily, 'let's see Google treat it then, shall we?'

'It said you could give it a thump with the family Bible.'

'I don't have a Bible.'

'That's all right,' I said, gloomily. 'I don't have a family. And as things stand, I probably never will.'

'Come and sit down, Max.'

I was suspicious. 'Are you going to hit me with *The Boys' Own Book of Doctoring*?'

He busied himself with something or other. 'Just come and sit down a moment. I agree with you about the family thing, but you're looking in the wrong direction, Max. Your mistrust of family life is not because of Ronan. It's because you yourself don't want it. I don't think you've ever admitted this to yourself but you don't. It's understandable. Bad memories. Bad experiences. But – you could have left St Mary's when Matthew was born. Or when you got him back from Ronan. Or at any time. But you haven't. I know you've been blaming Ronan, but you know as well as I do that if you'd wanted to – if you'd really wanted to – you could have just walked out of the gates with Matthew and Leon at any time. You didn't.'

270

He paused and then said quietly, 'I think you have to accept that normal life is not for you. It's not your fault. Some of it is in your nature – some of it is based on your life experiences. The thing is, Max, you'd be a lot less conflicted if you faced this. Drag it out into the open and confront it. Ask yourself – what *should* I do? And then ask yourself – what do I *want* to do? Answer those questions, make a decision and you're done. Doubt, uncertainty, fear, everything will just drop away. Yes,' he continued cheerfully, 'they'll be replaced by a whole new raft of doubts, uncertainties and fears, of course, but you can deal with all that easily enough. There – all done.'

'An ex-ganglion,' I said, looking down in surprise. 'Wow.'

'Yes,' he said, tidying his gear away. 'I'm always terrified by this procedure so I need to gabble away to take my mind off things. Thanks for listening. Did I say anything stupid?'

'Astonishingly, no,' I said slowly, searching his innocently beaming face for signs of deviousness and finding none. Perhaps he genuinely had been nervous. 'Happy to have helped. Have you seen Leon?'

Leon was waiting for me. I was really pleased to see him. Now that he was standing in front of me, I realised just how badly I'd missed him. I cleared my throat and said cheerfully, 'There you are. Where have you been?'

'Scrounging off Mrs Mack.' He looked down at me. 'What have you been doing to yourself?'

'Hardly anything,' I assured him. 'Almost nothing to concern you at all. You, on the other hand,' I said, changing the subject, 'look very well indeed.'

And he did. Having a beard suited him. He'd lost his pallor

and his light tan made his eyes look bluer than ever. He'd put on weight and muscle tone. There was no sign of his stick. He looked more relaxed and cheerful than for a very long time and, unwisely, I remarked upon this.

'Yes,' he said, smiling. 'These wife-free weeks have worked wonders.'

'Jolly good,' I said. I looked around curiously. 'Do you want to show me around the camp?'

'No.' He took my arm and we set off.

I was at a bit of a loss. 'Oh. Is it all . . . secret?'

We speeded up. 'No.'

'Restricted areas?'

We speeded up again. 'No.' We'd finished up outside his pod. 'This is where I live. Coming in?'

'Of course.'

The tiny area was typically tidy. I looked around. 'Are you here alone?'

'Ian bunks with me.'

'That's nice. How is he?'

'No idea.'

I looked around. 'Where is he?'

'No idea.'

'Oh. Is . . . um . . . something wrong? You seem very tense.'

'Ah. Is that what they're calling it these days?' He smiled down at me again and the penny dropped. We looked at each other. My heart began to thump. I was almost too afraid to move because if I'd read this wrong . . . if he wasn't ready . . . I thought about how much hurt I could inflict on both of us if I was mistaken.

He reached out his hand and said softly, 'Lucy . . .'

272

My legs turned to jelly. I'm such a wimp. I'm supposed to be a big, rufty-tufty, kick-arse, chimney-climbing historian and then my husband says my name and I just go to pieces. I took his hand and the next moment I was in his arms and he was holding me so tightly I was sure I could hear my ribs cracking again.

He was warm and solid and smelled of hot cotton, grass and oil. I breathed him in, suddenly filled with a sense of warmth and security and astonishment that this man loved *me*. And a sense of something else as well. I could feel him trembling against me.

'Leon . . .'

'I'm sorry,' he said, half laughing. 'This is my big moment and I'm about to disgrace myself utterly.'

'Just relax,' I said. 'You'll be fine. In fact, with luck, you'll be great.'

Now he did laugh. 'I *am* relaxed.'

'Are you sure?' I said. 'I don't think I've ever heard of anyone trembling with relaxation before.'

'I just don't want to . . . I don't want this to be over too soon.'

I patted his arm. 'Leon, I know you have a thing about ladies first but I really don't think that's the big issue just at this moment. Face it, if anyone deserves a free pass it's you, so you go ahead and make a start and I'll catch you up later.'

His eyes were very blue. 'It's not a race.'

'Says the man who always comes second.'

He laughed. I buried my head in his chest. Because – at long last and quite unexpectedly – this *was* his big moment and it had been a long time coming and I was suddenly and very unaccountably afraid. Of what, I had no idea.

I could hear the smile in his voice. 'Are you planning on coming out any time soon?'

I shook my head and burrowed even deeper. 'No, never. I'm going to spend the rest of my life like this.'

'Well, I don't think it's unpleasant, but I can see this could cause some comment throughout our working day.'

I shook my head again.

He laughed and stepped back.

I shut my eyes and refused to look at him because I was hot and bothered – natural consequences of spending time in someone's armpit, I think everyone will agree – and my hair was coming down.

He began, gently, to tuck it behind my ears. 'Look at me, Lucy.'

I did, briefly, and then shut my eyes again. My heart was thudding away and suddenly it was all too much and I was on the verge of disgracing myself.

He bent and whispered in my ear. 'I have doughnuts. Ta-dah!'

My eyes flew open. 'Are you serious? After what happened last time?'

'The Technical Section never quits.'

I looked around. 'They're not here, are they?'

He grinned. 'Would you like them to be? I could have them here in seconds.'

'That won't be necessary,' I said, gathering the faint remnants of my dignity around me. 'We don't want to frighten the horses.'

'I do,' he said softly, backing me against the console. 'I want to frighten the horses into a fit of the screaming abdabs.'

I gathered my scattered thoughts. 'Screaming what? Is that a technical expression?'

'It is indeed. It's what happens when we do this. And this. And . . . this.'

I took a deep breath and told my abdab to behave itself.

'So, what about it?'

'Sorry – I've lost the plot a little. What about what?'

'Doughnuts.'

'There was sugar all over the bed last time,' I said primly. 'We had to sleep on the floor.'

'Not a problem this time. *You* won't be sleeping at all.'

'Are you sure? I'm very tired, you know.' I yawned theatrically. 'Time for bed.'

'My thoughts exactly.'

I was swept off my feet. It wasn't unpleasant. I put my arms around his neck. 'Just in case you drop me.'

He set off towards the sleeping module.

'Wait. Stop.'

He spun us around. 'What? What's the matter?'

'You forgot the doughnuts.' I nodded towards the bag on the console.

'Seriously?'

'You're the one who brought them.'

'That's true, but I had imagined them more as an aid to foreplay than an actual snack . . .'

I seized the bag and peered inside. Two leaking jammy ones and a ring doughnut. All of them still warm. 'What's the ring doughnut for?'

He smiled down at me and my heart plopped about like a landed fish. 'You're really not bright, are you?'

'Ah.'

I do know that the accepted method of describing this sort of thing is to warble on about spinning galaxies, crashing waves, towering passions and so on, with a fair sprinkling of the word *thrusting*. There's usually quite a lot of throbbing, as well. My memories are exciting but jumbled so I wouldn't know anything about that. I do know we broke a cupholder.

And anyone who experienced a brief moment of concern regarding the fate of the jam doughnuts was perfectly justified in doing so. Their treatment was beyond cruel and unusual. The ring doughnut, though, was a star.

Afterwards, we both cried a little. I'm not saying any more.

28

Leaving them all again was unexpectedly difficult. My friends were here. It was peaceful. The weather was lovely. There was no stress, no danger. No one was shooting at anyone. No one was dying. Why wouldn't I want to stay here forever? I found I really didn't want to leave. I especially didn't want to leave Leon but, in the end, Leon left me.

'No, I can't tell you where I'm going,' he said, cheerfully, pulling on his boots.

'Why not?'

'Every husband should have secrets from his wife.'

'You're going after the teapot, aren't you?'

'With Mikey and Adrian, yes.'

I said nothing. Because once the teapot was back in play, a series of events would be set in motion from which there would be no returning. There wouldn't even be time to sit down and have a good think about what to do if everything went tits up. Once we did this – we were in it to the end. Whatever that end might be.

I took his hand. 'I'm sorry we didn't have longer together.'

He took mine in both of his. 'Max, a lot has happened to us over the years. One day one of us is going to have to live without the other. One of us is going to have to spend the rest of our life alone. It will happen, but we can take comfort from knowing that we never wasted a second of the time we had together. Every moment was worth it.' He kissed my hair. 'One day . . . perhaps not so long from now, this will be over and we'll be together again. I promise you.'

Time to be brave. 'I know.'

'Our lives will get better, Max.'

'I know.'

'And I love you.'

'I know.'

'Will you come and see me off?'

'Of course. Every wife always wants to know when her husband's safely out of the picture.'

'And I gather you're on the move, too.'

'Yes. Because of what's happening at St Mary's, Dr Bairstow's moved the schedule forwards. I'm going back to TPHQ.'

'Give my love to Matthew. How's he doing?'

'He broke the Time Map.'

'The boy's a vandal. He gets more like his mother every day.'

'And then showed them how to put it right.'

'The boy's a genius. He gets more like his father every day.' He began to lace up his boots again and then turned to look at me. 'Max – if this doesn't work . . .'

'I'm not even thinking about it. It will work. It has to work – therefore it will.'

'Is this the world according to the History Department?'

'Hey – it works for us.'

'That's a matter of opinion.'

We walked slowly to Number Six. Dieter, Adrian and Mikey were waiting for him.

'Have you got the signalling beacon?'

They nodded at the enormous pile of crates standing nearby, ready to be loaded. 'In there, somewhere.'

I blinked. 'Are you taking the kitchen sink?'

'Well, we're not sure what condition it will be in so we're taking everything we think we might need, plus supplies and items deemed essential by these two.'

'And the signalling beacon,' said Mikey. 'Because it's vital we can be tracked.'

Leon frowned. 'And you will be. A little more confidence in the Technical Section, please. The signal will work perfectly.'

'And it's configured to give more or less the same signal as our old radiation leak,' said Adrian, for whom the words 'radiation leak' in no way conveyed the same apprehensions of disaster as for normal people.

'So, you're back to a two-hour window then?'

'Yes, but we're used to that. It's not a problem.'

I turned to Leon. 'Will it still work?'

'If you mean your magnificent plan, isn't it a little late in the day for doubts?'

'I meant the teapot. It's been hidden for some time now.'

They all exchanged the glances common to those with a technical background. 'Yes, we're confident it will still work, but just on the off-chance it doesn't, Number Six will be there.'

I frowned. 'You can jump-start a pod?'

'We hope so. If not, we're taking Dieter in case we have to get out and push. Ready, everyone?'

I waved them off and went to find Dr Bairstow.

*   *   *

279

A day later, I would return to Rushford and Dr Bairstow was coming with me.

Markham escorted us back to Number Five. It was another lovely day which, somehow, made the damage to the back right-hand corner look even worse.

Markham recoiled – which I thought was a bit of an overreaction. 'Good Lord, Max, what have you done to it? Did Leon see that?'

'If he did, he was polite enough not to mention it.'

'Oh,' he said innocently. 'Do you think he might have had other things on his mind?'

I ignored him, saying thoughtfully, 'Do you think someone at TPHQ could slap a bit of duct tape on it?'

He grinned. 'Yeah, cos Leon will never notice that.'

I called for the door.

Markham put his hand on my arm. 'Just remember I'm not going to be around to rescue you this time.'

'What do you mean, rescue *me*? Surely it's always the other way around.'

He made a rude noise and then handed me a stun gun. 'Just in case.'

I took it gratefully.

'It's registered to me so don't lose it or it'll come out of my pay.'

Dr Bairstow turned to him. 'I am leaving you my unit, Mr Markham. Please try not to break it.'

'Do my best, sir, but you know what they're like.'

'I have every confidence that you will succeed.'

They turned to face each other. I'd never seen Markham look so solemn. 'Director, you are relieved.'

Dr Bairstow nodded. 'Director, I stand relieved. Good luck, Mr Markham.'

'Stay safe, sir.'

'I shall endeavour to do so, but I make no promises.'

We stepped inside. I offered Dr Bairstow the driver's seat but he refused, so I sat at the console and began to fire up the pod, very carefully laying in the coordinates. Partly because having him with me made me nervous and partly because this pod had made nine jumps – to Tilbury, London, Hunsdon, TPHQ, St Mary's, Jerusalem, Rushford, to the remote site and now this one back to Rushford. Leon had charged the batteries for me but it wasn't power that was the problem – it was accuracy.

Pods need servicing – there's no other reason for keeping the Technical Section in beer and bacon butties – but mostly they need regular realigning otherwise they begin to drift. The pods, that is, not the techies, although now I come to think of it . . . Anyway, it's not something we historians can do. We're not even allowed to change a light bulb. I think someone did once and the pod kept drifting a decade to the left until they discovered the cause of the problem. We'd done what we could with Number Five but it was all rather in the lap of the god of historians. Not an encouraging thought.

'Computer, initiate jump.'

'Jump initiated.'

The world went white. It was doing a lot of that recently.

We landed in Mrs De Winter's back garden again, to my secret relief. They must have been keeping a watch for us because the next moment we were through her back door and Sands was pouring the tea.

'Thank you, Mr Sands,' said Dr Bairstow, accepting a cup. 'I trust you are well.'

'Very well, thank you, sir.'

'I understand work is progressing on the film of your latest book, *The Time of My Life*.'

Sands beamed. 'Correct, sir.'

'Well, that is very exciting, to be sure,' he said, straight-faced. 'And how is it coming along?'

'Not too badly, sir. Obviously, a few small changes have had to be made. I think they felt St Mary's as an organisation was rather too sedate for the image they were trying to project, because "It's drama, darling". And so in the film they operate out of an underground complex known as Chrono One, which is buried under a desert in Florida; they time travel by means of amulets discovered in a mysterious vault under a sinister temple in Outer Mongolia; everyone is extraordinarily good-looking and well under thirty; the women all have big bosoms and – for what I am assured are very sound production reasons – they walk around in tiny vests and tight combat trousers; everyone carries at least two weapons; their commanding officer is losing a battle against drink and drugs and her husband is a secret traitor; everyone is having huge amounts of inappropriate sex with everyone else; they kill contemporaries at a rate of seven an hour; no one ever decontaminates because it slows down the action; and they've changed the title to *Split Second*.'

There was a thoughtful silence.

'I didn't know they had deserts in Florida,' said Dr Bairstow.

He spent the afternoon writing to the Time Police, inviting them to assist him in the recovery of St Mary's and the apprehension of the person responsible for the illegal Triple-S jump. We left him to it and sat in the garden for an hour. I tried not to keep falling asleep.

When he'd finished, Sands and Roberts went off to post the letter, Mrs De Winter tactfully disappeared and Dr Bairstow came to sit beside me in the sunshine.

'Dr Maxwell, I think now would be a very good time for you to return to your colleagues at TPHQ. I think it is safe to say that over the next few days, their attention will almost certainly be focused here. You will never have a better opportunity.'

I stared. Clever, clever Dr Bairstow, utilising recent events as a legitimate excuse to get the Time Police to St Mary's. Distracting them at the very moment when they should be paying most attention.

'I said I would clear the way for you, Max, and I think this will do it.'

I nodded and said very carefully, 'Sir, we are about to set in motion a series of events that, once initiated, cannot be stopped. I'm all set to go, but if St Mary's, for whatever reason, is unable to make the rendezvous then a lot of people might die.'

'I understand, Max. We'll be there. You have my word on it.'

I nodded. If Dr Bairstow said he'd be there then he would be. I held out my hand. 'In case everything goes tits up and I don't get a chance to say it, sir, it's been an honour and a privilege.'

'Well. I sincerely hope it won't go . . . er . . . tits up, Dr Maxwell, but St Mary's thanks you for your service anyway.'

I sighed. 'It's a shame, though, sir. I'd rather looked forward to having a go at the idiot Halcombe myself. I had plans to pull his brains out through his nostrils with a crochet hook.'

'I believe you may safely leave that with me, Dr Maxwell.'

'I was going to do it really, really slowly, sir.'

'Again, you may safely leave that with me, Dr Maxwell.'

'With added twist, sir.'

'Must I keep repeating myself, Dr Maxwell?'

'Sorry, sir.'

Sands dropped me off at TPHQ that evening. We landed in a quiet corner of Battersea Park. Somewhere near the little zoo.

'Wow,' he said, peering at the screen. 'The future.'

'Not for your eyes. You're too young.'

'I'm a bestseller,' he said indignantly.

'Trust me, you'll only get depressed.'

'Take care,' he said, as I opened the door.

'You too. And, for God's sake, look after Dr Bairstow. I know you'll have the might of the Time Police with you, but you know what they're like. Shoot first and call it Friendly Fire afterwards. And Halcombe might have a trick or two up his sleeve, as well. Or the Boss's friends in London might have got it wrong. Or no one turns up at the rendezvous point. Or . . .'

'Just go, will you. I'm hungry and Roberts promised to make cawl this evening.'

'Well, sorry,' I said, miffed. 'I wouldn't want to get in the way of your social life.'

He beamed. 'That's very thoughtful of you. Close the door on your way out. It's draughty.'

'How could I ever have forgotten what a complete pain in the arse you are?'

He laughed. I stepped outside and began to walk across the grass, halting by a vast clump of rhododendrons. I felt the wind stir my hair and when I looked back he'd gone. It had been good to see the two of them. I was on my own again and I suddenly felt very lonely.

I walked back along the river, wondering if the contents of Dr Bairstow's letter had yet been communicated to Commander Hay.

I reported in, applied for an appointment with Commander Hay and then went to my room. Someone had been busy in my absence. The files I'd requested were on the table in a lockbox. The red covers were marked *For Your Eyes Only* and were to be destroyed after reading.

I showered, changed out of my less than fragrant clothing and spent the afternoon reading. Commander Hay sent for me around half past four. A copy of Dr Bairstow's letter lay in front of her.

'Well,' she said, 'once again St Mary's has broken the rules.'

I shrugged. There was no point denying it. Captain Ellis would have reported back and Miss North was still here somewhere, subjecting the Time Police to the full force of her personality.

'A Triple-S infringement, Max.'

'I contained the situation as best I could, ma'am. I believe you have the perpetrators here, somewhere . . .' I paused invitingly, but she simply stared impassively, so I gave it up and let her get it off her chest.

'And now Dr Bairstow requests my assistance in what you informed Captain Ellis is, actually, an internal St Mary's matter.'

'That is true, ma'am, but unless these people are removed, there will be many more such infringements and it is very possible the Time Police will come to regard the days when Dr Bairstow commanded St Mary's as some sort of Golden Age.'

Some silences can be very expressive and this one easily conveyed how very unlikely that was ever likely to be. However, I'd made my point.

She sighed. 'We shall respond, of course. Captain Ellis will take four teams and a medical unit and render whatever assistance is required.'

'On behalf of Dr Bairstow, ma'am, thank you.'

She nodded.

'Regarding the other matter, ma'am, I believe the time has come to set that in motion. It's time to pick up the plan.'

She seemed amused. 'Yes, I think you've had time to get yourself into enough trouble here and Dr Bairstow has already initiated events at the other end.'

'He has, ma'am. Everything is ready.'

'Fortunately for you, this request for assistance will mean a large number of my people will be elsewhere.'

'Yes. I'm sure he didn't mean to be but, for once, Halcombe has been useful.'

She sighed. 'Get a good night's sleep, Max. It could be your last for quite some time.'

I did. I had a very pleasant evening meal and popped in to see Matthew. I had all sorts of messages from Leon, ranging from getting his hair cut to suggestions for the steering on his dirigible. I would have liked him to spend the night in our room, but it was a school night and not part of our normal routine. It was very important that everything looked absolutely normal.

I took the files to bed with me and read them through one last time. I made no notes. Then I fed everything through the lockbox auto-shredder. On my instructions, the computer turned out the lights. I lay in the dark and tried not to think of all the hundreds of things that could – and probably would – go wrong.

At least I didn't have long to wait. The next day started normally. I rose early and dressed. I had to wear uniform – it would look odd

286

if I didn't – and I couldn't pack a grab bag, so I wore two T-shirts and stuffed my finally useful Batman utility belt with various odds and ends I thought I might need.

I ate the most enormous breakfast, selling it to myself on the grounds that from this moment on I didn't know where my next meal would be coming from. And then I thought, don't be so ridiculous. It might not even begin today.

But it did.

I was in my carrel, head down and working hardish – the very model of a conscientious officer – when I noticed the buzz around me. Someone was running from carrel to carrel and I could hear cheering. Propelling my chair backwards so I could see what was happening, I stuck my head out and asked what was going on.

'They've got them,' said the officer in the next carrel excitedly. 'They've finally got them.'

'Who?' I asked in some alarm, half my mind still on Dr Bairstow and Leon and Peterson and everyone.

'Those little bastards.'

'What? What little bastards? Not . . . ?'

'Yeah. They got them early this morning. They finally ran them down – somewhere on the Chinese/Mongolian border. And their bastard pod, too. I shan't be sad to see the back of those little sods and I'm not the only one.'

'No, I can imagine,' I said casually. 'What will happen to them?'

He made that graphic throat-cutting gesture.

I was a picture of outrage. 'But they're children.'

'Well, no, they'll be tried, of course, but it's a foregone con-clusion, and then the short walk to Room 29. It'll all be done properly. We're not murderers,' said the man who was part of the organisation preparing to execute a couple of teenagers.

'Mm,' I said, heart racing. 'Well . . . must crack on.'

'Me too,' he said. 'See you in the bar this evening. There'll be a bit of a celebration.'

I watched my hands shut down my files and data stacks. I watched them place my pens in my pen mug. I picked up my notes and scrap paper and shoved it all in the auto-shredder. I left everything neat and tidy because I was never coming back and walked slowly out of the library.

My heart was thumping fit to burst. My hands were clammy. I didn't trust myself to take the stairs so I used the lift. The doors opened and I strode down the corridor. I was speeding up. I couldn't help it. By the time I got down to the lower levels, I was nearly running.

Just in time to catch them escorting Adrian and Mikey out of the pod bay on their way to . . . somewhere unpleasant, I guessed. Although it looked as if a certain amount of unpleasantness had been endured already. Mikey was crying. Her hair was all over the place and her clothing dishevelled. Adrian had a nasty bruise on his cheekbone and blood running from the corner of his mouth.

Bastards.

I pushed my way through the jeering crowd lining the corridor. There weren't as many as there could have been because four teams, a back-up unit and a medical team had been despatched to support Dr Bairstow at St Mary's. Nevertheless, they were being escorted by a detention squad; they're not usually selected for their social skills, but I didn't let that stop me. I pushed the nearest one against the wall. I only got away with it because it was so totally unexpected. He bounced off the wall and the next second was in my face.

I never gave him the chance. Rage is a very useful emotion.

It takes you straight through the narrow straits of common sense, right into death-wish territory without passing go or stopping to collect two hundred pounds. His visor was down and that blank-faced stare would have terrified me if I'd stopped to think about it. The only thing I could see was myself, reflected in his faceplate.

'You cowardly bastard. Typical Time Police. This is about your level, isn't it?'

He shoved me back. Considerably more effectively. I went flying into the crowd who helpfully pushed me back into the fray again.

'Come on then,' I shouted. 'Come and have a go if you think you're hard enough. I'm small. I'm female. That's what you like, isn't it? People who can't fight back. *Little girls*. No wonder you can't catch Clive Ronan. Too big a boy for you, is he? Worried he'll make you cry instead of the other way around?'

It suddenly dawned on me that everything had gone very quiet. I was winding up a prime example of a thoroughly nasty species and he was completely surrounded by his mates.

Fortunately, he ignored me. The squad reformed themselves around their prisoners and continued on their way. I was a fly they couldn't be bothered to swat. I was left with a group of grinning Time Police officers enjoying my mortification. Someone laughed. I tried to elbow my way through them and no one stepped aside. I really had to work at it, finally forcing my way through and arriving hot, dishevelled and furious, at the lift. I stabbed the button repeatedly because that always makes the lift appear more quickly, doesn't it? My temper was climbing to eruption point. Eventually, in its own time, the lift arrived. I stamped inside and called for the floor. It shot smoothly upwards.

I stormed down the corridor to Commander Hay, crashing

through the door into Captain Farenden's office. He was talking to two other officers and looked up, startled. 'Max – did you have an appointment?' He reached for his diary.

I ignored him and headed for her door.

'Hey, you can't go in there.'

I ignored him again and threw open the door.

Commander Hay and two unknown officers were pouring over a complex data stack. They looked up at my hasty entrance.

For a second, no one spoke – they out of surprise and me because I couldn't catch my breath.

Behind me, Farenden said, 'I'm sorry, Commander, I couldn't stop her.'

'It's all right, Captain, I think I can guess what all this is about.'

He shot me a look and then closed the door quietly behind him.

I had to be careful. I was certain he would be listening and there were two others out there with him as well.

I went straight to the point. 'You're going to kill them?'

She said coolly, 'Well, not me personally. And only after an inquiry, of course.'

'You mean a trial.'

'If you want to call it that.'

'After which you will kill them.'

'If they are found guilty.'

'Will they? Be found guilty?'

'If the evidence points to their guilt.'

'And who is presenting the evidence?'

'The Time Police.'

'And who presides over the trial?'

'The Time Police.'

'And who represents Adrian and Mikey?'

290

'An appropriate member of the Time Police will be appointed.'

'After which they will be found guilty.'

'Given the facts as they appear at the moment – very probably.' My voice was rising. 'And killed.'

She appeared to make an effort to remain calm. 'The Time Police will at all times . . .'

'You're going to execute a couple of children. If you added their ages together they probably wouldn't reach thirty.'

'Those children, as you call them, have been indulging in illegal time travel and . . .'

'And so you'll kill them. Why bother with a trial? Why didn't you save yourself the trouble and just shoot them as they exited their pod?'

I was shouting now, alternately thumping her desk and waving my arms around. She, on the other hand, was icy calm. At a nod from her, the other two officers began to shut down the data stacks. Neither of them looked at me. One of them went to speak and she stopped him with a gesture. I was about to find out how little I counted for in this organisation. She moved to attack.

'I confess, Maxwell, I find your indignation somewhat hypocritical. You had no hesitation in handing over Major Sullivan and his men and they at least had the excuse that they were acting under orders. These two are just a pair of delinquents racing up and down the timeline and it's only by enormous good fortune they haven't brought about some sort of temporal catastrophe. That, of course, doesn't register in any way with you, does it? But we are the Time Police and we do not tailor our policy according to the whims of St Mary's.'

'You can't . . .'

She cut across me. 'We can. And we will.'

291

'They're so young.'

'Not so young they didn't know what they were doing. No,' she held up her hand as I tried to speak. 'Enough. This is a Time Police matter and we will adhere to Time Police procedures. You elected to become a member of this organisation because it suited you to do so. We were supposed to serve your ends. Because we had a common cause I agreed to take you on. You agreed to abide by our rules and regulations. In typical Maxwell fashion, you have chosen to renege on the deal because, suddenly, a small part of it is unacceptable to you. Let me put this in words you can understand. Tough. Due to the excellent work of my people, two dangerous young criminals have been apprehended today. They are subject to Time Police procedures. As are you. I suggest, for your own good, that you take yourself off somewhere and have your hissy fit in private because you will not find a single soul in this building who has even the slightest sympathy for two stupid children who could have killed us all. Now get out.'

I stood, paralysed for a moment, while my brain struggled for words to express what utter bastards they were and failed miserably. I whirled about and wrenched open the door. Captain Farenden and the two officers with him were on their feet, hands on their weapons. He moved to intercept me. I heard her call, 'Let her go, Charlie.'

I shoved him aside, kicked a chair out of my way and stormed out. I heard her start to speak but the words were lost as I slammed the door behind me.

The corridor was empty. All the doors were closed but I could just imagine the ears pressed against them, laughing at the misfit from St Mary's getting her comeuppance. I stood for a moment, chest heaving to get my breath back, and then headed for the lift because the best thing in this sort of situation is never to give yourself enough time to think, otherwise common sense kicks in with a hundred good reasons why the daft course of action you propose to embark upon is foolhardy – if not terminal – and the best thing would be to sit down with a cup of tea and write a strongly worded letter of complaint instead. I decided that would be Option Two.

Option One was to try not to get myself killed.

I'd been here long enough to realise there were corridors and staircases less used than others and I utilised all of them, eventually fetching up in their subterranean areas again. These were the working bits of the building. Here were the generators, the recycling room, the boilers, the air-conditioning units and so on. It was heartening to see that even the most sinister organisation still needs space for unwanted office equipment, broken chairs and old photocopiers.

I snaked my way down a dimly lit corridor, emerging through a single door at the other end.

Over there, off to the left, was the Pod Bay. The medical facilities lay ahead and, to my right, an area that was officially off limits to me. Off limits to practically everyone, actually. I rather suspected Room 29 might be close by.

I stared thoughtfully. Time to take stock. I only had a sort of plan. I'd been devising various ways and means in my head but I'd always known the situation would be fluid and I'd been unable to devise a specific plan of action. Now . . . now the moment had arrived and I couldn't hang around thinking. I had to act. And I did, because I'd just had a brilliant idea.

Trust me, mankind might still be living in the technical age, but she who wields the clipboard is king. Or queen. One of the two anyway. And there was one hanging off a nail not three feet away.

Backing up, I wrenched it off the wall. It was supposed to be a maintenance record of some piece of electronics housed in the metal box nearby, but I needed it for something far more important than that.

I folded the sheet over and reclipped it. Yes, I know we're in the future but anyone who fondly imagines the paperless office had arrived should brace themselves for a big disappointment. Even these days, the clipboard reigns supreme, conferring dignity, gravitas and, above all, responsibility on the bearer. I had to work a bit at the gravitas and dignity but, trust me, I never have any difficulty being responsible for anything. And today was no exception.

I took three deep breaths, smoothed my hair, straightened my clothing, made a conscious effort to release the tension in my shoulders, marched down the corridor and tapped sharply on the door. Not a timorous *do you think you could let me in if it's not too much trouble please* tap, but a brisk *please don't keep me waiting because I'm very busy*. Polite, but peremptory.

The com box on the wall squawked. 'Yes?'

'Hi. I've just come from Commander Hay's office and I need to see our latest acquisitions, please.'

This could be easy.

'For what purpose?'

Or not.

'I've had previous experience with these two. The Commander has instructed me to exploit that and get some answers.'

'Turn to your right and face the camera.'

I turned to my right and faced the camera, flourishing my clipboard just for good measure.

Nothing happened for so long that I was convinced they were checking my story with Commander Hay, in which case there might be a teeny tiny problem. And then, just as I was beginning to wonder if I should walk away while I still had legs, the door hissed open. Of course, its opening could be the prelude to something unpleasant happening to me, but I'd just have to risk it. I could hardly ask them to let me in and then not go in, could I? Because that wouldn't be suspicious at all.

Telling myself I'd laugh about this one day, I stepped through into the Time Police Detention Centre.

29

Actually, such had been my fevered imaginings on the way down here, it was a bit of a disappointment. I'm not sure what I'd expected. Dank cells with manacled occupants screaming in torment, possibly. Or a bald, burly, leather-aproned man scrubbing blood off the walls. Sometimes, too much imagination is a curse. I was looking at a bright, modern detention facility, laid out like a racetrack, with what I assumed were offices and such-like down the middle and cells ranged in a rectangle around the outer walls.

Each cell's door was identical. Alongside each door was a keypad – so much for my plan to overpower the guards and take the keys – and over the keypad was a panel with the name of the prisoner currently benefitting from the facilities. As in a hospital, they'd put the most serious cases by the door. Those cells were occupied by Sullivan and his men. For the moment at least, they were taking priority over two harmless teenagers.

Apart from Markham's concealed stun gun, I was unarmed. I'd seriously thought about acquiring some weaponry – don't ask me how because they didn't leave that sort of thing lying around – but I'd decided against it on the grounds that although they might not have any problems shooting an unarmed person dead, they *definitely* wouldn't have problems shooting an armed person dead. Besides, I couldn't just march into the armoury with a shopping list.

An officer blocked my path. Female. I didn't make the mistake of thinking this would make things any easier. Her badge read: MSg B. Romano. She was built like a tank, but there was only one of her. I rather hoped a large number of her colleagues were off apprehending the idiot Halcombe and his minions at that very moment.

'Yes?'

I've always thought of Italian as a very melodic language, but not this time.

'Maxwell – to see the prisoners. I'm supposed to gain their confidence and encourage them to tell us everything.'

She relaxed a little. 'Well, I do not think it will take very much – the little one has not stopped crying since she got here.'

Good for Mikey.

'Let's hope I can capitalise on that,' I said, trying to look stern. 'Is there somewhere quiet I can take them?'

She looked around. 'There's an empty interrogation room over there. Number Two. Separately or together?'

'Together, I think. To begin with anyway.'

I stood as close to her as I dared and watched as closely as I dared. I'd talked to Markham about keypads and he was almost certain they would change the code every day, although, as he said, that was always the problem. People forget passwords. Just take a look at the number of yellow Post-it notes with today's passwords, key codes, whatever, plastered around people's work areas. It's forbidden but still people do it. Because the trouble is, he said in his capacity as oracle, although you had to have some-thing different every day, it still had to be something everyone could remember. Today's date usually figured prominently, he said, because everyone, with the possible exception of historians, always knew what today's date was.

Because I knew more or less what I was looking for, I reckoned I'd got it. She started with six figures – today's date, I fervently hoped – and two letters afterwards. Her initials, possibly? That would make sense.

Mikey was released first. Still tousled and weeping profusely, she was propelled into the interrogation room.

The door hissed closed. Adrian was next up. Romano checked I was standing well back and then opened his door. He looked past her at me, and I nodded slightly. He, too, was pushed into the interrogation room. I was surprised there was only one of her to handle two prisoners, but both of them looked so bedraggled and woebegone, and Mikey was weeping buckets. Obviously, no one expected them to put up any sort of fight. Just as they'd been instructed.

'Just one thing,' I said quietly, as I followed them into the interrogation room. 'Commander Hay wants the cameras off.'

'Why?'

I shrugged. 'She didn't tell me. She's given me five or six questions to ask – it'll take me about thirty minutes, I reckon – and then I'm to report straight back to her. All this is for her ears only.' I leaned closer and then lowered my voice. 'I suspect there are certain details she won't want made public. Such as how the two of them managed to evade us for so long.'

I think it was the 'us' that did it. She thought for a moment and then said, 'I can knock off the sound but not the camera. That's for your protection. In case they overpower you.'

Well, that was insulting. Between them, Adrian and Mikey had

298

the muscle power of cotton wool. Damp cotton wool. However, I nodded and contrived to look grateful.

As I'd hoped, she turned her back on me and reached up to the recording device on the wall. I pushed her hard. She smacked into the wall and I zapped her with my stun gun. She went down heavily, knocking over a chair. She would only be stunned for a minute but a minute was all we needed. And I was going to have to spend the rest of my life ensuring I never encountered Master Sergeant B. Romano again.

There were two cameras, one at each end of the room, so no chance of concealment. We had to work fast. Adrian and Mikey were already rolling her over. I ripped two zip-ties out of my utility belt. Adrian zipped her feet. Mikey took her hands and we rolled her under the table.

'Back in a minute,' I said, because I'd had an idea for a diversion.

I crossed to a random cell and peered at the keypad.

I banged in today's date, took a deep breath and then entered her initials. BR. She'd only entered two letters, I was certain of it. So, no rank and no middle initial.

The lock clunked open. I walked away. The door remained closed but was now unlocked. I wondered how long before the inhabitant investigated. As long as he diverted attention from us he could do whatever he liked with his unexpected freedom.

Mikey and Adrian were already at the outer door, waiting for me. Usually, having got into a secure establishment, getting out is easy, but this was the Time Police, after all. There was a keypad on the inside as well. My hand was trembling as I entered the code. How long before anyone noticed that not only had two prisoners disappeared, but that another one appeared to be perambulating the corridors? Would they automatically link the two circumstances? How much time would that buy us?

The lock clunked and Adrian grabbed for the door.

We pulled it to behind us and raced down the corridor. Up until now, things had gone according to plan but, from this moment, we were on our own.

Very, very cautiously, we emerged into another corridor. As we did so, the alarms went off. I never discovered if we had triggered something or whether they'd just realised two of their prisoners were missing.

The noise was overwhelming. It hurt my ears and made it difficult to think. We certainly couldn't hear ourselves speak. I think it must have been designed to be heard by the dead. The very deadest of the dead. We fled down the corridor hoping if anyone saw us they would think it was just panic. Actually, they wouldn't be far wrong. I was beginning to lose count of the number of laws I'd broken in the last week.

I eased open the door to the pod bay. Everyone was crowded into the office at the far end. I hoped they were busy trying to establish the cause of the emergency.

Adrian and Mikey's pod was parked quite close, up against the wall. I had no trouble picking it out. No one would have had any trouble picking it out. Pods come in many sizes and shapes. They may not all be small, anonymous, apparently stone-built shacks, but only one of them looks like a twelve-foot high teapot.

We sidled hastily through the door and it was lucky we did so because the bloody thing locked itself behind us. I suspected doors were locking themselves all over the building, cutting off any faint chance of escape. If we couldn't access the teapot then we were going nowhere.

Three mechs were standing, open-mouthed, in the office at the far end. One caught sight of us, put two and two together and shouted something at his colleagues. One spoke urgently into his com – the other two burst out of the office and came racing down the hangar. As I've already said, it was a big place and they were down at the wrong end. They were shouting at us. I could see their mouths opening and closing. They were waving their arms. I wondered whether they were armed. How much damage could weapons do in a place like this? They wouldn't worry about damage to people – people were expendable – but their precious pods weren't.

The teapot doesn't have a door. Or a ramp. It has a hatch at the top. And a ladder to access it. And there was no ladder. Shit – no bloody ladder.

Shit, shit, shit. I thought I'd thought of everything and I'd forgotten the hatch was about ten feet off the ground. It was just so typical of these two. They'd created and built just about the most sophisticated pod in existence. A pod that had, somehow, managed to bypass most of the safety protocols that were automatically built into both St Mary's and Time Police pods. Which was the main reason the Time Police had come down so hard on them, because theoretically, there was nothing to stop Adrian and Mikey pillaging the past and – and this is the important bit – loading up their pod with stolen treasure and auctioning it all off to the highest bidder. They'd never done so – in all fairness, I don't think it had ever entered their heads – but that wouldn't save them from the wrath of the Time Police. Which we would feel very soon if we didn't get a move on.

However, we still had the entry problem. Whenever they wanted to exit their pod, Adrian and Mikey opened the hatch and chucked out an enormous, heavy and very old-school wooden ladder. It wasn't even a modern aluminium folding affair. My own theory was that it doubled as a weapon. If they didn't like the look of you then they just dropped the ladder on your head and you were out of the game for the next week.

But – and this was the crux of the matter – the ladder was inside the pod.

Not for the first time, I'd underestimated the Time Police. They had one of those airplane ladders parked alongside. All ready for the mechs to start investigating the pod. It was one of those metal ones on wheels with a small platform at the top. Mikey was already wheeling it podwards.

At that moment the alarm stopped and the silence was almost as painful as the noise.

The leading mech shouted and at the same time, the tannoy clicked on. Commander Hay's voice echoed around the pod bay. This was not the Commander Hay determined to promote the softer side of the Time Police. This was the voice of Commander Hay who had fought in the Time Wars and seen her colleagues die.

'This is Commander Hay. Stand still and surrender yourselves. Do not do this. You will be fugitives forever. We will find you. We will hunt you down.'

I couldn't help myself. I shouted, 'Oh really? Before or after you fail to bring down Clive Ronan?'

I don't know why I did that – it wasn't as if she could hear me.

Down at the other end of the bay, I could hear doors banging open. Time Police officers were streaming into the hangar. We had three, maybe four seconds at most. Less if they used their sonic weapons.

'Come on,' screamed Mikey.

I turned. While I'd been wasting my time shouting at Commander Hay, they'd pushed the ladder to the pod and were opening the hatch. Mikey's legs were already disappearing inside.

'Come on, Max.' That was Adrian, lowering himself into the pod, his body lit by a strange blue glow as Mikey began to fire things up inside.

I raced up the ladder. As I reached the top I could feel the ladder vibrate. Someone was close on my heels.

I seized the edge of the hatchway intending to heave myself up and in but suddenly it receded into the distance. My fingers couldn't seem to get a grip. At the same time, I felt a sudden, sharp pain across my chest. I couldn't breathe in. I couldn't breathe out, either. I'd been zapped with one of their sonic thingies.

It's a dreadful sensation. Your body just shuts down. I couldn't breathe. My heart fluttered. The ladder swayed beneath me. One arm was already waving uselessly in the air. The other was clutching at the hatchway. I felt my fingers slacken. I was going to fall. Except I didn't know which way was up and which way was down.

Underwater sounds washed around me . . . I no longer had control over any part of my body. I couldn't see. I couldn't hear. I opened my mouth to tell them to get away without me but nothing happened. The fire in my chest was spreading. I was dying . . .

No, I wasn't – I was flying. Something caught at my wrist at exactly the same time as something caught at my ankle. They'd got me. They would pull me off the ladder. I'd crash ten feet or so on to the concrete floor and it wouldn't do me any good at all. If that didn't render me unconscious their boots soon would.

I tried to kick and at the same time someone grabbed my other wrist. I was being pulled in half.

My free leg was waving around like a flag on a breezy day. I had no control over it at all. I certainly can't take any credit but it connected with something and suddenly the pressure was gone. I was hauled through the hatch. Head first. It wasn't graceful. The hatch slammed shut behind me.

I'd like to think the two of them tried to catch me or at least break my fall, but if they did then they made a lousy job of it. I crashed on to the floor and lay, alternately stunned and dying. I had no idea what I'd fallen on, but I'd really bashed my shoulder on the way down and, believe it or not, I'd bitten my tongue as I landed. I could feel the metallic taste of blood.

Adrian and Mikey were yelling at each other. I could feel a vibration running through what I assumed was the floor. Lights flashed around me. This couldn't be good. Were we going to blow up? The noise rose to an ear-splitting whine. Adrian was counting down. I hoped to God everyone outside had got clear. There's a safety line for a reason.

'Now,' shouted Adrian. 'Jump. Jump. Jump.'

The whine became an escalating scream.

Bloody hellfire. I closed my eyes and waited for death.

Believe it or not – the world exploded in shards of purple.

30

Time for a bit of a recap, I think. To give me the chance to pull myself back together again.

Obviously, I hadn't broken our two young tearaways out of TPHQ. We'd been allowed to get away. Not that everyone had been in on the plan. Yes, the security chief – who wasn't going to thank me for letting one of his prisoners go free and tying up his Master Sergeant – had known about it. But not the Master Sergeant herself, who was probably going to spend the rest of her life looking for me.

The senior mechanic had known. The one who had so conveniently left the mobile ladder for us and made sure everyone was down at the far end of the pod bay.

And Commander Hay, of course. And probably Captain Farenden. And Captain Ellis.

And that was it. Anyone else we encountered would have done their best to take us down. Or take us out altogether. They hated Adrian and Mikey for making fools of them for years and I hadn't used my time there to make friends and influence people, either. If we had been caught, then the three of us would have 'fallen down the stairs' any number of times on our way back to the detention area.

Not that Adrian and Mikey's 'capture' had been entirely genuine, either. My unscheduled appearance at the remote site had been enough for Dr Bairstow – concerned we might find ourselves trapped between Ronan and the people in London – to bring forwards his plans. Leon had shot off with Adrian and Mikey to collect the teapot so they could be 'captured at last' by the Time Police. Something that, given the state of them when they eventually arrived back at TPHQ, they deserved considerable credit for.

Now for Phase Two. Here we were – fugitives in the wind and with the full force of the Time Police about to come down on us. And in possession of the world's most dangerous pod. Word would soon get out. We would be attracting all sorts of attention. From all sorts of people. And from one person in particular. Or so I hoped.

Mikey appeared in my blurred vision and bent over me.

'Max, how are you?'

'Hurrrr,' I said.

'I know – the take-off can be a little bit ... uncomfortable if you're not expecting it. Here, have some cheese.'

'Nnnnnn,' I said.

'You'll soon feel better, I promise you.'

I looked at the small cube of sweaty cheese.

'Nkyu.'

'Let me get you a blanket.'

I felt like granny being tucked up by her granddaughter. No, scrub that – great-granddaughter. But the cheese did help. I have no idea why. Slowly, the effects of the Time Police sonic gun wore off. My stomach settled, my eyesight was no more blurred than it usually was without my specs, and I could sit up and look around.

To begin with, I could hardly believe I was in a pod. The walls were circular. I could see two very narrow bunks – little more than planks, really. There were no lockers, but on the other hand they didn't own anything, so why would they want lockers? There was no bathroom. Not even a bucket that I could see. They did have some sort of console, which at the moment was buried under chocolate wrappers, spill-proof mugs, and a half-eaten sandwich which might have been there for some considerable time.

A pair of Adrian's underpants hung off some sort of joystick. He saw me looking, snatched at them and stuffed them away somewhere. There was a distinct sockiness in the atmosphere. You'd never think I was sprawled in just about the most dangerous piece of equipment in the world today.

The walls were covered in graffiti. They'd left notes and reminders to each other, jokes, odd bits of formulae, coordinates, to-do lists, insults, cartoons and so on. I tried to focus but my eyes were still wonky. I'd wait for the paperback edition.

They'd stuck Leon's signal beacon up on the wall. Given its purpose, which was to replicate the radiation signature for the Time Police to follow, I thought they'd have concealed it somewhere discreet. Under a bunk or something. I don't know why I thought that. The metal box was attached to the wall in full view of anyone who cared to look around. Apparently, they felt that standing a plastic model of a T-rex on the top constituted sufficient disguise to render it invisible and, just in case that didn't work, Adrian had stuck a scruffy piece of paper on the front with the scribbled message *Warning. Pre-set. Mikey, do not turn this off.*

The radiation leak was fixed but Leon's beacon would broadcast a very similar signal. The Time Police would be on it immediately. So once again our problem would be to stay ahead of them – because they would be hunting for us in earnest – and we would never be able to stay anywhere for longer than two hours. I wasn't looking forward to this one bit.

We had to do it though. We had to look authentic. Which meant continual jumping. And this pod lurched up and down the timeline as smoothly as the North Sea in a force eight gale. Adrian and Mikey were all right – they were used to it – but I foresaw much vomiting in my future. I hoped we had plenty of cheese.

'Time to get some distance between them and us,' said Adrian, and we had to endure a series of bone-breaking jumps as we endeavoured to build up a lead over the Time Police. I just lay on the floor with my eyes closed. They knew what they were doing. They'd been doing it for years. They probably thought it was fun. My job was simply to lie here and not die.

I lay and shivered as we bounced around the timeline. Without the cheese, I might have been pebble-dashing the walls with the enormous breakfast that had seemed such a good idea at the time. An hour into life on the run and I'd had enough already.

Finally, we came to rest. Don't ask me where.

'I think that should hold them for a while,' said Adrian, switching things off. Mikey raised the hatch, heaved out the infamous wooden ladder, and I wobbled up and out, sat on a nearby rock, took in deep breaths of some much-needed fresh air and waited for my outlying extremities to reassemble themselves in the correct place. This sort of thing was definitely for the young.

'We'll tidy up inside,' said Mikey, handing me another piece of cheese. 'You keep an eye on things out here.'

Out here was a featureless plain that stretched in all directions as far as the eye could see. I suspected I would be underemployed, but I appreciated them leaving me alone for half an hour or so. I was still shaking like one of those quivering trees and now that my sensible half had had time to catch up, I was beginning to realise how many times we'd nearly been shot.

My part in our adventure was temporarily over. I'd got them out. It was up to them to keep us safe.

I could hear the two of them firkling away inside, finally having time to uncover all the food and clothing left for them by a thoughtful Chief Technical Officer. Cries of delight and excitement wafted from the open hatch. I suppose that for two teenagers who, until taken in by St Mary's, had been slowly dying of radiation poisoning, starvation and hot pursuit, all this was luxury indeed.

Mikey appeared with a mug of tea and huge bar of chocolate. There was a note attached to the chocolate. *You'd better get this down you before you puke. Take care and see you soon, Leon x.*

Have I said how brilliant he is?

'Well?' I said, munching away. 'What do you think of your new facilities?'

'Oh yeah, fantastic, Max. There's tons of food. And you don't have to cook any of it. You just have to pull the heating tab. It's brilliant. And there's blankets. And some soap. All sorts of things.'

The hazards of the last thirty minutes appeared to have completely passed her by. On the other hand, she and Adrian had been running from the Time Police for years, so this really was a normal day for them.

'How long can we stay here?' I asked.

'Another hour. To be safe, another forty-five minutes. I've set the alarm. Gotta say, it's good to be back with the old girl again.' She patted the teapot's hull affectionately.

I felt depressed. If she regarded their pod as an old girl, in what light did she regard me? Ancient relic, probably. That was certainly how I felt.

Adrian joined us, munching on something that probably should

309

have been cooked first, but the teenage digestive system is different from that of normal people.

'Another two jumps, I reckon,' he announced thickly. 'Just to muddy the waters a little. If you think it's necessary, Max.'

'I honestly don't know, but I think we should err on the safe side.'

There's a phrase I don't use often, but I was beginning to appreciate its hidden benefits. Not for the first time, I wondered what the hell I thought I was doing. And when the next person enquired whether I was insane, the answer, sadly, was going to have to be yes. And there was no point in appealing to these two idiots. It was all a huge adventure to them.

I had a thought from the last time I'd been on the run from the Time Police. 'Try for somewhere meteorologically or geologically hazardous,' I said. 'Leon and I once lost them for a while at Pompeii. I know from experience that sort of thing causes their instruments some problems and even they weren't prepared to track us down in the middle of a volcanic eruption. With luck, by the time they re-calibrate, we'll be even further away.'

He nodded, swallowed the last of whatever he'd been eating, and with a dramatic swirl of his long coat, climbed back into his teapot.

Mikey and I sat in the sun a while longer.

'You all right with this next bit, Max?' she asked suddenly.

I nodded, because while you're not supposed to lie to the young, nodding doesn't count.

I spent the time gathering my scattered wits and getting my thoughts straight. I'd read the files left by Charlie Farenden. I knew where and when we should be. Just as soon as we had a decent distance between us and the Time Police. Commander Hay and I had discussed whether they should refrain from pursuit altogether – being caught prematurely would ruin everything – but she'd said we had to make it look as realistic as possible and I'd agreed. A large number of the Time Police were currently with Dr Bairstow who, at this moment, should be reclaiming St Mary's and kicking the idiot Halcombe down the stairs. I was sorry to miss that but even I can't be everywhere at once. And I was certain Mrs Enderby could supply Dr Bairstow with a crochet hook should he not have brought his own.

I believe we touched down briefly in Mughal India, to avail ourselves of their monsoon facilities and then hopped off to somewhere white. The whole world was white. The landing on that one was flawless but that was because we landed in twenty feet of snow.

I enquired whether they had a periscope, but with that teenage inability to understand sarcasm, Mikey had replied they had a camera on a stick and did I want to see?

I thanked them and declined.

And then, the time had come.

'OK,' I said. 'Let's get this show on the road.'

As I've said, there's such a thing as pod etiquette. You don't just shoulder someone aside in their own pod and lay in coordinates. That's rude. I gave the coordinates to Mikey and she laid them in.

I clutched my cheese like a talisman as the world shuddered violently and went purple again. When we landed, Adrian flicked on the screen.

Shit. Shit, shit, shit.

I was shocked. And surprised. And seriously concerned. I'm not familiar with London and I honestly hadn't realised we would be that close. Yes, we were on the other side of the river, but through a gap in the skyline, I could easily make out the Battersea Power

311

Station, dramatically lit against the night sky. Even as I watched, the nine p.m. London to Paris airship chugged majestically overhead, navigation lights flashing as it went.

'This is good,' said Adrian, confidently. 'They may not be able to pick up our signature this close.'

'Or, alternatively,' I said, drily, 'they could just look out of the window and wave.'

They agreed yes, that was perfectly possible, although not likely. I think they were beginning to see me as some sort of elderly aunt who needed to be reassured at every given moment. I looked at who was doing the reassuring and shook my head. Neither of them had even the faintest conception of self-preservation. I wondered if Mikey ever remembered she had been shot. That had been me once. When had I become so cautious? So careful? So prudent? I decided to blame motherhood. It changes a person – and not always for the better.

I needed to crack on.

I'm not going to give away any secrets, and the whole thing was redacted shortly afterwards anyway, but somewhere between Chelsea Square and Carlisle Square, there's a tall, narrow building that looks the very epitome of anonymous respectability and really, really isn't.

I'd seen plenty of photos and 3D images of the exterior. But very few of the interior layout. Apparently, recording devices did not function well inside. It had been made very clear to me that once inside this house, I would be completely on my own. Because although the building genuinely looked as if it had been picked up from 19th-century Cheltenham and dropped down here for the sole purpose of looking down on its neighbours, it was, actually, a sex club. A very, very exclusive and very, very expensive sex club.

Yes, all right, go on. Get it out of your systems. I don't blame you. Your reactions were as nothing to mine. Shock. Surprise. Alarm. Apprehension. Denial. Disbelief that such an establishment should exist in such an area. And, all right, just a very little curiosity.

Up until this moment, I'd given most of my attention to the breaking-out-of-Adrian-and-Mikey part of the assignment and spent comparatively little time on the getting-into-the-sex-club bit. I hadn't considered that to be particularly hazardous. Now, staring up at the discreetly flood-lit building, I rather thought I might have been wrong. At least I was familiar with the Time Police and their layout. Sex clubs were a bit of an unknown to me.

Even now, after all these years, my imagination always gets things wrong. In my youth I had always imagined Ancient Rome to be magnificently imposing, with gleaming white buildings and wide, paved roads, gracious porticoes and impressive temples. The reality is that most of it was made up of tall, badly built tenement blocks, and narrow streets stuffed full of beggars, vomit, and mule shit. Their much-vaunted public fountains were not much more than receptacles for rotting vegetables, dead cats and the like. And that was when they weren't being used as public urinals.

I think I thought a sex club would be a scarlet and black, shabby, garishly-lit, music-blaring, everyone having a great time sort of house, with scantily clad young men and women draped suggestively over the front steps and possibly even – given these enlightened days – some scantily clad young livestock.

What I got was a gracious, five-storey Regency building with wrought iron balconies, reminiscent of a spa town in its heyday. Far from being accessorised with over-friendly . . . staff . . . the

313

only people visible were two enormous black men, beautifully dressed in exquisite black suits, black shirts, black ties and the obligatory sunglasses – which must surely have rendered them nearly blind at this time of night. They were standing on either side of the imposing double front doors, occupying exactly the position where more traditional establishments would have placed carefully cultivated bay trees in carefully understated wooden tubs.

They stood, motionless, their hands clasped in front of them, just like those Secret Service agents detailed to protect yet another unfortunate US president against the inevitable. I wondered if they were armed. It seemed safest to assume they were.

I halted unthreateningly at the foot of the steps and we all regarded each other. I think it would have been impossible to overestimate their disinterest.

Slowly, very slowly, I climbed the shallow steps.

There was no response.

I made my voice as authoritative as I could. 'Good evening. My name is Maxwell. I'd like to speak to Mr Atticus Wolfe, please. I shan't keep him long.'

The one on the left said, 'Why?' and his voice was so deep my chest rumbled.

I pushed my specs back up my nose. I was wearing the ones that made me look both intelligent *and* sexy. 'Because, according to my list, Mr Wolfe is the fourth most powerful person in London.'

He blinked. 'What?'

'Well,' I said confidingly, 'I did consider the Lebedev brothers, the *third* most powerful people in London – I should imagine they're very nervously watching out for Mr Wolfe in their rear-view mirror, wouldn't you? – but having considered the situation,

I thought I'd have more luck with Mr Wolfe. As fourth on the list, he's not quite in the top three, but he is the best of the rest and I feel will be more appreciative of the advantage I am about to offer him.' I beamed.

'What?'

I leaned towards them, deliberately waited two heartbeats and then said very softly, 'Please tell him I can give him his heart's desire.'

Their expressions never changed, but I had the definite impression they thought this highly unlikely.

Their next words proved it. 'Get lost.'

'OK.' I turned to go, saying over my shoulder, 'My compliments to Mr Wolfe. Tell him Max from the Time Police said she's sorry we were unable to do business together.'

I made it all the way to the bottom of the steps confident they would call me back and they didn't. Bollocks. This wasn't going to work and I didn't have a Plan B. Back to the pod to think again.

'Wait.'

I stopped and turned. The one on the right was disappearing through the front doors into the brightly-lit hall beyond. The other moved to a more central position and stared impassively down at me.

I made no move to climb back up the steps – not least because I reckoned at least three cameras were watching me – and remained where I was, taking the time to admire the litter-free pavements, the well-lit houses around the square, and the expensively authentic reproduction street lights. There was a very great deal of money invested in these few square yards. Sadly, none of it was mine. Nor ever likely to be.

I don't know for how long I waited there until the door opened.

And stayed open, letting a bright shaft of light illuminate the steps. The guard was holding it open for me to enter.

I walked slowly up the steps, edged past the remaining security man who made no effort to move out of the way, and oozed into the hall. The door closed behind me, shutting out the hum of the city.

This was my first sex club and I was very, very impressed. Don't judge me. Captain Ellis had briefed me on what I might expect to find.

'Relax, Max – there's no sex on the premises – that would be illegal. There's no gambling, either, because that would require a licence. It's a house offering excellent food, drink and "company" to any member who requests it. The "company" can be of either sex and is, without exception, well-educated, intelligent, personable, charming, and able to hold their own in any conversation from football to free-market economies. Introductions are made and there is pre-dinner conversation. During an excellent and very expensive meal, which will be added to the member's monthly account, a great deal of fine wine will be consumed, and the member and however many of the "company" he or she feels they can comfortably accommodate, are put into a taxi and driven to a mutually agreed private destination. All the action takes place well away from club premises. No one will be swinging naked from the chandeliers.'

I'd asked if the 'company' were employed and hired out by the house.

He shook his head. 'Nothing so crude. The house provides only the venue. Several attempts at prosecution have failed to prove that the "company" is in any way employed by Mr Wolfe. His argument is that he provides an environment for friends to meet, dine, and get to know each other better. He maintains that what happens after they leave his establishment is none of his business. Which it isn't. Except, of course, for the vast sums he rakes in afterwards. From both hirers and hirees. His commission.'

'And they pay? Everyone pays?'

'Of course they do. Apart from the fact he'd send the boys round to break more than their legs, it's a highly profitable enterprise for everyone. The "company" – once they've been carefully vetted, of course – have the entrée to a tip-top establishment frequented by the very best people. And the very best people have access to good-looking, intelligent, amenable, and above all very friendly experts in their field who are more than happy – for a generous remuneration – to cater to their every whim. And, best of all, the authorities are thrilled because some very top people are members of this club and it makes it easy for them to keep tabs on who's doing what to whom.'

It didn't sound too bad and I said so.

He frowned. 'Max, you need to be aware that Atticus Wolfe is a very astute man. He plays by the rules – as long as they suit him – and that has made him an extremely rich man. And a very powerful one. He's not one of your backstreet thugs who's dragged himself up by his bootstraps. He's intelligent and cultured. Marlborough and Sandhurst.'

'Sandhurst?'

'Yes, but not for very long. After being invited to resign his commission he diverted his undoubted talents into other, less structured, areas.'

'And you are bringing him to my attention because . . . ?'

'Because we in the Time Police have, for some time, suspected him of being implicated in several serious Time infringements.'

'Details?'

'We're convinced he's been the money behind several illegal pods and their use. Our Mr Wolfe has a penchant for the past. He's invested a great deal of money in the attempted retrieval of various items. Unsuccessful retrieval, so far. We've managed to hoover up his associates but never been able to pin anything on him. But we don't believe he's given up and that, Max, is what makes him so ideal for your purposes.'

I'd taken that nugget of information and run with it and now, here I was, in my by now quite shabby uniform, lowering the tone of an establishment that was, officially, definitely not a sex club. I wondered what Dr Bairstow would say.

Accustomed as I was to the lived-in look of St Mary's and the bland sterility of the Time Police, the inside of a sex club was a bit of a revelation to me.

Given the neighbourhood it was a good bet it wouldn't be furnished with sticky flooring and easily washed vinyl seating. The lighting wasn't low to the point of non-existence. Nor were there any discreet areas where more advanced 'conversations' could take place.

Everything was open plan. I don't know if that was a metaphor or not. There were different levels, but everywhere was visible from where I was asked to wait, just inside the door.

I stood in a wide, welcoming hallway. The floor was of a dark parquet, covered by a Turkish carpet whose rich colours glowed like jewels in the soft light. The walls were panelled with Regency-style wallpaper and there was art on the walls. Good art. A skilfully chosen mix of traditional and modern stuff and it worked very well. There were leather chesterfields and armchairs scattered around for those whose strength had presumably failed them after the short march from the door. The leather looked soft and buttery and was worn just enough to be fashionable.

Shaded wall lights highlighted the paintings and a glittering crystal chandelier hung from the ceiling. Over in the corner stood a grand piano. A real one, not a digital one, which is what you mostly see these days. I think it was a Bechstein. A man in evening dress played 'Spiegel im Spiegel'.

Members were deftly relieved of coats, umbrellas and other paraphernalia by staff who emerged, did the biz and then faded away again. No one was left alone for a second. From the hallway they were escorted into the main area which was where things started to get interesting. If they'd pre-booked – or whatever the expression is – then their "company" would be ready and waiting for them, welcoming them with a charm and enthusiasm so professional that it actually looked genuine. If they hadn't pre-booked, or had just dropped in on spec, they were introduced to a group of three or four equally professionally charming people sitting in the lounge area. I never saw how it worked, but somehow, a choice would be made, those who hadn't made the cut would discreetly fade away and the guest left to enjoy the "company" of their choice.

Everything was smooth and quiet. There were no scenes. No raised voices. Everyone was happy and smiling and relaxed. I couldn't help thinking what the St Mary's version would be like. For a start, there would be Angus.

Of course, this elegant mix of traditional and modern concealed what I was convinced would be state of the art security. This building would be regularly swept for listening devices and hidden cameras. They would have that special glass that blocked wi-fi. There would be very few electronics. And no tills, of course, because no money changed hands. Not here, anyway. I bet if you wanted to pay your membership fees in cash then you'd need to bring the money in a security van.

They kept me waiting for a while. I'd thought they would,

and it gave me time to look around and note the position of any emergency exits should I require them later.

All the staff – and there were a lot of them around – wore dark suits, white shirts and ties. Women wore dark dresses and good jewellery. Most had put their hair up. A door on each side of the hall led off to the restrooms. One of the doors opened and I caught a glimpse of a beautiful room with sofas, dressing tables laden with expensive toiletries, and even more attendants.

Two wide shallow steps led down into the bar. It was gleaming and mahogany and ran all the way down the right-hand wall with well-stocked glass shelves on the wall behind. Two barmen were mixing cocktails. They wore white shirts and black waistcoats and looked extremely smart. And they were very good-looking. As were all the staff. No one waited at the bar. I rather had the impression that standing at the bar was a bit of a no-no. There were about twenty people in the room and all of them were seated. Drinks were served at the tables.

Most people sat in pairs – one man, one woman, or the occasional same-sex couple. Everyone was in evening dress. I passed some time trying to work out who might be the member and who the "company", but such was the quality of the establishment it was impossible for me to tell. I suspected most of the women were "company" but that was only because they were, all of them, good-looking, impeccably dressed, and listening with every appearance of rapt attention to whatever their companions were saying.

Everywhere was the low hum of conversation. Drinks were served promptly and empty glasses whisked away almost before they could be set down.

Looking through the bar, I could see the dining room beyond – a beautiful vision of white tablecloths, shining cutlery and winking

321

glasses. There were fresh flowers on every table. One or two tables were occupied. Waiters – all male – stood against the wall, waiting.

The lighting was quiet, rather than low. Well, they wouldn't want anyone falling down the steps, would they? Men who, in other, lesser establishments would be bouncers, stood in discreet corners, their hands clasped lightly in front of them. And every single one of them was looking at me.

I felt very conspicuous and considerably underdressed. Which I was. I'd tidied my hair and washed my face but I suspected that might not have been enough. I was surprised they'd left me lying around like this where anyone could see me.

I turned my attention back to the bar again, watching the people in there. Yes, I know I should have been concentrating on the job in hand, marshalling my arguments and anticipating what might happen, but I couldn't help wondering at what point the . . . arrangements were made. If it wasn't all pre-arranged then was it before dinner? After? During? What would happen if the 'company' you'd selected fell short? Suppose you changed your mind. Did you hand them back and request another? And, if so, did you have to buy them dinner, too?

One or two heads were beginning to turn my way. I wondered if they thought someone had ordered in a bit of rough.

Before I had too much time to worry that I'd failed to make the social grade in a sex club, another man presented himself to me. This one was black again; although not as enormous as the man-mountains outside, he wore the same black get-up and had an earpiece.

His voice was quiet and very courteous. 'Good evening, madam. How may we be of assistance?'

I took my cue. Quiet and courteous back again. Standing up, I said again, 'Good evening. I was hoping for an opportunity to speak to Mr Wolfe. No, I don't have an appointment and I'm afraid this isn't a matter about which I would care to speak to anyone other than Mr Wolfe himself.'

'I am Mr Wolfe's personal assistant, madam. You may speak to me with confidence.'

Time to give in gracefully. I leaned towards him and said very quietly, 'My name is Maxwell, late of the Time Police. I have an offer which I think might interest Mr Wolfe,' and stepped back again to watch his reaction.

He stood very still for a moment. He would want me out of public gaze and as quickly as possible. I wondered how he would do it.

'I wonder if you would be more comfortable in one of our private salons, madam?'

I smiled. 'I'm sure I would, but I should perhaps warn you that my non-appearance at a certain place and at a certain time will cause others considerable consternation . . . and cause *you* extreme inconvenience.'

'I do not doubt it, madam, and I am certain Mr Wolfe will do everything in his power to ensure you make your rendezvous. My suggestion that you repair to a salon was based solely on the need for discretion.'

'Thank you, Mr . . . ?'

'My name is Khalife,' he said solemnly. 'Demiyan Khalife at your service, madam. This way, please.'

The small salon turned out to be quite large. By my standards, anyway. I really must tell Dr Bairstow about all this and see if we couldn't get St Mary's remodelled along the same lines.

I seated myself on a very comfortable sofa. This was obviously some kind of waiting room. A selection of magazines was laid out on the coffee table, just like at an upmarket dentist. Accustomed as I was to the Spartan living conditions of the Time Police, I looked around for the drinks machine in the corner. Obviously, there was nothing like that here. The door opened and a waiter enquired whether there was anything I needed.

I shoved aside my overwhelming urge for a margarita. I needed to lay off the booze if I was going to get through this, so I asked for a glass of water. He reappeared a moment later bearing a tray with a glass that he set before me as if it were the Hope Diamond.

I thanked him.

The glass was smoked and heavy and the ice clinked expensively. It wasn't until I swallowed that I realised how dry my mouth was. Still clutching the glass, I extricated myself with some difficulty from the sofa and wandered around the room, checking out the art. Here it was mostly modern. I was unfamiliar with the artists, and I was peering at a small landscape, trying to make out the signature, when the door opened behind me. Mr Khalife was back. And with a young woman in a sharply tailored suit.

'I hope, madam, you will not be offended.'

I'd been warned to expect this. 'Of course not.'

She was very thorough, going over every inch of me. I had to take my top layers off. Mr Khalife studied the wall, which I appreciated. She ran her fingers over every inch of my skin, examined my clothes minutely, and ended by passing a wand over them and me. She paid particular attention to my hair and ears, eventually saying, 'Thank you, madam. May I assist you to redress?'

I'd never had anyone help me to put my clothes back on before. Leon sometimes assists in getting them off but that's because he's the impatient one in our relationship. 'Thank you, but I can manage.'

She nodded and I scrambled back into my clothes, trying not to think about the CCTV because it wasn't anything I could do anything about so no point in worrying.

When I'd finished, she left the room, saying to Mr Khalife, 'Nothing.'

He turned around. 'Dr Maxwell, would you care to come this way?'

My heart sang. I had what I needed.

Still clutching my drink, I followed him across the hall and through a door marked 'Office'.

If this was an office then I wanted one just like it. Another thing to talk to Dr Bairstow about. There was more fine art on the walls. Very fine art. I itched to get over there and have a closer look. Concentrate, Maxwell.

A complete arsenal hung from one wall. Spears, daggers, knob-kerries, swords, shields, slings and other weapons. None of this was my speciality but the period looked medieval and most of them appeared to be of African or eastern origin.

Another wall was floor-to-ceiling books. And not just posh but unread, leatherbound, carefully selected to make you look good, bought by the yard books, but real ones. Some looked new. Good to know books make it into the future.

A beautiful Persian carpet occupied the centre of the floor, surrounded by gleaming parquet. Three bronze lamps stood in the corners, sending out a soft, warm gleam which was reflected off the curtains, themselves shot through with bronze thread.

The fourth corner was occupied by a magnificent ebony statue of an African warrior. Two huge masks hung either side of it.

They looked Greek. I couldn't take my eyes off them. They were genuine – I was convinced of it.

There was a proper working desk, not some magnificent edifice hewn from an endangered forest somewhere. Two cardboard jacketed files lay open before him. I remembered there was probably no wi-fi. Behind the desk was the most imposing object in the room: the man sitting behind it.

I've never been a portrait painter. I've done a couple of Leon, one of which he quite liked, but Matthew never sits still long enough for me to get a good likeness of him. Looking at this man, I could see why an artist would be inspired. I guessed from the width of his shoulders that he would be tall. His hands were beautifully shaped. His grey suit was the best I'd ever seen. His skin was the darkest I'd ever seen – and he had light grey eyes. I was transfixed. Speechless.

Someone coughed. For God's sake, Maxwell, focus.

'I beg your pardon. I was distracted by your wonderful masks.'

He smiled and it was a genuine smile. 'Do not apologise, Dr Maxwell. I am perfectly accustomed to taking second place to the treasures in this room. Allow me to introduce myself. Atticus Wolfe.'

'Maxwell,' I said. Which he knew but I couldn't think of anything else to say.

He didn't rise from his desk or offer to shake hands. That was fine by me.

We looked at each other. He was an extraordinarily handsome man. His bone structure was superb. His skin so dark as to be almost black except it wasn't black. Black was far too dull a word. There was deep, deep purple in the shadows under his eyes, olive green in the hollows in his temples, and his brow gleamed rich

326

brown and crimson. A golden light caught his cheekbones and the bridge of his nose. His shaved skull was the most perfect shape. Even his hands, long and slim with tapering pianist's fingers, were elegant.

I blinked and became aware I was staring.

'Well, Dr Maxwell – I believe you have a proposition for me?'

I did it all wrong. We should have danced around each other – neither of us committing ourselves to anything that could be construed as illegal in a court of law. There should have been elegant repartee and oblique allusion while we took stock of each other. There wasn't any of that.

I blurted out, 'Have you ever had your portrait painted?' And it would have been hard to say which of us was most surprised by the question.

He glanced up at Mr Khalife, who had moved to stand behind his right shoulder in a manner that rather reminded me of Commander Hay and Captain Farenden, and then back at me.

'No, I have not.'

'Well, if you ever do, would you consider offering me the commission?'

'Is that what you wished to speak to me about?'

'No. I have just never met someone who would make such a spectacular subject.'

He leaned back and smiled. 'And how would you represent me?'

I thought of the statue, the African artwork. In for a penny . . . in for a pound.

'Could you stand up, please?'

He looked surprised and for a moment I thought I'd gone too far, then he cast an amused look at Mr Khalife and came out from behind his desk to stand in front of me.

327

The two men outside had been colossal but this man wasn't far off. He was powerfully built, but not bulky. His head gleamed under the light from the chandelier.

'I see you leaning on your spear. The day is ending. Your lion skin hangs over one shoulder. Jebel Barkal stands behind you. You are watching the sun set. You are alone.'

There was no reaction of any kind.

I stopped, stepped back and muttered, 'Sorry.'

He stood for a moment longer and then motioned me to a sofa. It was as comfortable as the others. He sat at the other end and we turned to face each other.

'So that is how you see me.'

It was how he saw himself but no need to tell him that.

'Yes, but I regret I have allowed myself to become distracted.' As if any man minds being a distraction. 'It is on another matter that I have come this evening.'

'Yes,' he smiled, a man enjoying a joke. 'I believe you have something unusual for me.'

He knew I wasn't wired. I had no such comfortable conviction. I was certain there were two, maybe three cameras in this room. Hidden eyes would be watching my every move.

'I do. You should know, however, that despite my uniform, I no longer work for the Time Police. We have . . . parted company.'

'May I ask why?'

'They were pursuing a course of action of which I did not approve.'

'I see. Do you frequently disapprove of those around you?'

'No, but on this occasion, yes.'

He waited.

I swallowed. 'There is, in existence, a pod. The Time Police have

328

been pursuing it and its occupants for a very long time. Eventually, they were successful. They proposed to execute them. I disagreed with this policy – *deeply* disagreed with this policy – and so I facilitated their . . . departure. And that of their pod.'

I stopped and waited again, but he still said nothing so I ploughed on. 'I must now speak frankly.'

'Please do.'

'We are fugitives. The Time Police will never rest until they have recaptured us. We need protection and sanctuary. Not many people are able to provide this. The Time Police are powerful. We need someone even more so and who, for a remuneration, would be prepared to offer us what we need.'

'And what form would this remuneration take?'

'In return for our safety, we would undertake to . . . work for this person.'

'In what capacity?'

'Well, it occurs to me that, for example, should this person collect certain objects that are not always easy to procure, we could be instrumental in obtaining some very choice items for him.'

He made a dismissive gesture. 'But you are describing something that cannot happen. Everyone knows that nothing can be taken from the past. The Time Police make that very clear to everyone. There are safeguards, protocols and so forth. And consequences.'

I looked him in the eye. 'All of that is very true. But perhaps you should ask yourself *why* the Time Police are so interested in this particular pod. *Why* they have pursued it for years. And *why* they are dealing so harshly with its owners.'

'The Time Police are interested in every illegal pod. And they deal harshly with everyone.'

I said softly, 'But this pod is . . . special. And its inventors even more so.'

There was a very long silence. No one moved. On the other side of the door, people were having a perfectly normal evening – having dinner, meeting exciting new people, booking an evening's adventurous sex – 'you bring the Pyrex and I'll bring the goat' – while in here, I was breaking the few remaining rules left to me. After all, I'd changed – sorry, re-routed – History, so why not now start to plunder it?

He said very slowly, 'In what way is this pod so special?'

I lowered my voice. I might as well make it as difficult as possible to those listening in. 'Let us assume that during the pod's construction, certain protocols were either not built in or somehow bypassed. It was not deliberate. No one is quite sure how, but this pod is able to remove items from the past. Successfully. By which I mean no one dies. Unless they're caught by the Time Police, of course. In the interests of full disclosure, I must point out that anyone taking on this pod will immediately find themselves in the gravest danger.'

He stood up abruptly and returned to his desk. To show my independence, I remained where I was, but I suddenly felt very isolated and afraid. For something to do, I sipped my water and took stock.

These were intelligent men. Intelligent enough to know that power speaks for itself. That they had no need for shouting and violence to intimidate others. Polite and quietly spoken they might be, but only up to a point. At this moment it didn't suit their purposes to hurt me but that could all change in a heartbeat and I had no back-up of any kind.

I rather thought I was safe for the moment. There was no point in them killing me now. If I didn't make the rendezvous, Mikey and Adrian would simply jump away and re-join St Mary's. They wouldn't be happy, but they'd promised. Everyone would be very sorry the plan hadn't worked and then sit down to think of something else.

On the other hand, Mr Wolfe, or more likely, Mr Khalife, might decide he could prise the location of our rendezvous from me, turn up in my stead, somehow overcome the two of them and try to seize the pod. I was sure Adrian and Mikey, veterans of Time Police pursuit over the years, would be more than equal to that, but that wouldn't benefit me. It dawned on me that, at that moment, I really was in a very bad position. On the other hand, it wasn't the first time I'd been without back-up. Could be the last, though. I thrust that thought away.

Mr Wolfe seated himself slowly and precisely, straightening the few items on his desk that had somehow managed to disarrange themselves in his absence.

'I have sources, Dr Maxwell, and yet I have heard nothing of this.'

'And you won't. The Time Police will lock this down as tightly as they can. There's no way they will want word of this pod getting out. And certainly not that they had it and let it go. They will concentrate every resource on recapturing us. We need a protector. The strongest there is.'

'Forgive me, Dr Maxwell, but I would like to be absolutely clear on this. You are telling me that you possess a pod able to remove items from their own timeline?'

He'd got the phraseology exactly right. More than ever, I was convinced I had the right man and this would succeed.

I nodded, and then said, 'Sorry – for the benefit of hidden microphones, I just nodded.'

331

Another silence fell. Both of them possessed the gift of complete stillness and the knowledge of how to use it. Suddenly, Atticus Wolfe pulled open a drawer, pulled out a piece of paper and held it out to me.

I looked at it and then looked at him. Surely, he didn't expect me to sign something?

'A preliminary sketch.'

'I'm sorry?'

'You wanted to paint my portrait. I believe the established procedure is to begin with preliminary sketches.'

'Here? Now?'

'Why not?'

So – no pressure then. I wondered if this was a test. If I made a good job of the sketch then he would continue with our transaction. If not . . .

I stood up and approached his desk. I stirred his pen pot until I found a pen I could use, said, 'With your permission,' and pinched his blotter to use as a makeshift drawing board. Even more cheekily, I plonked myself down in his visitor's chair directly opposite him and asked if he could turn slightly to his left.

There was a lot resting on this. I told my hands to stop shaking and my heart to slow down. I didn't rush into it. I made myself spend some time just staring at him. Looking at the planes and angles of his face. He sat perfectly still, showing no signs of impatience. No one spoke.

I started with the inside corner of his right eye because if I could get that right then the rest should follow, and then spread outwards. The bridge of his nose, his other eye. The flare of his nostrils. The angle of his cheekbones. The set of his eyebrows.

I didn't rush, but I didn't have to. I had some trouble with the curve of his mouth and in the end, I left it very loose – just a line and a shadow. Actually, the whole drawing was fairly loose. I concentrated on the shadows, using the white paper to suggest the highlights. The precise planes of his face slowly began to emerge. I was lucky. The likeness was there from the very beginning. Given the circumstances under which I was working, I could so easily have made a mess of it. I narrowed his eyes slightly, emphasised his cheekbones – which were magnificent anyway – and worked away in silence.

Complete stillness had descended upon the room.

Pushing my luck, I got up, moved around the desk to peer closely at his eyes. Mr Khalife stirred very slightly and I decided that was enough.

Ten minutes later, I was done. And I wasn't displeased. Although that wasn't any credit to me. Some faces just scream out to be painted and I couldn't screw them up if I tried, but this was good work. Even I was satisfied. Although I wasn't the important person here.

I laid it on the desk in front of him. His own face looked up at him. Still and stern, looking slightly away at something only he could see.

The room filled up with another long silence. I think it was a deliberate ploy to unsettle visitors. It certainly unsettled me.

Finally, he stirred. 'Perhaps we could discuss some specifics.'

I looked at the clock on the mantelpiece. I had thirty-five minutes before I needed to depart. I had decided against informing Mr Wolfe of our two-hour deadline. I certainly didn't want to give him information he could use against me. And it would be our protection against the inevitable moment when he decided he

333

didn't need us any longer and would go it alone. Fat lot of good that would do him. One hour and fifty-five minutes later he'd find himself looking at some seriously irked Time Police officers. No need to bother him with that information either.

On the other hand, I had only thirty-five minutes, so I kept calm and asked what he had in mind.

'You will bring me something.'

Success!

'All right.' I stood up.

'Something unique. Something that could not possibly have come from say . . . a museum or a private collection somewhere.'

Ah. I wondered if he'd been caught like that before. Someone had stood before him proudly flourishing some artefact that they had, in fact, lifted from a museum just down the road.

'All right.'

He said again, 'Something specific.'

'If you are thinking of someone's famous jewels, then no. Too difficult. And too easily traced.'

'I was thinking of, possibly, something from the *Titanic*.'

My stomach clenched. 'Absolutely not.'

He swept on. 'I want proof, Dr Maxwell. Something unique. A one-off. Not something that could have been stolen from a collection or a museum. Some headed notepaper, perhaps, from the passengers' lounge.'

Oh, for crying out loud. I had no doubt Adrian and Mikey would be up for it but there was no way I was going anywhere near the *Titanic*. Pods have slightly less buoyancy than the Great Pyramid encased in lead and the Atlantic goes a long way down.

'Well,' I said, to gain time. 'That's certainly . . . specific.'

'I have been deceived in the past, Dr Maxwell.'

334

By whom, I wondered, and tried not to think about what could have happened to them.

'Something that could not possibly have come from this time.'

'Righty-ho.' I headed for the door.

'Where are you going?'

'To procure something specific and unique. Something that will impress even you, Mr Wolfe.'

'And what would that be?'

'A surprise.'

I reached the door. Not to my surprise, Mr Khalife was there before me.

'Are you going to check to see I haven't stolen an ashtray?'

'Mr Wolfe has not given you permission to depart.'

'I don't need his permission to depart.'

He said very gently, 'Such discourtesy so early in our relationship.' He was close enough to see the line of sweat on my top lip.

'I know,' I said. 'Believe me, I'm as shocked as you, but no doubt Mr Wolfe is excited to see what I shall bring him, so I'm prepared to make allowances.'

'I think Mr Wolfe feels his interests would be best served by you remaining here for the time being.'

'I'm sure he does but, as I said before, if I am not at a specific place at a specific time then the offer is withdrawn.'

'You are fugitives. You need protection. You need Mr Wolfe.'

'You are correct. I am a fugitive. And I do need protection. But not necessarily Mr Wolfe's protection. If I am not at the rendezvous point, my colleagues will simply make the same offer to a . . . excuse me, I have trouble with this name . . . Mr Spirios Panagopoulos, who is not, I believe, unknown to Mr Wolfe.'

'And how will this trouble Mr Wolfe?'

335

'It will not trouble Mr Wolfe at all. Except that then Mr Pana-gopoulos will possess what Mr Wolfe does not.'

'It is you, I think, who will be the loser.'

'I'm on the run from the Time Police,' I said, bitterly. 'I'm a dead woman walking. And perhaps you are right. Perhaps even Mr Wolfe cannot protect me from them. Perhaps it would be in all our best interests if I simply walked away and we all pretend this meeting never took place.'

'Twenty-four hours.' His voice came from the other side of the room.

I turned back to Mr Wolfe, still sitting at his desk. 'I beg your pardon?'

'You have twenty-four hours.'

Twenty-four minutes would more than do it but no need to tell him that either. I didn't want to make this look too easy.

'Very well. Good evening, Mr Wolfe. Mr Khalife.'

I reached for the door but he was ahead of me again. 'Allow me, Dr Maxwell.'

'Thank you.'

I had a feeling turning my back on Mr Wolfe would be consid-ered unwise as well as discourteous so I nodded and backed out of the room into the hall.

The place had filled up since I'd arrived. There were more people in the bar now – still all sitting at tables. No one was standing at the bar. No one was alone. Everyone had at least one companion. Some of the conversations had become animated. Behind them, in the dining room, more tables were occupied. Waiters were flying to and fro with laden trays. I wondered how much a meal here cost. Which obviously led me to wonder how much an evening with one of Mr Wolfe's 'company' cost. And he earned at both ends of the transaction. He took his cut from both the donor and the recipient of whatever services had been negotiated and at comparatively little risk to himself. I reminded myself this was only a small part of his trade. The public face of his occupation. The working conditions of those hundreds of women further down the scale would hardly bear thinking about. A short life of violence, hardship and disease was their lot.

Mr Khalife escorted me personally to the front door. 'Goodnight, Dr Maxwell.'

'Do you have delivery facilities here?'

He seemed surprised. 'Why would you ask?'

'In twenty-four hours I will have a delivery for Mr Wolfe.'

'May I ask the nature of the delivery?'

'You may, but I think Mr Wolfe should be the first to know, don't you?'

For a moment, he regarded me with no expression at all and I went cold all over. I forced myself to smile politely. 'It has been a pleasure to meet you this evening, Mr Khalife. I shall see you again soon.'

'Within twenty-four hours, Dr Maxwell.'

I smiled in what I hoped was an enigmatic manner, although I've been told that really doesn't work for me. Someone – I've no idea who – flung open the front door with a flourish and I was back out in the cold night air.

I said a polite goodnight to the two well-dressed thugs on the door. I'm an historian and it's one of our basic rules – always be polite to the man with the machine gun/spear/army/clipboard/vicious dog/whatever.

They both ignored me. As far as I could see, neither of them had moved at all during my visit inside.

I trotted carefully down the steps, turned left and strode confidently up the street. Past the lighted windows, now with their curtains drawn. Back towards the hum of traffic in the distance.

I turned a corner and was out of their sight. I took a firm grip on some expensively ornate railings and sucked in great lungfuls of oxygen. The sweat was pouring off me. I could feel cold damp patches under my arms, in the small of my back, even the creases of my knees. The night was cool but that wasn't why I was shivering. There had been no threats, no hostility, not even raised voices, and yet, throughout the entire interview, I had been conscious of such a sense of menace. I had never met two men who frightened me more. Not even the two massive men on the front door. Atticus Wolfe had terrified me from the moment I walked into his office. As had his so-called personal assistant. Of Demiyan Khalife's loyalty to his boss there could be no doubt. There was a closeness there. A bond. Complete loyalty to one another. I wondered if they had grown up together. It seemed likely. I wondered whether they were aware they both possessed the same facial marker – the Kushite fold that had given me so much trouble in Mr Wolfe's sketch.

I had no doubt that had Atticus Wolfe so much as lifted his little finger, I'd be face down in the Thames by now. And I'd probably never have known anything about it.

I took two or three more deep breaths and straightened up before someone rang the police and reported a strange woman hugging their railings. This was a well-to-do area – they would be here in seconds. I set off again.

I was almost certain I would be followed. Not a problem at this stage. In fact, I couldn't blame Mr Wolfe for his suspicions. I walked briskly, only looking behind me to cross the street.

No one was in sight but I was convinced they would be there somewhere.

I took the long way back, cutting down narrow streets full of smart houses with window boxes and expensive curtains. They were tiny, narrow-fronted houses that would have cost more than both Leon and I would ever earn in our entire lives. Just down here was an alleyway between two houses. An iron bollard prevented vehicular access. I turned down the alley. Being between two high brick walls with no way out was not comfortable. I'd once had a very unpleasant experience in a narrow Whitechapel alleyway. Still, I'd survived that. I could survive this.

I listened for footsteps but could hear nothing. If they were there then they really were very good. At the end I stopped and looked back. The alleyway was empty. I felt rather silly. Then I worried that perhaps they hadn't believed me. Perhaps I wasn't important enough to warrant the effort. Perhaps no one was following me at all.

I pulled myself together. No – of course they were. Somewhere, they were here.

And so were Adrian and Mikey. The alleyway opened up into a wider area – one of those funny spaces where two alleyways converge and no one can think of anything useful to do with such a tiny space. I could see the teapot against the far wall. Initially, I'd been concerned its unusual shape would promote comment but fortunately it bore a really very startling resemblance to the public conveniences dotted around the area. It was still a little early, but I wondered how many slightly confused and increasingly desperate revellers had tried to gain access.

The hatch was down and locked. There was no sign of life. They were under strict instructions. I stood some ten feet away where they could see me. There was a pause which I chose to believe was them carefully surveying the area to make sure I was alone, although with those two I wasn't optimistic.

The hatch opened and their heavy ladder thudded to the ground. I clambered up and in. The hatch closed behind me.

'Any chance of a cup of tea?'

A steaming mug was placed in my hands.

'You cut that rather fine,' said Adrian. 'Should we go?'

'Whenever you're ready.'

I hung on tight to my tea as the world shuddered and went purple.

32

The next landing was better. Or possibly the vast amounts of cheese I'd consumed were beginning to kick in.

We made no move to disembark. I'd warned them to be very careful.

'They once suffered an invasion by Clive Ronan,' I told them. 'A lot of people died. They're rather keen to prevent a repeat of that. There is every possibility they'll shoot first and apologise afterwards.'

They nodded.

We sat quietly while armed guards surrounded the teapot and then, when we reckoned everything had settled down a little, I raised the hatch and slowly peered outside. 'Good afternoon. I'm here to see Director Pinkerton. I do have an appointment.'

We were at St Mary's, but not my St Mary's. A future version. I'd been here before and I was here now because they owed me. We'd landed on what used to be the South Lawn and now was just pastureland. Wild flowers grew everywhere. I rather liked it. The gardens were much less extensive than I was used to, but the building itself was considerably larger.

A familiar figure approached. She was wearing her orange jump-suit. Before being appointed director, she'd been the unit's Chief Technical Officer and I guessed she hadn't completely given that up.

She put her hands on her hips and stared up at me. 'Max, welcome.'

Why is no one ever pleased to see me?

'What ho,' I said cheerily, because it would have annoyed Markham, had he been here. 'Can I introduce my travelling companions? This is Adrian and this is Mikey.'

Their heads popped up alongside mine. Rather like meerkats, as Pinkie said later, but less cute. Adrian and Mikey smiled and waved. No one smiled and waved back.

We climbed down slowly, Mikey very carefully securing the hatch behind her. They weren't as irresponsible as they looked. We were taken around the front of the building and in through the main doors. Wisely, Pinkie had decided she didn't want either of these two having a good look at Hawking and its contents.

'We could do with recharging our batteries if that's possible,' said Adrian. 'We have solar chargers, but direct power is quicker and easier.'

She nodded. 'Do you use an Edmondson connection or a Parissa fitting?'

'Neither,' he said, ruthlessly reducing technician mystique to something understandable by small dogs and historians. 'Bog standard caravan plug. Have you got one of those?'

'I'm sure we'll be able to find something somewhere,' she said gravely and two technicians peeled off to rifle their stores for something that probably hadn't been used for some considerable time. Not at St Mary's anyway.

Mikey and Adrian might be unknown quantities but I was an honoured guest. Pinkie took us to her office. In Dr Bairstow's time it had been full of books and ancient prints. In Pinkie's it was full of engineering diagrams.

Our escort was dismissed and we were alone.

She hadn't changed since the last time I'd seen her, which hadn't been that long ago. We'd gone off together one Christmas and done something that was outrageous even by St Mary's standards, and which I can't tell you about even a little bit because the only reason the Time Police allowed us to live afterwards was because we signed an incredible number of documents promising to take the secret to our grave. And beyond the grave, as well, according to Clause 18(b).

Her air of pugnacious belligerence was somewhat muted these days, although I suspected it wasn't far away and could easily be resumed should she find it necessary. She had a square face and sandy hair which she was still wearing in a thick braid over one shoulder.

I made formal introductions.

'Wow! Director Pinkerton! Awesome!' They beamed at her and she thawed a little. It's hard not to respond to blatant hero worship. Even Dr Bairstow had succumbed, after all.

Pinkie turned to me. 'Are these the ones all the fuss has been about?'

'I expect so,' I said, since Adrian and Mikey were too busy staring around to reply.

I know we're supposed to treat teenagers like proper people, but they don't always make it easy. They were wandering around her office, examining diagrams and plans. 'Wow! This is so cool.'

I wasn't sure I should let them – contaminating the timeline and all that – but on the other hand, it kept them out of mischief for a few minutes so I left them to get on with it.

'You know why we're here, don't you, Director?'

'Well, I think most of us were rather hoping you'd come for

a shower and change of clothes, but yes. They're crated up and ready.'

'That's great, thank you.' I paused. 'Although a shower would be nice.' I poked Mikey, staring in awe at a diagram of an exploded pod. I mean the diagram was exploded – not the pod. For the time being, anyway.

'What? Oh, yes, a shower.' She focussed on a bemused Director Pinkerton. 'Do you have any cheese?'

I don't think she quite knew how to respond to that. 'Not on me, no.'

'A nice shower,' I said brightly to Mikey, 'and our clothes laundered while the pod is loaded.'

'A nice shower and our clothes laundered and then *we* load the pod,' said Adrian firmly, obviously not prepared to have just anyone accessing his beloved teapot.

Dr Pinkerton nodded gravely. 'I think that can be arranged.'

'Who have you got for us?'

'Hillary and Donald.'

'A breeding pair? Excellent.'

'Max . . .'

'You'll get them back,' I soothed. 'They're worth far too much for anything to happen to them. Which is more than can be said for these two and me. Out of all of us, Hillary and Donald are the most likely to emerge unscathed.'

'Do you have time to eat?'

Adrian and Mikey, who always had time to eat, gazed at me imploringly.

'Of course,' I said. 'But first – a shower.'

They laundered our clothes for us which was pretty good of

344

them. I should imagine there was some muttering over my TP uniform, but I got it back and in considerably better condition than when I'd taken it off. I know the Time Police have self-cleaning clothes but even they hadn't been able to cope with life on the run. In a teapot. With teenagers.

We also tucked into fried chicken, chips and salad – no one ate the salad – and a satisfying number of cups of tea.

I felt a hundred times better as we headed towards the pod. Two large crates awaited us, each covered by a tarpaulin.

'It keeps them quiet,' said Pinkie. 'They think it's night.'

Actually, according to my internal clock, it was about two o'clock in the morning, but time is relative.

'Max . . .'

'So how many dodos do you have now?' I asked, hoping to change the subject. I really didn't want her telling me how risky this whole business was. I knew how risky this whole business was. No one knew better. And we hadn't even got started yet.

'Nearly one hundred,' she said, wearily. 'Yes, they have the infant-nurturing skills of Herod the Great, but that's offset by their extraordinary fertility. We lose a lot of eggs – mostly they get trampled – but a significant number survive long enough to hatch. We have so many now that we've actually put together a plan to return a group of them back into the wild.'

'Not to the 17th century,' I said, alarmed.

'Oh, no. Contemporary time. I think it's scheduled for next Thursday. We release them at, say, nine o'clock in the morning, an eminent ornithologist on an expedition from the University of Thirsk makes the discovery of a lifetime at, say, eleven-thirty, and the whole shebang is on the six o'clock news that night, complete with pictures of cute dodos and an incoherent ornithologist. Apparently, there's been an unknown colony in that remote location all this time.'

'And no one ever noticed?' I said in disbelief.

'Apparently not.'

'Will they be safe, do you think?'

'Well, let's hope everyone is a little wiser the second time around and the only shooting is done with long-range cameras.'

'Yes, indeed. What do they eat, by the way?'

'Everything. You will want to be careful what you leave within beaking range. Hillary, they tell me, is particularly fond of hard-boiled eggs.'

'Isn't that like some form of cannibalism for them?'

She nodded. 'Eating one's young.'

'Eating one's young is a hugely underestimated weapon in the parental arsenal.'

We broke off to watch the two rather large crates being man-handled towards an aperture not designed for such an object.

I turned to Mikey. 'Are we going to be able to get them in?'

'Oh yes,' she said cheerfully. 'And it'll be much easier getting them back out again.'

I doubted that but she seemed confident enough so I let it go.

I thanked Pinkie, who told me for God's sake to take care, Max.

We climbed aboard, they detached the umbilicals, and off we went again.

As I had suspected, getting the crates out again wasn't the plain sailing Mikey had reckoned, but no one dropped a dodo, no one fell off the ladder and no one put their back out. We stood, hot and panting, in the intersection between the alleyways which now constituted our head office.

346

'You'd better be ready to shoot off,' I said. 'Just in case.'

Adrian set his foot on the bottom rung and then turned to me. 'Are you sure you'll be all right, Max?'

'I'll be absolutely fine,' I assured him. 'Give it five minutes and then off you go,' and I set off for my second visit to a sex club.

The front was shut up. Even the bouncers had disappeared so I went around the back. The sign said *Ring for Deliveries* so I did. Mr Khalife himself opened the door. Considering the hours they must keep here, I wondered if he'd even been to bed.

'Delivery for Mr Wolfe,' I said, cheerfully.

He stared at me. I wondered if he'd ever expected to see me again.

'Got a flatbed?'

They did. They had a flatbed. A very smart affair, remotely operated, that could cope with steps and sharp corners. Perhaps they used it to manoeuvre drunken patrons discreetly out of the door and into a taxi. He clicked his fingers and two men followed us down the road, around the corner, down the alleyway and into the little space that we were now calling our own. The teapot had disappeared and just the two tarpaulin-covered crates remained.

He twitched aside the canvas. Hillary – or Donald – stared sleepily back again. He did the same with the other crate and Donald – or Hillary – grockled a protest. Khalife's face was expressionless. If he'd been expecting or hoping I would fail, I couldn't see it.

He clicked his fingers again. I didn't even have to load the crates myself. So far, being a member of the criminal classes was working out quite well for me. The two blokes loaded the dodos and we all set off back to the sex club.

How many books have you read that include the words dodos and sex club in the same sentence?

He motioned the men to take them inside, barking at them in a language I didn't understand when they banged the flatbed against the wall.

This house was much bigger than it had looked from the outside, being narrow but deep. There were rooms and corridors in all directions. The old servants' quarters, I guessed. And they had a goods lift. I tried not to think about some of the things that might have been transported in it.

Obviously, plebeian crates and the peasants escorting them were never going to make it all the way to Mr Wolfe's office. We finally came to rest in a small bare room at the end of a long corridor. At a word from Mr Khalife, the two men disappeared. We awaited Mr Wolfe in silence.

He made us wait, but not too long. The door opened and in he came. He wore a lighter grey suit which made his skin look darker than ever. I had no idea what time of day it was. There was light outside but that was the extent of my knowledge. I also knew that despite the quick wash and brush up at Pinkie's St Mary's, I was looking tired and scruffy.

He greeted me courteously. 'Dr Maxwell.'

'Mr Wolfe.'

He stared at the crates. 'And here we have . . . ?'

Here we go.

'As discussed, something specific. In fact, I've exceeded the brief. Not one but *two* unique specimens. Two members of an extinct species that could not possibly have originated from anywhere except their own time. Please regard them as a gift to you, a demonstration of good faith and an example of things to come.'

'May I see, please.'

Mr Khalife carefully removed the tarpaulins. Donald and Hillary gazed incuriously at Mr Wolfe, who stared impassively back again.

'Dodos,' I said. '*Raphus cucullatus*. Extinct since the 17th century. You now possess the only two specimens in existence. At this moment in time.'

He peered at them. I hoped to God he hadn't expected Tutankhamun's death mask. With Tutankhamun still wearing it.

'Male and female,' I said, to break the silence.

He straightened up. 'Remarkable. Quite remarkable. And these two – how much would you say they were worth?'

'Hard to say,' I said, not having a clue.

'But a considerable sum, you would think.'

'Indeed, yes. The sort of money anyone would pay for the last two of their kind.'

He nodded to Mr Khalife, who took a small gun from his pocket, pointed it at the nearest bird – and fired.

The shot sounded enormously loud in the small space. I jumped out of my skin and then stared, appalled, at the bloody bundle of feathers that had once been a dodo.

I opened my mouth to demand to know what the hell he thought he was playing at but, fortunately, before I could make matters worse, my brain kicked in. Because, unknowingly, he'd done me a favour. Brought me up short. Now, I realised just how dangerous this man was. How violent. How unpredictable. Of course, he was. He was the ruthless head of a large criminal organisation and I'd fallen victim to his charm. I'd been seduced by the civilised surroundings and the good suit. I'd forgotten who and what I was dealing with. And a dodo had had to die to remind me.

This man was a cold-blooded criminal. A brutal thug who had clawed his way to the top in a brutal world. His hands would not be clean. I'd fallen for the charm, just as he'd intended me to. This . . . establishment of his was just the acceptable face of his activities. He was a trafficker. For every well-turned-out woman present last night there would be hundreds more held against their will and forced to work in a dark and degraded world. This man dealt in death and terror and violence and, just because he was good-looking and intelligent and charming, I'd very nearly forgotten who he was, who I was, and why I was here. I wouldn't make that mistake again.

I did manage to remain calm. But only just.

'You seem upset, Dr Maxwell.'

Somehow, I kept my voice steady. I shrugged. 'I don't like waste.'

'But now I have more than doubled the value of the remaining bird.'

I let my anger show. 'They were a breeding pair. You could have charged a fortune for every egg. They would literally have been the dodos that laid the golden eggs.'

'But then others would have their own dodos. They might set up their own breeding programmes. Mine would no longer be exclusive. And I must always have exclusivity.'

I would not give in. 'A problem easily solved by only selling the males.'

'But a cross-species manipulation with, for example, turkey DNA . . .'

I brought out the phial. 'Dodo contraception. If you had given me time to explain.'

Silence. Here we go . . . Now the fun would start.

He said very softly, 'You will get me another.'

'I don't think so.'

'That was not a request.'

Mr Khalife was behind me. With his gun. I said quietly, 'But that *was* a refusal.'

'I do hope we're not going to fall out so soon in our relationship.'

'What we do is not without risk and I am reluctant to take that risk if you're going to shoot everything we bring back.'

'My problem, Dr Maxwell, is that I am not completely convinced these are what you claim them to be.'

'I don't understand. They are – were – a pair of dodos.'

'Of that I have no doubt – it's their point of origin I dispute.'

'I'm sorry, I'm not with you.'

'How do I know these are what you claim them to be?'

I stared. I heard my voice say, 'What do you think they are – camels?' And now I needed to tread very carefully indeed.

He said thoughtfully, 'Perhaps *I* should make the next choice.'

'What next choice?'

'My choice. I will decide what you will bring back for me.'

'No,' I said slowly.

Mr Khalife stiffened. I'd gone too far. I wondered if anyone had ever said no to Mr Wolfe before.

Mr Wolfe made a slight gesture in his direction, turned to me and said, 'No?'

'This is ridiculous. I moved heaven and earth to obtain those specimens for you and not only did you shoot fifty per cent of them but now you're saying you don't believe they're genuine. This is a business arrangement and as such requires a degree of trust from both parties.'

Mr Khalife said softly, 'I could shoot you where you stand.'

I sighed. 'You'd have to join the queue.'

More silence fell. I moved my position slightly so I didn't have to look at the dead dodo. The other one – his mate – was shifting its weight from foot to foot in agitation and making soft grockles of distress. I picked up the tarpaulin and threw it over the cage. The grockling ceased.

Mr Khalife was between me and the door. No one had come to investigate the shot. I was well and truly up the River of Excrement and my canoe had no visible means of propulsion.

OK. Time to make things worse. I said, 'I propose a practical demonstration.'

'I don't understand, Dr Maxwell.'

'I'm offering to take you on a jump. To prove we are who we say we are. Are you up for it?'

He spread his hands. 'Why would I do such a thing?'

'It's the only way you can assure yourself that whatever we bring back is completely and utterly genuine.' I held his eye. 'And exclusive.'

He made no reply for a long time and then said, 'What sort of trip?'

Now I had to be careful. If I told them what I proposed, and if Clive Ronan *was* involved somehow, then an ambush would be easy and I'd had enough of that.

'Egypt,' I said. 'The funeral procession of Tutankhamun. What do you think?'

'What will I see?'

I tried to put myself in his shoes. What would he want to see?

'Ancient Egyptians. Processions. Grave goods.'

He looked unmoved.

'Gold. Probably quite a lot of gold. You could think of it as a preview. A chance to scope out future opportunities.'

He nodded, his face giving nothing away. I was certain, sooner or later, he was going to double-cross us but I could hardly complain because I fully intended to double-cross him.

I walked to the door, not looking at the dead dodo. 'Ten a.m. tomorrow morning. Mr Khalife knows where. Wear something loose and flowing.'

'Are you insane? Why would I trust you?'

I shrugged. 'Trust me – don't trust me. Your choice. We will wait five minutes. No longer. If you're not there you will never see us again. Take your dodo and do with it as you please.'

Well, they were never going to let me go, were they?

'I think not, Dr Maxwell. I rather think we should discuss your continued presence here and how it will ensure future good behaviour from your colleagues.'

I shook my head. 'You haven't met my colleagues, so I'll forgive you, but trust me, they have absolutely no conception of the words "good behaviour". And they're certainly not stupid. They'll land, wait for five minutes and then leave. Then you'll be stuck with me and I can produce any number of teachers and ex-employers to testify I'm the most awkward sod in existence. There are two blokes back in 1400 who still wish they'd never clapped eyes on me. You'll have no choice but to shoot me, dispose of the body, and hope the Time Police never put two and two together and use it as the excuse they've been waiting for.'

Listen to me defying organised crime.

His face was carved from stone. 'I am not convinced you and the Time Police have completely sundered your relationship.'

Shit. Stay calm, Maxwell. 'Best you don't shoot me then. Not until you're completely certain. They get very upset when people shoot one of their own. And it's not as if they're not itching for an excuse to take you down.'

All true, according to the Time Police file.

He stared for a moment. 'How did they ever come to recruit you?'

'Seconded,' I said, because telling the truth is a Good Thing.

'From where?'

'St Mary's.'

He was incredulous. 'A religious establishment?'

'Well, there is often a great deal of futile god-invoking going on so yes, if you like, an establishment with a religious interest.'

He stared at me some more. I stared back. How much of a risk-taker was he? A big one, I suspected. You didn't get where he was without pushing your luck.

'So,' I said. 'Ancient Egypt – yes or no?'

'No,' said Mr Khalife.

'Why there?' asked Mr Wolfe.

'Because I think you'll like it.'

'No,' said Mr Khalife again.

'Yes,' said Mr Wolfe.

Mr Khalife was not happy. 'Sir . . .'

'Peace, my friend. You will be accompanying me.'

I frowned.

'A problem, Dr Maxwell?'

'We have space issues. You are neither of you small men. I might have to scrunch you up more than is commensurate with your dignity.'

'Mr Khalife will gladly make the sacrifice.'

Mr Khalife was a very unhappy man. Guess who was going to get the blame for that.

He was even less happy at seventeen minutes past eight the next morning. I know we'd said ten a.m. but seventeen minutes past eight is such a much more innocuous time of day.

We had landed in their back yard when they were expecting us in the alleyway. And we were early. I've become an expert in avoiding ambushes.

I took a quick look around. This was the bit of the club the punters would never get to see. It seemed deserted enough. We'd parked next to piles of empty crates and in front of a long row of wheelie bins. It was tidy – there were no bodies or vomit and no one was being knee-capped. Nocturnal establishments don't tend to be lively at seventeen minutes past eight in the morning, but I had a good stare around at the blank walls and empty windows, just to be on the safe side.

I rang for deliveries again and scampered back to the pod.

If they'd had anything sinister planned for us then nothing showed in their faces although they were neither of them very cheerful. I had no idea whether it was because their plans had been foiled or if it was just early morning grumpiness.

It got worse. I hadn't tried to prepare them for their first sight of the pod because how many ways are there to describe a twelve-foot high teapot that don't actually include the words twelve-foot high teapot? I've never heard such an eloquent silence. Not even from Dr Bairstow who does that sort of thing quite well.

They were going to be even more unhappy when they realised we weren't going to Ancient Egypt.

I was pleased to see they'd obeyed the 'wear something flowing' directive. Both wore dazzling white jellabiyas. I wasn't sure how accurate they would be where we were going, but Jebel Barkal was a cosmopolitan place and they shouldn't stand out too much. Their turbans were traditionally long – to be used as a shroud should they fall in battle – which could be quite useful if we found ourselves in difficulties. Not that we would. I had no intention of straying much more than ten feet from the teapot. This would be the safest jump ever.

First things first.

'Right,' I said, channelling official tour guide. 'Let's have your guns.'

That got the sort of reaction you would expect.

'No,' I said firmly. 'No. Absolutely no guns. This is my world. If you want to survive then you do as I say. No guns. If you shoot someone and they turn out to be an ancestor then you might never have been born at all, in which case you never got to shoot your ancestor and at this point we're dealing with the P-word.'

There was a thought-filled pause and then a slightly baffled Mr Khalife said, 'Do you mean penis?'

I sighed. This was going to be a very long day.

I said patiently, 'No, I mean paradox. Not that it would get that far because History would have taken you out long before you'd be allowed to create such a thing. Trust me – I've seen it happen. So – no guns. Or knives.'

I'm pleased and proud to say I've caused the opposite sex a

356

great deal of trouble and grief over the years and today was no exception. Their very lack of expression spoke volumes.

'I mean it,' I said. 'You will be putting yourselves in extraordinary danger if you carry any sort of weapon.'

'Then how do we defend ourselves?' enquired Mr Wolfe.

'Well, you'll have Mr Khalife here to do that for you and I'll do as I always do, which is run like hell.'

OK – so we hadn't scored highly with the teapot. Our scores had plummeted further when I made them give up most of their weapons – I say most, because even I wasn't stupid enough to assume they didn't have a couple of knives, hand-grenades and small thermo-nuclear devices concealed somewhere about their persons – but I think it's safe to say their first sight of Adrian and Mikey took our score right down to *nul points*.

The two sides stared at each other. Adrian was wearing his dramatically long coat – I suspected he intended to be buried in it – and Mikey was in her favourite disreputable old flying jacket and flying helmet and had completely unnecessary goggles on top of her head. They beamed politely at our prospective passengers who stared stonily back again. I would not have thought it possible for Mr Khalife to look any more unhappy, but he managed it.

He turned to me. 'Are you insane?'

I was tempted to come back with my usual response, 'No, Dr Stone had me tested,' but I suspected an imminent sense of humour failure.

He pointed a disbelieving finger. 'These are children.'

Shaking my head, I said, 'It's a well-known fact that most physicists have done their best work by the time they're thirty.'

Huge apologies to physicists everywhere.

'It's the same with temporal dynamics.' I tried to remember

when I'd been more authoritative on a subject I knew absolutely nothing about. At this rate I'd be able to run for parliament. 'These two designed, built and operate this tea . . . this pod. It is far in advance of anything yet produced, which, I believe, was what interested you in the first place. If, however, you have changed your minds . . .'

'Sir?' said Mr Khalife and they exchanged a look.

Mr Wolfe smiled. 'My friend, I have never known you to give bad advice, but I think a small compromise here might benefit everyone.'

He meant a hostage.

Adrian, Mikey and I had discussed this. It made sense. Accidents aside, there was nothing to stop us spiriting the two of them off into the wide blue yonder and never bringing them back. Adrian had volunteered, saying he could do with a bit of a holiday, warned Mikey the teapot was still a couple of decades out and not to forget to compensate for drift.

I saw no signal, but two men appeared from the back door. I recognised the two bouncers from last night. They kept their distance but we all knew why they were there.

'Oh great,' said Adrian in excitement. 'Can I be the hostage? Pleeeease. Do you have the Sports Channel? Can I play my guitar? Any chance of a McBurger or three?'

He started to walk towards the two men. 'Hi, my name's Adrian. What's yours?'

They stared over his shoulder to Mr Wolfe who smiled slightly. 'Why not?' He raised his voice. 'Give him everything he wants.'

'Cool,' said Adrian, with enthusiasm.

'Bummer,' said Mikey. 'Is it too late for me to be the hostage?'

'Can we get a move on, please?' I said, motioning Mikey back

358

to the pod. Wolfe and Khalife stood stock-still. Had it all been too easy?

'Come along,' I said, making chivvying gestures. 'Let's get this show on the road.'

Mikey waved at Adrian who waved back again. I wondered if either of them had even the faintest idea of how much danger he was in.

I climbed up the ladder. Then Wolfe. Mr Khalife brought up the rear.

Mikey helped me inside. Wolfe and Khalife swung themselves down like athletes. I reminded myself I was the brains of the outfit – not the brawn.

They looked around. I could feel their surprise.

I know I've already described the unlikely interior of their teapot. Nothing much had changed except now it was redolent with the results of dodo travel-sickness. I felt quite nostalgic for cabbage.

We sat them down facing the wall because, as Mikey explained, having no safety protocols wasn't always a good thing and we could land anywhere. She added cheerfully that there was nothing to stop us rolling a hundred feet down a sand dune and that it had happened once before, although it had been hilarious because Adrian had been eating spaghetti at the time and she'd practically had to cut him free. She finished by telling them that if they were facing the wall then they couldn't see if anything went wrong and ignorance was bliss and to trust her.

I think at this point they were so bemused at this charmingly informal approach to time travel that they'd have gone along with anything. If they'd seen pods before I couldn't help wondering what they'd been expecting this time. Banks of sophisticated equipment? Flashing lights? Steely-eyed operatives feeding complex mathematical and temporal equations into some kind of super-computer? Trust me – you don't need any of that. Which was just as well because we didn't have any of that.

I joined them on the floor, hoping they would find my presence reassuring, rather like goats and racehorses, but I could have been kidding myself. I said, 'You might want to brace yourselves.'

I think they were already braced, but they found a little extra from somewhere.

I heard Mikey talking to the computer. The teapot shuddered and the world went purple.

It was bad for me. I can only imagine what it must have been like for them. I pushed at Mr Khalife. 'Get off me.'

He heaved himself up. Wolfe was staring at the floor with the intent expression of someone concentrating on keeping his insides inside. I could now add grey to his impressive list of skin colours.

We gave them a moment to regain their composure. I remember thinking that if this didn't cure them of wanting to accompany us on all future jumps then nothing would. Alternatively, of course, they could just think of someone who had annoyed them recently – they had a long list, I was willing to bet – and despatch them in their place.

Mikey was rummaging for the cheese. 'Here you are,' she said cheerfully, holding out a handful of sweaty lumps.

Their silence was eloquent.

'No,' I said. 'She's right. At the moment, you're suffering nausea, headaches, disorientation, and poor coordination. You will go on to experience feelings of disconnection and the fear of being lost. To say nothing of the sheer weight of time bearing

360

down upon you as you struggle to find your place in it. All that will pass. Cheese will help.'

I think they felt it was one of those situations where the cure is worse than the disease, but they wouldn't be where they were if they weren't tough and resilient. They took the cheese, munched for a moment and then looked around.

'Just take your time,' I said. 'You don't want to spoil the experience by vomiting over your own feet. Or even worse – my feet. Mikey – how are we doing?'

'Spot on,' she said, shutting things down. 'I was easily able to compensate for the drift. Adrian's such an old woman. Whenever you're ready, Max.'

I stared at the screen. It wasn't as big as the ones I was accustomed to, but the resolution was excellent.

Mr Wolfe had pulled himself together. 'Where are we?'

'Aha,' I said. 'A typical rookie remark. Your first question should always be, "When are we?"'

Actually, the first question was frequently *What went wrong?* closely followed by *When are we leaving?* and *Whose fault was it this time?* but no need to bother them with that now.

I indicated the screen with a flourish. 'Behold.' And that's not a word you get to say every day of the week. Not in normal everyday conversations anyway.

They beheld.

The sun was just coming up and turning everything to liquid gold. Long, long purple shadows stretched towards us.

'Again, I ask. Where are we?'

'The land of Kush. Around 720BC.'

There was a bit of a pause. '*Not* Egypt?'

I said, 'Not Egypt, no,' watching his face carefully for signs of

361

disappointment at a possible failed ambush, but as far as I could see there was just non-comprehension and irritation and I get that all the time in my normal working day so it was water off a duck's back, really.

'And you have brought me here because . . . ?'

'Several reasons. I've never been here before and I've always wanted to come. It's the time of the Black Pharaohs. And – something you may find interesting – it's almost certainly the land of your ancestors.'

Mr Wolfe said, 'My family comes from Chelmsford.'

'I daresay,' I said, 'but your ancestors were Kushite.' I indicated with my finger. 'You both have the Kushite fold.'

Even I could see that, despite my enthusiasm, Mr Wolfe was underwhelmed.

'This is not Egypt.'

'No, this is the country that rules Egypt.'

He stared again. 'I would have preferred Egypt.'

Bloody ingratitude. Five minutes into his first jump ever and he's moaning already.

'You mean Egypt with its pyramids and monuments? Its stele and temples? Its wealth and influence? Its riches? Its treasures?' I paused. 'And its gold.'

He nodded and said firmly, 'Yes. That Egypt.'

'Egypt has no gold. Well, yes, they do, obviously, lots of it, but what I'm trying to say is that gold is not mined in Egypt. This is the land of Kush. Where Egypt's gold comes from. My thinking was that it would be easier – although not today, of course – for us to steal a little gold at source, so to speak, rather than wait until it found its way up to Egypt. Where they really don't take kindly to that sort of thing at all. And their punishments are not much fun.

You know – impalement. And while I'm the first to enjoy a good laugh, believe me, there are no funny historian-on-a-stick jokes.'

They took a moment to think about this. I could practically hear their brains working. Passengers apart, I have to say, I was beginning to see the attractions of the shadier side of time travel. You could go where you pleased and do as you pleased when you got there. There were no rules. And not least, actually being able to call it time travel without fear of incurring the wrath of Dr Bairstow. I took a moment to wonder what was happening at St Mary's and then dragged myself back to the here and now. There was nothing I could do for my colleagues. I needed to concentrate my attention here. I had to keep these two off-balance. Keep them always slightly unsure of what was going on. Not enough to frighten them, because frightened people are dangerous, but just vaguely disoriented and unsettled. And very dependent on me and Mikey.

I indicated the hatch. 'Gentlemen, are you ready?'

I didn't bother waiting for a reply. Mikey sprung the hatch and I climbed up, heaving their bloody stupid ladder as I went. There surely must be some good reason why they lugged this bloody great heavy thing around with them when surely a neat, folding aluminium affair would have been easier, lighter, more convenient, and less prone to braining anyone unfortunate enough to be passing below.

I climbed out into the brilliant sunshine, down on to the gritty sand and waited at the bottom for them to join me.

They made a business of straightening their robes and turbans which fooled no one. They were using the time to pull themselves together and get their bearings. I gave them a while, because I still remembered my first jump. The heart-thumping excitement. The

363

trepidation. The anticipation. And underlying everything – the faint fingers of fear.

Eventually, when I judged they were ready, I said softly, 'Gentlemen.' I waited until I had their full attention and then stepped aside to show them.

There it was – directly in front of us.

Jebel Barkal. The Sacred Mountain.

It's not a big mountain as mountains go, but it's loaded with symbolism, mostly due to its shape which – depending on which direction you were approaching it from, or even how much barley-beer you'd been drinking – resembled either the Uraeus as depicted on the crown of Egypt, or a giant penis, or a sitting god, or a man wearing a crown. Obviously both the Kushites and the Egyptians believed in getting good value from their landscape.

Now, with the rising sun sweeping across its flanks, it was easy to see any or all of those shapes in the constantly changing shadows. The mountain glowed gold, peach, crimson and purple. A fitting home for a god.

At its base reared any number of magnificent public buildings, built of a combination of the ubiquitous mud bricks and local sandstone, gleaming red in the sunshine and each one far grander and finer than anyone who thought only Egypt could manage this sort of thing would have believed. Chief among them and towering over everything was the magnificent Sanctuary of Amun with its tall pylons, colourful carvings and bright pennants snapping in the crisp, early morning breeze. The pylon was more than three storeys high and today its gates stood open, giving a view along a pillared avenue, bright with colours, ending in yet another colossal pylon behind which towered yet another pylon. Behind that, if memory served, stood the enormous hypostyle hall and the inner sanctum:

the holy of holies where the god lived. The sanctuary towered above everything except the mountain behind it – from which it seemed to have grown.

Kings – Egyptian and Kushite – came here to be crowned. To give their reigns validity in the eyes of the god. At the height of the ceremony, the king would make his way to the inner chamber – the place where the god dwelt – to meet with him alone. This was their most sacred place.

Other gods had their temples here as well. Isis, Hathor and so on. I could have stared all day, but I had a job to do. I turned to Wolfe and Khalife.

'I'm not sure how much you want me to be a tour guide. I can explain what you are seeing here or I can shut up and leave you to form your own impressions. It's up to Mr Wolfe.'

'Information – any information – is always useful, Dr Maxwell.'

'Well,' I gestured at the mountain. 'This is Jebel Barkal. The Sacred Mountain. One of the Thutmoses – I can't remember which one – decreed it to be the home of the mighty god Amun. An act which came back to bite Egypt much later when the Kushites claimed Amun had declared them the rightful rulers of Egypt. Their king, Piye, swept into Egypt to begin the 25th dynasty. There are statues of him everywhere. And of the women he left behind to rule in his name. You can tell they're Kushites because of their crown – a cap designed to represent the shape of the mountain and the double Uraeus of Egypt and Kush. All the statues have what's known as the Kushite fold. As do you. Apparently, they were very proud of it.' I watched Mr Khalife raise his finger to his face. 'And of their Kushite roots. Every single one of them was returned here for burial.'

I gestured at the largest building. 'The Sanctuary of mighty

Amun-Ra. Only the foundations and the pillars are of sandstone. All the rest is mud brick. Like all the buildings around here – including the pyramids. The temple complex is vast – hall upon hall – going right back to the mountain itself.

'The avenue of kneeling ram-headed statues . . .' I gestured, '. . . are the personal symbol of Amun, and lead to the huge wooden doors over there. There are also temples to the female gods, Hathor and Nut. Whether gods or mortals, the Kushites did not discriminate between men and women.'

I gave them a moment for that revolutionary concept to settle.

'What are those people doing?' enquired Mr Wolfe.

A number of broom-wielding slaves were engaged in an unending battle against the encroaching sands.

'Keeping the desert at bay. Keeping the temple clean out of respect for the god. Speaking of which . . .'

I had no idea to which particular religion Messrs Khalife and Wolfe subscribed but, speaking as an historian, it never does any harm to pay one's respects to any local deities who might be knocking around and I needed all the help I could get. I mean, you'd have to be a complete idiot to announce there was no such god as Amun-Ra when standing only a couple of hundred yards from his sacred mountain, wouldn't you?

I turned to the mountain, placed my hand on my heart and made the gesture of respect.

Wolfe and Khalife watched expressionlessly.

I said softly, 'Women touch their heart – men touch their brows.'

Somewhat to my surprise, they did so. Good – they weren't stupid enough or arrogant enough to assume they knew everything. I began to feel faint stirrings of optimism. This could turn out well.

So, the appropriate god propitiated, I led them away for what, with luck, would be a little harmless tourism.

Yeah – right.

The early morning breeze was blowing stinging sand at us. Simultaneously and quite instinctively, I think, they wound the long ends of their turbans around their faces. I myself was enveloped in what appeared to be some sort of tablecloth. Don't ask me why the teapot terrors would own such a thing; I certainly didn't want to dwell on some of the uses it might have been put to. I pulled it across my face and we set off.

We wandered around the public buildings. Mr Wolfe punctuated our perambulations by enquiring as to the portability of any treasures within. I told him what he wanted to hear, secure in the knowledge it would never come to that.

We pushed our way through gathering crowds and wandered the streets pretty much as the fancy took us. Away to my left, I could see a line of greenery which must be cultivated land lying alongside the River Nile. Kush was rich and fertile, easily able to support kings, priests and its formidable army. We weren't close enough to identify the individual crops but I could see clumps of date palms silhouetted against a cloudless blue sky. Small groups of hobbled donkeys stood beneath them, taking advantage of the shade. Early morning it might be, but the sun was already very bright and I was beginning to sweat under my tablecloth.

The town was waking up. There was lots of early-morning bustle. Shops were opening around us with goods being laid out ready for the first customers. Those who had no shopfront exhibited their goods under the shade of convenient trees. Awnings were being slung across narrow streets to ward off the white-hot sunshine.

A small group of people had gathered outside the fishmonger's, waiting to get their fresh fish before it went off in the heat of the day. Ancient shutters slammed back against the walls. Women and children were drawing water from the public well in the open space in front of a minor temple. Up at rooftop level I could hear someone shaking out their sleeping mats. Sand and dust filtered down. Others were sweeping it off their doorsteps. The narrower streets were unpaved and sand and grit had piled in heaps against the walls, driven by the incessant wind.

Off to my right, more lines of donkeys were being watered and a small boy was tossing handfuls of some sort of green stuff at their feet.

We wended our way through the residential streets of mud-brick houses, most of which were single storey with high windows and flat roofs. One seemed to grow from another. I wondered if each sprawling unit housed generations of the same family. All living on top of each other and with never a moment's respite. I was congratulating myself that neither Leon nor I were burdened with relatives when I remembered St Mary's. All of us living on top of each other all day long. I did have an extended family after all. I wondered again how they were getting on.

After nearly an hour, we had circled back almost to our starting point. The Sanctuary of Amun.

'Pyramids,' said Wolfe, looking to his left. 'They are smaller than I expected.' He sounded disappointed.

'Smaller and steeper,' I said, 'but many more of them.'

Khalife never stopped looking around, missing nothing. 'Is something about to happen?'

He was right. Something was going on. The slaves had finished brushing sand from the approaches to the temple and were clearing away their gear. More were approaching bearing garlands of flowers which they began to set up around the entrance. Men that I assumed were lower-ranking priests appeared. They wore the usual fine, light linen tunics. Slaves wore loincloths of what looked like coarse wool. Some were virtually naked, their skins leathery from the fierce sun. Most of the people, men and women, seemed to wear some kind of linen tunic, but not all. Looking around at the people beginning to assemble, this was a very cosmopolitan society. Kush was a trading nation and there were representatives from many different countries. We weren't conspicuous at all. There were groups of obvious Egyptians, with their black eyes and wigs. There were nomads from the desert, muffled in long, flowing robes. Some had only their eyes visible. Were they in town for the ceremony or just passing through? Sadly, I'd never know. This was not a fact-finding tour.

The space in front of the temples was beginning to fill up with people as the hard, white sun climbed higher in the cloudless sky. I wondered if this was a regular ceremony to thank the god for the new day before the noonday temperatures drove everyone back inside again, or whether today was a special day for the god.

Many people were pouring into the space now. Men, women and children. Most wore flowers in one way or another – a garland round their neck or a wreath in their hair. Even some slaves had a bedraggled bloom behind their ear. Some of the children held carefully assembled little posies. There was excited chatter every-where. Bakers, brewers and confectioners around the square were doing a roaring trade. All the signs were here. This was a holiday. All right, not a funeral procession, but as good as.

Behind me I could hear some sort of commotion. Horns sounded and men shouted. I spun around to see what was happening. The

Time Police and their bi-hourly appearances were never far from my thoughts. Do I mean bi-hourly? I never know whether that means two hourly or twice an hour. And I didn't want to call up Mikey. It might not be important but I wasn't sure I wanted Wolfe to know she and I could talk to each other. Not that it mattered because we'd be gone in less than an hour, regardless.

I was recalled to the present by a series of horn blasts. One after the other. There was nothing melodic about them at all – their tone was strident and attention-grabbing. All chatter stopped and people moved back, opening up a wide space in front of the Sanctuary of Amun.

The enormous wooden doors were being thrown open. Straining slaves pushed them back against the walls. The entrance was in deep shadow and I couldn't see anything. No one else was looking anyway. All eyes were staring in the opposite direction. Craning my neck, I could see some sort of procession approaching, threading its way between the buildings to the sound of pipes and cymbals, slowly making for the ram-flanked ceremonial avenue. This was good. This would give Wolfe and Khalife a bit of spectacle to look at. Trust me, there's nothing wrong with the Kingdom of Kush – nice people, magnificent architecture and so on – but, as Mr Wolfe had several times pointed out, it wasn't Egypt. I'd overestimated the interest they would have in observing their possible ancestors. There's obviously no money to be made out of ancestors.

'What is happening here?' enquired Mr Wolfe.

'Some sort of religious ceremony,' I said, quietly. 'Dedicated to Amun-Ra, obviously. He's the big cheese around here. I think the procession is arriving.'

It was on the tip of my tongue to ask him whether he wanted to give it a miss and have a poke around the town while the bulk

of the people were observing the ceremony. The unspoken impli-
cation being that there might be something interesting – all right,
valuable – to pick up, but before I could say anything, the temple
guards appeared, each with his own wicked-looking spear and
khopesh, so I decided not to offer them the option.

The procession was headed by a huge ram, his coat immaculate,
whiter than white. They must have been up all night preparing
him. A garland of flowers hung around his neck. His impressive
horns were tipped with gold. He would be the sacrifice. Over the
clashing cymbals and blaring horns, we could hear the cheers of
the people as they threw down their flowers for him to walk upon.

The ram seemed calm enough. He'd almost certainly been given
drugged food. He walked placidly to the temple, his oiled hooves
sending up little puffs of dust and sand. Two garland-laden acolytes
paced solemnly alongside, each holding him on a golden rope,
although he wasn't giving any trouble.

Behind him came half a dozen white horses, similarly garlanded.
They weren't as tall as modern horses, but they were very good-
looking animals, small heads on arched necks, prancing along on
delicate hooves. Unlike the Egyptians who only used horses for
pulling chariots, the Kushites rode theirs. As a nation they were,
apparently, quite fond of horses, and the Pharaoh Piye, having
conquered Egyptian Hermopolis, had had some harsh things to
say when he saw the condition of the royal stables and the horses
therein. These, however, were beautiful beasts. Only the best for
the great god.

Behind the horses came a long line of donkeys – whitish and
not quite so beautifully presented. I wondered if there was some
kind of animal hierarchy here. And bringing up the rear, to my
amazement, some ten or twelve camels. Supposedly, there were

371

no camels in this area until the Persians introduced them around 520BC. I did think about sharing this fascinating piece of information with my travelling companions but something told me my enthusiasm would not be shared.

Each camel was wearing an elaborate harness, decorated with coloured beads, strands of wool, flowers and ribbons. They plodded along, staring disdainfully down their nostrils and looking very unimpressed. Although, to be fair, it's quite hard for a camel to look enthusiastic about anything. Their enormous soft feet spread over the sand, which, despite the best efforts of the slaves, was already beginning to cover the paved court again. It was obvious the ram was marked out for sacrifice but whether the other animals were also for sacrifice, or only present to escort the ram to the god, or whether they were a gift to the temple was not clear. In the end, it didn't turn out to be that important.

With a final flourish of horns, a trill of pipes and a clash of cymbals, the procession halted at the entrance to the Sanctuary. The actual ceremony would be performed by the priest, in private inside the temple, but the dedication would be public.

People shuffled into rough queues, clutching their offerings. Everything from gold to small loaves of bread. There were lots of flowers in the form of either wreaths or garlands. Little piles of grain were carefully carried in clay dishes. Many people offered up tiny, delicately carved wooden rams. This was the closest to the real thing a poor person could get and even that wouldn't be cheap. Wood was expensive in desert cultures.

All these were people's gifts to the god. Gifts representing their hopes and fears and their dreams. To protect a brother or a son in the army. To save a sick child. To ensure a safe childbirth. The people lined up for their votive offerings to be blessed by the priests and accepted. The air was heavy with the smell of dust and incense from the temple.

Silence fell. The sun beat down. Sensibly, I stood in Mr Khalife's shadow.

Two figures appeared at the entrance to the temple. Both wore intricate headdresses of feathers. There's a saying, 'They dripped with gold,' and in this case, the saying was spot on. Both Mr Wolfe and Mr Khalife instantly became much more cheerful. One figure was male and one female – the male on the right and the female on the left. They stood together, with equal status.

A complete silence fell over the crowd. This was obviously a very holy moment. A holy silence to attract the attention of the god. The sacrifices would be dedicated, the rites carried out and then it would be everyone off for an early lunch.

'What is happening?' enquired Mr Wolfe again, reminding me I was derelict in my duties as tour guide.

I whispered, 'The animals will be dedicated to the god and then ritually sacrificed.'

He lowered his voice. 'To what end?'

'It could be anything. To ensure the future prosperity of Kush. Ditto the Pharaoh Piye and his family. To ensure a good harvest. Or that the Nile will behave itself this year. Or that the livestock will be fertile. Or that there will be no sickness this summer. Or that the Assyrians won't invade . . . anything, really.'

He nodded gravely and turned to watch the crowd again. He seemed quiet and engaged. I began to wonder if I'd been worrying unnecessarily.

Unfortunately, while I'd been talking to Mr Wolfe, I'd forgotten about Mr Khalife. In the 8th century BC we might be, but he hadn't forgotten his primary function, which was to protect Mr

Wolfe from any and all peril. Unfortunately, in my job there's usually quite a lot of peril scattered about. I'd done what I could. I'd selected a peaceful country not in the middle of any wars. There was no current sickness. The country was prosperous and law-abiding. The people were pleasant. I thought I'd covered all the bases. Wrong again.

It wasn't completely Mr Khalife's fault, but the results were pretty spectacular, just the same.

We were waiting with the crowd. Wolfe and I stood together, with Mr Khalife in his favourite position just behind Wolfe's shoulder, when there was a commotion. No one spoke – obviously the silence was sacred and could not be broken without angering the god – but suddenly people were jumping aside. Children were grabbed and hoisted off the ground. Something was wrong. I tweaked Wolfe's jellabiya, just to alert him to something happening and then the crowd parted in front of us and I finally saw what everyone was trying to get away from.

A snake. And a big one, too, with a lighter underbelly and darker mottling along its back. Some sort of cobra, unless I was mistaken, and sadly I didn't think I was, because a good historian reads up on the local flora and fauna before setting out on an illegal operation accompanied only by a cheese-munching teenager and two of the most untrustworthy men in London.

I had no idea how the snake had suddenly found itself among this crowd of people. I suspected its normal habitat was in the lush green area alongside the Nile and it had perhaps been brought here accidentally in a basket of green stuff. Its only idea was to get as far away as it could as quickly as it could, but there were legs and feet everywhere and it wasn't happy. Head up, it was hissing loudly and rhythmically. A bit like one of Lingoss's steam inventions.

374

People were scuttling away, still preserving the sacred silence, and the snake suddenly found itself in a wide, empty space, which cobras hate. It put its head down and moved. Fast. Straight towards us. I'm always amazed at how rapidly snakes can shift. I think this one just wanted off the hot stones, which was understandable, and into the cool, damp shadows as soon as possible.

I'm not sure if Wolfe, still watching the priests accept the offerings, was even aware of the snake, but Khalife was. In his defence, his actions were probably instinctive. He stiff-armed Mr Wolfe aside and interposed his body between him and the snake. Which didn't pause for a moment.

Neither did Khalife. Groping in the recesses of his robe he pulled out the gun I'd been pretty sure he hadn't surrendered. A small, short-barrelled, stocky affair.

I cursed and moved but I was centuries too late.

Three or four loud shots reverberated off the buildings. The snake disintegrated, splashing snake goo all over everyone's pristine robes. Especially mine. People screamed – not at the snake but at the noise. They would never have heard anything like it. I was willing to bet at least half of them thought their god was suddenly among them and they were terrified.

If it had just been the people who were terrified then it might not have been too bad. I wondered how many of them would even make the connection between the short stick-affair in Khalife's hand and the shattered snake. Perhaps not many. However, it wasn't the people we had to worry about because if they were terrified, the animals were doubly so.

The donkeys weren't too bad. In a crisis, donkeys tend to close their eyes and stand still. They're the technicians of the animal world. Horses tend to be a bit more skittish. A couple of them were snorting, rearing and plunging and as I looked, one tore free from his handler and, tail kinked up over his back, was off and heading for the far horizon. He had no idea where he was going – all his attention was on getting away. Horses are probably the historians of the animal world. Of course, once one goes, they're all off. Half the time they'll come back when they're hungry. Just like historians.

In a moment they were all dragging their handlers through the crowds, knocking people down as they went. Shouts and screams marked their progress, all attempts to maintain the sacred silence forgotten. Their handlers, rather than be dragged along, let go before they incurred serious injury, and their horses bolted.

It wasn't the horses that were the main problem, though. It was the camels. Yes, I know, not an animal noted for light-hearted frivolity. And I know they have the reputation for being nasty-tempered buggers who will bear a grudge until the end of time – a bit like the Time Police, now I come to think of it.

I'd never actually seen a camel stampede before so the day wasn't completely wasted, and as an historian it's my job to pay attention to whatever is in front of me – unless it's Peterson, of course, when I just watch his mouth open and close . . . open and close . . . until someone wakes me up.

No one could have slept through this. I've never seen such destruction. Not even when Professor Rapson attempted to repro- duce Leonardo's multi-cannon affair and managed to demolish not only the bin store, but also Mr Strong's bicycle, which was leaning against it at the time, and Bashford's beloved Ford Prefect, also resting against it, while it recovered from a massive emissions test failure. I mean the failure was massive, not the emissions – although they were as well.

I'm not tall and from my comparatively low vantage point, there were camel legs everywhere. Suddenly each camel had considerably more than just four legs and every single one of them operated entirely independently of the other three. My world was suddenly full of horny knees and windmilling legs as they struggled to get their giant feet off the ground.

They don't look where they're going, either. People here might be unfamiliar with the hazards of rapidly perambulating *Camelus dromedarius* and their poor sense of direction, but they scattered anyway. You really wouldn't think such an ungainly animal could move so fast. Or do so much damage.

Stalls and tables never stood a chance, crashing to the ground to the sound of shattering pots and angry cries. Carefully assembled offerings were scattered in panic and trampled underfoot as people did what they always do in a crisis. They screamed and ran.

I myself was transfixed. I had no idea camels had such enormous feet. They're like hairy dinner plates with toenails.

It seemed as if every dog in the city was barking furiously and was either running in to snap at the camels' heels or indulging in a spot of canine opportunism, grabbing everything edible within reach and making off with it, dodging the giant feet coming down around them like pile-drivers.

Squawking chickens achieved powers of flight they hadn't known they possessed, massively evacuating their bowels to help them reach escape velocity.

Three camels raced past me, their tethers swinging. I caught a confused glimpse of pendulous lips and disdainful nostrils and then I was enveloped in a choking cloud of gritty dust. My eyes stung. The smell of camel was shutting down my sinuses. Something hard caught me a massive wallop and I flew through the air to land with a crash on the only area of the square *not* covered in soft sand. On the other hand, there wasn't a layer of even softer panicking-animal excrement either, so it could have been worse, I suppose.

I picked myself up before something four-legged ran over the top of me or something two-legged beaked me to death. Don't tell him I said so, but Markham's view of the entire animal kingdom as malevolent beasts all hell-bent on the destruction of mankind by lunchtime might not be so far out after all.

I looked around to see the last three or four camel bottoms disappearing out of sight, closely pursued by a group of shouting men I assumed were their owners. Personally, I'd have let them go and taken myself off for a stiff drink. I suspected we might have delayed the re-introduction of camels to this area by several hundred years.

I rotated my shoulder to check it was still working and adjusted my dress. I really should find the causes of all this trouble and remove them from the vicinity with all speed.

The ceremony was ruined. Stalls and tables were little more than matchwood, the goods displayed upon them scattered over a wide area. Metalwork was dented and misshapen. Bolts of linen had been unravelled and dragged through the shit. Flowers had been crushed. There was even the traditional one sandal. People were emerging from doorways or picking themselves up. The temple guards reappeared and tried to look as if they hadn't been the first to leg it to safety.

Slowly and cautiously, the priests came back. A lot of them. And they weren't happy. Not happy at all. The guards straightened their headdresses and began to look about them for someone to blame.

Time to go.

Khalife had Mr Wolfe against a mud-brick wall and was standing in front of him, gun drawn, looking for trouble.

Definitely time to go.

'Well,' I said conversationally as I approached. 'I never thought I'd meet anyone who could cause more inadvertent destruction than the last outfit I worked for, but I have. Congratulations. Neither of you has a Markham or a Bashford in your ancestry, do you? Please give me the gun, Mr Khalife.'

He was looking over my shoulder. 'We may need to defend ourselves.'

'Mr Khalife, you have already ruined an important ritual, caused massive damage and lightly injured most of the population, and all you did was shoot a snake. Imagine the carnage if you shoot a guard. Give me the gun.'

'But how will we get away?'

'Successfully. Believe me, I was doing this before you were born.'

I held out my hand. He glanced at Mr Wolfe, who nodded. Reluctantly, he handed it over to me.

I stuffed it away. 'Thank you. Right. Mr Khalife, you will go first. Mr Wolfe in the middle. I'll watch our backs. Yes, Mr Khalife, I know, but it will look strange to see a woman leading two men and we really don't want to draw attention to ourselves right at this moment. The pod isn't far. Along the wall here, turn right and just keep going. *Now*, if you please.'

I bundled them out of the square and into the quieter but still animal product-littered streets, intent on getting them back to the teapot as soon as possible. The town was in an uproar. The priests were outraged at the heresy and screaming at the guards. The guards were looking around for someone to blame. Amun-Ra himself probably wasn't that happy either and, just to add to my problems, the Time Police were out there somewhere, almost all of them ignorant of my wonderful plan and searching for us just as hard as they could, eager to get their hands on us and our pod.

As, I hoped, was Clive Ronan. Because if Atticus Wolfe wasn't in the process of selling us to the highest bidder then he wasn't the charming, amoral, vicious, opportunist thug I took him for. Because that's what Wolfe did – he bought and sold things. Including people. Especially people. And if Clive Ronan was unable to ensure that, by fair means or foul, he was the highest bidder then he wasn't the ruthless, murdering bastard I took him for, either.

The only question was when.

I rather thought we'd be safe for this jump. Wolfe had been unaware of this destination. Even if he was already in contact with Clive Ronan there was nothing he could have told him. I rather suspected that the reason for Wolfe's presence today was not so much his desire to forge a good working relationship, nor his greed for gold, but the need to check out his merchandise prior to putting us on the market. I was almost certain he'd been approached, either directly or indirectly, by Clive Ronan who, I hoped, would be completely unable to pass up the opportunity of acquiring a pod with such interesting design features, and possibly me along with it. He would make Mr Wolfe an offer he could not refuse. I couldn't help wondering what sort of price Wolfe would get for us. And, hard on that thought, how long he'd be allowed to enjoy it. Or even whether Wolfe wasn't the king of double-cross and would do for Ronan without me having to lift a finger.

Life's quite interesting sometimes, don't you think?

I had every confidence that somehow, Clive Ronan knew what I'd done. He would know I'd had a screaming row with Commander Hay. He would know I'd stolen the pod, rescued Adrian and Mikey, and that the three of us had gone on the run with no

380

thought for the long-term consequences. All that was so like me. The need for a sanctuary would soon drive us to someone like Atticus Wolfe. A man who dealt in commodities.

And Wolfe knew who I was. Right from the very beginning he'd known who I was. Right from the moment Khalife had addressed me as Dr Maxwell when I'd deliberately only introduced myself as Maxwell. They'd been expecting me. I didn't know how he was linked to Ronan – that wasn't my concern because the Time Police would be all over that – but he was and, with an enormous amount of luck, he and Wolfe would be each other's downfall.

That was how I'd sold my plan to the Time Police. This would give them both Clive Ronan and Atticus Wolfe. People they'd been itching to get their hands on for a very long time. And then the civil authorities could dismantle Wolfe's empire, Adrian and Mikey could enjoy a more conventional lifestyle – because that was the price I'd demanded – and I could take Matthew home. Everyone would be a winner. I'm such a bloody genius.

Well, I would be if I lived long enough.

I'd discussed this thoroughly with Adrian and Mikey, who, after all, were taking an even bigger risk than me. We'd sat down at St Mary's, before I even left for the Time Police, to thrash out the details. Despite me telling them their capture by the Time Police might not be pleasant, they'd been unsurprisingly gung-ho about the whole thing.

'The only thing is,' said Adrian, 'will Wolfe actually be willing to part with the pod? Surely he'll want to hang on to it.'

Mikey shook her head. 'We're more trouble than we're worth. He'll see that very quickly.'

'Plus,' I said, 'he'll get a good price for it.'

'If Ronan actually holds up his end of the deal.'

381

'Not our problem,' I said. 'And it's a good deal for Atticus Wolfe. I suspect his plan will be to shelter Ronan and take a cut of everything.'

'I can't see Clive Ronan sharing. Not in the long term.'

'Neither can I but it doesn't matter. Wolfe is bait for Ronan. Our job is to manufacture the perfect moment and then the Time Police will have both of them. And, if the gods are on our side, we'll survive to see it.'

Adrian and Mikey grinned at each other. 'Cool.'

So now, here I was, ushering two amateur time travellers back to the comparative safety of our teapot-shaped pod. Before the temple guards decided we were worth investigating. Or we were trampled by a runaway camel. Or another snake turned up. Or a scorpion. I mean, the list just went on and on. Besides, I was gasping for a cup of tea.

Rather contrary to expectations, the teapot was exactly where we'd left it. Mikey must have been watching the screen because she raised the hatch as we approached and dropped down the ladder, enquiring, 'What did you do?'

'I don't know what you mean?'

'I heard the gunshot from here. Who did you shoot?'

'Mr Khalife will be delighted to answer all your questions. After you, gentlemen.'

He turned to me. 'Give me back my gun.'

'At the end of the assignment, Mr Khalife. Once we're home you may shoot whomever you please. Excluding me and Mikey, of course.'

'Disappointing,' was all he said as he climbed the ladder.

Mikey had the kettle on and we settled down for the traditional autopsy and allocation of blame.

Mr Wolfe appeared puzzled by our little ways. 'Should we not be thinking of returning home, Dr Maxwell?'

I grinned. 'A true historian never goes back looking anything other than cool, calm, collected and completely on top of things. A cup of tea usually does the trick.'

'Even after a camel stampede?'

I managed to look superior. 'Call that a stampede? I was in the Cretaceous once and not only did hundreds of dinosaurs run straight over the top of us but they knocked the pod off a cliff as well.'

He blinked. 'You've been to the Cretaceous period?'

'Many times,' I said, loftily. And then, in the interests of accuracy, 'Well, five times, actually.'

'And me,' said Mikey sunnily. 'Loads of times. It's good fun.'

He was regarding us in astonishment. 'You've seen dinosaurs?'

Ah, the magic of dinosaurs. And now I had to tread carefully. I'd planted the seed, now I had to lure him in . . . Is that a mixed metaphor? I never really paid a lot of attention at school.

I shrugged. 'A few. Some of them from a safe distance. Some of them rather too close for comfort. Some of them actually from underneath. And I once stared down a T-rex.'

They stared at me.

I waved it aside with becoming modesty. 'It wasn't fully grown.'

Mr Khalife spoke again. 'I require my gun, if you please.'

We were sitting cross-legged on the floor. Mikey was young enough to put her legs in any position she pleased and both Khalife and Wolfe had lowered themselves with an ease that irritated me. My bloody knees were killing me and one foot had gone to sleep. I let an edge creep into my voice.

'Did I not explain how important it was to do no harm? The implications it could have for the future? For *your* future?'

He wasn't listening. 'Give me back my gun.'

I snapped, 'I told you – when we're safely home. You have no idea how much damage a bullet could do in here. Unless you want to remain in this time and place forever, of course.'

We glared at each other. You might say there was a bit of an atmosphere.

I took a deep breath and then turned to Mr Wolfe. 'Look, I don't think this is going to work. I think the time has come to admit we're not right for each other. We'll drop you off. You hand back Adrian – and I suspect your people will be only too pleased to see the back of him – and we both walk away. No harm done.'

Mr Wolfe said slowly, 'I don't think so.'

I shrugged. 'I do.'

'Dr Maxwell, I have complete faith in you and your equipment.'

'Do you? I rather got the impression there hadn't been enough gold around to pique your interest.'

'On the contrary, you have more than addressed my concerns as to your authenticity. I am very willing to offer you all the support you require.'

'Such as?'

'A secure base from which to operate. And financial backing. You need never worry about money again.'

That would be because we wouldn't live that long, but never mind that now.

'Research facilities,' put in Mikey quickly.

He nodded with all the ease of a man who has no intention of keeping his word. 'I shall be delighted to provide you with what-ever you desire. You have a proven track record in innovation and achievement and I am confident I would soon see a return on my investment.'

It's interesting, isn't it, how language is such a giveaway. If his offer was genuine he'd have said, '. . . *will* soon see a return . . .' or '. . . *shall* soon see a return . . .' *Would* was rather too provisional for me.

'Remuneration?' I said quickly, channelling greedy historian.

He smiled comfortably. 'Oh, I don't think we should talk about that now. Obviously, you won't be cheap and my initial outlay would be enormous, but I think we might consider allocating you a small . . . a very small percentage of whatever you manage to . . . retrieve. Once my start-up costs have been recovered, of course.'

I sighed. A moving portrayal of an historian who is slowly realising she might have bitten off more than she can chew but it's too late to do anything about it now. Sometimes I think there should be more Oscars on my mantelpiece.

'Well,' I said slowly, apparently willing to be persuaded. 'We could start small, I suppose. A few trinkets here and there. Something from Marie Antoinette, perhaps. Or Martin Luther's *Ninety-five Theses* hot off the church door . . .'

'No,' he said flatly. 'I don't do starting small, Dr Maxwell. You will start large and then get larger. I want something big. Spectacular. Priceless. Something that will put me at the very top. Something unique.'

'Well,' I said dubiously, 'I could bring you the *head* of Marie Antoinette if you like, but I should warn you it won't keep well.'

'Bigger,' he said. 'Much, much bigger.'

Silence fell in the pod. I stared at my feet apparently deep in thought.

The silence ticked on. The urge to say something was overwhelming but it had to come from him. I'd planted the seed . . . I made myself stay silent. Not to over-egg the pudding. Just let him find his own way . . .

'You mentioned dinosaurs, Dr Maxwell.'

I offered up a quick thank you to the god of historians and then scowled horribly. 'Are you saying . . . ? No. Absolutely not. Out of the question.'

'Perhaps I should explain,' he said gently, 'that the consequences of saying "no" to me are not pleasant.'

'By all means,' I said, sweat breaking out all over again. 'And then I can explain the consequences of trying to capture a dinosaur, subdue a dinosaur, ward off its deeply unhappy friends, get it up the ladder and into the pod. Then I can describe the injuries even quite a small dinosaur can inflict when it really puts its mind to it. Yes, Mr Wolfe, I can understand the attraction but, believe me – it's not worth the risk.'

He shook his head. 'I don't think you understand me, Dr Maxwell.'

'Well, there's a coincidence. I was about to say exactly the same thing to you.'

Mr Khalife slapped my face. Not hard but hard enough. The sound rang around the pod. I'd threatened Mikey with all sorts of death if she intervened. But her gasp of surprise was very realistic. I put my hand to my face, apparently too shocked to speak.

Khalife's eyes glittered. 'You are an intelligent woman, Dr Maxwell, but your manners need work. Mr Wolfe is accustomed to more respect.'

I let my hand drop. 'Not if he keeps coming up with daft ideas like that one.'

It was going to be a clenched fist this time.

Wolfe held up his hand. 'One moment, my friend. It is possible that Dr Maxwell has misunderstood me. Of course, I can see the difficulties she so vividly outlined, but it occurs to me that all that could be bypassed simply by bringing back . . .' he paused for effect, his eyes gleaming – possibly with excitement but more probably greed, '. . . a dinosaur *egg*.' He sat back, well pleased with himself. 'Small, portable, non-violent, perfect.'

I said suspiciously, 'And what would you do with this egg?'

'That need not concern you, Dr Maxwell. In fact, I really think all our lives will be much easier if you just confine yourself to . . . shall we say, acquisitions . . . and leave the distribution side of the business to me.'

I needed to struggle. Just a little. 'I don't think . . .'

'Very wise, Dr Maxwell. In fact, your role will not require you to think at all. Simply to do as you are told.'

I very badly wanted to tell him better men than he had tried and failed at that, but now was not the time. Hopefully I would live long enough to see him dead at my feet.

'The Cretaceous period lasted for millions of years, Mr Wolfe. How would you have me narrow down such a long period of time?'

'As you yourself said, you've been there before so it's not completely unknown territory.'

The thought flashed through my mind. Could it possibly be that *he* thought he was steering *me*?

I said slowly, 'A colleague and I once spent some time there, carrying out an in-depth survey. Flora, fauna, geology, climate – all that sort of thing. I'm familiar with that particular part of the Cretaceous so I suppose I could revisit. It would have to be some six months or so later – to avoid running into myself.'

I paused, staring at nothing, apparently considering ways and means.

He waited patiently. Not a man to over-egg his pudding, either.

'Yes,' I said, eventually. 'I suppose it could work – I would know my way around the area, be familiar with the livestock and so on, and there won't have been any major geological changes in just a few months.'

He nodded. 'You cannot be more precise as to the date?'

'Well, not really – dates hadn't been invented then and it's a very long time ago so I'm afraid that's about as precise as I can get.'

It was precise enough. Ronan knew when Sussman and I had been in the Cretaceous. He'd be perfectly prepared to jump to approximately the right time and wait for as long as it took. The incentives were all there. Me, of course, but mostly, this pod. The pod that would make him more than rich. Oh yes – he'd happily wait for us to turn up.

Knowing perfectly well why he was asking and curious as to what he would say, I said, 'Why are you asking?'

I was expecting something vague and meaningless so his answer came as a bit of a shock. 'I rather thought I might join you.'

It would be hard to say whether it was me or Mr Khalife who was most alarmed.

He silenced our babble of protest. 'Who could resist a dinosaur?'

I said flatly, 'I mentioned a colleague. Perhaps I should tell you he didn't make it back home. Well, not all of him. I only ever found his boot. His foot was still in it.'

He waved that aside. 'Mr Khalife will keep me safe.'

I could already see Khalife mentally loading for elephant. God knows what sort of arsenal he'd bring with him. And he'd use it, too. I'd seen dinosaurs slaughtered once. I had no desire to see it again.

But, I had to get Ronan to the Cretaceous. I needed him to die there and there would never be a better opportunity than this. All my planning, step by careful step, had brought me to this point. Surely I could cope with two extra passengers. I should give in ungracefully and just do my best to prepare for whatever might go wrong. Because it would.

I counted slowly to ten and then said reluctantly, 'Well . . .'

'A wise decision, Dr Maxwell. I foresee this will be a very profitable enterprise.'

For him – yes. For us – probably not so much.

I changed the subject slightly. 'Will you try to hatch the egg?'

'An interesting experiment, don't you think?'

'What will you do with it if you're successful?'

'He could feed it the other dodo,' said Mikey, who had yet to master some aspects of polite social interaction. 'Max – we agreed – after what they did to Donald – or Hillary – no more livestock. They can't be trusted.'

They both ignored her. She was just a little girl.

'Hush, Mikey,' I said in my *let the grown-ups sort it out* voice. The one that pushes teenage buttons everywhere and one of the very few weapons in the parental armoury. She subsided in a really very realistic sulky heap.

Messrs Wolfe and Khalife exchanged glances. I pretended not to notice. Because I didn't care. I was off to the Cretaceous and that was all that mattered.

That part of the assignment settled, now it was time for the bread and butter matters. I looked at Mikey. 'How are we doing for power?'

'Fine.'

I began to unwind my pins-and-needles-ridden legs. 'No time like the present then. Let's go.'

Wolfe held up a hand. 'I applaud your enthusiasm, Dr Maxwell, but I need to return to my office. I have important meetings planned.'

'Mr Wolfe, you could spend ten years in the Cretaceous and still be back in time for your important meetings. We should go now.'

He shook his head. 'I have a great deal of material to prepare and I am tired and have things to see to. Tomorrow. We will . . . what is the expression? . . . jump? We will jump tomorrow at six p.m.'

Which would give him more than enough time to hold his 'meetings' and get all his players into place. I sighed heavily and nodded. Not happy, but unsuspicious. Yet another award-winning performance.

And back to the sex club – a phrase Jane Austen inexplicably omitted to use in any of her books – because the next task was to get Adrian back, although I suspected they would be only too happy to let him go. We might even find him waiting for us on the pavement.

We landed in their back yard. Right next to the wheelie bins again.

'Anything?' I said to Mikey and she shook her head. The proximity alerts stayed silent.

We waited.

'What are we waiting for?' enquired Mr Wolfe, testily.

'Adrian.'

And here he came. Very happy by the looks of it and definitely very chatty. He was escorted by the two bouncers who were looking particularly glassy-eyed. That's the problem with teenagers. Either you can't get a word out of them as they squat, sullen and suspicious, in their own filth – or bedroom, as they describe it – or you can't shut them up at all and your ears melt in self-defence.

Mikey sprung the hatch and I gestured politely to our guests. Sorry – employers. We dropped the ladder and they descended.

Adrian was *still* talking. 'Remember, it's a lot easier if you can bypass the start-up procedures in the first place because then it will disable both firewalls and update automatically. After that – you're straight in. Oh, hello.' He waved. Mikey and I, both peering out of the hatch, waved back.

I eased Khalife's gun out of my pocket and held it out of sight. I didn't think there would be any trouble, but just in case . . . Clive Ronan was never far from my thoughts.

Mr Khalife turned back. 'My gun.'

I nodded at Adrian. 'My hostage.'

Wolfe nodded at Khalife who nodded at the two men who would probably have nodded at Adrian had he actually stopped talking long enough to notice.

Traditionally, of course, the two sets of hostages walk slowly towards each other, pause as they meet, and then continue on their way. Adrian obviously hadn't read the Hostage Handbook.

'Hello, Mr Wolfe. Hello, Mr Khalife. Did you enjoy it? Where did you go? Did you bring anything back? Donald's laid an egg so we got that wrong. How was the pod? Did it drift at all? Mikey doesn't always compensate properly, you know. Tell me you didn't end up in the Gobi Desert? I got bitten by a scorpion there once and Mikey was shot on the Chinese border. Well, actually, she was shot in the shoulder but you know what I mean. Oh – are you not stopping?'

They weren't trotting, because that would be undignified, but there was a briskness to their walk.

391

Adrian clambered up the ladder, turned at the top and waved. 'Thank you for having me.'

Have I mentioned they both had beautiful manners?

Mr Wolfe called up, 'Tomorrow then, Dr Maxwell. Six p.m.'

Yeah – like I was going to turn up at a pre-arranged time and walk straight into Clive Ronan.

I smiled, waved an acknowledgement, checked the safety catch and chucked Mr Khalife's gun to him.

He caught it neatly, shot me a look that could have meant anything, and the two of them disappeared into the house.

'We should go right now,' I said, once again letting my fear of untimely ambush envelop me in the warm, fuzzy blanket of paranoia.

So, we went.

Obviously, there was no way we were going to do anything as daft as turning up at the right place at the right time. Who would do something that stupid?

We landed at the wrong time and in the wrong place. Always listen to your paranoia. It's keeping you alive and almost certainly has more sense than you do. We watched for a while and when nothing dreadful happened, shoved out the ladder.

'Why?' I asked in mild exasperation.

They seemed bemused. 'Why what?'

'Why this old, heavy wooden thing?'

They looked at it as if seeing it for the first time. 'What's the matter with it?'

'It's old, heavy and wooden.'

They didn't seem to understand.

I tried again. 'You could get something better.'

'Better than what?'

The ladder hit the ground with a thump, failing to maim any passers-by. 'Than this.'

'What's the matter with it?'

I know when I'm being wound up. 'Nothing. For you two, it's just perfect.'

Adrian grinned. 'Yeah, most people see it our way sooner or later. Right, I'm off over the river to give myself up to the Time Police and tell them what's happening.'

'Remember,' I said, because all sorts of things could go wrong, 'demand to speak to Commander Hay. She will be expecting you. Behave yourself. Don't provoke them into shooting you and . . .'

'Yes, all right,' he said impatiently. 'Mikey, look after the pod and don't forget to . . .'

'Just go, will you,' she said in exasperation.

He clambered down and disappeared, his coat flapping dramatically around him.

'They're going to be awfully surprised when he knocks on their door,' said Mikey. 'Do you think they'll just shoot him out of hand?'

I shook my head. 'I think I'm the one who's most likely to be shot out of hand. Remember – hatch down and locked. If neither of us comes back then jump to St Mary's and hand yourself over to Dr Bairstow.'

If he was there.

I went to climb out of the hatch. I should get a move on. Adrian could be crossing the river by now.

She grinned. 'Wish I could see their faces when he gives himself up.'

'It's not too late for you to go with him so be careful what you wish for.'

She grinned. 'Nah – you'd never be able to pilot this thing by yourself.' She patted the wall affectionately.

'You do know Dr Bairstow has promised to destroy it when all this is over, don't you?'

'I do. But it's not over yet.'

'And never will be unless I get a move on.'

'Good luck, Max.'

'See you in ten minutes.'

There was no one on duty at the front door. Well, it was only twenty past eleven in the morning. I looked but couldn't see a bell anywhere. Presumably if the door wasn't opened for you by a massive bloke in a suit then you didn't get in at all.

Obviously, a subtle approach was required.

I stepped back to give myself room and pounded on the door. 'Hey, open up. It's me. Get a move on – it's time to go.'

I reckoned twelve to fifteen seconds. They opened the door in nine.

I stepped well back out of grabbing range, although there were people in the street and I wasn't too worried. They still needed me. It was when we arrived in the Cretaceous that my warranty would suddenly run out.

Mr Khalife stared down at me. 'You are early, Dr Maxwell.'

'Dodging the Time Police,' I said, backing down the steps. 'We're going now. If you want to come with us be in the alleyway in five minutes. If you're not there we will go without you.'

I turned away.

'Wait,' he said. 'Mr Wolfe is not ready.'

394

'Then tell Mr Wolfe he can come next time,' and trotted back along the pavement. I had my hand on my stun gun the whole time just in case Ronan had men here already waiting for us to turn up. He himself, I suspected, would be waiting for us in the Cretaceous. Just in case we slipped through everyone's fingers here. Belt and braces. And he'd want to make sure of the teapot.

Mikey flung out the ladder as soon as I turned into the alleyway. I clambered up and we heaved it in and waited. Who would appear? Wolfe or Ronan. And who would arrive first?

It was Wolfe.

34

They say that smell is the most evocative of all the senses. I stuck my head out of the hatch and the stink hit me square in the face, taking me back. Right back. Back to the time when I was Miss Maxwell. When I'd never even heard of Clive Ronan. When life was bright and exciting and I and everyone I knew were all going to live forever. When I'd only just met Leon. When Kal was still at St Mary's. When Helen was still alive. And Davey Sussman.

For a moment, everything blurred. Which is a pretty dangerous thing to have happen when you're only a small, pink, not very hairy mammal at the bottom of the Cretaceous food chain. I blinked away days that would never come again and concentrated.

We'd landed on flattish ground which was good because this teapot, while well-stocked with loud, chest-rumbling music, chocolate and steampunk literature, was fairly deficient in the whole *let's do our best not to tip over on landing* hydraulic-leg department.

There's a penalty to be paid for flat, however, and the ground beneath us, and all around, appeared to be one massive swamp. The smell – as I've already mentioned – was breathtaking and for all the wrong reasons. Rotting foliage, stagnant water, wet earth, the heady tang of dinosaur manure and, over everything, the sulphur of over-active volcanoes. I was certain I would never need my sinuses irrigated again. In fact, I think they'd stopped working forever.

The other thing I'd forgotten was the heat. Dear God – it was hot. And humid. Every pore began to exude at an industrial rate. Where's rot-proof clothing when you need it?

It was never silent here – day or night. Off in the distance something shrieked – but only very briefly. Something else roared and the shriek was cut off in, well, mid-shriek, I suppose. There was a moment's silence as something started on its lunch and then the roars, grunts, moos, and bellows of everyday life in the Cretaceous started up again.

I did a very careful three-sixty-degree survey, taking my time about it. Mikey reported the proximity alerts were silent and I couldn't see any movement. We were safe for the time being.

The ground was muddy and I could see animal tracks criss-crossing each other as dinosaurs had passed and repassed as they went about their everyday business of eating and being eaten. There were trees growing through the mud, grey and green with moss and hanging lichen. Their aerial roots entwined each other in a chaotic and impassable tangle. I bet a million tiny creatures lived in there.

Broken or dead trees leaned at crazy angles and rotting logs were slowly returning to the swamp from which they had emerged. Higher and dryer ground lay about a hundred yards to the north, easily accessed by hopping across the humps of wet mud standing a few feet above the brackish black water.

Have I mentioned the smell?

Our landing site was both good and bad. Good because anything big scouting around in search of lunch would probably not fare well in all this tangle of undergrowth, roots and low-hanging branches, and bad because even the worst of mothers wasn't going to build a nest and park her eggs here. We would need to head for the higher ground and scout around a bit.

I ducked back down into the pod.

'Well,' I said to our guests. Sorry – employers. 'We're here.'

They made to get up. A small corner of my mind noted they'd recovered from this jump considerably more quickly than the one to Jebel Barkal. I reminded myself yet again – these were intelligent and adaptable men. Oh – and ruthless. Don't forget ruthless. And brutal. And cold-blooded. I shut myself up before I came to my senses and took us all home.

'Before you go,' I said, 'a quick briefing. No – I mean it. I need to prepare you for what you'll find here and you, Mr Khalife, will need to know the best ways to keep Mr Wolfe from harm.'

They both subsided.

'Right. First things first. This is a hostile environment. Nothing out there is your friend. This is the Cretaceous period. Top predators are the Tyrannosaurus and various raptors – Troodons, Deinonychus, and so on. They're fast and intelligent. You'll never see them coming. If you do see one raptor then you can be sure the other five are hidden nearby and ready to pounce. And most of them will be behind you. And they don't kill you first. They just eat you. I've seen it happen. You can only pray you go quickly. A T-rex, especially the smaller male, can be outrun, but not on the straight so don't run in a straight line. Zigzag around whatever you can. Their heavy tail slows them down and prevents them cornering too tightly. Get within range of the jaws, however, and you can zigzag until you drop and it won't do you any good at all.

'And don't make the mistake of discounting the herbivores. A lot of them are plated and a swipe from an Ankylosaur's tail can kill even a T-rex. We'd never find enough of you to take back home. Be aware that even the more placid dinosaurs can absent-mindedly stand on you. Especially since some of them don't see very well.

So, regard everything as hostile and dangerous. Everything here hunts by sight or smell or both. Well done for wearing camouflage gear but don't touch anything if you can help it. Don't drop rubbish. Don't piss against trees. And don't make a noise. Bear in mind that they're all masters of camouflage and that by the time you spot a dinosaur it's already too late. And don't drink the water. When we leave the safety of the pod, your first task will be to cover yourselves in mud. And keep replenishing as we go. You need to look and smell less mammally. Any questions?'

Mr Khalife brandished his weapon so he obviously hadn't been listening to a word I'd said. Boys and their toys.

'Mr Khalife,' I said. 'If you are in a position where you must kill something you'll probably only get one chance. One shot. Make it count. But be aware that if you do shoot something – even if you only wound it – the smell of blood will bring ten or twenty predators down upon us in minutes. And if that happens, nothing can save us.'

He held my gaze and rammed home a magazine.

I should have realised then, but I didn't. In my own defence, I had a lot on. I thought I'd covered everything, but that I missed.

They shouldered their way past me without a word and climbed down the ladder. Now that we were officially working for them there was a definite difference in their behaviour towards us. I exchanged glances with Mikey. She nodded.

Once outside, I handed them each a small pack containing water and some of those ghastly high-calorie biscuits that are supposed to keep you on your feet for hours – and trust me, they do, because you just want to get the assignment over and done with so you won't have to eat another one. If you want a comparison, try eating a raffia coaster. Very similar in size, shape and taste.

I left Mikey in the pod. No one was going to do anything to me when Mikey could just close the hatch and jump away, leaving them there forever. And Wolfe and Khalife wouldn't risk that. Not until they were certain Ronan was here. So, for the moment at least, I was quite safe. Safe being a relative term.

I made them cover themselves all over in smelly swamp mud. It wouldn't do us a lot of good against a flock of raptors – and there was always the possibility of every frog within a hundred yards deciding we smelled good enough to be their annual breeding ground and having multiple frog sex all over us – but it was the best I could do.

I didn't like having them behind me, but there wasn't much I could do about that, either. I went first. Mr Wolfe was in the middle, and Mr Khalife brought up the rear with his gun. Well, his three or four guns, probably. With luck, that would not become an issue.

We splashed gently through the muddy water. Or possibly the watery mud. Things plopped into the water all around us. I could hear water dripping from broad leaf on to broad leaf. There were giant insects everywhere. I could hear the drone of their silver wings. The dragonflies were an iridescent blue and green and purple and, to my eyes, the size of small donkeys. They dive-bombed us unmercifully until we moved away from their territory. Vicious buggers.

We moved slowly for many reasons. The ground was squidgy and I didn't want too much splashing. Splashing often indicates an animal in distress and would attract all sorts of attention. I was constantly peering through the trees for signs of movement. Listening for heavy breathing. Watching the skies overhead for Pterosaurs – although they'd nearly all gone by now. And scanning the water for that ominous bow wave heading in our direction.

Giant crocodiles, giant lizards, giant snakes – they'd all be around somewhere. I couldn't see anything but I was pretty sure a hundred eyes would be watching us.

I felt happier once we were out of the swamp. We clambered out to firmer ground and I took a quick look around. We were on a broad, flat plain that encompassed the swamp. Flowering plants and their heavy scents attracted even more insects. Either heavy, droning single flies or irritating clouds of midge-like bugs – they all headed straight for us. The trick is not to wave your arms around because this enrages them and they go off and bring back their mates.

Away to my left, the ground began to rise. Magnolias and other flowering plants grew in riotous clumps everywhere. Palms erupted out of the tangled undergrowth. Further up there were conifers doing well on the higher ground. Above them reared bare mountains and behind them, smudgy on the horizon, the ominous cone-shape of volcanoes, source not only of the nostril-searing sulphur smell, but the acid rain that had dissolved great holes in the broad-leaved plants around us.

There was no grass – it hadn't evolved yet – but stretched in front of us, bordering the swamp, was a vast area of trampled horsetails. Which was good, actually, because nearly everything in the Cretaceous was much bigger than we were and having to fight our way through shoulder-high horsetails would be both tiring and dangerous. You never knew what might be lurking only three feet away.

I motioned them down and we dropped to a crouch – all of us keeping watch over the others' shoulders.

'This is good,' I whispered, gesturing at the trampled vegetation. 'I think this might be a Hadrosaur feeding ground. They're

401

like cows. They move slowly, grazing as they go. See the trampled plants? The bad news is that where you get prey you get predators. I propose we move further up – into the treeline up there. It will give us cover and we might be lucky enough to find a nest.'

'And see a dinosaur,' said Mr Wolfe, firmly. I suspected, as with Jebel Barkal, the Cretaceous might not be living up to his expectations.

'Very probably, yes. Follow me.'

We zigzagged uphill for a hundred yards or so, easing ourselves past clumps of laurel, ficus and cornus, and into the trees. It was no cooler here. The air was still and close. The sun made dappled patterns on the forest floor. Very pretty but it was going to be a bugger to spot a well-camouflaged predator.

The forest was very quiet. Very quiet indeed. There were no normal forest noises. The silence had a listening quality to it. I gestured and we all dropped to the ground again.

I breathed. 'There's something here.'

Once again, we all watched each other's backs. We knelt for a while, watching and waiting. I could feel my knees sinking into the damp soil. In the distance, I could hear the sound of something trampling the undergrowth and breaking branches. Something big was crashing through the trees and causing a fair amount of noise and damage as it went. Something that didn't care who knew it was here.

Wolfe went to stand up and I pulled him back down again which left Mr Khalife in something of a quandary. The disrespect I'd shown by manhandling Mr Wolfe battled against my having prevented him doing something unwise.

We sat for a while, inhaling forest smells. If I closed my eyes

I could almost imagine Davey Sussman standing behind me. So, don't close your eyes then, Maxwell.

The noise gradually ceased. Whatever it was had moved away. Gradually, sound and movement came back into the forest and now I had a decision to make. When Sussman and I had done our study here, we'd been stuffed with equipment. I don't just mean the star-mapping instruments and the geological stuff and all that, but we'd had proximity meters which would tell us if anything was moving close by. We'd had blasters with which to defend ourselves. We'd had Professor Rapson's spray that was supposed to fool predators into thinking we were just perambulating vegetation. And yet Sussman had still died. His fault – but he'd died, nevertheless. Now I had nothing. I had a short-range stun gun. I had two amateurs who could turn on me at any moment and probably would. And I had a teenager in a teapot.

Stop feeling sorry for yourself, Maxwell. You have a job to do so get on with it.

I stood up slowly and looked around. Everything looked normal enough – for a predator-laden environment, that is.

I whispered, 'Come on,' and we set off. The trail was easy to find. There were broken branches and vivid, lighter scars where bark had been torn off tree trunks. The scrapes were about the height of Mr Wolfe. So probably not a T-rex then. Too short. Nor raptors. Too tall. Raptors are always smaller than people think. Except for Deinonychus and I definitely didn't want to meet any more of those. I wondered if I'd encounter the pack that did for Sussman. It was possible, I suppose. I was in roughly the same area as before, although at the other end of the valley, but these creatures roam. And if I did meet them, would they remember the smell of human? Something else not to think about.

We walked quietly, in single file. A few leaves fluttered down around me and I cursed myself for not remembering to keep looking up.

There are other perils here besides being eaten. I had forgotten the weather.

In the early Cretaceous, the weather was pretty stable. Warm and wet most of the time, even the poles were pleasant places at which to live. However, as time went on, Pangea split into two land masses, Laurasia and Gondwana. These, in turn, were breaking up into the continents we know today. The Tethys Sea was disappearing as these continents began to form. Sea levels were falling, weather patterns began to develop and the endless days of gentle, balmy weather were long gone. Late Cretaceous weather could be very exciting indeed.

All this is just a long-winded way of saying that the wind was getting up. I tilted my head back and looked up at the sky. The tops of the trees that I could see were tossing and swaying. As I watched, more leaves floated down. The sun had disappeared. Dark oily clouds scudded across the narrow slice of sky visible between the trees. A storm was coming.

I'd been caught in a tropical storm once before and although Leon and I had found new and exciting ways to pass the time, that certainly wasn't an option with these two. The decision I had to make was whether to leave the comparative safety of the forest and try to get back to the pod or hunker down here until it was over with. Which might take some time.

I remembered I was only an employee and such decisions were now above my pay grade. Turning to my employers, I said, 'There's a storm approaching. They can be savage. We'll probably be quite safe here among the trees or we can make our way back to the pod

404

and wait it out there. In this situation I would appreciate Mr Wolfe's instructions.' And waited to see how he would handle the situation.

Perfectly, as it turned out.

'Your recommendation, Dr Maxwell?'

More leaves fluttered down. The wind was doing more than sigh in the treetops.

'To stay put. We're safe enough here. Everything will do as we do and take shelter until it's over.' I couldn't help adding, 'There will be a great deal of sound and fury but please try not to be too alarmed.'

They both turned identical stares on me.

'There's a clearing ahead. We'll check it out and then find ourselves some shelter. Please be aware that any place that looks desirable is almost certainly already occupied by something that won't be willing to give it up.'

The clearing hadn't been large to begin with, but whatever had been crashing around the landscape had made it bigger. Big enough to accommodate the huge, cone-shaped pile of mosses and lichen pulled down from the trees and piled up in the centre. Small branches formed a solid base at the bottom and the top was covered with broad, bright green, freshly gathered leaves.

A nest. Just what we'd been searching for and now found by accident. Looking at it, it was very easy to believe that many dinosaurs had evolved into birds. Apart from the fact it was built on the forest floor and about four feet high, it looked just like a bird's nest. I had no idea what type of dinosaur had built it so we needed to be very careful. A species that believed in hands-off parenting and was already some distance away would be my first choice. Still, time to earn the pay I probably wouldn't live long enough to collect.

'Ah,' I said, every inch the obsessed, oblivious historian. 'We're in luck. This is just the job.' Out of sheer bloody-minded reck-lessness, I added, 'We could be back home in thirty minutes, Mr Wolfe. You'll make your meetings after all.' And pretended not to notice the flicker of consternation in his eyes.

Inspecting it more closely, I suspected a Sauropod nest. They tend to lay their eggs on the fringes of a forest so the hatchlings can penetrate further in where the trees are too close together for the bigger predators to get at them. By the time the young emerge some years later, they're almost big enough to fend for themselves.

I made Wolfe and Khalife wait under the trees while I approached with huge caution. Mother could be anyone and anywhere. I squatted and waited for the longest ten minutes of my life.

Nothing happened.

Khalife appeared beside me. 'Mr Wolfe is wondering at the delay.'

'My compliments to Mr Wolfe. The delay is caused by a cau-tious historian endeavouring to ascertain whether Mum is still in the vicinity. May I suggest you alleviate Mr Wolfe's impatience by attempting to remove an egg yourself; then we shall almost certainly find out very quickly.'

We looked at each other for a moment. I was half braced for another slap and then he surprised me by grinning suddenly. 'I shall advise Mr Wolfe I am leaving this matter in your capable hands.'

But he was right. I couldn't hang around forever. Even if Mum had pushed off, any number of predators could be on their way. Or might even be here already. I was hugely reluctant – not only because of the physical risk, but because it was going against all my principles and training. I tried to tell myself that if I survived the next hour or so I could always put it back.

Carefully, my head practically rotating, I approached the nest. It looked solidly built and easily able to hold my weight. I stood on tiptoe and leaned over. What would I find? If only a few eggs had been laid then the nest might well belong to a T-rex or one of the larger predators. If I uncovered ten or more eggs then I was probably looking at a Hadrosaur or Sauropod nest with, if the god of historians was really with me, absentee parents.

I counted five eggs and what looked like another five on the bottom layer. Like a box of chocolates. *And* they were laid on their sides rather than vertically. So probably not a T-rex. I reached out and gingerly touched an egg. Sadly, it was warm and still covered in some sort of birth fluid so these eggs were freshly laid – very likely by whatever we'd heard thrashing around in this vicinity. However, no sign of Mum now, so, fingers crossed, it was probably almost safe to remove one.

I got my hands underneath one and lifted. It was about the size and rough shape of a rugby ball. I went to slip it inside my jacket and something made me look up. To this day I don't know what. Instinct, perhaps.

It wasn't that large and, at first, I thought it was a raptor, but it wasn't. Standing motionless between two trees was a T-rex. Perfectly camouflaged, its skin colour and mottling rendered it almost invisible among the pine trunks. I hadn't heard it approach so it must have been there for some time. Waiting to see if Mother came back, perhaps, and now, reassured by the lack of a maternal presence, it was about to make a move on the nest.

And me.

It was a small specimen. A young male, I guessed. Living alone and fending for himself. He stood, head tilted to one side because my scent was unfamiliar to him and he couldn't work out what I was. He'd learned to be cautious. A bigger specimen would have barged in and gobbled up me, the eggs, and probably my two employers as well.

Not that I was in any way reassured by his stillness. Trust me, a T-rex is no less terrifying when it stands still and just looks at you.

I froze. The typical instinct of the small terrified mammal faced with a dangerous predator.

We looked at each other.

I'd forgotten that giant head. Those teeth. And how their breath stinks of rotting meat. And those cold, intelligent eyes.

As it turned out, freezing was not the wrong way to go. He was young and inexperienced and I don't think he knew whether to go for the unknown – me – or concentrate on the tangible prize – the nest of eggs. If he was very hungry, he might only be aware of the eggs. Which turned out to be a good guess because ignoring the unfamiliar and strange-smelling mammal, he went straight for the nest.

He took two giant steps into the clearing, swung his head and demolished the whole careful structure there and then. Eggs, nest material and an historian flew in all directions. I hit the ground with a bit of a thump. I lay, winded and wondering whether to move or not. Half the bloody nest fell on top of me as well. Which turned out to be a good thing because he missed me so completely he very nearly trod on me in his rush to get to the eggs.

Male Tyrannosaurs don't have an easy life. They're smaller and lighter than the much more aggressive females. They tend to live solitary lives, only getting together with a female whenever she feels like it. The females are belligerent in their better moods and deadly in their worst. They'll tolerate a male for a short period while he does the business, but outstaying his welcome will result in him finding himself on the lunch menu.

This one, nowhere near fully grown, was even more battered and scarred than usual, and hungry enough to abandon caution.

Dinosaur eggs are robust. They have to be. An egg laid by a giant Sauropod has a long way to drop before it hits the ground, so the eggs rolling in all directions across the forest floor were undamaged. He dipped his head, seized one in his jaws and gobbled it whole. He crunched the next one and I watched liquid egg run out from between his teeth.

He must have been starving because he was head down, snatching at the eggs as fast as he could find them. I needed to get out while his attention was elsewhere. Especially before he discovered that fresh meat could also be on the menu today.

The nest was almost completely demolished. There was no cover of any kind and any moment now he'd be sniffing around the forest floor looking for any eggs he might have missed.

I waited until his back was to me, and he was nosing at an egg wedged under a root, wriggled out from under the pile of moss and branches and rolled across the clearing, under his tail, and into the trees. I took two seconds to get my breath back and groped for my stun gun, all prepared to defend myself and two worthless specimens of humanity.

I don't know what happened next. He wasn't large but he was still a threat and he was between me and Wolfe and Khalife. I don't know if one of them moved. Or tried to run. Or what. I only know he lifted his head suddenly and stood stock-still. It was a terrifying moment. He stood completely motionless, like a statue, and lowered his head. I could hear the air whistling in and out of his nostrils and I knew he'd sensed them.

Whether he hesitated for that vital second because he was trying to assimilate their unfamiliar smell – I don't know. Whether, if they'd stood their ground and not moved, he would have gone back to his eggs – again, I don't know. I only know that he hesitated just long enough for Khalife to raise his gun and fire.

Three sharp shots cracked around the clearing.

At first, I couldn't think why he bothered. Even I could see his gun didn't have anything like enough stopping power to put down a T-rex – but, as it turned out, he didn't need to stop a T-rex. He only needed to stop Mr Wolfe, whose chest exploded in a spray of red blood and tissue.

There was a moment's complete silence while everyone tried to work out what was happening – Wolfe, me and the T-rex – and while we were doing that, Khalife turned to run. The T-rex might have followed him but the smell of blood was just too much for him. Lowering his massive head, he sniffed at the body almost at his feet. Wolfe lay on his back. Red, shiny blood had sprayed everywhere, dripping down tree trunks and lying in pools on the ground. The clearing was very quiet. I could hear Wolfe's agonised attempts to breathe.

The T-rex lowered his head. I saw his nostrils flare.

Atticus Wolfe wasn't yet dead. But there was nothing I could do. I was on the other side of the clearing. The T-rex was between him and me. I saw him feebly lift his arm – whether in an appeal for help or in an effort to ward off the inevitable, I don't know, and he didn't live long enough for me to find out. The T-rex drew his lips back from his teeth, and made a sudden lunge. There was a gurgling scream. I woke up and turned away. Get out of here, Maxwell. Now.

I turned and ran in the opposite direction from that taken by

Khalife. He might have a gun but I was betting I'd last longer than he would because he would be blasting off at everything in sight and that was just plain stupid. I was convinced he wouldn't last an hour. Actually, realistically, neither would I because everything – climate, flora, fauna, ex-employers, Ronan – absolutely every bloody thing in the world was out to kill me.

I zigzagged around the trees, not so lost in headlong flight that I forgot to have a bit of a think as I ran.

Had Wolfe and Khalife been Ronan's distraction? To get me out of the way while he went after the pod?

Or, out of self-protection, had Khalife killed Wolfe, Medea-like, so he could distract the T-rex and make his escape, leaving me, unarmed, on my own, and with a life expectancy of seconds?

Or was this Khalife's power play? His bid for Wolfe's job?

Or was he working for Ronan and eliminating Wolfe on his instructions?

It didn't matter whether he was acting on Ronan's orders or not, Wolfe was now well and truly out of the game. I felt a stab of regret. I saw his beautiful room full of beautiful things. And then I remembered all the things he must have done to acquire those beautiful things. And who he must have done them to.

Forget him. He was no longer relevant. I had other things to think about. Was Ronan actually at the teapot this very moment? Mikey wouldn't open up under any circumstances but I had a sudden vision of a little packet of something explosive fitted around the hatch. Just enough to get it open, shoot Mikey, dump her body and jump away.

I dodged around trees, leaped over tree roots and tried not to break my neck in this mad gallop downhill.

And, just for the record, there was absolutely no bloody sign of any bloody back-up of any bloody kind any bloody where.

I was trying not to think about it because I had a lot on at the moment, but ever since I'd arrived here the thought had shouldered its way to the front of my mind and refused to leave.

They weren't here because they hadn't made it. Neither St Mary's or the Time Police had prevailed over Halcombe and his slimy forces. In my worst moments I saw them all, dead and dying. I could be the last member of St Mary's left alive. And not for very long at this rate.

I stopped, my chest heaving, put a hand on a tree trunk for support – both mental and physical – and listened hard. Nothing. No one was behind me. I needed to get back to the pod. I changed direction and ran. As fast as I could.

I ran through the trees, dodging from side to side, trying to look in all directions at once and wondering if I was in more danger from the visitors or the inhabitants of this world. Finding myself a safe-ish area where three trees grew so closely together they were almost one, I wedged myself inside them, took one long look around and then crouched low. I tapped my ear and whispered, 'Mikey.'

She whispered back. 'Yes?'

I said, with no little exasperation, 'There's no need for *you* to whisper.'

'Oh. No. Sorry.'

'It's all kicking off. Lock yourself in. Remember the code word.'

'Max, you should get back. The weather's turning really nasty.'

And it was. Now that I'd stopped running, I could hear the shushing noise of the wind in the trees. Leaves and small twigs swirled around me.

I said, 'Wolfe's dead.'

'Was it Khalife?'

I nodded, cursed myself for an idiot, and said, 'Yes.'

'Great,' she said sunnily. 'Adrian owes me a million pounds. He's going to be really pissed off.'

It was on the tip of my tongue to say, 'You knew what he had

413

planned?' but that implied that I hadn't, which, while true, wasn't something I wanted to admit.

'Let's hope you live long enough to collect from him. Anything moving near you?'

'No, nothing. I haven't seen a thing. I think we're building up to a storm and everything seems to have gone to ground. What are you going to do now?'

'Well, I'm pretty sure it's a trap and they'll be expecting a panic-stricken historian to be careering back to the pod as quickly as she could get her legs to move. I suspect they'll wait for you to open the hatch for me and then it'll all hit the fan.'

'See you in a minute, then.'

'Maybe. I'm going to work my way back to you and see what happens. Remember . . .'

'I know – don't open the hatch. Not for anyone or any reason.'

'Not even . . . ?'

'Not even if it's you.'

'Unless . . . ?'

'Unless you give the password.'

'Because . . . ?'

A teenage sigh gusted through my earpiece. 'Because . . . *we are not alone.*'

I tried to remember the days when I never took anything seriously, either.

'See you soon, Mikey.'

'Good luck.'

'You too.'

I stood up cautiously, checked around, and headed downhill again, eventually emerging from the trees and into the open ground. I noticed the difference immediately. The weather had seriously deteriorated over the last twenty minutes. The sun was gone and heavy, rain-laden clouds seemed only inches above my head. The wind was stronger here, lifting my hair and blowing it back off my face. Dust, leaves and small twigs swirled in miniature dust devils.

I wasn't sure what to do but cowering here wasn't going to help. I had a T-rex behind me, Demiyan Khalife somewhere off to my right, Clive Ronan probably between me and the pod, and the deteriorating weather. I really couldn't afford to hang around to see which of them killed me first.

The low-hanging clouds bulged with moisture. Somewhere in the distance, lightning flickered pink and thunder rumbled. The storm was almost upon us. I could smell rain in the air.

I had a sudden thought. Ronan might not hang around if he thought his life was in danger, not even for a magic pod, and if he came after us again it could be at a time and place of his own choosing and the advantage would be his. I had to prevent that happening. I couldn't do all this again. I had to force him to make his move here. It's typical, isn't it? We think we're so wonderful with our careful, complex plans. I'd moved heaven and earth to assemble all the players at the right place at the right time and then the bloody weather steps in and ruins everything.

This wouldn't be a light shower. You could stand under Niagara Falls and still not get as wet as you would in a Cretaceous rainstorm. Torrents of muddy water would be sweeping down this hillside within minutes. The level of water in the swamp would rise dramatically. Whether it would be enough to sweep away the teapot I had no idea but, whereas I had no problems with Khalife or Ronan being stranded here in the Cretaceous, I had several issues with the same thing happening to me. I'd get back to Mikey and we'd do a sideways jump to further up the hillside. Maybe high enough to put us up in the coniferous zone. Well out of harm's way. If you *can* actually be out of harm's way in the Cretaceous.

Yes. That was a plan. Get back to the pod as soon as possible, check on Mikey, jump to safety, wait out the storm and then have another go.

The weather was worsening by the moment. The air was stifling – the humidity unbearable. With a flash that turned the world pink, giant lightning forked across the sky, followed instantly by the sound of tearing clouds. This thunder didn't rumble – it ripped across the sky. The bang hurt my ears, still not completely recovered from London Bridge.

And at that moment the rain came down. Straight down, because it was far too heavy to be driven by the wind. I felt as if some prehistoric weather god had pulled the plug and emptied the contents of her bath all over me. I was drenched to the skin in seconds.

There were lots of downsides to this situation but the worst was visibility. I could barely see a yard in front of me. The ground turned to instant quagmire and, what with that and the buffeting rain, I was hard put to keep my feet. Yes, I needed to get out of this, back to the pod, jump to safety, have a cup of tea and a re-think, wait out the storm, and then we'd have another go.

As I came to this decision, Mikey spoke in my ear.

'Problem, Max. The water's rising quickly. And it's racing. Lots of white water. There's trees and all sorts of things sweeping past. I'm worried we might be . . .'

She broke off.

'Mikey?'

No response.

'Mikey, can you hear me?'

Nothing.

Shit. Shit, shit, shit.

I set off in what I vaguely hoped was the right direction and the first thing that happened was that Mr Khalife popped up – literally from nowhere. I never saw him coming at all which was a bit of a shock and I was angry with myself. I needed to concentrate more. He could have been Ronan, or a couple of Deinonychus, or a T-rex, or even an absent-minded duck-billed Hadrosaur trying to get out of the rain. Too much was going too wrong too quickly. I needed to concentrate on one thing at a time. Prioritise, Maxwell.

He was only a couple of feet away but I had to shout to make myself heard. 'We need to get back to the pod. Follow me.'

Like me, he was soaked to the skin and having some difficulty keeping his balance. His gun was holstered so I felt no particular fear. I can still run faster than most people I know.

And then the bastard slid his hand out of his pocket. He had a stun gun. Worse – he had my stun gun. What? I had no idea when he could possibly have picked my pocket. I certainly hadn't noticed anything. He was obviously a very skilled thief.

Turning his head, he called, 'You can come out now, Mr Ronan,' and fired it at me.

A hot pain jagged across my chest. My legs buckled and down I went into the mud. The tiny part of my brain that was still working told me it might be a good idea to stay put. Just for a moment. So, I did.

I lay still – no hardship there – and felt the rain hammer down on my face. It was surprisingly painful.

I could hear something splashing towards me. I couldn't look up. All I could see were black combats very like my own, and some good boots.

They stopped a safe distance away. I didn't blame him. Mr

Khalife had just shot one employer and presumably would have no difficulty doing it again should the situation arise.

And, whether he realised it or not, Mr Khalife was in some considerable danger as well. He wouldn't be the first to think he'd negotiated himself a very good deal with Clive Ronan only to find that actually he hadn't. I was rather fuzzily aware that I might be the safest person here.

Khalife gestured at me. 'As you requested, Mr Ronan.'

'No – not as I requested. She was taking you back to the pod, you moron. Another five minutes and we'd have her and it. Saving ourselves a lot of time and trouble.'

Khalife stopped smiling. 'It will not be far away. Easily found.'

There was a pause. Thunder cracked and rolled again. I imagined Ronan peering sarcastically through the driving rain. 'Where?'

Khalife gestured downhill. 'Over there. She will take us. When she has recovered.'

'Are you insane? This woman has more lives than a herd of cats. I want her dead at my feet before we go anywhere.'

'She is only a woman.'

'Get her up.'

I was hauled to my feet. My legs buckled again and down I went back into the mud. Khalife yanked me up again. And not gently. I was beginning to go off him in a big way.

Ronan said something which, given the distance, the torrential rain and the by-now almost permanent ringing in my ears I didn't catch but I felt Khalife shake his head.

'No. The price is doubled now. This woman has value to you and I have the woman. The transaction is simple.'

'It certainly is,' said Ronan, and shot him.

Down went Khalife and again, so did I.

Ronan approached, very, very cautiously.

I tried to blink away some of the mud and rain out of my eyes and there he was. He looked down at me. I looked up at him. We regarded each other.

'Now look what you made me do,' he said, quite mildly.

I stared at Khalife. His eyes were open. I saw him blink. His dark blood pumped into the swirling water and was carried away. That wasn't good. Even setting aside the normal predators, there was a T-rex out there somewhere. I managed to slur, 'Should get out of here.'

He nodded calmly. 'I'm aware,' and I remembered him leaving Davey Sussman dying in his own blood. To be torn apart by a herd of Deinonychus.

I could see most of him now – well, as clearly as anyone not wearing her glasses in a tropical rainstorm and with a face full of mud can see anyone.

Brace yourself for entirely understandable bad language. Where the fuck were the Time Police? No matter what was going on at St Mary's, they could have sent a small team, at least. I loved the way everyone had blithely assured me they'd be here when I needed them and then, presumably, found somewhere more exciting to be.

And what of Mikey? Was she, even at this moment, being swept over a Cretaceous waterfall?

Or St Mary's and Dr Bairstow? Where the fuck were all these people? I don't know, you work hard at uni, you get your qualifications, you sign up for a nice indoor job with adequate access to chocolate and just look how it all turns out.

He threw his gun to someone beyond my range of vision. I knew he wasn't alone because, through the noise of the storm, I could catch men's voices on the wind and hear their blasters whining. He leaned down and hauled me up out of the swamp.

I was none too steady on my feet but he had hold of the scruff of my T-shirt, easily holding me upright. He was unarmed. Now was my opportunity. In my mind, I tensed every muscle and hurled myself at him. What actually happened was that my left arm waved vaguely for a moment and then fell to my side again. I had a vague idea I might be dribbling. Can I refer you to my previous comments on historians and good career choices?

If he was heading for solid ground then he was going to have to put his back into it. Everywhere was water. Fast-flowing water. And not just water – branches, debris, the occasional small dinosaur or mammal body . . . We really needed to get out of here. Dirty water was cascading down from higher ground bringing small rocks and boulders with it. A liquid landslide.

I spared a thought for Mr Khalife. I couldn't see him anywhere. Was he underwater? Had he been washed away? Was he, at this moment, something's lunch? It occurred to me that no matter how badly my day was turning out, Wolfe's and Khalife's had turned out worse. Not that I was doing that well . . .

I peered blearily at Ronan and slurred, 'Ever wished you'd never got up this morning?'

He shook me, rather as a terrier shakes a rat, which did me no good at all. I added nausea to my long list of things to be unhappy about.

'No, you don't, Maxwell. You don't try to smarm or charm your way out of this one.'

Movement was coming back into my uncooperative lips. 'What, you mean identifying a common bond and using that to establish a relationship? Like we did in the desert?'

His voice was harsh. 'When you betrayed me?'

I shook my head and nearly overbalanced. 'When you did good work, Clive. When you remembered you were once an historian. When you saved my life . . . and I saved yours.'

'Yes, well, I expect we both regret that now.'

I made an effort. 'Clive, for the last time – it wasn't me. I didn't tip off the Time Police.'

'Well, not you, obviously. It was that bastard Bairstow.'

'It wasn't,' I said, my mouth still feeling as if I'd spent the morning at the dentist. 'He was as taken aback as any of us. It was just a coincidence. The Time Police had been chasing you ever since you took me from St Mary's.'

He actually seemed offended. 'Oh, before that, surely?'

'Well, yes, I expect so, but only in a kind of half-hearted "We'll get you one day, Ronan" way. It was only after what you did to Helen and . . . and Matthew . . . that everyone really started having a go at you.'

'And look how that turned out. You nearly lost everything, didn't you? Husband . . . son . . . friends . . .'

'I got them all back. You'll never win. You know it.'

His grip tightened. I was making him angry again but my instinct was to keep him talking. If he was talking and listening then he wasn't shooting. There was still time for the less than timely Time Police to amble into the picture. And Mikey was brave and resourceful and would think of something, with luck before she was washed into the nearest ocean.

'And really, you know, Clive, you've only got yourself to blame. If you'd just settled down somewhere quiet you'd probably have got clean away. You could have used your future knowledge to make yourself a fortune. You could have been rich and powerful and comfortable but instead you raced up and down the timeline destroying this and killing that – really you couldn't have been any more obvious, could you? It's almost as if . . .'

I stopped deliberately. The wind no longer shrieked at us but the heavy rain still ran down his face. We looked at each other.

'Almost as if what? Don't stop now, Maxwell.'

Shit. Well, in for a penny . . .

I took as deep a breath as I could manage. 'Almost as if you wanted to draw attention to yourself. Almost as if you wanted to be caught. Almost as if you . . .'

He slapped me with his free hand. 'Shut up.'

'Almost as if you wanted to die . . .' and I knew that I had touched a nerve.

He was furious. Gobs of spittle flew from his mouth. He was white-faced with rage. His eyes glittered. He had no gun – possibly a safeguard against me making a death-or-glory grab for it – but he was powerful enough to snap my neck where I stood. One hand still held me up – the other curled around my throat.

A deadly voice said, 'As long as I outlive you.'

I honestly thought my last moment had come. I had nothing to lose.

I hurled myself at him – although, again, the word 'hurled' might be slightly overstating my uncoordinated lurch. And I slipped as I lurched. My foot slithered backwards in the mud and instead of launching myself forwards as I'd planned, I lost my balance and fell. Which turned out to be a Good Thing.

It couldn't have been Ronan so it must have been one of his men who fired his blaster at me. Something hot sizzled over my shoulder. Whoever it was, they were far enough away to miss but close enough to give me a painful burn.

I lost all momentum and fell heavily, but I did manage to drag Ronan down with me. Which turned out to be a very Bad Thing because he immediately tried to drown me in the mud.

I was so pissed off with today. How much more could go wrong?

He forced me on to my front, grinding my face down into the mud. I screwed up my eyes and tried to close my mouth but the pressure was too great. And I could feel watery mud being forced up my nose and into my mouth. My instinct was to swallow and that wouldn't be good. His weight was on my back and I could barely move. I flailed helplessly and, typically, it was at this point that Mrs Partridge's words came back to me. When I'd sat in her office all those weeks ago. When all this had seemed like such a good idea.

'You must not make the mistake of thinking that because the circumstances are the same, the result will be the same.'

I heard the alarm in her voice – the warning – and suddenly, now that it was too late, I realised I might have made a huge mistake. Yes, Ronan had died here in another world, but I'd been in this world long enough to know that while events often played out in a similar fashion – the results weren't always exactly the same. Ronan and I had been trapped in a tropical storm in the Cretaceous period and he'd died. Now – today – Ronan and I were again trapped in a storm in the Cretaceous period but this wasn't Ronan's end. It was mine.

423

36

Typical Ronan, he didn't go for any of the complicated ways of ensuring my death. All this tying me to the railway track and retiring to twirl his moustaches and gloat wasn't his style at all. He simply pushed my face in the mud and put his knee on my back.

There wasn't a thing I could do about it. I kicked my legs but they were underwater and all that happened was a great deal of splashing. I flailed my arms but I couldn't reach him. There was nothing to catch hold of. Nothing with which to get a purchase. Instinctively I put my hands down to try to push myself up and all that happened was that they sank more deeply into the warm, wet mud.

Mud was everywhere. My eyes were full of it. As were my mouth and nose. I hadn't had a chance to take a deep breath before he attacked me and my heart and lungs were pounding. The next breath I took would probably be my last. Even my ears were full of mud, although I could still hear the floodwaters roaring past. I was panicking.

It was at this moment that I accepted that the Time Police weren't coming. No one was coming. I was alone. I'd been too clever and one of the complicated elements of my wonderful plan had failed to mesh with the others and everything was crashing to the ground.

I could feel my heart thumping inside my head. And inside my chest. I tried twisting from side to side. Nothing happened. He was a big, strong man. He knew what he was doing. His weight was in all the right places. I was as helpless as a baby. There was nothing I could do to save myself. In desperation, I pushed down even harder.

Something moved beneath my hand.

I thought I'd been panicking before but that was nothing to this. Something squirmed under my hand. And then it writhed about and twisted around my wrist and arm. Whatever it was, it was very thick and very strong.

And then it bit me. A sharp red pain shot up my arm.

My panic went into overdrive. Instinctively, I tried to scream and my mouth filled with more mud and grit and God knows what. Most of it went down my throat and that was when my body kicked my brain into touch and took over.

Facing imminent choking, my entire body heaved in one huge paroxysm that dislodged Ronan's knee. The weight shifted. Desperate for air, I twisted somehow and he toppled off me. The pressure eased. I could move my head. I twisted to one side, got my head free and coughed and coughed, spitting mud and stuff until finally, I could suck in some Cretaceous air.

But only for a second. He wasn't going to let me go. I could feel his fingers scrabbling for my throat but the best thing about a Cretaceous downpour is that it's as bad for everyone. He couldn't see either. And he was as hampered by the rushing water and mud as I was. Neither of us could see what we were doing. Neither of us could get a grip on the other.

Not unsurprisingly, I think, I'd forgotten about whatever it was I'd disturbed under the mud but just when I could have done without the distraction, the thing wrapped around my arm tightened its grip. It was like having one of those old-fashioned blood-pressure cuffs which had malfunctioned and wasn't going to stop until it had cut my arm in half.

At the same time the something bit me again – on the back of my hand this time. The same sharp pain flashed. I had no idea what was attacking me – other than Ronan, of course – and terrified that something was about to eat my entire arm, and in an attempt to dislodge it, I flung that arm around in a wide arc.

I hit something that could only have been Clive Ronan. I heard him yell. The next moment he'd rolled away from me.

Whatever was around my arm slackened its grip. I couldn't see a thing for all the gunk in my eyes. I had no idea what was attached to me. A giant leech, perhaps, black and glistening with mucus, and with an orifice as big as my head. Or was this just one arm of a multi-tentacled Cretaceous monster the size of Penge? Whatever it was, I didn't want it anywhere near me. For once in his life, Ronan could perform a useful function and act as alternative host.

I struggled to get up but the rushing water was strong and I couldn't get any further than kneeling. Screaming fit to burst, I flapped my arm wildly, shouting, 'Get off. Get off. Get off.' Which of them I was talking to was anybody's guess but my tactics were successful. The snake-like creature slackened its grip. I don't think it was anything I did. I suspect it had been ripped from its nice, safe refuge deep in the mud and it didn't like what was currently happening to it. Its instinct would be to lash out at everything in sight and at that moment everything in sight was Clive Ronan.

In one sinuous movement it unwound itself from my arm and plopped on to Ronan. As it did so, a head emerged from the coils, piranha-shaped and with huge, inward-pointing teeth far out of proportion to its mouth, followed by, as far as I could blurrily make out, yards and yards of snake body.

Behind the front end – or the teeth end, as I liked to think of it – protruded two stubby, fin-like legs. Whether this was some snake creature evolving to be a land animal, I had no idea. Or perhaps it had given up on land and was becoming a water-based creature? A gigantic eel, perhaps, or a transitional snake. As far as I could see – which wasn't far – it was about twelve feet long, as thick as my arm, and an oily blackish-brown.

Ronan instinctively tried to bat it aside and it didn't like that at all. Perhaps I was splashing too much as I struggled to get away, because the next moment it had abandoned me completely and was slithering across his upper body, teeth bared and looking for trouble. Ronan twisted, and in his efforts to get away, fell backwards on top of me.

I opened my mouth for a scream that was half shock, half terror, half Ronan's crushing weight driving the breath from my body again, and half regret that I wasn't better at maths.

Unlike me, Ronan didn't waste time screaming and flailing. Baring his teeth, he seized the snake between head and fins and began to squeeze with both hands. And now it really was a Clash of the Titans. The thing hissed and spat, snapping at him with those giant teeth and squirming in his grip. Pulling itself further out of the water it attempted to encircle Ronan in its thick coils. Really, I suppose it was just a case of who would do for the other first. From a safe distance, it could have been interesting and I rather thought that now might be a good time to achieve that safe distance. With an effort, I heaved myself out from beneath Ronan and tried to crawl away. Not a lot of me was working that well, and it's difficult crawling through mud because it just wants to pull you downwards rather than forwards, but I'd achieved nearly six or seven inches when the pair of them, still locked together in mortal combat, crashed down on top of me and I was face down in the mud *again* with one hugely pissed-off snake indiscriminately biting both of us.

Something was happening. Something other than the life and death struggle going on over my head, I mean. The ground was moving. Literally moving underneath me. A surge of colder water swept over me and did what I could not – dislodged Clive Ronan.

I knew what this was. I've been caught in a flash flood before. They're not tsunamis – there's not a lot of height – but they just don't stop. They sweep everything before them and that's what kills you. Being walloped round the head by a socking great tree trunk. Or caught under an impenetrable mat of debris and branches and unable to get your head above water to breathe, or tossed and turned by the power of the uncaring water as your body is slowly battered into tiny pieces.

I vaguely recall being washed along, turning and rolling as the current took me. I could hear a roaring in my ears. I needed to get out of here. I needed either to drag myself to solid ground, or find something sturdy to hang on to until the worst was past.

The water was carrying me along. Sadly, there wasn't enough of it in which to swim but too much to stand up in so I was bounced along the ground, colliding with what felt like every rock and tree stump in the Cretaceous period. I tried to hang on to something but it was all moving with me.

Heaven knows where I would have ended up eventually, but a lucky collision with a tree stump somehow pushed me out of the main flow. Suddenly, the current was lessened and there was ground beneath me.

428

I forced my arms and legs to move. Whether through terror or because the effects of my own stun gun were wearing off, I found I could slither along fairly easily. I wriggled along, very much like a snake myself, feeling more and more optimistic with every moment. Suddenly, there was a chance I might make it after all.

Something caught at my leg. A hand. He was still there. Still doing his best to kill me. And this time I was finished. I had no more fight left in me. I thought I saw the snake, too, twisting and turning in the torrent. That was it then. One of them was bound to get me. This was the end.

So, obviously, that was when the Time Police turned up, took one look at the situation and shot us all.

Bastards.

They must have had their sonics on a stronger setting this time because it was more than just the chest pain and disorientation. I think I lost consciousness altogether. I know I fell back into the water.

I remember someone grabbing me under the arms and tugging hard. I remember the water didn't want to let me go. Someone rolled me into the recovery position. There was a lot of shouting. Something very exciting was happening somewhere close by. Someone who looked very much like Dr Bairstow fixed an oxygen mask over my face. I lay back and gulped it down, grateful for the feel of the now-gentle rain washing me clean.

I opened my eyes to a calmer world. Clouds flew high above me, twisting and swirling as the wind pulled them apart to reveal the familiar blue sky. I lay on my back and watched them. There was something I should be doing but for the life of me I couldn't remember what it was. The shapes and movement were really rather interesting though. Shades of grey. If I were to paint it I rather thought I'd lay in a magenta background and then swirl the grey over the top. The background would be hidden but it would still be there, affecting the other colours and bringing hidden drama. I was rather reminded of that interesting philosophical conundrum – can redness exist without the colour red? Or something like that. I wondered if the person who had asked the question had been an artist. You may not be able to see the colour but it's there all the same and . . .

It was only when someone poked it that I realised there was a dead snake on my chest and that's not weird at all, is it? I became aware of sound coming back to my world again. Was it perhaps an *acoustic* snake? What a good idea.

'Max? Max, can you hear me?'

I tried to indicate that of course I could hear them because I had an acoustic snake on my chest.

Someone was trying to lift me out of the extremely comfortable, warm Cretaceous mud. I said, 'Mind the snake.'

Someone said, 'Kill it, quick.'

'Ah,' I said, my lips mumbling the words. 'The Time Police are here. Everyone prepare to be slaughtered immediately.'

'Max, can you hear me?'

'Don't kill the snake.'

'Well, we can't leave it there. Have you seen the teeth on it?'

The snake took matters into its own hands – so to speak – lifted its head, stared around, not surprisingly decided it didn't want any part of this living on land business and, in one lightning movement, wriggled off me and back into the safety of the swamp.

I told them they'd probably set evolution back by about fifty million years.

'Can you sit up?'

Stupid question. Why would I even want to? I lay very still, quietly returning to the primordial ooze from which we'd all emerged once upon a time. It was good stuff. I don't know why we'd ever left it in the first place.

A different voice said, 'Max?' and suddenly the primordial ooze lost its charms.

'Leon?'

A wonderful voice said, 'Here,' and if it hadn't been for Ronan, a disillusioned snake, various raptors, the Time Police, the entire Cretaceous period and Dr Bairstow, we would have been completely alone.

I mentioned this to Leon.

'Yes,' he said, shunting aside to make room for yet another Time Police medic, 'I think we should resign ourselves. This is as alone as we are ever likely to be.'

I took his hand. 'For God's sake, Leon, don't ever, *ever* let me do anything this stupid again.'

431

He lifted my head and shoulders out of the mud and held me tightly. And painfully. 'If you tell me how that can be accomplished I shall be very happy to comply.'

I said, 'You're very hard,' and someone snorted.

I raised a wobbly hand and tapped on his armour. 'Hello there.'

He was wiping the mud off my face. His own hands were filthy and he was depositing more than he was taking off but he's a hero so it's allowed. 'Hello yourself.'

I looked around. There seemed to be an awful lot of people about. What on earth was going on? And then I remembered.

I tried to sit upright, failed miserably, and croaked, 'Ronan?'

He held me even more tightly. 'We did it, Max. We've got him.'

I could hardly believe it. 'Oh my God. He didn't get away? We got him?'

'We did. We've done it. At last.'

I repeated stupidly, 'We've done it?'

'We have, sweetheart. We've done it. It's all over.'

'We've got Ronan?'

'We have indeed.'

It wasn't going in. 'We've done it? We got him?'

'We've got him. He can't hurt us any longer.'

I stared up at him, tears beginning to well up. Shit, I was going to cry in front of the Time Police. 'I can't believe it.'

'Well, you should. He's only just over there. Look.'

I turned my head. Ronan, securely zip-tied, lay unconscious on the ground. Two medics bent over him.

And then everything came rushing back. 'Mikey?'

'Alive and well and discreetly remaining inside her pod. Everyone is being very tactful about her being a wanted fugitive.'

I was a touch bewildered. 'I'm sure I saw Dr Bairstow. Did I see Dr Bairstow?'

'You did. He's here, too. He wanted to be present at . . . well . . . the end.'

'He pulled me out of the water, I think. I owe him.'

'And I'm sure he will remind you of it for the rest of your life. Which won't be long if we don't get you out of here. Can you stand up?'

'Of course,' I said happily, not having a clue whether I could or not.

There was rather a nasty sucking sound as I was lifted out of the mud. I said, 'That wasn't me.'

He smiled for me alone, ran his finger down my cheek and said, 'You have swamp hair.'

There were Time Police pods everywhere. I could see a big medical pod, two detention pods and a normal one, all parked on the plain between the swamp and the forest. Apparently, it had been the Time Police pods that had crushed the horsetails, not a herd of dim-witted, barely sentient duck-billed Hadrosaurs. Although, as I pointed out to them, the resemblance was so great it was an easy mistake to make. No one shot me but I couldn't see me getting away with this much longer.

'Why didn't you make yourselves known?'

'We were waiting for Ronan to show up.'

Fair enough, I suppose. They weren't bothered about me. I was just the means to the end.

'And once the storm started we couldn't get a precise location on you. And then you got washed away so we had to chase you downstream. Really, Max, you didn't make it easy for us at all, did you?'

433

I said, 'Wolfe and Khalife are dead.'

'No loss.'

One of the doctors finished with Clive Ronan, stood up and squelched over.

'Well then, Dr Maxwell. How are you feeling?'

'Absolutely fine,' I said, swaying in the wind.

'Good,' he said, and turned away. 'But we'll have you in the medical pod just in case.'

I was all set to argue but Dr Bairstow turned up, not armoured but wearing jungle camouflage.

'Good afternoon, Dr Maxwell.'

'Hello, sir. I thought I saw you earlier but decided you must have been a vision.'

He nodded. 'An easy mistake to make. Are you injured?'

'Not even a little bit, sir. All ready to return to St Mary's.'

'I think there may be a small delay. You and I are both required at TPHQ. It would seem there are statements to give and reports to write.'

'Oh. OK.'

Captain Ellis appeared. 'Max. Good to see you on your feet.'

'Yes, it's always nice to be out of the mud. We got him, then?'

He didn't look at me. 'We did, indeed.' He hesitated and then said, 'Sir, may I respectfully remind you about the other matter.'

I knew immediately what he was talking about. This was about Adrian and Mikey. Because part of the price to be paid for all the Time Police help and support was the teapot. Dr Bairstow had agreed to destroy their pod if the Time Police agreed to leave Adrian and Mikey alone. And no prison sentence, either, which was the other part of the deal. They'd spend some time at St Mary's, instead. The living conditions were more spartan but the food was better. They'd both accepted with enthusiasm.

'Dr Bairstow, sir, whenever you're ready.'

'I am at your disposal, Captain. Max?'

'Ready, sir. Will it take long?'

'I shouldn't think so, will it, Captain?'

'No,' said Ellis, watching them cart Ronan away. 'No time at all.' He turned back to Dr Bairstow and said stiffly, 'Again, sir, and with respect, you gave your word.'

Dr Bairstow eyed him for a moment. 'I did. You may witness the matter being set in hand immediately.' He turned to Leon. 'Chief Farrell, please instruct Mr Dieter to proceed with the disposal of the illegal pod as directed.'

'Yes, sir.'

'And then I would be grateful if you could retrieve all our young people and return them to St Mary's.'

'Yes, sir. If you don't need me, Captain?'

'No, thank you, Chief. Commander Hay has asked me to pass on her congratulations and thanks for all your assistance.'

Leon nodded and walked away. He doesn't like them much.

'This way, please.'

Dr Bairstow and I were ushered into the medical pod. Ronan was already there, strapped to a table. Still unconscious. And surrounded by various pieces of equipment.

I took a seat, my mind still buzzing. I just couldn't get it to sink in. We'd done it. We'd actually got him. We'd got Clive Ronan. I couldn't believe it. We'd finally got him. There he was. Clive Ronan himself. Unconscious and under restraint. We'd got Clive Ronan and his pods and his men and he could never do us any harm again.

I was struggling with the implications for all of us. From now on the only hazards we would face would be those of our normal working day. The only foe would be History itself. Our only problems would involve getting this year's funding from Thirsk. And avoiding the next bloody idiot they foisted upon us, of course. But the point was that these were normal worries. Normal hazards. Normal problems. Because we'd got him. We'd got Clive Ronan.

There was the usual uneventful landing. I wasn't going to miss that. St Mary's does these things much better and in a couple of hours I would be back there telling them so. There would be sausages and margaritas and arguments. And Leon, of course. Every inch of my body ached and I was pretty sure my snake bites would go septic and I'd lose my arm but, despite all that, we'd got Clive Ronan, and the knowledge gave me a little warm glow inside. Because we'd got him.

Ronan was disappeared off to somewhere or other, but I was treated inside the pod because all my injuries were minor. They said. And no, I wasn't going to lose my arm. The snake hadn't even been venomous they said, making a bad job of concealing their disappointment.

Dr Bairstow collected me and we were escorted to Commander Hay's office. Because we were being escorted, I kept my voice down.

'Do I gather everything went well at St Mary's, sir?'

'You may.'

'Dr Peterson?'

'Resuming his duties.'

'Casualties?'

'Minimal. They surrendered almost immediately.'

'Halcombe?'

'Time Police custody.'

I left it there, passing the time by pointing out libraries and various places of interest I thought he might find noteworthy. He was very quiet but I was talking so much I never noticed.

Commander Hay stood up as we entered. She and Dr Bairstow greeted each other formally. Also present were Captain Ellis and the ubiquitous Captain Farenden.

As we entered, her overhead lights came on. I hadn't noticed – having had other things on my mind – but the afternoon was very heavy and overcast. Bad weather was brewing. I could almost imagine the storm had followed me back here from the Cretaceous.

Somewhere, something beeped. Farenden looked down at his scratchpad. 'Flood warning, ma'am. The Thames Barrier is being raised and the Tower already has its defences up.'

'Very well, Charlie. Get ours up as well.'

Climate change had left London vulnerable to flooding. All the buildings along this stretch of the Thames had their own protection.

Farenden left the office. I could hear him talking to someone out of sight.

We were asked to sit down. They'd even found some tea from somewhere. It didn't taste quite right but I was so euphoric I could probably have drunk even coffee and never noticed.

God help me – I expected congratulations. I don't mean me personally, but I thought there'd be a general *well done, everyone* air to the meeting and there wasn't. It was as I finished gulping down my tea that I became fully aware of their silence. I put down my cup and saucer very carefully and very quietly and waited.

Dr Bairstow sat, straight-backed as he always did, his hands resting on his stick. Other than greeting the commander, he hadn't said a word.

As I said, I expected a quick congratulatory chat, then I'd be shunted off to give a statement or two and that would be it. For the time being, anyway. Later, there would be a trial, at which we would be expected to give evidence, followed by, barring some sort of satanic intervention, an execution. Given their willingness to do away with Adrian and Mikey, I think I assumed the trial would be a bit of a formality.

None of that happened.

I knew I'd get nothing from Commander Hay's face so I watched Captain Ellis instead, standing at her shoulder. Their backs were to the darkening window outside and their faces unreadable.

I suddenly had a very bad feeling. Instinctively I pushed my cup and saucer well out of harm's way and said, brightly, 'So, what's next? When is the trial?'

The silence dragged on. I could feel Dr Bairstow, tense and still beside me, and then Commander Hay said, 'There will be no trial. Clive Ronan was released twenty minutes ago.'

38

With a flash of lightning, the storm broke. Thunder rumbled at the same time and the rain that had nearly killed me in the Cretaceous came back for another go. I had forgotten how much more violent the weather is in the future and it poured down now, hard and heavy. Within seconds the view from the window had completely disappeared. I could see only water cascading down the glass. Inside, the ceiling lights automatically brightened.

I found I'd surged to my feet. I don't know why. I don't know what I thought I was going to do. I didn't even remember doing it. I was vaguely aware that Dr Bairstow had risen with me. The world was whirling around me. A band tightened around my chest and I couldn't get my breath properly. I could hear my own pulse pounding in my ears. I sensed rather than heard Captain Farenden come back into the room and stand behind me. Not too close, but close enough to get to me should he have to. I suppose I should have been flattered he thought I was capable of doing any damage to anything, but actually I could barely think at all. One moment I'd been right up there, experiencing the euphoric high of a hard-earned triumph and the next moment everything – including me – had come crashing to the ground. I kept hearing her voice. 'Clive Ronan was released twenty minutes ago.' Released. Twenty minutes ago. They'd let him go. *They'd let the bastard go.*

I couldn't keep silent. I said through clenched teeth, 'People have *died* . . .'

She remained icy calm. 'This is a dangerous business. People have always died.'

My voice was harsh. 'And will continue to do so, thanks to you. Unless you're a violent criminal, of course, in which case you can look forward to a very privileged existence, courtesy of the Time Police.'

She didn't bother with me. 'Dr Bairstow . . . if you please.'

He held her glance for a very long time and then slowly sat. I followed suit. I could feel my eyes burning. For two pins I'd happily have toasted the other half of her face.

I felt Captain Farenden station himself at my shoulder. Ellis had his hand on his gun. I said to Dr Bairstow, 'You must forgive their timidity, sir. The odds are against them. There's only three of them, and they're not that heavily armed.' I turned to Commander Hay and said, 'We're happy to wait a moment while you summon reinforcements.'

Dr Bairstow's voice was very quiet. 'If you have some sort of explanation for your . . . behaviour . . . then I suggest you make it now.'

'I do not believe I am obliged to justify my actions to St Mary's.'

'You are not, madam, but I don't believe your organisation has forgotten the last time you were foolish enough to cross our path. Yours is not an organisation with friends. And there is considerable dissent within your own ranks. You would do well to consider carefully before antagonising St Mary's as well. We all worked together successfully to bring down Clive Ronan, but we could just as easily work against you.'

Nothing could beat the might of the Time Police, but there was enough of a threat there to cause her concern. And I was all for it. I could start now if they liked.

I said, 'Jamie Cameron, Mary Schiller, Helen Foster ... *Matthew* ...'

She cut across me. 'Yours is not the only organisation to have sustained losses at Ronan's hands.'

I was on my feet again, spitting the words at her. 'Yeah, but you're the only organisation who *let him go*.'

And with those words it all came boiling up inside me again. I saw that small, neat bullet hole over Helen's eye. Saw her crumple to the ground. Matthew holding out his little arms to me. Hot, burning bile rose in my throat. The desire to lash out . . . to do some damage . . . to these bungling, gutless, witless fuckwits, prancing around in the silly black uniforms they think make them look so important . . . I looked over at Ellis. 'That's why the Time Police have to shoot so many people, isn't it? Before anyone actually finds out how pathetically useless you really are.'

'Dr Bairstow, I don't think any useful purpose is being served by rudeness.'

'I would be astonished to hear the Time Police is even familiar with the expression "useful purpose". This does not happen often but I find myself in complete agreement with Dr Maxwell. And I know you will accept this in the spirit in which it is meant, madam, but if, under your management, the Time Police continue to betray their allies in so spectacular a manner, you will very soon find yourself with none at all.'

'As usual, St Mary's is commenting from a position of complete ignorance.'

'On the contrary, madam, I am perfectly well aware of your reasons for releasing Clive Ronan. It is your concealment of those

441

reasons that is falling under heavy criticism. Particularly from Dr Maxwell. The only question now is whether I allow her the pleasure of a little light violence before returning to St Mary's.'

I turned to Dr Bairstow. 'You knew . . .'

He said quietly, 'I hesitate, in the face of such overwhelming stupidity, to utter even a word in their defence but, yes, I know why they've let him go. And, Max, when you are able to think clearly, so do you. What I am taking issue with, at this moment, is the very poor judgement shown in not preparing you, of all people, for what *must* happen.'

I took two or three deep breaths and then sat back down again. The emotional temperature in the room dropped a little.

'Go on then,' I said to her. 'Amaze me with tales of your cunning and intelligence. And believe me, I will be amazed.'

Her eyes narrowed. 'You are treading a dangerously fine line.'

'Only for you.'

'I think you forget for whom you work.'

'For St Mary's. Always have – always will.'

'I could have you shot where you sit. And very possibly will. Believe me, no one here will lift a finger.'

Dr Bairstow stirred. 'Not an absolutely correct statement, madam. I would lift several fingers.'

'And suffer the appropriate response.'

'Dear me,' he said mildly. 'Do you propose to strengthen your position by assassinating the Director of St Mary's? I think if you take the time and trouble to think things through, you will find that might not be your optimal course of action.'

More rain lashed against the windows, sounding very loud in this quiet office. My insides were beginning to settle. I nodded at her. 'Go on then. Justify your actions.'

'It isn't a case of justifying our actions,' she said angrily. 'In this instance the Time Police . . .' and subsided as she regained control. She took a deep breath. 'I shall explain. There will be no discussion because the deed is done but I think you will see the necessity.'

I said again, 'Go on.'

She pushed herself back from her desk a little and said, 'Have you ever heard of smartdust?'

I looked at Dr Bairstow who shook his head for both of us.

'It is – was – an offshoot of biotechnology subsequently hijacked by . . . some people who found a better use for it. It was originally developed for endoscopic imaging but is now used mainly for monitoring and surveillance.'

'And this has to do with Clive Ronan – how?'

'The product was adapted to monitor people's brains. Not their thoughts, unfortunately, although some work has been done in that direction, but rather to be able to see which areas of the brain are active and to what extent.'

She paused. 'We've taken things one stage further. Under anaesthetic, smartdust is inhaled by the subject . . .' She meant victim. '. . . Where it lodges in the brain. I won't bore you with the science because I don't understand it myself. But – and this is the important bit – at a previously designated moment, the smartdust embedded in the cerebral cortex can be . . . activated.'

'What do you mean – activated?'

'In this case – detonated.'

I stared in puzzlement.

Dr Bairstow intervened. 'It means, Max, that Ronan is walking around with a bomb inside his head.'

She nodded agreement.

I was bewildered. 'But why?'

'Because during the course of his life he has done many wicked things – and some he has yet to do. It is not a case of preventing those from occurring – they have already happened to you and others and he must, therefore, remain at liberty to commit them. They occur in your past but his future. If he dies prematurely, your past – everyone's past – will slowly unravel. To prevent this happening, he has been released.'

She straightened something on her desk. 'Thanks to smartdust, he can be closely monitored and after he's cleared his backlog of outstanding actions . . . when he reaches the point where he can no longer do anyone any harm . . . hundreds of thousands of microscopic bomblets will detonate.'

'And blow his head off.'

'No. The explosion will be internal – we don't want any unnecessary casualties. To all intents and purposes, he will have some kind of neural event – a stroke, perhaps – and die instantly. Whatever conclusions are drawn, you may rest assured that he will be very, very dead.'

'But until then . . . after all this effort . . . he'll still be out there, running riot, killing everyone in sight.'

Her expression hardened. 'I have already explained . . .'

'Not to my satisfaction. Nor that of anyone else who has suffered at his hands.'

She slammed her hand on the table. 'Oh, for God's sake, Maxwell, grow up. What did you think was going to happen? How did you think the problem of his future crimes would be solved? You surely weren't so naïve as to think it would all tidy itself quietly away.'

An icy hand clutched at my heart. Because she was right. I'd known about this problem. I'd always known about it. Back in the days when we were dealing with Mary Stuart, I'd known about it. And now I needed to be honest with myself. I hadn't forgotten it. I'd done worse than forget it – I'd buried it. Buried it deep. Out of sight – out of mind. If I'd considered it at all – and I hadn't – at some point I'd just thrust the thought into a room in my mind and slammed the door on it. I think I'd rather hoped that someone above my pay grade would have come up with a solution and saved the day and, of course, that was never going to happen. Could never happen. An older Clive Ronan had done things in my past but his future. They'd been done to me but he hadn't done them yet. Effect before cause.

I was still boilingly furious, but a good part of it was now directed inwards. I'd just assumed someone would have thought of some way out of this problem. They were the Time Police after all. They operated under different rules. They were technically advanced. They'd think of something. But they hadn't. Because there was nothing to think of. There was no way around the problem.

I was angry at the world, at the Time Police, and at myself. I stared at the floor as my mind flew around like a trapped bird, injuring itself looking for a way out that didn't exist.

Dr Bairstow remained silent, giving me all the time I needed.

Eventually, I said, 'Does he know?' Meaning Ronan.

She shook her head.

'But how can you keep it from him? He must know he's been in surgery.'

'He and his men were brought back unconscious and kept that way. They'll be dumped back in the Cretaceous again. We'll wait around, discreetly keeping them safe until they regain consciousness and then leave him to get on with the rest of his life. What's left of it.'

I persevered. 'But the damage he could do.'

'The damage he *must* do . . .'

'And then he dies?'

'And then the smartdust activates and he dies, yes.'

I sat quietly, unsure how I felt about any of this.

She said more gently, 'Max – you agreed to this.'

'I agreed to his capture. Because I thought someone here might have the answer. That some giant mind had figured it out.'

'They have. We have. The smartdust will be activated on a certain date. An unknown date. We have to leave him free to perform the actions that he must perform.'

'You free him to perform more atrocities.'

'Atrocities that have already happened, Max. He just hasn't done them yet. We call it closing the circle. When all the circles are closed – bang.'

'Which will be when?'

She shrugged. She wasn't going to tell me. Probably she herself didn't know. That knowledge would be confined to only a very, very few people and I wasn't one of them. I hadn't even been important enough to be included in their plans.

Outside, the wind was getting up. I could hear it shrieking around the building. The windows here didn't rattle the way they did at St Mary's. Suddenly, I wanted very much to be back among my own people. Back with Leon and Matthew, sitting in our room where the windows rattled properly and even leaked a little if the wind was in the wrong direction. I suddenly felt very tired and I badly wanted to go home.

I stood up. 'With your permission, sir, I'll leave you to finish dealing with these people. I'll collect Matthew and meet you downstairs.'

The atmosphere in the room changed immediately.

39

I've often suspected I'm not a nice person. That there's a part of me that is best kept hidden. It erupts from time to time – people get hurt – but not, thank God, very often. I don't know if other people are the same. Whether we all have hidden demons that must continually be controlled, repressed or contained, for fear of what would happen should they break free, even for one moment. Something told me that moment had come. Because something bad was about to happen.

She reached under her desk and behind me, something thunked. She'd locked the door.

I turned very slowly to look at Farenden. His face gave nothing away. I turned back again to look at Ellis. The same. Both of them had their hands on their guns. I couldn't see the commander's hands but I was willing to bet she had some pretty substantial weaponry tucked away under her desk, too.

At some point, Dr Bairstow had risen. 'Commander, I beg you to reconsider this course of action.'

'I am sorry, I cannot. Nor should I. Nothing has changed. Clive Ronan is still out there. Matthew must remain here under our protection.'

I said, flatly, 'You will surrender my son. Now.'

She sat back. 'I could not do so even if I wished. He is not here.'

'More lies.'

'I can assure you that is true.'

'I don't think you are in a position to assure anyone of any truths ever again. You stand exposed as a liar, Commander. Frankly, I wouldn't believe you at the moment if you told me it was raining.'

She flushed. Good – I'd made her angry.

'Matthew is currently enjoying a school expedition in the Wye Valley. Canoeing, I believe.'

'Too convenient for belief.'

'Max, we have an agreement.'

'That Matthew remained here with his parents' permission. That permission is now revoked. You are now committing a crime.'

'To remove Matthew now would expose him to great danger.'

'And that's why you deliberately let Clive Ronan go. He's your excuse for hanging on to Matthew.'

She ignored that. 'Your best course of action would be to leave Matthew with us until Ronan is terminated. For his own good. You must see that. If you don't, we have emergency powers designed to cover this situation.'

She tapped at her scratchpad and passed it across for us to read.

I expect Dr Bairstow read it. I was too busy planning my next move. Over the desk. Knock aside Ellis's gun. Somehow. Avoid whatever she had concealed under the desk. Somehow. Avoid being shot in the back by Farenden, still behind me. Somehow. Get out of this locked room. Down to Matthew's dormitory. Seize Matthew. If he was there. Get him through miles and miles of featureless Time Police corridors. Somehow. Down to the pod bay. Avoid mechs, security people and sundry passing bodies. Steal a pod. Get it to accept my instructions. Escape back to St Mary's. Somehow.

It was never going to happen.

There was silence as all the other occupants in the room waited for me to come to this inevitable conclusion.

Or I could die in the attempt and take as many of them with me as I possibly could.

I watched them stiffen as all the other occupants in the room came to this inevitable conclusion.

I looked at her . . . measuring the distance . . . calculating the risk.

Dr Bairstow put his hand on my shoulder and twisted me round to face him. 'Dr Maxwell, you will remain still and silent. That is a direct order. Please indicate your understanding.'

I was angry. 'What are you doing, sir?'

'Saving lives.'

He was afraid. I could see it in his eyes. Whether for me, for them, or the situation in which we found ourselves, I had no idea.

'Say nothing, Max. Not a word.'

I don't think I could have. I started to shake. I've no idea why. Rage? Shock? Imminent death? Hers, I mean, not mine. Because I would do this. I'd lost Matthew once. There was no way I would leave him again.

Part of my mind – the probably slightly saner part – was telling me not to make this situation worse. To allow the arrangement to carry on as before. He would live here with frequent visits from both sides. Not to put myself in a situation where neither Leon nor I would have any access to our son. The larger part of my mind was telling me to kill them where they stood. Another part flew back to the Egyptian desert. I stood in the wavering heat haze and heard Ronan's voice.

'Because, my dear Max, you dance on the edge of darkness . . . and I don't think it would take very much for you to dance my way.'

There was a connection between us. Or there had been. I was the one he'd sought out with his offer of peace. He'd saved my life, I'd saved his. Yes, there was a connection between us and I felt it now.

A long time ago, Ronan, too, had once been desperate to escape and take a loved one with him. He'd killed and injured friend and foe alike in his doomed attempt to escape with Annie. She'd died in the crossfire. Now, suddenly, I too, could feel all the desperation, all the panic, all the helplessness that the sudden and brutal loss of a loved one could entail.

I couldn't leave Matthew behind. He was mine. He was my son. Part of me. And I certainly wouldn't leave him alone with these people. To watch him grow up in their image. A tiny voice said I probably wasn't going to be allowed to watch him grow up at all. The thought exploded inside my head. I'd lost him once and now I was going to lose him again.

No. I would see them all dead at my feet before I allowed that to happen.

As if he could read my mind, Dr Bairstow tightened his grip. 'Dr Maxwell, you will remain silent. You will not move. You will not utter another word. That is a direct order with which you will comply.'

Actually, I had no choice. My mouth was full of bile. I could feel it burning the back of my throat, leaving a bitter taste in my mouth. Because I'd been played. The Time Police never had any intention of ending Ronan. And they'd never had any intention of relinquishing Matthew, either. They'd played me from the moment I walked through their front door.

Dr Bairstow turned towards the door, his hand still on my shoulder.

'Madam, we are leaving. By the time we reach the door it will be unlocked. We will not encounter any obstacles on our way to the pod bay where a pod will be ready and waiting for us. Failure to comply with any of these instructions will result in a blood bath. You will have to kill both of us and then account to the world for your actions and I can assure you all of St Mary's – in every place and every time – will unite in publishing your wrongdoing to the world. Your attempts to separate a mother from her child for no good reason – in fact, no reason at all – will attract the harshest censure.' He paused and then said, meaningfully, 'Colonel Albay would be so proud.'

And now she hated both of us.

I took advantage of her sudden silence, leaning over her desk until we were eye to eye and my voice was deadly. 'And then . . . Leon will come for you.'

There was just a very tiny flicker in her eyes. I turned away.

Dr Bairstow took my arm, saying in an undertone, 'Say nothing to anyone, Max. No matter what the provocation.'

I nodded.

The door thunked open while we were still a good three paces away. I felt him relax a little.

We crossed Farenden's office. He and Ellis had fallen in behind us.

Dr Bairstow walked me through the building. I would never have made it without him. The corridors were lined with silent officers, watching us as we walked. I had no idea how they knew but they did. No one said a word. I found I couldn't look at any of them, let alone speak.

We reached a junction in the corridors. Right would lead to the lift – left to the dormitory areas. My feet stopped of their own

452

accord. Dr Bairstow tightened his grip. I felt Ellis and Farenden move up behind us.

Dr Bairstow turned his head. 'Step back or I will not be responsible for the consequences.'

They stepped back.

'Come along, Max. Only a little further.'

My feet turned right.

Ellis and Farenden stayed well back in the lift. I suppose if I'd been going to try anything then that would have been the place, but Dr Bairstow had steered me into a corner and held my arm in a grip of iron. I stared at the floor indicator, watching the numbers change, my mind in a whirl, completely unable to formulate any sort of action plan. I couldn't think of any way to prevent this happening. Because once I was out of TPHQ, I was pretty sure I'd never be allowed back in again. The thought was unbearable and I shifted my weight. His grip tightened even further.

The doors opened before I could do anything suicidal.

A pod was ready and waiting for us. One of the smaller ones. A crew stood inside. We were formally handed over. An officer motioned us up the ramp.

I stopped dead at the foot. Once I climbed into this pod there would be no coming back. I looked back over my shoulder, measuring distances, calculating chances . . .

The officer gestured with his gun. 'Into the pod.'

My legs wouldn't move.

The officer poked me with his gun. 'Move.'

'If you do that again,' said Dr Bairstow, pleasantly, 'I will make you eat it.'

Good, we were going to make a fight of it.

The same thought had obviously occurred to Ellis and Farenden.

453

Ellis stepped forwards. 'Thank you, Lieutenant. You can dismiss your men. Captain Farenden and I will take it from here.'

'But sir, my orders are to . . .'

'Don't make me thank you again, Lieutenant.'

They exited the pod and stood back. Although none of them put down their weapons.

Dr Bairstow said, 'Come along, Max.'

I couldn't move. This was my Rubicon. If I stepped into this pod then I'd lost Matthew forever. I remembered our Friday nights with holos and pizza. I remembered him huddled on the end of my sofa after he'd broken the Time Map. I remembered him playing football with Markham and the Security Section. I remembered him showing Leon his dirigible plans. I remembered his skinny little body with the scars and the healed burns, the hollows of his temples, the way his hair always seemed to need cutting. I remembered his rare, swift smiles. I remembered him saying to Leon, 'Mummy's awesome.'

Dr Bairstow said softly, 'Time to go, Max.'

His voice broke the spell. My feet moved. I walked slowly up the ramp and into the pod.

They didn't hang around. Ellis sat himself at the console. 'Initiating jump procedures.'

'Jump procedures initiated.'

And just like that, it was all over.

40

We touched down in complete silence. In every sense of the word. No one spoke and our landing was as light as thistledown.

Ellis said, 'Ramp,' and cool, crisp air flooded into the pod. I stared out at St Mary's, unchanged in the autumn sunshine.

Markham had an armed team waiting. He always had a team waiting. Just in case – and it would seem that today, just in case had arrived.

'Max ...' We walked down the ramp. I stood on St Mary's ground. The fight had gone out of me.

Dr Bairstow pitched his voice for everyone to hear.

'Mr Markham.'

'Sir.'

'I shall be making a formal announcement later today, but you and your team should be aware these people are no longer welcome at St Mary's. Should you find any member of the Time Police on these premises without express permission from me then you may regard them as being here with hostile intent and shoot them.'

'A pleasure, sir.'

Ellis stepped forwards. 'Dr Bairstow ...' and at once the security team brought up their weapons.

'Can we start now, sir?'

'If they are still here in thirty seconds, then yes.' He turned to

Ellis and Farenden, both standing very still. 'You are no longer welcome here. The behaviour of the Time Police in this matter has been deplorable. You appear to be completely unaware of the standards of behaviour to be expected from friends and allies. You are entirely without honour. You have exercised your might and your power over individuals who cannot respond in kind. These are the marks of a bully. You have manipulated and exploited my people, all of whom acted in good faith. Since it is a well-known fact that bullies are physical cowards, I warn you now, in future, to avoid St Mary's. There are people here with scores to settle and who would welcome the opportunity to do so. Now get out.'

Ellis looked past him to me.

I said, 'I wish I'd left you in the dust at Pompeii.'

He turned very white. 'Max . . .'

Markham brought up his gun. 'Security Section, prepare to fire.'

There was the sound of whining blasters.

Farenden touched his shoulder and said something. Not taking his eyes from me, Ellis stepped back. The ramp came up. The last I saw of him he was still staring at me. Then the ramp closed. There was a brief swirl of wind and they were gone.

Dr Bairstow still had hold of my shoulder. I found I couldn't move.

Markham shouldered his gun and approached. 'Max, are you hurt? Should I alert Sick Bay, sir?'

'Thank you, Mr Markham, but no. Where is Chief Farrell?'

He gestured over his shoulder. 'Hawking, sir.'

'Thank you. Come along, Max.'

The pressure on my shoulder increased and I was walked towards Hawking. Markham on one side, the Boss on the other. The big doors were open to let in the welcome sunshine.

'I hope you understand, Max, that my priority was to make it as difficult as possible for the Time Police ever to come back here.'

I wasn't listening. They were just words. All my effort was in putting one foot in front of the other.

It was only as I stepped inside and saw that Hawking was fully occupied that I remembered they'd had some trouble here themselves. I should ask. I should find out about Halcombe and Peterson and all that had happened here and I would. I remember, I wasn't even surprised Leon hadn't been there to greet me. My fuel tank was empty and I was running on fumes.

Dieter was talking to Polly Perkins, both of them pouring over a diagnostic printout. 'Good afternoon, sir. Max.'

'Chief Farrell?'

'Number Eight, sir.'

We walked in silence. I became aware my legs were growing heavier with every step. I so badly wanted Leon. I wanted to feel his arms around me. I wanted to close my eyes and let go – even if only for a second.

And I dreaded seeing Leon. Dreaded seeing his face when I told him what the Time Police had done. That I'd had to come home without Matthew. That Ronan was still free. That people had died and would continue to do so.

'Just a little further, Max.'

We reached Number Eight. He handed me up on to the plinth, said, 'Mr Markham, a word if you please,' and the two of them disappeared down the hangar.

I took a deep breath, lifted my chin and stepped into the pod.

It was déjà vu all over again.

Leon stood alone in the middle of the pod. I made myself look

457

at him. I must have looked terrible. Filthy dirty, exhausted, utterly finished.

He didn't come to greet me. My heart, just beginning to slow down, started to race again. Something was wrong.

We looked at each other for a moment and then, slowly, he stepped to one side and I saw he'd been standing in front of Matthew.

He was here. Matthew was here. He was here. Right here. Right now. Standing in front of me. He was still wearing a red life jacket. I stared, first at Leon and then at Matthew. I think I wondered if I'd finally gone insane.

We all stared at each other, and then Leon said, 'I'll be back in a moment,' dropped a kiss on the top of my head and left the pod.

I had to put a hand on the console to steady myself. I had to swallow twice before I could say, 'Matthew?'

We looked at each other and then . . . he held out his arms to me.

I dropped to my knees, partly to hug him close, but mostly because my legs had abandoned me and gone off to look for someone who would take better care of them.

I don't say this anything like often enough, but my husband is a hero. And my boss isn't bad, either. I've never been more glad to work for someone who knows everything and plans accordingly. He'd known the Time Police weren't to be trusted, probably right from the moment I'd first laid my plans in front of him. And he'd planned for just that eventuality. Yes, Halcombe had been a minor blip but there isn't much Dr Bairstow can't incorporate into his schemes. He'd known they wouldn't – couldn't – execute Clive Ronan and from that he'd inferred they wouldn't release Matthew.

I was willing to bet he'd had Leon scooping up Matthew before we'd even had our row with Commander Hay. Matthew had been gone before she knew it.

Now, I remembered his instructions to Leon. 'Chief Farrell, I would be grateful if you could retrieve *all* our young people.' Not *both* our young people, but *all* of them. Adrian, Mikey ... and Matthew. And he'd issued the instruction right in front of the Time Police. I made a mental note to congratulate him on style.

Matthew was regarding me with some severity. 'You're very wet.'

'So are you.'

'And you smell.'

'Sorry about that but I've been fighting off dinosaurs.'

I peered at him, hoping for at least a flicker of a *Wow! My mum is so cool* expression but there was nothing.

'*I've* been canoeing.'

It was obvious which he rated more highly.

I'm a mother. I know my duty. 'Wow, that is so cool.'

'I turned my canoe over.'

'Wow,' I said again, my conversational repartee fast dwindling. I leaned against the console for support. My legs were still in the Cretaceous and I'd left my temper back at TPHQ where, I hoped, it was still roaming the corridors seeking whom it might devour. What was left of me in the here and now was definitely feeling a bit ropey.

I hugged him even more tightly. He was taller than he'd been last time we'd done this. The Time Police had looked after him well. I sighed. The immediate future was going to be choppy. 'And now you smell, too.'

'Will I have to shower? Again?'

His tone implied he'd exceeded his weekly quota already.

459

'If I have to then so do you.' I climbed to my feet. I really, really needed a cup of tea. The proper stuff. No more brown water for me.

There was going to be a major row, of course. A major, major row. Once the Time Police discovered Leon had removed Matthew from his school trip they would . . . what? What would they do? What could they do?

We'd find out soon enough. On the other hand, we're St Mary's and we drink proper tea. It occurred to me that I was a little light-headed.

Hawking was full. Every single pod was in. And the teapot was here as well. Again, I heard Dr Bairstow giving his word it would be destroyed. Well, they'd broken theirs, as he knew they would, and he'd broken his. I wasn't going to lose any sleep over it.

The hangar was full and black umbilicals snaked everywhere. I told Matthew to watch where he was going.

He wasn't listening. I don't know why I bother.

We were heading towards Leon and Dr Bairstow, talking together at the far end of Hawking, when Adrian's head appeared out of the teapot. He was calling down to Mikey, who appeared from behind the pod, scratchpad in hand.

Matthew stopped dead, staring, and, not expecting it, I nearly fell over him.

The moment dragged on and then he said, 'She was here before.'

I nodded. 'She was. At the croquet match.'

'Who is she? And who is he?'

My spidey-mother senses woke up.

Quite casually, I said, 'Brother and sister. Adrian and Amelia Meiklejohn. She goes by Mikey.'

He stared some more. He has a very intense stare. And you can't rush him. I waited.

460

'Why is she called Mikey?'

'Because anyone calling her Amelia suffers immediate and cat-astrophic damage to their nose.'

He stood stock-still and watched her. Reaction had set in. I was sick, cold and desperately, desperately thirsty but I'm a mother. I know my duty.

Mikey was jumping about in her scruffy flying jacket, calling readings up to Adrian. The sunlight from the open door caught her short blonde hair and turned it into a halo of gold. She looked like a dancing angel.

I'm not psychic but I suddenly foresaw a whole new raft of problems.

She stowed her scratchpad, climbed up the ladder and, still shouting at Adrian, disappeared inside.

Matthew watched her go and then said, quite casually, 'I'm going to marry her.'

'Good choice,' I said, equally casually. 'Shall we go and find your dad?'

THE END

ACKNOWLEDGEMENTS

Thanks to Kate Foti for allowing me to use her idea to rename TB2 as Tea Bag 2.

Thanks to Rebecca Lloyd, my editor, for her support and patience.

Thanks to Phil Dawson, who advised me on Time Police procedures, sex-clubs and smartdust.

Thanks to everyone at Headline for all their support and encouragement.

Thanks to everyone at Accent Press for being amazing.

JUST ONE DAMNED THING AFTER ANOTHER

'So tell me, Dr Maxwell, if the whole of History lay before you . . . where would you go? What would you like to witness?'

When Madeleine Maxwell is recruited by the St Mary's Institute of Historical Research, she discovers the historians there don't just study the past – they revisit it.

But one wrong move and History will fight back – to the death. And she soon discovers it's not just History she's fighting . . .

HEADLINE

WHITE SILENCE

'I don't know who I am. I don't know what I am.'

Elizabeth Cage is a child when she discovers that there are
things in this world that only she can see. But she doesn't want
to see them and she definitely doesn't want them to see her.

What is a curse to Elizabeth is a gift to others –
a very valuable gift they want to control.

When her husband dies, Elizabeth's world descends into a
nightmare. But as she tries to piece her life back together,
she discovers that not everything is as it seems.

Alone in a strange and frightening world, she's a
vulnerable target to forces beyond her control.

And she knows that she can't trust anyone . . .

HEADLINE

DARK
LIGHT

The thrilling sequel to White Silence

Betrayed, terrified and alone, Elizabeth Cage has fled her home. With no plan and no friends, she arrives at the picturesque village of Greyston and finds herself involved in an ages-old ceremony that will end in death.

And that might be the least of her problems – the Sorensen Institute would very much like to know her whereabouts. And Michael Jones is still out there, somewhere, she hopes. No matter how far and how fast she can run, trouble will always find Elizabeth Cage.

HEADLINE

HISTORY WILL NEVER BE THE SAME AGAIN...

BOOK ONE

BOOK TWO

BOOK THREE

BOOK FOUR

BOOK FIVE

BOOK SIX

BOOK SEVEN

BOOK EIGHT

BOOK NINE

BOOK TEN

SHORT STORIES

THE CHRONICLES OF ST MARY'S